KU-306-655

INSIDE THE O'BRIENS

Joe O'Brien is a Boston cop; his physical stamina and methodical mind have seen him through decades of policing the city streets, while raising a family with his wife Rosie. When he starts making uncharacteristic errors — mislaying his weapon, having trouble writing up reports, slurring speech — he attributes them to stress, though he finally agrees to see a doctor. The unexpected, terrifying diagnosis is Huntington's disease. Not only is Joe's life set to change forever, but each of his four grown-up children has a fifty per cent chance of inheriting the disease. Observing her potential future play out in her father's escalating symptoms, his yoga-teacher daughter Katie wrestles with how to make the most of the here and now, and how to care for her dad who is, inside, always an O'Brien.

Books by Lisa Genova
Published by Ulverscroft:

LOVE ANTHONY

46 853 264 4

SPECIAL MESSAGE TO READERS

THE ULVERSCROFT FOUNDATION
(registered UK charity number 264873)
was established in 1972 to provide funds for
research, diagnosis and treatment of eye diseases.
Examples of major projects funded by
the Ulverscroft Foundation are:-

- The Children's Eye Unit at Moorfields Eye Hospital, London
- The Ulverscroft Children's Eye Unit at Great Ormond Street Hospital for Sick Children
- Funding research into eye diseases and treatment at the Department of Ophthalmology, University of Leicester
- The Ulverscroft Vision Research Group, Institute of Child Health
- Twin operating theatres at the Western Ophthalmic Hospital, London
- The Chair of Ophthalmology at the Royal Australian College of Ophthalmologists

You can help further the work of the Foundation
by making a donation or leaving a legacy.
Every contribution is gratefully received. If you
would like to help support the Foundation or
require further information, please contact:

THE ULVERSCROFT FOUNDATION
**The Green, Bradgate Road, Anstey
Leicester LE7 7FU, England
Tel: (0116) 236 4325**

website: www.foundation.ulverscroft.com

Lisa Genova graduated valedictorian from Bates College with a degree in Biopsychology and has a Ph.D. in Neuroscience from Harvard University. With more than half a million copies of her critically acclaimed *New York Times* bestselling novels in print, she has captured a special place in contemporary fiction, writing stories that are equally inspired by neuroscience and the human spirit. She lives with her family on Cape Cod, Massachusetts.

Visit her online at: lisagenova.com

Follow her on Twitter: @LisaGenova

LISA GENOVA

INSIDE THE O'BRIENS

Complete and Unabridged

CHARNWOOD
Leicester

First published in Great Britain in 2015 by
Simon & Schuster UK Ltd
London

First Charnwood Edition
published 2016
by arrangement with
Simon & Schuster UK Ltd
London

The moral right of the author has been asserted

Copyright © 2015 by Lisa Genova
All rights reserved

A catalogue record for this book is available
from the British Library.

ISBN 978–1–4448–2851–1

Published by
F. A. Thorpe (Publishing)
Anstey, Leicestershire

Set by Words & Graphics Ltd.
Anstey, Leicestershire
Printed and bound in Great Britain by
T. J. International Ltd., Padstow, Cornwall

This book is printed on acid-free paper

For Stella
In loving memory of Meghan

If you bring forth what is within you, what you bring forth will save you. If you do not bring forth what is within you, what you do not bring forth will destroy you.
— The Gospel of Thomas, saying 70

Once you can imagine these things, you can't unimagine them.
— Joe O'Brien

PART I

Huntington's disease (HD) is an inherited neurodegenerative disease characterized by a progressive loss of voluntary motor control and an increase in involuntary movements. Initial physical symptoms may include a loss of balance, reduced dexterity, falling, chorea, slurred speech, and difficulty swallowing. The disease is diagnosed through neurological exam, based on these disturbances in movement, and can be confirmed through genetic testing, as a single genetic mutation causes this disease.

Although the presentation of physical symptoms is necessary for diagnosis, there exists an insidious 'prodrome of HD' that may begin up to fifteen years before the motor problems appear. Prodromal symptoms of HD are both psychiatric and cognitive and may include depression, apathy, paranoia, obsessive-compulsive disorder, impulsivity, outbursts of anger, reduced speed and flexibility of cognitive processing, and memory impairment.

HD is typically diagnosed between the ages of thirty-five and forty-five, proceeding inexorably to death in ten to twenty years.

There is no treatment that affects the progression and no cure.

It has been called the cruelest disease known to man.

1

Damn woman is always moving his things. He can't kick off his boots in the living room or set his sunglasses down on the coffee table without her relocating them to 'where they belong.' Who made her God in this house? If he wants to leave a stinking pile of his own shit right in the middle of the kitchen table, then that's where it should stay until he moves it.

Where the fuck is my gun?

'Rosie!' Joe hollers from the bedroom.

He looks at the time: 7:05 a.m. He's going to be late for roll call if he doesn't get the hell out of here pronto, but he can't go anywhere without his gun.

Think. It's so hard to think lately when he's in a hurry. Plus it's a thousand degrees hotter than hell in here. It's been sweltering for June, in the high eighties all week, and barely cools down at night. Terrible sleeping weather. The air in the house is a thick swamp, today's heat and humidity already elbowing in on what was trapped inside yesterday. The windows are open, but that doesn't help a lick. His white Hanes T-shirt is sticking to his back beneath his vest, pissing him off. He just showered and could already use another.

Think. He took a shower and got dressed — pants, T-shirt, Kevlar vest, socks, boots, gun belt. Then he took his gun out of the safe,

4

released the trigger lock, and then what? He looks down at his right hip. It's not there. He can feel the missing weight of it without even looking. He's got his magazine pouch, handcuffs, Mace, radio, and service baton, but no gun.

It's not in the safe, not on his dresser, not in the top drawer of his dresser, not on the unmade bed. He looks over at Rosie's bureau. Nothing but the Virgin Mary centered on an ivory doily. She sure ain't going to help him.

St. Anthony, where the fuck is it?

He's tired. He worked traffic detail last night over at the Garden. Friggin' Justin Timberlake concert got out late. So he's tired. So what? He's been tired for years. He can't imagine being so tired that he would be careless enough to misplace his loaded gun. A lot of guys with as many years on the force as Joe grow complacent about their service weapon, but he never has.

He stomps down the hall, passes the two other bedrooms, and pokes his head into their only bathroom. Nothing. He storms into the kitchen with his hands on his hips, the heel of his right hand searching for the top of his gun out of habit.

His four not-yet-showered, bed-headed, sleepy teenagers are up and seated around the tiny kitchen table for breakfast — plates of undercooked bacon, runny scrambled eggs, and burnt white toast. The usual. Joe scans the room and spots his gun, his loaded gun, on the mustard-yellow Formica counter next to the sink.

'Mornin', Dad,' offers Katie, his youngest,

5

smiling but shy about it, sensing that something is off.

He ignores Katie. He picks up his Glock, secures it in its holster, and then aims the crosshairs of his wrath at Rosie.

'Whaddaya doin' with my gun there?'

'What are you talking about?' says Rosie, who is standing by the stove in a pink tank top and no bra, shorts, and bare feet.

'You're always movin' my shit around,' says Joe.

'I never touch your gun,' says Rosie, standing up to him.

Rosie is petite at five feet nothing and a hundred pounds soaking wet. Joe's no giant either. He's five feet nine with his patrol boots on, but everyone thinks of him as being taller than he is, probably because he's barrel-chested and has muscular arms and a deep, husky voice. At thirty-six, he's got a bit of a gut, but not bad for his age or considering how much of his life he spends sitting in a cruiser. He's normally playful and easygoing, a pussycat really, but even when he's smiling and there's that twinkle in his blue eyes, everyone knows he's old-school tough. No one messes with Joe. No one but Rosie.

She's right. She never touches his gun. Even after all these years of his being on the force, she's never grown comfortable with having a firearm in the house, even though it's always in the safe or in his top dresser drawer, where it's trigger-locked, or on his right hip. Until today.

'Then how the fuck did it get there?' he asks, pointing to the space next to the sink.

6

'Watch your mouth,' she says.

He looks over at his four kids, who have all stopped eating to witness the show. He narrows in on Patrick. God love him, but he's sixteen going on stupid. This would be just the kind of knucklehead move he would pull, even after all the lectures these kids have endured about the gun.

'So which one of you did this?'

They all stare and say nothing. The Charlestown code of silence, eh?

'Who picked up my gun and left it by the sink?' he demands, his voice booming. Silence will not be an option.

'Wasn't me, Dad,' says Meghan.

'Me either,' says Katie.

'Not me,' says JJ.

'I didn't do it,' says Patrick.

What every criminal he's ever arrested says. Everyone's a fuckin' saint. They all look up at him, blinking and waiting. Patrick shoves a rubbery slice of bacon into his mouth and chews.

'Have some breakfast before you go, Joe,' says Rosie.

He's too late to have breakfast. He's too late because he's been looking for his goddamn gun that someone took and then left on the kitchen counter. He's late and feeling out of control, and he's hot, too hot. The air in this cramped room is too soupy to breathe, and it feels as if the heat from the stove and six bodies and the weather is stoking something already threatening to boil over inside him.

7

He's going to be late for roll call, and Sergeant Rick McDonough, five years younger than Joe, is going to have a word with him again or maybe even write him up. He can't stomach the humiliating thought of it, and something inside him explodes.

He grabs the cast-iron skillet on the stove by the handle and sidearms it across the room. It smashes a sizable hole in the drywall not far from Katie's head, then lands with a resounding *BANG* on the linoleum floor. Rusty brown bacon grease drips down the daisy-patterned wallpaper like blood oozing from a wound.

The kids are wide-eyed and silent. Rosie says nothing and doesn't move. Joe storms out of the kitchen, down the narrow hallway, and steps into the bathroom. His heart is racing, and his head is hot, too hot. He splashes cold water over his hair and face and wipes himself dry with a hand towel.

He needs to leave now, right now, but something in his reflection snags him and won't let go.

His eyes.

His pupils are dilated, black and wide with adrenaline, like shark eyes, but that's not it. It's the expression in his eyes that has him arrested. Wild, unfocused, full of rage. His mother.

It's the same unbalanced gaze that used to terrify him as a young boy. He's looking in the mirror, late for roll call, glued to the wretched eyes of his mother, who used to stare at him just like this when she could do nothing else but lie in her bed in the psych ward at the state hospital, mute, emaciated, and possessed, waiting to die.

The devil in his mother's eyes, dead for twenty-five years, is now staring at him in the bathroom mirror.

SEVEN YEARS LATER

2

It's a cool Sunday morning, and Joe is walking the dog while Rosie is at church. He used to go with her and the kids whenever he had off, but after Katie received her confirmation, that was the end of it. Now only Rosie goes, and she's disgusted with the whole pathetic, sinful lot of them. A big fan of tradition, an unfortunate quality for someone who only gets a full weekend off every seven and a half weeks and hasn't seen Christmas morning with his family in six years, Joe will still attend Mass on Christmas Eve and Easter when he can, but he's done with the weekly sacrament.

It's not that he doesn't believe in God. Heaven and hell. Good and evil. Right and wrong. Shame still guides many of his daily decisions. *God can see you. God can hear what you're thinking. God loves you, but if you fuck up, you're gonna burn in hell.* The nuns spent his entire youth hammering those paranoid beliefs through his thick skull, right between the eyes. It's all still rattling around in there with no way out.

But God must know that Joe's a good man. And if He doesn't, then one hour once a week spent kneeling, sitting, and standing in St. Francis Church ain't going to save Joe's immortal soul now.

While he'll still put his money on God, it's the

Catholic Church as an institution that he's lost faith in. Too many priests diddling too many little boys; too many bishops and cardinals and even the Pope covering up the whole disgraceful mess. And Joe's no feminist, but they don't do right by women, if you ask him. No birth control, for one thing. Come on, is this really a mandate from Jesus? If Rosie wasn't on the pill, they'd probably have a dozen kids by now, and she'd have at least one foot in the grave. God bless modern medicine.

That's why they have a dog. After Katie, he told Rosie no more. Four is enough. Rosie got pregnant with JJ the summer after they graduated from high school (they were lucky pulling out worked as long as it did), so they had a shotgun wedding and a baby before they turned nineteen. JJ and Patrick were Irish twins, born eleven months apart. Meghan arrived fifteen months after Patrick, and Katie came screaming into this world eighteen months after Meghan.

As the kids got older and went to school, life got easier, but those early years were ugly. He remembers giving Rosie many unreciprocated kisses good-bye, leaving her home alone with four kids under the age of five, three of them still in diapers, grateful to have a legitimate reason to get the hell out of there, but he worried every day that she might not make it to the end of his shift. He actually imagined her doing something dreadful, his experience on the job or stories of what his fellow officers had seen fueling his worst fears. Regular people end up doing some crazy shit when pushed to their limits. Rosie probably didn't get a full night's sleep for a decade, and their kids were a handful. It's a miracle they're all still alive.

Rosie wasn't on board at first with the Infield Plan, as Joe called it. Insanely, she wanted more babies. She wanted to add at least a pitcher and a catcher to the O'Brien roster. She's the youngest of seven kids, the only girl, and even though she hardly ever sees her brothers now, she likes being from a big family.

But Joe made his decision, and that was that. He wasn't budging, and for the first time in his life, he actually refused to have sex until she agreed with him. That was a tense three months. He had been prepared to take care of business in the shower indefinitely when he noticed a flat, circular container on his pillow. Inside, he found a ring of pills, a week's worth already punched out. Against God's will, Rosie ended their cold war. He couldn't take her clothes off fast enough.

But if she couldn't have any more babies, she wanted a dog. Fair enough. She came home from the animal shelter with a shih tzu. He still thinks she did that just to spite him, her way of getting in the last word. Joe's a Boston cop, for cripes sake. He should be the proud owner of a Labrador or a Bernese mountain dog or an Akita. He agreed to getting a dog, a real dog, not a prissy little rat. He was not pleased.

Rosie named him Yaz, which at least made the mutt tolerable. Joe used to hate walking Yaz alone, out in public together. Made him feel like a pussy. But at some point he got over it. Yaz is a good dog, and Joe is man enough to be seen out in Charlestown walking a shih tzu. As long as Rosie doesn't dress the pooch in one of those friggin' sweaters.

He likes walking through Town when he's off duty. Even though everyone here knows he's a cop, and he's carrying his gun concealed beneath his untucked shirt, he feels unburdened when he's not wearing his tough police persona along with the uniform and badge that make him a visible target. He's always a cop, but off duty, he's also just a regular guy walking his dog in his neighborhood. And that feels good.

Everyone here calls the place Town, but Charlestown isn't really a town, or a city for that matter. It's a neighborhood of Boston, and a small one at that, only one square mile of land tucked between the Charles and Mystic Rivers. But, as any Irishman will tell you about his manhood, what it lacks in size, it makes up for in personality.

The Charlestown Joe grew up in was unofficially divided into two neighborhoods. The Bottom of the Hill was where the poor Irish lived, and the Top of the Hill, up by St. Francis Church, was home to the Lace Curtain Irish. People at the Top of the Hill could be just as poor as the bastards at the Bottom, and in most cases they probably were, but the perception was that they were better off. People here still think that.

There were also a few black families in the projects and some Italians who spilled over from the North End, but otherwise Charlestown was a homogenous hill of working-class Micks and their families living in tight rows of colonial and triple-decker houses. The Townies. And every Townie knew everyone in Town. If Joe was ever doing anything out of line as a kid, which was often, he'd hear somebody yelling from a stoop or open window, *Joseph O'Brien! I see you, and I know your mother!* People didn't have to involve the police back then. Kids feared their parents more than they did the authorities. Joe feared his mother more than anyone.

Twenty years ago, Charlestown was all Townies. But the place has changed a lot in recent years. Joe and Yaz plod up the hill, up Cordis Street, and it's as if they've turned the corner and stepped into another zip code. The town houses on this street have all been refurbished. They're either brick or painted in a glossy palette of approved historical colors. The doors are new, the windows have been replaced, neat rows of flowers bloom in copper window boxes, and the sidewalks are dotted with charming gas lamps. He checks out the make of each parked car as he presses on up the steep hill — Mercedes, BMW, Volvo. It's like Beacon Fuckin' Hill here.

Welcome to the Invasion of the Toonies. He doesn't blame them for coming. Charlestown is perfectly situated — on the water, a quick hop over the Zakim Bridge to downtown Boston, the Tobin Bridge to the north of the city, the tunnel to the South Shore, a quaint ferry ride to Faneuil Hall. So they started coming, with their fancy

17

corporate jobs and their fat wallets, buying up the real estate and classing up the joint.

But the Toonies don't typically stay. When they first come, most of them are DINKs — Double Income, No Kids. Then, in a couple of years, they might have a baby, maybe one more to balance things out. When the oldest is ready for kindergarten, that's when they leave for the suburbs.

So it's all temporary from the start, and they don't care about where they live as much as people do when they know they're staying until they get put in a box. The Toonies don't volunteer at the Y or coach the Little League teams, and most of them are Presbyterian or Unitarian or vegetarian or whatever friggin' wacky thing they are, and so they don't support the Catholic churches here, which is why St. Catherine's closed. They don't really become part of the community.

But the bigger problem is the Toonies have made Charlestown desirable to outsiders, and they've bloated the housing market. A person has to be rich to live in Charlestown now. Townies are a lot of great things, but unless they've robbed a bank, none of them are rich.

Joe is third-generation Irish in Charlestown. His grandfather, Patrick Xavier O'Brien, came over from Ireland in 1936 and worked in the Navy Yard as a longshoreman, supporting a family of ten on forty dollars a week. Joe's father, Francis, also worked in the Navy Yard, earning a hard but respectable living repairing ships. Joe's not breaking the bank on a cop's salary, but they get by. They've never felt poor here. Most of the next-generation Townies, however, no matter what they do for work, will never be able to afford to live here. It's a real shame.

He passes a FOR SALE sign in front of a freestanding colonial, one of the rare few with a courtyard, and tries to guess the outrageous listing price. Joe's father bought their house, a triple-decker at the Bottom of the Hill, in 1963 for ten grand. A similar triple-decker two streets over from Joe and Rosie sold last week for a cool million. Every time he thinks about that, it blows his friggin' mind. Sometimes he and Rosie talk about selling their place, a giddy, fantastical conversation that sounds a lot like imagining what they'd do if they won the lottery.

Joe would get a new car. A black Porsche. Rosie doesn't drive, but she'd get new clothes and shoes and some real jewelry.

But where would they live? They wouldn't move to some monstrous house in the suburbs with lots of land. He'd have to get a lawn mower. Rosie's brothers all live in rural towns at least forty-five minutes outside of Boston and seem to spend every weekend weeding and mulching and doing something labor-intensive to grass. Who wants that? And he'd have to leave the Boston Police Department if they moved to a suburb. That ain't happening. And realistically, he can't drive that kind of car around here. Talk about being a target. So he really wouldn't get the car, and Rosie is fine with her fake diamonds. Who wants to worry about lost or stolen jewelry? So although the conversation starts out heady, it

19

always loops into a big circle that lands them firmly right back where they are. They both love it here, and for all the money in the world wouldn't live anywhere else. Not even Southie.

They're lucky to have inherited the triple-decker. When Joe's father died nine years ago, he left the house to Joe and Joe's only sibling, his sister, Maggie. It took some serious detective work to track Maggie down. Always Joe's opposite, she made it her mission to leave Charlestown immediately after high school and never returned. He found her living in Southern California, divorced, no kids, and wanting nothing to do with the house. Joe understands.

He and Rosie live on the first floor, and twenty-three-year-old Patrick still lives with them. Their other son, JJ, and his wife, Colleen, live on the second floor. Katie and Meghan are roommates on the third floor. Everyone but Patrick pays Joe and Rosie rent, but it's minimal, way below market value, just something to keep them all responsible. And it helps pay off the mortgage. They had to refinance a couple of times to put all four kids through parochial school. That was a huge nut, but there was no way in hell his kids were getting bused to Dorchester or Roxbury.

Joe turns the corner and decides to cut through Doherty Park. Charlestown is quiet at this sleepy hour on a Sunday morning. Clougherty Pool is closed. The basketball courts are empty. The kids are all either in church or still in bed. Other than an occasional passing car, the only sounds are the jingling of Yaz's tags and the change in Joe's front pocket playing together like a song.

As expected, he finds eighty-three-year-old Michael Murphy sitting on the far bench in the shade. He's got his cane and his brown bag of stale bread for the birds. He sits there all day, every day, except for when the weather is particularly lousy, and watches over things. He's seen it all.

'How are ya today, Mayor?' asks Joe.

Everyone calls Murphy Mayor.

'Better than most women deserve,' says Murphy.

'So true,' chuckles Joe, even though this is Mayor's verbatim reply to this same question about every third time Joe asks.

'How's the First Lady?' asks Murphy.

Murphy calls Joe Mr. President. The nickname began ages ago as Mr. Kennedy, a reference to Joe and Rose, and then at some point it morphed, skipping from father to son, defying actual US political history, and Mr. Joseph Kennedy became Mr. President. And that, of course, makes Rosie the First Lady.

'Good. She's at church praying for me.'

'Gonna be there a long time, then.'

'Yup. Have a good one, Mayor.'

Joe continues along the path, taking in the distant view from this hill of the industrial silos and the Everett shipyard on the other side of the Mystic River. Most people would say the view is nothing special and might even think it's an eyesore. He'll probably never find a painter parked on this spot with an easel, but Joe sees a kind of urban beauty here.

He's descending the steep hill, using the stairs instead of the switchback ramp, when he somehow missteps and his view is suddenly nothing but sky. He skids down three concrete steps on his back before he has the presence of mind to stop himself with his hands. He eases himself up to sitting, and he can already feel a nasty series of bruises blossoming on the knobs of his spine. He twists around to examine the stairs, expecting to blame some kind of obstruction such as a stick or a rock or a busted step. There's nothing. He looks up to the top of the stairs, to the park around him and the landing below. At least no one saw him.

Yaz pants and wags his tail, eager to move along.

'Just a sec, Yaz.'

Joe lifts each arm up and checks his elbows. Both are scraped and bleeding. He wipes the gravel and blood and eases himself to standing.

How the hell did he trip? Must be his bum knee. He twisted his right knee a couple of years ago chasing a B&E suspect down Warren Street. Brick sidewalks may look pretty, but they're bumpy and buckled, brutal to run on, especially in the dark. His knee hasn't been the same since and seems to just quit on him every now and then without warning. He should probably get it checked out, but he doesn't do doctors.

He's particularly careful going down the rest of the stairs and continues down to Medford Street. He decides to cut back in and up at the high school. Rosie should be getting out soon, and he's now feeling a stabbing pinch in his lower back with each step. He wants to get home.

As he's walking up Polk Street, a car slows down next to him. It's Donny Kelly, Joe's best friend from childhood. Donny still lives in Town and works as an EMT, so Joe sees him quite a bit both on and off the job.

'Whaddya drink too much last night?' asks Donny, smiling at him through the open window of his Pontiac.

'Huh?' asks Joe, smiling back.

'You limpin' or somethin'?'

'Oh yeah, my back is tweaked.'

'Wanna ride up over the hill, old man?'

'Nah, I'm good.'

'Come on, get in the car.'

'I need the exercise,' says Joe, patting his gut. 'How's Matty doin'?'

'Good.'

'And Laurie?'

'Good, everyone's good. Hey, you sure I can't take you somewhere?'

'No, really, thanks.'

'All right, I gotta go. Good to see you, OB.'

'You, too, Donny.'

Joe makes a point of walking evenly and at a rigorous clip while he can still see Donny's car, but when Donny reaches the top of the hill and then disappears, Joe stops the charade. He trudges along, each step now twisting some invisible screw deeper into his spine, and he wishes he'd taken the ride.

He replays Donny's comment about having

too much to drink. He knows it was just an innocent joke, but Joe's always been sensitive about his reputation and drinking. He never has more than two beers. Well, sometimes he'll finish off his two beers with a shot of whiskey, just to prove he's a man, but that's it.

His mother was a drinker. Drank herself into the nuthouse, and everyone knew about it. It's been a long time, but that shit follows you. People don't forget anything, and who you're from is as important as who you are. Everyone half expects you to become a raging alcoholic if your mother drank herself to death.

Ruth O'Brien drank herself to death.

This is what everyone says. It's his family legend and legacy. Whenever it comes up, a parade of memories marches closely behind. It gets uncomfortable real fast, and he swiftly changes the subject so he doesn't have to 'go there.' How 'bout them Red Sox?

But today, whether due to a growth in bravery, maturity, or curiosity, he can't say, he allows this sentence to accompany him up the hill. *Ruth O'Brien drank herself to death.* It doesn't really add up. Yes, she drank. In a nutshell, she drank so much that she couldn't walk or talk a straight line. She'd say and do crazy things. Violent things. She was completely out of control, and when his father couldn't handle her anymore, he put her in the state hospital. Joe was only twelve when she died.

Ruth O'Brien drank herself to death. For the first time in his life, he consciously realizes that this sentence that he's held as gospel, a fact as verifiable and real as his own birth date, can't literally be true. His mother was in that hospital for five years. She had to have been as dry as a bone, on the permanent wagon in a hospital bed, when she died.

Maybe her brain and liver had been soaking in booze for too many years, and it turned them both to mush. So maybe it was too late. The damage was done, and there was no recovering. Her wet brain and soggy liver finally failed her. Cause of death: chronic exposure to alcohol.

He reaches the top of the hill, relieved and ready to move on to an easier street and topic, but his mother's death is still pestering him. Something about this new theory doesn't ring true. He's got that unsettled, hole-in-his-gut feeling that he gets when he arrives at a call and he's not getting what really happened from anyone. He's got a good ear for it, the truth, and this ain't it. So if she didn't drink herself to death or die from alcohol-related causes, then what?

He searches for a better answer for three more blocks and comes up empty. What does it even matter? She's dead. She's been dead a long time. *Ruth O'Brien drank herself to death.* Leave it alone.

The bells are ringing as he arrives at St. Francis Church. He spots Rosie right away, waiting for him on the top step, and he smiles. He thought she was a knockout when they started dating at sixteen, and he actually thinks she's getting prettier as she ages. At forty-three, she has peaches-and-cream skin splashed with freckles, auburn hair (even though these days the color comes from a bottle), and green eyes that can still make him weak in the knees. She's an amazing mother and definitely a saint for putting up with him. He's a lucky man.

'Did you put in a good word for me?' asks Joe.

'Many times,' she says, flicking holy water at him with her fingers.

'Good. You know I need all the help I can get.'

'Are you bleeding?' she asks, noticing his arm.

'Yeah, I fell on some stairs. I'm okay.'

She takes hold of his other hand, lifts his arm, and finds the bloody abrasion on that elbow.

'You sure?' she asks, concern in her eyes.

'I'm fine,' he says, and squeezes her hand in his. 'Come, my bride, let's go home.'

3

It's almost four thirty, and the whole family is sitting around the kitchen table set with empty jelly jar glasses, plates, and silverware on the threadbare green quilted place mats Katie sewed in home ec ages ago, waiting for Patrick. No one has seen him since yesterday afternoon. Patrick bartends nights at Ironsides, so presumably, he was there until closing, but he never came home last night. They have no idea where he is. Meghan keeps texting him, but, no surprise to any of them, he's not answering his phone.

Joe noticed Patrick's empty, perfectly made twin bed on the way to the bathroom early this morning. He paused before continuing down the hall, his focus drifting above where Patrick's head should've been to the poster on the wall of Bruins center Patrice Bergeron. Joe shook his head at Bergy and sighed. Part of Joe wanted to go in and mess up the blankets and sheets, make it look as if Patrick had been home and was already up and out, just so Rosie wouldn't worry. But that's not a believable ruse anyway. If Patrick had come home, he'd still be in there, passed out until at least noon.

It's best if Rosie knows the truth and is allowed to express her concerns. Joe can then listen and nod and say nothing, concealing his own darker theories beneath a veiled silence. What Joe is capable of imagining is far worse than anything Rosie might cook up. The lad drinks too much, but he's twenty-three. He's young. Joe and Rosie have their eyes on it, but the excessive drinking isn't where either of their real worries lie.

Rosie's terrified that he's going to get some girl pregnant. This highly religious woman actually slips condoms into her son's wallet. One at a time. Poor Rosie is gravely mortified each time she checks inside and finds only a couple of bucks and no condom, often many times in the same week. But she always resupplies him, sometimes with a little cash, too. She then makes the sign of the cross and says nothing.

Although Joe wishes Patrick had a steady girlfriend, someone with a name and a nice face and a pretty smile who Patrick cared enough about to bring home to Sunday supper, Joe can live with the womanizing. Hell, part of him even admires the boy. Joe also can forgive him for not coming home at night and for the time he 'borrowed' Donny's car and totaled it. Joe's more worried about the drugs.

He's never held this kind of suspicion with the other three kids and has no direct evidence that Patrick is using. Yet. He can't help finishing that thought every time with a 'yet,' and so therein lies Joe's worry. Whenever Joe's working the midnight shift and gets called to the Montego Bay boat launch or some other secluded parking lot to arrest some punks for drug possession, he finds himself first searching the young faces for Patrick's. He hopes to God he's wrong and is being unnecessarily paranoid, but there's a familiar attitude in these kids that reminds him too much of Patrick, an apathy and recklessness beyond the normal sense of invincibility of young people. It worries Joe more than he'd like to admit.

He's not a stranger to arresting family, and it's no fun. He caught his brother-in-law Shawn literally red-handed, stained head to toe in exploded red dye, with a thick, crisp stack of one-dollar bills sandwiched between two fifties shoved inside the pocket of his hoodie — only minutes after a bank was robbed in City Square. Another brother-in-law, Richie, is still doing time for drug trafficking back in the late nineties. Joe remembers eyeing Richie through the rearview, handcuffed and staring out the backseat window of his cruiser, and Joe felt ashamed, as if he'd been the one who committed a crime. Rosie was heartbroken. He never wants to put another relative in the back of his car again, especially not his own son.

'Meghan, text him,' says Rosie, her arms crossed.

'I just did, Ma,' says Meghan.

'Then do it again.'

Rosie's concern is deteriorating to anger. Sunday supper is nonnegotiable for the kids, especially on a Sunday that Joe is home, and to be this late is approaching unforgivable. Meanwhile, Rosie will keep cooking the food that was already overcooked a half hour ago. The roast beef will be dry, tasteless leather, the mashed potatoes will be a bowl of gray glue, and the canned green beans will have been boiled beyond recognition. As he's done for twenty-five years, Joe will get through supper with a lot of salt, a couple of beers, and no complaints.

The girls have a harder time with Sunday supper. Katie is vegan. Each week she passionately lectures them about animal cruelty and the outrageously disgusting practices of the meat industry while the rest of them, minus Meghan, all shovel in heavily salted mouthfuls of overcooked blood sausage.

Meghan typically rejects most of the meal because of fat and calorie content. She's a dancer for the Boston Ballet and, as far as Joe can tell, eats only salads. She usually picks at the obliterated canned vegetable while the rest of them, minus Katie, fill up on meat and potatoes. Meghan's not too thin, but her eyes always look so hungry, following the movement of their forks like a caged lion stalking a family of baby gazelles. Between the two girls, you need a degree from college to learn and memorize all the rules and restrictions surrounding their diets.

JJ and his wife, Colleen, will politely eat anything Rosie puts in front of them. God bless them. That takes some highly skilled manners.

Joe and JJ are a lot alike. They share the same name, the same stocky build, and the same sleepy blue eyes. They both have pasty white skin that blooms an unflattering carnation pink whenever they get excited (the Red Sox win) or angry (the Red Sox choke) and that can sunburn in late-afternoon shade. They both have the same sense of humor that at least half the time Rosie thinks isn't one bit funny, and they both married women who are far too good for them.

But JJ is a firefighter, and that's the most striking difference between them. For the most part, Boston firefighters and cops consider themselves brothers and sisters, here to protect and serve this great city and her people, but the firefighters get all the glory, and that bugs the piss out of Joe. Firefighters are always the big heroes. They show up at someone's house and everyone cheers and thanks them. Some of those guys actually get hugged. The cops show up and everyone hides.

Plus firefighters get paid more and do less. It drives Joe nuts when they respond to fender benders where they're not needed, messing up traffic, getting in the way of BEMS and the police. Joe thinks they're bored and trying to look busy. *We got it, guys. Go back to the house and take another nap.*

To be honest, he's actually grateful that JJ didn't become a cop. Joe's proud to be a patrol officer, but he wouldn't wish this life on any of his kids. Still, sometimes Joe feels strangely betrayed by JJ's career choice, the way a Red Sox player would feel if his son grew up and became a New York Yankee. Part of Joe is busting with pride, and the other part wonders where he went wrong.

'What's goin' on, Dad?' asks Katie.

'Huh?' asks Joe.

'You're all quiet today.'

'Just lost in thought, honey.'

'Havin' two of them in there can be tough,' ribs JJ.

Joe smiles.

'Now I'm thinkin' you should go get me a beer,' says Joe to JJ.

'Me, too,' says Katie.

'I'll have one,' says Colleen.

'No beer until supper,' says Rosie, stopping JJ at the fridge.

Rosie looks up at the kitchen clock. It's now five o'clock. She continues to stare at the time for what feels like a full minute and then, without warning, slams her wooden spoon down on the counter. She unties her apron and hangs it on the hook. That's it. They're eating without Patrick. JJ opens the fridge and retrieves a six-pack of Bud.

Rosie pulls what used to be roast beef out of the oven, or the 'taste extractor' as Joe likes to call it, and Meghan helps her transport the entire meal to the small, round table. Everything is overcrowded — elbows bump neighboring elbows, feet kick opposite-facing feet, bowls touch plates, plates touch glasses.

Rosie sits down and says grace, and then everyone rotely says 'Amen' and begins passing food.

'Ow, Joe, quit bumping me,' says Rosie, rubbing her shoulder.

'Sorry, honey, there's no room.'

'There's plenty of room. Stop fidgeting so much.'

He can't help it. He had three cups of coffee this morning instead of his usual two, and he's feeling on edge, wondering where Patrick is.

'Where's the salt?' asks Joe.

'I got it,' says JJ, who showers the food on his plate and then hands the shaker over to his father.

'Is that all you're having?' Rosie asks Katie, looking at her big white plate sporting only a modest mouthful of wilted gray beans.

'Yeah, I'm good.'

'How about some potato?'

'You put butter in it.'

'Just a little bit.'

Katie rolls her eyes. 'Ma, I'm not just a little bit vegan. I'm vegan. I don't eat dairy.'

'And what's your excuse?' asks Rosie, referring to Meghan's similarly empty plate.

'Do you have any salad?' asks Meghan.

'Yeah, I'd like a salad,' says Katie.

'There's some lettuce and a cucumber in the fridge. Go ahead,' says Rosie, sighing and waving the back of her hand at them. 'You girls are so difficult to feed.'

Meghan pops up, opens the fridge, finds the two ingredients and nothing else, and sets herself up at the counter.

'How about some cow?' offers JJ, extending the platter of roast beef under his sister's nose.

'Stop it. That's disgusting,' says Katie, pushing the plate back toward him.

Meghan returns to the table and portions half the salad onto Katie's plate, the other half onto hers, and then dumps the empty bowl into the sink. Meanwhile Joe works at cutting his roast beef with the same level of effort a lumberjack might use to saw through a tree. He finally frees a piece and watches his girls happily crunching

33

on their salads as he chews on a salty roof shingle.

'You know, the farmers who grew that lettuce and cucumber probably used fertilizer,' says Joe, wearing the straightest expression he's got.

Katie and Meghan ignore him, but JJ cracks a smile, knowing where this is going.

'I'm no farmer, but I think they use cow manure for fertilizer, don't they, JJ?'

'Yup, they sure do,' says JJ, who has never stepped foot in a garden or on a farm in his life.

'Stop,' says Meghan.

'The lettuce and cucumber seeds use nutrients from the cow manure to grow. So basically, if you do the math, that salad you're eating is made of cow shit.'

'Gross, Dad. Really gross,' says Katie.

'I'd rather eat the cow than the cow's shit, wouldn't you, JJ?'

JJ and Joe have a good laugh. For many reasons, the women in the room are not amused.

'Okay, that's enough,' says Rosie, who would normally find Joe's teasing at least good-natured. She doesn't understand the whole vegan thing either. But he knows that she's still fuming about Patrick's unknown whereabouts and is too distracted by his absence to think anything is funny. 'Can we please talk about something other than shit?'

'I have the dates for *Coppélia*,' says Meghan. 'It runs August tenth to the twenty-fourth.'

'Me and Colleen are going on the first Friday,' says JJ.

'Colleen and I,' says Rosie. 'That works for me. Katie?'

'Uh, I'm not sure yet. I might have plans.'

'Doing what?' asks Meghan in a dismissive tone that Joe knows Katie will find offensive.

'None of your business,' says Katie.

'Lemme guess. Ironsides with Andrea and Micaela.'

'My Friday nights are just as important as yours. The whole world doesn't revolve around you.'

'Girls,' warns Rosie.

Growing up, Katie was Meghan's dutiful shadow. As Joe remembers it, he and Rosie always parented them as a single unit. Except when it came to dance, Joe and Rosie referred to the girls together so often, their individual names seemed to blur into a single third moniker. *Meg-an-Katie, come here. Meg-an-Katie are going to the parade. Meg-an-Katie, time for supper.*

But since high school, the girls have been drifting apart. Joe can't put his finger on exactly why. Meghan's so consumed with her rigorous ballet schedule; even though the girls live together, she's not around much. Katie could be feeling left behind. Or jealous. They all do make a pretty big deal over Meg. Joe listens politely whenever other parents in Town brag about their daughter who works at the library or the MBTA or who just got married. He beams when they're done, when it's finally his turn. *MY daughter dances for the Boston Ballet.* No other parent from Town can top that. He realizes just now that he doesn't mention anything about his other daughter.

Katie teaches yoga, which Joe will admit he knows virtually nothing about except that it's today's latest fitness craze, like Zumba or Tae Bo or CrossFit but dressed in a New Age, hippy-dippy, cultlike kind of following. He thinks it's wonderful she's doing something she enjoys, but Joe can tell she's dissatisfied. He's not sure whether it's with yoga or all the attention they give Meghan or a boyfriend Joe doesn't know about, but there's a tension in the posture of Katie's voice that seems to be squeezing tighter each week, a chip on her shoulder that she wears like a favorite accessory. She was such an easygoing kid. His baby girl. Whatever's going on, he assumes it's just a phase. She'll work it out.

'Dad?' asks Meghan. 'Are you coming?'

Joe loves watching Meghan dance, and he's not ashamed to admit that it always makes him cry. Most little girls say they want to be a ballerina, but it's a wish in the same category as wanting to be a fairy princess, a whimsical fantasy and not a real career goal. But when Meghan said at the age of four that she wanted to be a ballerina, they all believed her.

She began with lessons at the local dance studio and then entered the free Citydance program when she was in the third grade. She was focused and tenacious from the start. She received a scholarship for the Boston Ballet School when she was thirteen and was offered a contract in the corps de ballet when she graduated high school.

Meghan works hard, harder than any of them probably, but Joe also believes that she was born to dance. The stunning beauty of those spins, whatever they're called, the impossibility of how high she holds one leg in the air while the rest of her is balanced on one big toe. He can't even touch his toes. Meghan has Joe's eyes, but thank God that's about it. The rest of her comes from Rosie or is a gift straight from God.

He missed *The Nutcracker* this year. He'd seen her in it many times before, although not in this role in the Boston Ballet, Meghan would be quick to point out. And he got called in for an evening shift when he was supposed to see *The Sleeping Beauty* in April. He knows he's disappointed her. It's one of the worst things about his job, missing out on Christmas mornings and birthdays and his kid's Little League championship game and every Fourth of July and too many of Meghan's dance recitals.

'I'll be there,' says Joe.

He'll work it out. Meghan smiles. Bless her for still believing in him.

'Where's the water?' asks Rosie.

Joe spots the water pitcher on the counter.

'I got it,' he says.

The pitcher is heavy, real crystal, probably one of the most expensive things they own if Joe had to guess. It was a wedding gift from Rosie's parents, and Rosie fills it with water, beer, or spiked iced tea, depending on the occasion, every Sunday.

Joe fills the pitcher at the sink, returns to the

table, and, still standing, requests everyone's jelly jar one at a time, ladies first. He's pouring water into Katie's glass when he somehow loses hold of the handle, midair, midpour. The pitcher drops, knocking Katie's glass out of his other hand, and both hit the table, instantly shattering into hundreds of the tiniest pebbles of glass. Meghan screams and Rosie gasps, her hand over her mouth.

'It's okay. Everyone's okay,' says JJ.

His right hand stuck in place as if still holding the pitcher, Joe assesses the damage. The pitcher is destroyed beyond recognition. Everything on the table is wet and seasoned with crumbs of glass. He finally unfreezes and rubs his fingers and thumb against the palm of his hand, expecting them to feel greasy or wet, but they're clean and dry. He stares at his hand as if it doesn't belong to him and wonders what the hell just happened.

'Sorry, Rosie,' says Joe.

'It's all right,' she says, unhappy but resigned to the loss.

'I have glass in my food,' says Katie.

'Me, too,' says Colleen.

Joe looks down at his plate. He's got glass in his mashed potatoes. What a mess.

'Okay, nobody eats anything,' says JJ. 'Even if you can't see any glass, it's not worth taking the chance.'

As Katie is cleaning up the floor with a dustpan and broom and Rosie and Meghan are clearing the plates of ruined Sunday supper, Patrick strolls in, yesterday's clothes rumpled and hanging on his skinny frame, smelling of stale beer, cigarettes, and mint, a box of Dunkin' Donuts under his arm.

'You're late,' says Rosie, her eyes two formidable laser beams fixated on boring a hole through the center of her boy's forehead.

'I know, Ma. I'm sorry,' says Patrick.

He kisses his mother on the cheek and sits down at the table.

'I don't even want to know where you were,' says Rosie.

Patrick says nothing.

'There's no excuse for missing Sunday supper.'

'I know, Ma. I didn't miss it, I'm here.'

'Oh, you missed it,' says JJ.

Katie smacks Patrick on the shoulder, a signal to lift his elbows off the table so she can wipe it down with a sponge.

'Where's the food?' asks Patrick.

'Dad thought supper needed more water and a dash of glass,' says Meghan.

'Be thankful you're not a klutz like your father,' says Joe.

Patrick proudly sets the box of Dunkin' Donuts on the table. Today's O'Brien family Sunday supper. JJ dives in first and pulls out a Boston Kreme. Katie peeks into the box expecting to be disappointed, but instead her face lights up.

'You got me a toasted bagel with peanut butter.'

'Course I did,' says Patrick. 'And an egg-white veggie flatbread without the flatbread for Meg.'

'Thanks, Pat,' says Meghan.

Rosie's posture softens, and Joe knows that Patrick is forgiven. Joe chooses a jelly donut and a cruller. Donuts and beer. He pats his protruding belly and sighs. He's going to have to start watching his figure if he wants to live to be an old man.

He takes in the ordinary scene at their modest table, at his grown children and wife, everyone happy and healthy and here together on a Sunday afternoon despite all their quirks and faults, and a wave of gratitude swells inside him so suddenly, he doesn't have time to brace himself. He feels the full magnitude of it pressing against the inner wall of his chest, and he exhales hard through clenched teeth to relieve some of the pressure. Underneath his tough-cop, macho exterior, he's soft as a jelly donut. As he turns his head and wipes the wet corners of his eyes with the heel of his hand before anyone can see, he thanks God for all that he has and knows that he is truly blessed.

4

Joe's been patrolling the hilly streets of Charlestown, riding alone in his cruiser for a few hours now. It's a typical day tour, which of course is an oxymoron, and Joe knows it. There's no such thing as a typical tour. It's one of the things he loves and hates about his job.

He loves it because it means he's never bored. Not that every minute of every shift is enthralling. Most shifts crawl through hours of mind-numbing tedium, beginning with roll call and the ridiculous daily song and dance of locating the damn four-digit number on his assigned car among a sea of identical parked cruisers, then driving the same familiar streets, nothing at all happening. And then, invariably, something does.

A call will come in. Someone is breaking into a home on Green Street, some husband is beating the crap out of his beloved wife, there's a pileup involving a tanker trailer hauling jet fuel on the northbound expressway, another bank robbery, several purses were stolen from an office in the Schrafft Center, there's a bar fight outside the Warren Tavern, there's a gang fight outside the high school, there's a sunken car in the harbor with a body in it, someone jumped off the Tobin Bridge. It can be anything, and it's never the same. Every burglary, every assault, every domestic is different, and different means never

41

boring. It means that with every call, there's the chance Joe will be summoned to use any and all of his training and skills.

Responding to a call also gives him the rare chance to experience what he loves most about his job — when he really helps someone out, when swift and decisive action results in a win for the good guys, when they take the bad guys off the street and keep this corner of the planet just a little bit safer. If that sounds like a corny after-school special, so be it. It's why Joe keeps showing up for roll call, and he'd bet box seats behind home plate at Fenway that every officer worth his salt feels the same way.

But it's a double-edged sword, because each call also brings the greater possibility of steering Joe directly into the mouth of what he hates most about his job. Every day, police officers see the hairy, smelly underbelly of humanity, the most depraved and evil shit human beings are capable of, shit civilians thankfully can't imagine. A call comes in. A man in Roxbury strangled his wife, stuffed her in a trash bag, and then threw her off the roof of his apartment building. A mother in Dorchester drowned her three-year-old twin boys in the bathtub. Two bombs on Marathon Monday.

He has his training and the stress unit to help him deal with whatever it is, and as have all his fellow officers, Joe's made a fine art out of telling crude jokes and acting callous, a standard and fairly transparent arsenal of self-defense mechanisms aimed at keeping the vile carnage he's witnessed from penetrating him. But it does. And it changes him. It changes all of them.

The trick is not to let it affect Rosie and the kids. He remembers the body of a teenage girl, shot twice in the head, left rotting in a Dumpster in Chinatown. Even lifeless and discolored and covered in flies, the girl looked so much like Meghan, Joe couldn't take it. He had to use every ounce of willpower he possessed to suppress the urge to puke right there in front of everyone. He did what he had to do, holding it together, stuffing the revulsion down, moving through his duties on autopilot. Hours later, alone in his cruiser, he noticed his hands gripped around the steering wheel, shaking so violently that the entire car shimmied.

When Joe got home that night, Rosie asked, 'How was your day, sweetie?' Probably the most innocent and banal question in most marriages, it's a can of fuckin' vipers for Joe, and he ain't opening it. That night, like so many others, he gave Rosie a kiss and a vague 'Good' and went to bed.

He had nightmares about that young girl in the Dumpster for months but never mentioned a word of any of it to Rosie. She often complains about his silence and wishes he'd share more with her. He knows that good communication is important for a healthy relationship, and officers suffer a higher-than-normal rate of divorce, but he'd never burden her with the horrors he's seen. Once you can imagine these things, you can't unimagine them.

So no shift is typical and no call routine, but so far today, nothing's happened. He slows down

43

in front of his house on Cook Street. No sign of anyone. Even though it's almost noon, Patrick is probably still sleeping. Meghan was up and out earlier than Joe. He checks the time. Katie is teaching a yoga class at Town Yoga in a few minutes, the noon Hour of Power. He'll drive by her next. JJ may or may not be on duty now, Joe can't remember. Colleen is at work. She's a physical therapist at Spaulding. And Rosie is working today. She's a part-time receptionist for a dermatologist practice in the Schrafft building. He smiles, imagining his family doing what they should be doing. All is well.

He hasn't seen the other cruisers here since earlier in the morning. Only four officers cover Charlestown — one two-man car, the rapid, and two one-man service cars. Joe's grateful he's alone in a service car and wasn't assigned to a rapid today. He's not in the mood for conversation, and a lot of the guys, especially the young rookies, are real Chatty Cathys and never shut the fuck up. Maybe he's just turning into a crotchety old man of forty-three, but Joe finds more and more that he prefers the solitude and quiet of a service or tango car to the chitchat of a rapid.

Joe drives by the Bunker Hill Monument and slows to study the makeshift memorial where a nineteen-year-old boy was shot to death last week — a wooden cross, red, white, and blue balloons, a baseball glove, a teddy bear, his school picture. Joe sighs. Such a waste.

Charlestown is a relatively safe neighborhood. They don't typically see a lot of violent crime,

44

and almost never any homicides. But there's that word again. Typical. There's no such thing.

Charlestown's crime cocktail consists mostly of drugs, thefts, domestics, and bar fights. In recent years, Joe's seen a lot of muggings in Charlestown. That kind of shit didn't happen here when he was growing up. Not that people then were above stealing. Almost every kid Joe knew was related to someone who'd committed a real crime, and burglary was probably the most popular. But there was a code of ethics with respect to stealing, if that's possible. Robbing a bank or an office building was fine because it was considered a 'victimless' crime. Robbing a person or someone's house was never okay.

Joe remembers Billy Ryan, the scariest thug he knew, berating Mark Sullivan for lifting fifty bucks from an apartment on Belmont Street. *That's Kevin Gallagher's house. You robbed Kevin's mother? You piece of shit, what's wrong with you?* If memory serves Joe right, Billy actually shamed Mark into breaking back into Kevin's house to return the money. Billy robbed a bank the next day.

Joe drives by Dougherty Park. The courts are empty, but the pool is packed. It's ninety-seven degrees today. Hazy, hot, and humid. The hospital ERs will be clogged with heatstrokes and heart attacks. Even with the AC on full blast, Joe's sweating. His T-shirt and underwear are soaked through, the wet cotton clinging to his skin. The relentless rays of the sun assaulting him through the windows and windshield coupled with his Kevlar vest and navy blue police

45

uniform make Joe feel as if he's a hothouse tomato dying on the vine. It could be worse. He could be on his feet, outside on the black pavement, directing traffic.

He winds his way down to Main Street and pauses in front of Town Yoga. There are no windows to peek through, so he can't actually see Katie. He has no idea what goes on in there, but if he had to guess, it has something to do with women dressed in tight black pants contorting themselves into pretzels. Katie's been hounding him for well over a year now to take one of her classes, but he always gives her some excuse wrapped in a joke. *I would come, hun, but I pulled my third chakra yesterday, and the doctor said 'No yoga for a month.' I'm wicked bummed.*

He unwraps his tuna sub and scarfs it down, barely tasting it. He's got the last bite stuffed in his mouth when a call comes in. A robbery in progress at 344 Bunker Hill Street. Unit 31. Joe wipes the mayonnaise from his lips with the back of his hand, hits the buttons by his hip for lights and sirens, and takes off.

He knows the address. He was just over there. It's the old school building, now a swanky condo property filled with Toonies, across the street from the park and pool. Unit 31. Third floor.

Does it face the street or the back of the building? If it's a back unit, does it have a balcony? A fire escape? Will the suspect exit there or through the interior of the building? Stairs or elevator? If the suspect's a Townie, he could easily be brazen or stupid enough to walk right

46

out the front door. The back of the building has a parking lot. Perfect spot for a getaway car. Depending on what's being stolen, the suspect could be in a car or on foot. The building has a basement garage. A great place to hide. Is there more than one suspect? Is this a random, opportunistic hit or a targeted break-in? Is anyone home? Probably, but hopefully not. It's the middle of the day, and this building is primarily populated by young professionals. It's summer, so maybe the resident is away on vacation. But the caller, a neighbor, is home, so it's possible the resident is also. An elderly parent. A retiree. A mother and baby. Someone who called in sick. Will the suspect be armed?

Joe kills the siren and then pulls over a couple of houses before the building. He's the only car on the scene. Fuck. He doesn't know what he's about to face in there. Ideally, officers go into this kind of situation with the odds in their favor, a show of force so they don't have to actually use any. But Joe can't just wait in his car until the other officers get there. He has to get out and deal with what's happening, whatever it is. His adrenaline spikes.

Joe pulls out his gun and holds it pointed down by his side as he enters the building and ascends the stairs to the third floor. He turns right: 35, 37. Wrong way. He pivots and hastens left. He stands in front of the door to unit 31, and Joe's heightened senses go to work. The unit faces the back of the building. The doorframe next to the deadbolt is splintered, forcibly broken. The call is real. Joe's heart rate escalates.

He stays quiet and listens. His own heavy breathing. Air blowing from the air-conditioning vents. Talking. Male voices. A conversation.

He backs up and, in the most muted yet clear voice he can manage, radios this information in.

'We have at least two in there. Unit faces the rear. We need someone to cover the back.'

A few seconds later, Officer Tommy Vitale, Joe's oldest, closest friend on the force, is standing beside him. The other officer from Tommy's rapid unit must be outside, covering the rear of the building. Joe and Tommy connect eye-to-eye, and then Tommy nods. Joe turns the doorknob, and they enter the unit.

They immediately slice the room. Joe rushes diagonally left, and Tommy moves right, both heading for the walls on opposite sides of the room. Joe stands with his back to the dining room wall, and Tommy positions himself against the wall in the kitchen. They see no one so far.

They're in one of those modern, open-floor-plan condos, and they can see into the living room. It's a mess. Drawers dumped and emptied, papers and junk all over the floor. Beyond the living room is an open glass sliding door leading to an outdoor balcony. And bingo, there are the two suspects. Teenage boys.

Both Joe and Tommy advance, guns pointed at the boys' chests.

'Boston PD! Drop the bags and show me your hands!' yells Joe.

The boys are in T-shirts, long, baggy shorts, sneakers, baseball caps, and dark sunglasses. Both are carrying black backpacks. Joe is trying

48

to figure out whether the boy on the left is armed while still aiming his gun at the center of the boy's chest when this moron decides to make a break for it and vaults the railing.

A third-floor unit is thirty feet up. Joe's not sure what this genius was thinking would happen when he landed, but he's probably broken both legs and possibly his back. He's lying on the pavement, and his screaming turns to a pitiful squeal when Officer Sean Wallace flips and cuffs him.

'So is it your turn?' asks Tommy, cocking his head toward the railing.

The kid drops the bag and holds his bare hands in the air.

'At least this one has a brain in his head,' says Tommy as he cuffs him. 'Size of a pea, but he's got one.'

Joe searches the rest of the condo to be sure there aren't any other pals in on the heist. The two bedrooms, the two bathrooms, and the home office are all empty. The bedrooms don't look too bad, but the home office is gutted.

Joe returns to the balcony.

'The rest is clear.'

Tommy is patting down the prisoner; he's searching for a weapon but doesn't find one. They see this a lot, especially in the summer, when school is out and the kids have too much time on their hands. These teens break into someone's house, steal whatever they can get their hands on, and pawn it for cash. The cash is always for drugs. If Joe doesn't catch them stealing, he catches them buying. If he doesn't catch them buying, he catches them using or doing something stupid while using. And after they're out on bail or parole, he catches them again. Round and round they go.

Joe eyes the young man cuffed and slouched before him. He's hanging his head, so Joe can't get a good look at his face under the rim of his baseball cap, but Joe recognizes the heavy ink on both arms — the Irish and American flags, a navy ship, a heart, and a four-leaf clover. It's Scotty O'Donnell, the younger brother of Robby O'Donnell, who grew up with Patrick. Robby was a star basketball player in high school and stayed out of trouble. Scotty's older sisters were all honor-roll students. His mother goes to church with Rosie, and his father works at the post office. He comes from a good family.

'Scotty, what the hellaya doin'?' says Joe.

Scotty looks down at his sneakers and shrugs.

'Look at me when I'm talkin' to you.'

Scotty lifts his head. Tommy removes Scotty's sunglasses, and Scotty's eyes are defiant, admitting nothing, not nearly scared enough.

'Y-gonna bring shame to your poor mother. She's gonna have to come down to the station and bail your dumb ass out. She doesn't deserve that.'

The ambulance is now here, and the EMTs are lifting the Olympic hurdler onto a stretcher. Officer Wallace will have to accompany this kid to the hospital and guard him through any X-rays and procedures he might need.

'You want this one?' asks Tommy.

'Yeah, I'll take him in,' says Joe.

'I'll wait for the detective.'

Joe looks down at the black backpack, and an unexpected, additional surge of adrenaline pulses through him, sending every muscle and nerve in his body back into high alert, twitching, ready to pop. It's probably going to be a long time before any Boston cop can look at a young man with a backpack and simply see a kid with a schoolbag and not a potential terrorist with a weapon of mass destruction.

Loud, sudden noises aren't any better. Every officer was called out for duty on July fourth. Less than three months after the marathon bombing, security for a public event attracting three hundred thousand civilians to the Esplanade lawn in celebration of the nation's freedom was through the roof. Joe hadn't seen anything like it in all his years on the force. The night went off without incident, but every firework *boom* made Joe's heart seize and his right hand recoil to his hip. Over and over and over. He tried all night to override this automatic startle response, to anticipate and stifle the reflex, but he was frustratingly powerless over it. *Boom.* Seize. Recoil. The grand finale was friggin' torture. He can still taste the cold beers he drank with Tommy and the guys at the end of that shift. Best fuckin' beers of his life.

'You wanna take a look in there?' asks Joe, nodding to the bag.

'Be my guest,' says Tommy.

'Ladies first.'

'Pussy.'

'I'm busy with Scotty here.'

51

Tommy squats by the backpack and unzips it in one fast motion, as if ripping off a bandage. The bag contains what they of course knew it would — an iPad, jewelry, a camera, some painted figurines, and not a pressure cooker filled with nails and ball bearings. Joe exhales and only then realizes that he'd been holding his breath.

Tommy zips the bag and hands the evidence over to Joe. They share a quick, knowing look of relief.

'Those pearls a present for your girlfriend, Scotty?' asks Joe.

Scotty says nothing.

'I didn't think so. Let's go.'

Joe slings the backpack over his left shoulder and directs Scotty out of the condo with his left hand. As Joe walks Scotty to his cruiser, he's feeling satisfied that he, Tommy, and Sean did everything right and made two lawful arrests. He's relieved that the boys weren't armed, that he, Tommy, and Sean are all walking away in the same condition they were in when they got the call. He's happy for the owner of the condo, who has a real mess to clean but will get all of her things back. He's worried for Scotty's poor mother, imagining the phone call she's about to receive. But more than anything, he's pissed at Scotty for unnecessarily scaring the shit out of him with that backpack. Protecting the top of Scotty's head with his hand, Joe grabs hold of Scotty's skinny shoulder, squeezes it hard, then shoves him into the cruiser a little more roughly than necessary.

'Ow,' says Scotty.

Joe slams the door shut and smiles. That felt good.

⋆   ⋆   ⋆

Joe had entered the sally port at the station with his prisoner at around one o'clock. He searched Scotty two more times; took off his sneakers, socks, hat, and earring; logged his basic information, including name and height and weight; took his prints; gave him his phone call; and tossed him into the juvi holding cell. It's now four o'clock, the end of Joe's shift, and he's still sitting at a computer, writing up the report.

Reports are a royal pain in the ass, but they're a necessary and critical part of the job. Joe knows he'll never write the great American novel, but he takes pride in the accuracy of his reports. His narratives tend to be long and thorough. He takes this shit seriously. A seemingly minor, inconsequential detail might turn out to be the crucial piece of evidence in court, the linchpin needed for nailing the guy, even years later. Look at the Whitey Bulger case. Those prosecutors are using specific language from police reports filed decades ago to convict this scumbag.

So getting all the facts down is imperative. Leave something out and there might just be enough crawl space for someone like Whitey to wiggle through, free on a technicality. And then all that work and time and money go down the drain, polluting the harbor with the rest of the

53

sewage. When training young recruits, Joe can't stress this point enough. The reports need to be meticulous.

Even so, a straightforward B&E like this one should take no longer than an hour. But Joe's still not done. He was interrupted numerous times by guys wanting to hear all about the B&E bust, which Joe eagerly recounted. True to his Irish heritage, Joe loves to tell a good story, especially if it has a happy ending like this one. And he only received Sean Wallace's hospital notes on the other prisoner thirty minutes ago. But all distractions and delays aside, he's having a hard time concentrating and isn't at all confident that he's properly pieced together the precise sequence of events and every detail.

He has to incorporate the information from the detective, the photographs of the room, and the interview with the neighbor who made the 911 call. He has to decipher Sean Wallace's friggin' chicken scratches about the kid in the hospital — the name of the attending doctor, the tests, the diagnosis, and the treatment. He has to capture every element in methodical order so that the suspects can be properly identified, so the arrest can be proven lawful.

He stares at the computer screen, at the sea of words in all caps with no paragraphs, and his brain swims. Think. What happened, and then what happened next? He can't think. He's tired. Why is he so tired? He looks at his watch. His shift ended five minutes ago, and there's no way he's getting the fuck out of here anytime soon.

A small voice inside his head urges him to give

54

up. *It's good enough. Wrap it up and go home.* But Joe knows better. He's been trained to ignore that voice, to beat it into bloody submission if he needs to. He never gives up. Not on anything. Plus, he knows if the report isn't done properly, his supervisor won't approve it.

He rubs his eyes and focuses on the screen, pushing on. There's the list of property stolen, exceeding $250, making this a B&E daytime and a larceny. There are the digital photos showing the state of the kitchen and living room, the bedrooms, the bathrooms, and the home office. The hospital report. There's the cracked wood in the doorframe by the dead-bolt lock, making this robbery a B&E. They found two boys on the balcony. He needs to describe exactly what they were wearing, what they were carrying. The tattoos on Scotty's arms. One jumped, one stayed. There's who responded to the scene and the neighbor who called it in. There's the owner of the unit who wasn't home.

This is a simple B&E. Joe stares at the screen, drumming his fingers on the desk as he reads and rereads his report. His report is a mess.

This is a simple B&E. Then why the hell isn't it simple?

*   *   *

It's six o'clock, and Joe should be home with Rosie. He should be sitting in his living room chair with his ugly feet up on the coffee table in front of the window air conditioner with a cold beer in his hand, getting ready to watch the Sox.

55

But instead he's standing in the middle of the street, at the intersection of Beacon and Charles, between the Common and the Public Garden, directing rush-hour traffic. He finally finished that damn B&E report at five o'clock, a whole hour after his shift ended. Then, probably because he was still hanging around and the duty supervisor needed bodies, Joe was ordered to work traffic detail at the Concert on the Common from five thirty until midnight.

The temperature is still hugging a muggy ninety degrees, and he's standing on black pavement — wearing a navy-blue uniform topped with a fetching lime-green vest, surrounded by bumper-to-bumper traffic emitting foul-smelling exhaust and even more heat — exactly where he was grateful not to be earlier. Murphy's Fuckin' Law. He should've knocked on wood.

It's a gnarly intersection at this time of day even without the attraction of the free outdoor concert. There are too many cars trying to leave the city all at once, too many walking commuters, twelve separate locations where pedestrians can step off a curb. The men are in suits and ties and the women are in heels, and they're all pissed off because it's too hot, and there are too many sweaty people standing too close to each other all waiting to cross the street, and the wait is taking too long, and they've just worked eight hours and want to get home already. Lucky them. At least they're on their way. Although Joe is here to help them in their cause, no one appreciates it, and in fact, by the time he waves them across the street, most of the pedestrians, if they bother to look at him at all, shoot him a poisonous glare as if he's personally to blame for all this misery. It's a friggin' thankless task.

And because of this, poor Rosie is home alone tonight. Again. She knows this drill all too well. Such is the life of a cop's wife. If he thinks about how many nights he's missed with Rosie, if he actually does the math, a task that would require a calculator because the number is so large, he might weep right here in the middle of Boston. So he doesn't think about it. He only thinks about getting through tonight and getting home to her when it's over.

At least they didn't have any special plans. It's bad enough to come home at the end of a sixteen-hour day to a lonely or disappointed wife, but if he misses a wedding or a christening or a holiday, then he faces resentment, and that's much harder for Joe to make good on. When they don't have plans, Joe can erase Rosie's loneliness or disappointment with a heartfelt hug and a kiss. Chocolate and wine also help. She knows it wasn't his fault he got ordered to overtime, and in his arms, she remembers to be grateful that he made it home alive. But if he misses a planned event, there's nothing other than time that can melt Rosie's hostility, as if he would ever choose to stand alone in the middle of the street for seven hours after working a full-day tour, directing angry pedestrians and motorists nearly running him down in ninety-degree heat.

* * *

It's now eight o'clock, and the concert doesn't end for another two hours. Then, hundreds of people will be leaving the Common, and Joe will be busy again, but for now, he's mostly hanging around, waiting. Other than directing the two sets of tourists who asked him how to get to Cheers, he's had little to do since rush hour. He's been on his feet for two and a half hours, and he can feel every ounce of the thirteen-pound gun belt around his waist. He's exhausted, his back and feet are killing him, and his very soul is aching to sit on that bench he can see beneath the weeping willow tree in the Public Garden. It might as well be in California.

He continues to stand and tries to listen to the music. It's jazz, but too far in the distance to hear fully. A brassy note floats by here and there, but Joe's ears can't string enough of them together to decipher a melody, nothing he can whistle along to, and the effort only frustrates him.

He notices a percussion sound, like a maraca shaking, in addition to the jazz notes, but the sound is separate, out of sync, closer. He tunes in to the noise and discovers that it's coming from him. It's the handful of coins, change from the crappy day-old ham-and-cheese sandwich he bought at 7-Eleven for dinner, jingling in his side pants pocket. The cause of the jingling has Joe curiously stumped until it finally registers. He's hopping back and forth on his feet as if he were standing barefoot on hot coals.

He didn't even realize he was moving. He thought he was standing perfectly still.

Maybe he has to take a piss. He checks. He doesn't. He's too dehydrated from sweating in this hideous heat.

It must be an adrenaline hangover from the B&E bust. Of course the perceived threat is long over, but Joe knows from experience that those powerful juices can still be hitting every GO button in his body hours later. Anytime he has to take out his gun, his body floods with adrenaline, a visceral rush that feels a lot like chugging three Red Bulls. He can be twitching and vibrating, muscles ready to pounce into action for the rest of the day. It must be that.

He imagines the people on the Common, couples drinking wine out of plastic cups, kids dancing barefoot in the grass, everyone enjoying the live music. He wishes he and Rosie could be there among them, sitting on a blanket, eating a picnic dinner, relaxing together. Then he pictures Fenway, only a couple of miles up the road, and wonders how the Sox are doing. He pivots on his restless feet, turning away from the concert he can't quite hear or attend, away from the bench he can't sit on, away from the baseball team he loves, toward the direction of Bunker Hill, near where Rosie is waiting for him, and imagines getting home to her.

Four more hours and he'll be home. Four more.

He turns back toward the Common, only now his focus drifts past the jazz concert to the city beyond it, and a thought creeps into his consciousness like spilled ink bleeding onto paper, eventually soaking the whole sheet through.

The Opera House!

Joe checks his watch, and his heart sinks fast and heavy like a rock in water. Possibly at this very moment, Meghan is performing her solo in *Coppélia*. JJ, Colleen, and Rosie are in the audience, and there's a disgracefully empty seat next to Rosie where Joe said he'd be.

Fuck.

Joe stands in the street, his feet already jumpy, desperate to bolt through the Common to the Opera House just beyond it, but he might as well be paralyzed. He can't go. He's on duty. He missed it.

Yes, he was ordered to overtime, but he could've asked his supervisor for a favor. He could've tried to make a deal with another officer, offering to take a future shift for him or her in exchange for tonight. Someone would've helped him out.

He pats his chest pocket for his phone, but it's not there. He looks over to his parked cruiser. He's pretty sure he left it on the seat. He was so frazzled by that friggin' B&E report that he forgot to call Rosie to let her know about being called to overtime. He hasn't checked his phone in hours. Christ. There will be many unread, increasingly angry texts from Rosie waiting for him.

When he didn't come home from his shift on time, she probably worried about him. But Joe knows that when she saw nothing on the evening

60

news and didn't get a phone call, she stopped worrying. She most likely concluded that he got ordered to overtime or was out having a drink with the guys. Either way, he didn't return Rosie's texts, and he missed Meghan's dance. She's now definitely and rightfully pissed.

And Meghan. He promised he'd be there. He let her down. Again. That last thought punches Joe low in the gut.

He wipes his sweaty forehead, shakes his head, and looks down at his boots, wishing he could kick his own ass for forgetting about tonight. He sighs and looks up, staring in the direction of the Opera House, imagining his beautiful daughter dancing on the stage, and prays for forgiveness.

5

The Sox are in the World Series, and everyone in New England is high on hope. They're on a nine-game winning streak, taking Game 1 last night, trouncing the St. Louis Cardinals 8 – 1. Things are looking good, an attitude no sane Bostonian would've dared possess before 2004. But the Curse of the Bambino has been reversed, and Sox fans are now a crazy bunch of cockeyed optimists.

Tonight is Game 2 at Fenway, and Red Sox Nation is feverishly giddy with preparation, doing their part to ensure another win — donning their B caps, buying Fenway Franks at Stop & Shop and cases of beer at the package store, going unshaven and wearing their mismatched socks pulled up to their knees, or following whatever superstition has been clinically proven to work its juju. Joe is wearing his new Pedroia shirt under his Kevlar vest. And then there are those lucky bastards who have tickets to the game. Joe can't even bear to think about them.

Joe loves the Red Sox, but it's a complicated, bittersweet relationship for a Boston cop. Like every kid in the city, Joe grew up worshipping the team. He collected cards and taped posters of Jerry Remy and Carlton Fisk to his bedroom wall. He played Little League, second base, and his glove was his most prized possession. He took better care of it than he did his bike or his teeth. He can still remember the heavenly smell of it — leather and oil and dirt. He'd rub his glove down with linseed oil, darkening every inch of the leather, stick a ball in the pocket, tie it up with string, and pound the hell out of it until it was as buttery smooth as a baby's bottom. He remembers wearing his glove for good luck while watching the games on TV in the living room with his dad and Maggie, fetching cans of Schlitz from the fridge for his dad during commercials, everyone standing for the seventh-inning stretch and singing 'Take Me Out to the Ball Game,' many times staying up way past his bedtime in pajamas, especially if the Sox made it to the postseason.

Whether they had won or lost, Joe has nothing but fond memories of watching the Sox in the fall as a kid. He has no such memories of the Sox as an adult. At least not of the home games. Each home game in the postseason means crowd control and overtime duty. It means riot training in Dorchester before the game, and it means standing *outside* Fenway during and after the game. It means no beer and no lucky glove. It means his kids didn't grow up with the kinds of memories Joe did, of watching the postseason Sox in the living room with their dad.

When the Sox are playing a home game in October, all Boston police officers get called to duty. All days off are canceled. And that means never seeing the game.

In his most selfish, shameful moments, Joe finds himself wishing they'd lose, that the Series would end, and then Joe wouldn't have to stand outside Fenway like a knight banished from his castle, tortured by each eruption of cheers, excluded from experiencing the excitement on the other side of the green wall. Of course, he doesn't really want the Sox to lose, and he knocks on wood as soon as he catches himself tempting fate with such evil, renegade thoughts.

He tries to keep it positive. Joe always wishes for a clean sweep on the road. That would be the ideal scenario. The Sox would win, *and* he'd have the chance to see it on TV. Everyone wins. But that's never how it goes for Joe or the Sox.

Tonight's game starts at 8:07, which means that this morning, Joe finds himself at the old National Guard Armory in Dorchester. The hangar is huge, a vast amount of empty space surrounding the collection of officers gathering in the middle of the gym. The height of the room is as impressive as its girth. The windows running the length of the building are set too high to see anything out of but sky, and the ceiling is at least forty feet up. Joe spots a pair of pigeons sitting on one of the rafters.

He's standing in the center of the gymnasium floor among forty-nine other officers from every precinct, guys he typically only sees at parades and funerals. Joe spends a few minutes catching up with Darryl Jones and Ronnie Quaranto, two of his best buddies from his Police Academy days. Darryl's daughter is getting married. It's costing him a fortune, and he can't stand the groom. Otherwise, no complaints. Ronnie's looking forward to a much-needed vacation next week with his wife, a cruise in the Caribbean.

Joe finds the familiar face of his best friend, Tommy Vitale, but then does a double take. His lip. In the twenty-four years Joe has known Tommy, he's never once seen Tommy's upper lip.

'Hey, Magnum, should we file a missing report for your furry pet?' asks Joe.

Tommy combs the naked skin beneath his nose with his fingers.

'It was time for a change. Whaddaya think?'

Tommy turns to the side, offering Joe his profile, and smiles.

'I think you should've gone the other way, grown a full beard to cover up that ugly mug.'

'Amy likes it. Says I look like a young Robert De Niro.'

'Tragic that she's going blind at such a young age.'

Tommy laughs.

'Naw, you look good. Ten years younger.'

'Really?'

'I've never been more attracted to you.'

'It feels weird. I can't stop touching it.'

Joe spits out a laugh. It takes Tommy a second, and then both he and Joe are giggling like teenage boys.

The sergeant calls an end to the happy reunion. The fun and games are over. It's time for three hours of tedious, military-style drills, crowd-control training for tonight's potential post-game riot.

Everyone lines up in full gear, wearing helmets and gloves, holding three-foot service batons and gas masks. It's a delightful fall day outside, sunny with a crisp, gentle breeze rolling in off the Atlantic, but it's friggin' summer in Florida in this gymnasium. Joe's Pedroia shirt is already damp, and the tag is irritating the top of his back. He chastises himself for not remembering to cut the tag out.

They're standing arm's length apart in a stack formation. Joe is positioned in column number two, lucky number thirteen — twelve taller guys in front of him, four shorter guys behind. Sergeant Ferolito, a former marine, is bellowing out commands, his gravelly voice echoing throughout the hangar and Joe's helmet.

'Column number two, line formation, on me. *MOVE!*'

The point man moves first. Odd numbers advance forward and shift left, even numbers shift right. Sticks and boots stomp the ground in unison. Step, together, step, together, step. It's an intimidating drumbeat, a thunderous trotting that grows exponentially as more officers peel off, like a herd of large animals in a controlled stampede. The uniforms ahead of Joe weave like braided hair, creating a brand-new line configuration. The choreography is precise and allows no room for error. It requires a remarkable amount of attention and coordination, the closest thing to dance Joe knows, which makes him admire Meghan all the more.

It's Joe's turn, and he's supposed to cut right foot first to the left. He's been repeating the mantra 'Odd men are never right' amid a sea of crisscrossing bodies ahead of him. But now that it's his turn, his right foot jumps out, as if he were an impulsive dog on a leash sniffing out the irresistible aroma of a squirrel *over there*, and it jerks Joe to the right. This move fucks up the line of officers behind him, as they all copy Joe's mistake and line up behind him like misplaced dominoes. It also fucks up the progress of the remaining guys in column three, who correctly cut left only to collide with a wall of bodies who weren't supposed to be there.

'Well, that was ugly,' says Ferolito. 'Everyone, back in stack. You're gonna do it again. O'Brien, you need a lesson in right and left?'

'No, sir,' says Joe.

'Good, then kindly get your head out of your ass.'

They all arrange themselves back in stack formation. Sergeant Ferolito keeps them there, pacing with his hands clasped behind his back, saying nothing, holding his order, the corners of his mouth lifted in a devious smile. Meanwhile, Joe is having a hell of a time keeping still. His body is a can of shaken soda, ready to spray in all directions.

And he can't stop thinking about the friggin' tag. The sensation is somewhere between a tickle and an intense itch, but it might as well be a knife stabbing him in the back for all the attention it's demanding. He'd like to rip the friggin' tag off his shirt right now. Pedroia had better hit a homer tonight.

He has to stop thinking about the tag. He stares at the head of the guy in front of him. It's Ronnie Quaranto's head. He narrows in on the bulge of fat in the back of Ronnie's neck and counts to himself, concentrating on each number and Ronnie's neck pudge and not the tag, holding himself steady. He's on thirty-six, clenching his fists, his teeth, even his ass, when Sergeant Ferolito finally barks out the command.

'Column number two, line formation, on me. *MOVE!*'

Ronnie proceeds right, Joe's cue to move, but the relief in Joe is so overwhelming, he loses focus. He's supposed to be the mirror image of Ronnie, and so he should cut left and land in a straight new line, but again, his body seems to have an impetuous mind of its own, and Joe steps right. Again, the officer behind Joe is then faced with the dilemma of what to do — go to the right, as he would have if Joe had done what he was supposed to do, or follow the rule and do the opposite of what was done directly in front of him — and he can't ponder this decision over a leisurely cup of coffee. It must be now, immediately, in precision with fifty pairs of boots and service batons beating against the hangar floor. He chooses to mirror Joe. The formation is fucked up. Again.

'O'Brien,' calls out Sergeant Ferolito. 'Are you aiming to be here all day?'

'No, sir.'

'Cuz I'm sure as hell not. Let's do it again.'

On their way back into columns, Joe makes eye contact with Tommy. Joe answers Tommy's raised eyebrows with a quick shrug and then finds his spot. Everyone is still, waiting for the sergeant's order. Everyone but Joe.

Joe keeps shrugging as if he's got hiccups in

his shoulders, and it's causing a noticeable swing of his baton, which knocks into the leg of the officer next to him. He tries pulling his wrists down and pinching his shoulder blades together, but his shoulders keep popping up. He can't stop them.

Be still, goddamn it. But the effort somehow recruits his feet, and now he's shrugging his shoulders *and* shifting back and forth on his feet, dancing in place. He bumps into the guy to his right, then the guy to his left. Good God, if someone doesn't kick the shit out of him soon, he's going to do it himself.

'O'Brien, I'm getting tired of hearing my voice say your name. You got ants in your pants?'

'No, sir,' says Joe.

'We're all going to wait right here until everyone is perfectly still.'

Joe squeezes every muscle he can find, trying to transform his entire body into an inanimate object, imagining himself as a wooden plank. He holds his breath. Sweat drips off the tip of Joe's nose like a leaking faucet. He resists the urge to mop his face with his gloved hand. That tag is still pissing him off. He promises himself the satisfaction of annihilating it later. A phlegmy tickle rakes the back of his throat, begging him to cough. He swallows several times until his mouth goes dry, but it won't go down. He will not cough. Joe knows discipline.

But there's a mightier urge to move building deep inside him, emanating from an elusive, nonspecific origin, denying him a target to aim at. He's not a plank. He's a rubber balloon, blown to thin capacity and not tied off, and someone else, someone with a sick sense of humor, is pinching the neck, threatening to let go.

His shoulders shrug again. What the *fuck*. Sergeant Ferolito is standing before the formation, his feet wide and arms crossed over his chest, his dark eyes staring Joe down. It feels as if the eyes of every officer are on Joe, even though Joe knows the only officers actually looking at him are Sergeant Ferolito and the guy directly behind Joe.

He can't imagine what's causing these bizarre muscle spasms. He hasn't been lifting weights or furniture or exerting himself in any way out of the ordinary. He mostly stands on his feet, sits in his cruiser, sits in the living room chair, or sleeps.

Maybe he didn't do anything to cause it. Joe sometimes gets spasms in his toes, especially the two next to his big toe. Without warning or instigation, they'll pinch together in an unnatural, rigid position, out of line from the rest of his foot, and stay there in a gnarled pose, impervious to any attempt at relaxing them, for several agonizing minutes. But these shrugs feel more like hiccups than toe cramps. Sudden, involuntary, exaggerated bursts of movement. Shoulder hiccups. He's never heard of such a thing. And what's up with his antsy feet?

Maybe he's getting too old for this shit. He's one of the oldest officers here. He's forty-three and feels every year of it lately. Never a slender man to begin with, Joe's probably carrying an extra twenty pounds around his middle, his protruding gut the likely cause of his chronically aching back. He makes unattractive old-man noises, grunting and groaning when he gets out of bed in the morning and whenever he goes to stand after sitting for too long. He'd like to think he could still do twenty consecutive pull-ups and beat JJ in an arm wrestle, but he wouldn't put money on it.

Most of the guys here are in their twenties or thirties. This job is for the young. But Tommy isn't having a problem. Jonesie and Quaranto are older. Who is he kidding? This can't be about age or strength. He's being ordered to keep the fuck still, not to do twenty pull-ups. Then what is it?

He shrugs.

'Jesus Christ, OB,' someone mutters.

The acoustics in this cavernous hangar are awful, distorting pitch and amplitude, causing every sound to echo, but he's pretty sure that was Tommy. This has to stop. Joe tries to take a deep breath through his mouth, but his chest is a concrete wall, his lungs a couple of bricks. He's breathing like a panicked gerbil. Sweat is pouring off his nose. His head is baking beneath his helmet. That fuckin' tag.

He shrugs.

Joe declares war on himself. He clenches his hands so hard that he can actually feel the length of his veins straining in his forearms. He clamps his jaw, flexes his ass and his quads, tightens his stomach, and envisions a fifty-pound sandbag sitting atop each shoulder. His heart races, his head is boiling in sweat, and he doesn't breathe.

His shoulders shrug. He jostles against the guys on either side of him.

Mother of God. Joe closes his eyes. He can hear his heartbeat throbbing in his red-hot ears. The guy breathing behind him. Cars whizzing by outside. Pigeons cooing in the rafters. Joe unclamps his teeth. He listens to the manic rhythm of his heartbeat in his ears and coaxes it to slow down. He relaxes his face, softens his stomach, his back, his legs. He sips in a breath of air and then another. He listens and breathes and waits. His shoulders stay put. His feet remain planted. He listens and breathes and waits. His shoulders stay. They stay. Please stay. Stay.

Sergeant Ferolito calls the next drill.

6

The tasty smell of fried peppers and onions wafts over from the sausage cart on the corner, and Joe wants another sub. He's not particularly hungry, but he's bored, and that tangy, sweet aroma is undeniably alluring. Intoxicating. He inhales, and his mouth waters. He inhales, and every thought in his head becomes saturated in greasy onions. Women should forget about those fancy, expensive perfumes that all smell like some old lady's garden. They should dot their wrists and necks with drippings from Artie's Famous Sausages. Men would be all over them.

It's now almost ten, and Joe, Tommy, and Fitzie have been standing together at their post on Lansdowne Street in the shadow of Fenway since four thirty. There's nowhere to sit, nothing to read, nothing to do but stand, wait for the game to end, and imagine what's going on inside the ballpark. It's worse than standing in the women's intimates department at Macy's, waiting for Rosie while she's in the dressing room trying on a bra or some other piece of clothing Joe is too embarrassed to imagine in public. This is taking forever.

Using their cell phones while on duty is frowned upon, but they all sneak it. Fitzie pulls his from his chest pocket and reads a text.

'Shit.'

'Whaddaya got?' asks Joe.

'Cardinals up, one nothin'.'

'What inning?' asks Tommy.

'Toppa the fourth.'

'Okay, okay,' says Tommy. 'Still plenty of time.'

Joe nods and prays to his Pedroia shirt. He sways back and forth on his feet, alternating his full weight between them for a moment, then rolls heel to toe. He's been standing for over five hours straight, and his feet are begging him for any relief he can offer.

'You're like a friggin' Weeble Wobble over there,' says Tommy. 'Will you stay still? You're makin' me nervous.'

'Sorry, man; my feet kill,' says Joe.

Fitzie nods. They've all been on duty since seven thirty this morning.

'I'm ready for my couch,' says Fitzie.

'And a cold beer,' says Joe.

They all nod. Joe imagines the first few minutes of being home tonight, the gratifying relief of finally pulling his exhausted feet out of his tight, heavy boots, the clean scent of citrus as he pushes a wedge of lime down the glass neck of a Corona, the sweet, cold, beautiful taste of it. Lying down on the couch. A soft pillow beneath his head. Highlights from the game on the TV.

Joe's reverie is broken when he catches the pointed look on Tommy's face, clearly not imagining a couch or a cold beer. Tommy's stroking the bare skin above his lip, studying Joe.

'You and Rosie taking any vacation time soon?' asks Tommy.

'Nah, nothing on the calendar. How 'bout you and Amy?'

'Just up to New Hampshire to see her folks.'

Joe nods.

'You hear Ronnie talking about that cruise he's going on?' asks Tommy.

'Yeah, sounds real nice.'

'Yeah,' says Tommy, thinking something over. 'Everything okay with you, man?'

'Me? Yeah, I just want to get off my friggin' feet.'

Tommy pauses, watching Joe. Joe's lifting and dropping his heels, stepping side to side. He knows he's bugging the shit out of Tommy with all his moving around, but he can't help it.

Beer. Couch. Soon.

'What was with you this morning at riot training?' asks Tommy.

'I dunno,' says Joe, shaking his head. 'I'm getting too old for this shit.'

Tommy pinches his lips together. 'I hear ya. I'm gonna go get another heart attack sub. You hungry?'

'No, but I'll have one.'

After Tommy turns the corner onto Brookline Avenue, a mammoth roar erupts from the ballpark.

'Yes!' says Fitzie to his phone.

'What happened?' asks Joe.

'Big Papi hit a two-run homah, knocked Pedroia in. Sox up two – one.'

'Yes!' says Joe, thanking his shirt. 'What inning?'

'Bottom of the sixth.'

Joe feels like a kid, hooting and high-fiving Fitzie despite the bone-compressing agony in his back and feet. Good. Joe hopes that he never loses the little boy inside him, that naive spirit who will always root for the Red Sox to win, whose cheering will always drown out the miserable complaining of Joe's old-man feet. A win for the Sox is a win for the good guys. It's Superman defeating Lex Luthor, Rocky knocking out Apollo Creed.

After being gone for what seems like ages, Tommy returns with three hot dog buns overstuffed with sausage, peppers, and onions, steaming and dripping with grease, and Fitzie tells him about the homer. Joe consumes his sub in four uninterrupted, brutish bites and immediately regrets not going slower. He should've savored it. He inhales deeply through his nose while eyeing Fitzie's sub, only half-gone, and feels the hot pang of jealous desire mixed with a pinch of indigestion.

Fitzie licks the grease from his fingers and pulls out his phone. 'Fuck.'

'What is it?' asks Joe, wiping his hands on his pants.

'Buncha friggin' wild throws. Cardinals up four – two.'

'What inning?'

'Toppa the seventh.'

'Shit,' says Tommy. 'Come on, two more runs.'

'My feet can't take extra innings,' says Joe.

Five years ago, he would've said 'heart' instead of 'feet.'

'We're still in this,' says Tommy.

No more runs go on the board that inning. Joe hears the distant karaoke of thirty-seven thousand people singing 'Sweet Caroline.' The words fade out and then gallop back with the chorus. '*So good! So good! So good!*' Joe sings in a murmur along with them, feeling happier and less excluded as he does so.

Almost done. Aside from the cops and street vendors, no one is outside now. Everyone is either in the ballpark or in the bars, glued to the tight game. If the Sox lose, the Series will be tied up. The fans will spill out of the park and the bars hanging their heads, disappointed and a little heartbroken, but they probably won't do anything to land a starring role on the late-night news. Boston sports fans are passionate and loyal and a touch crazy, but they're surprisingly nonviolent. Boston doesn't see the kinds of riots other cities suffer after their beloved team loses. Everyone will likely want to walk it off, go home, and go to bed. It's still early in the Series, only Game 2, still plenty of time. Sox fans want to live to tell their grandkids the wicked-awesome story of *how* they won as much as they want to win, so a loss tonight isn't the end of the world. There won't be any flipped cars, smashed windows, looting, or rioting.

Unless they win. While Bostonians tend to be quiet, humble losers, they don't always display their most gracious, flattering side when their team wins a big game. Joe thanks God that tonight isn't a Saturday. With Saturday games, people drink all day and plan to sleep in on Sunday. When the Sox win a postseason game on a Saturday, everyone is typically fifty shades of drunk, gloating and looking for either a party or trouble, and it's a long night of crowd control for the Boston Police.

But tonight is Thursday night. Everyone who has a job has work in the morning. The kids have school. Win or lose tonight, the Sox will go on to play Game 3 in St. Louis. Most everyone will be looking to go home as quickly as possible when this is over. Joe hopes.

He wiggles each aching foot and does a few deep knee bends. His shoulders shrug, like earlier, but instead of fighting it, Joe uses the opportunity to stretch one arm above his head and then the other. He scratches his head. He twists his torso side to side, trying to take the vertical pressure off his spine, even for a second, and groans. His back isn't any happier than his feet.

'Hey, Jane Fonda,' says Fitzie, reading his phone. 'Bottom of the ninth. Still four – two. Two outs.'

Joe closes his eyes, prays to God and his lucky shirt, and knocks on his service baton, wishing for the Sox to win. The street is eerily quiet, as if all of Boston is holding its breath.

'Just struck out Nava,' says Fitzie. 'Game over.'

They all hang their heads and say nothing, a solemn moment of silence before they have to get to work. It takes only a handful of minutes for the sold-out crowd to begin pouring out of Fenway. The police have already blocked all side streets with barricades, creating a narrow channel banked by officers. The goal is to disperse the crowd and herd everyone out of the city. Soon, thousands of people are walking past Joe, all in the same direction. It's a fast-moving river with only one way for the fish to swim.

A young boy, probably around six, meets Joe's eyes as he passes by on his father's shoulders. Joe nods and smiles. The boy's eyes widen, startled, as if he never expected Joe to move, as if Joe had been a statue that suddenly animated. The boy then slumps his shoulders and turns his face away, resting it on the top of his dad's head. The father is holding his boy's leg with one hand and his wife's hand with the other.

Family after family inches by, and Joe regrets that he didn't get to spend more time like this with Rosie and his kids when they were young. In twelve years, he'll be retired. JJ and Colleen should have a few kids by then. Joe knocks three times on his baton. The girls will hopefully be married with kids, too. He knocks again, once more for Rosie.

It worries Rosie that the girls are so unsettled, dancing and Downward-Dogging without a steady boyfriend, not even a prospect for marriage in sight. Both the yoga and dance worlds are predominantly populated by women. It seems that the few eligible men who are in the ballet company are gay or from Eastern Europe, owning last names Rosie can't even spell, and the yoga students who aren't women are Toonies. Rosie's long-held assumption that her daughters would someday marry nice Irish Catholic boys from the neighborhood is growing more and more far-fetched, absurd even. As long as they eventually marry someone. And he isn't a Protestant.

In twelve years, Patrick might even be settled or at least living somewhere else. Hopefully all of Patrick's progeny will be legitimate.

Retirement and grandchildren. He'll be fifty-five, still plenty young enough to enjoy kids. He'll take them to Fenway and spoil the hell out of them.

Lansdowne is now empty but for a handful of dumb fish who resisted the current. Six college-age boys remain in the middle of the street. Joe gathers from three of the T-shirts and two of the hats that they go to Boston College. They're all drunk, laughing and hawking spit, being loud and moronic. Probably not BC's best and brightest.

The street is lined shoulder-to-shoulder with cops who've been standing for seven hours straight, all desperate to go home, and these six idiots are in the way of that happening. Joe sighs, knowing that their minutes are numbered, wishing they'd save everyone the time and trouble and beat it now. Joe and his fellow officers will give the boys only a touch longer to celebrate, to sober up a bit. There are no more beers to be had in the middle of the street, and no bathrooms. Even Artie's sausage cart is gone by now. There's nothing interesting going on here. Maybe they'll leave of their own accord. Joe knows they won't.

At last, Jonesie steps out of formation, into the street. It's finally time to nudge things along. The night will now end one of three ways — full cooperation, the paddy wagon, or an ambulance.

Jonesie is a six-foot-four grizzly bear of a guy who grew up in a tough section of Roxbury. He saunters into the middle of the street and approaches the biggest of the six boys, probably only five feet ten. He's wearing a preppie striped golf shirt, jeans, and boat shoes.

'Game's over, boys,' says Jonesie. 'Time to call it a night.'

'We have a right to stay here if we want to,' says one of the other, shorter kids.

'Come on now,' says Jonesie. 'Everyone went home. Time to wrap it up here.'

'It's a free country,' says the redhead, the most visibly drunk of the crew.

The kid standing nose-to-nose with Jonesie stiffens his posture and stares straight into Jonesie's eyes. He ain't budging. Jonesie adjusts his stance a bit wider and leans in real close to the kid's face.

'Listen, Chester,' says Jonesie. 'You and your pals need to go on home. *Now*.'

Maybe it's because Jonesie invaded the kid's personal space, maybe it's a matter of alpha male pride, maybe it's because Jonesie spit out his *t*'s and *p*'s, maybe it's because he called the kid Chester. Joe never knows for sure what exactly trips the trigger, but he and every other cop watching this scene knew Chester would bite the bait. Chester takes a swing at Jonesie, and Jonesie easily dodges the blow. He then grabs Chester by the arm, turns and pins him stomach down to the ground, and cuffs him.

Joe and ten other officers march into the street in a wedge formation, heading directly toward the remaining kids with an intimidating suggestion of force.

'This ain't campus security, boys,' says Tommy. 'This is Boston PD. Unless the rest of you want to join Chester down at the station, I suggest you go home right now.'

The boys hesitate for half a second and then, like a flock of birds who decide to take flight in unison, they wordlessly abandon Chester and scurry down Lansdowne, out of town. Good boys. Joe smiles and checks his watch. Time to go home.

* * *

It's just after midnight when Joe parallel parks his car on Cook Street. His good mood dials up a notch as he appreciates this small but significant victory. Parking in Charlestown can be a nightmare. It's practically routine to 'get home' only to spend the next half hour hunting for a spot that will invariably be six blocks away and at the bottom of the hill. And then it starts raining. But not tonight. Tonight Joe found a space first try in full view of his house.

He steps out of the car, and every muscle in his body screams in protest. *No more standing!* He pushes the heels of his hands against his lower back, forcing his torso vertical. It takes considerable effort. He feels as if he's aged thirty years in one night, as if he's the Tin Man and every joint in his body could use an injection of WD-40. And nothing can save his poor feet.

As he approaches his front door, he's

surprised to notice the windows glowing amber yellow behind the drawn shades. The living room light is on. He checks his watch again, even though he knows the time. Patrick is still bartending at Ironsides. Rosie's a morning person and usually can't last past ten, but sometimes she has insomnia. Sometimes Joe will come home at midnight to find her ironing. Rosie irons everything — clothes, underwear, sheets, towels, doilies, and every so often the lace curtains. The ironing board is a permanent fixture in the living room, as much a part of the decor as Joe's chair and Yaz's dog bed. If she's not ironing, she's lying on the couch, snuggled under a blanket, watching QVC or Oprah. Rosie has at least ten years of *The Oprah Winfrey Show* recorded on VHS tapes. Sometimes she's asleep in that same scenario, the TV light flickering on her angelic face. But the light in the living room windows isn't flickering. The overhead light is on.

Joe turns the cold brass knob of the front door and pushes it open. The foyer light illuminates the bottom steps of the stairwell leading to the second- and third-floor units, but aside from that, the front of the house is dark and quiet. Joe closes the door, turns the deadbolt, and tosses his keys onto the small wooden table to the left of the door. They land at the feet of the Virgin Mary.

Above Mary, a white marble font is fixed to the wall, filled with holy water. Rosie blesses herself and anyone in arm's length every time she leaves or enters the house. She refreshes the water every Sunday. Joe berates himself for forgetting to anoint his Pedroia shirt this morning before he left for roll call. Maybe that's why the Sox lost. He'll be sure to bless his Ortiz shirt for Game 3.

He steps onto the threshold of the living room and then stops in his tracks. Rosie is up, but she's not ironing or lying down on the couch, watching QVC or Oprah. The TV is off. She's sitting cross-legged, like a small child, her knitted ivory afghan draped over her shoulders and around her lap, holding an empty wineglass with both hands. An empty bottle of Chardonnay sits on the coffee table next to a full bottle of tomato-red nail polish. He notices her shiny red toenails peeking out from under the afghan.

She's still wearing eye makeup and her gold cross necklace. She's not in pajamas. She smiles when she sees him, but he can tell it's a lie, and the heavy expression in her eyes turns the bones in Joe's legs to Jell-O.

'Who?' he asks.

Rosie takes a deep breath.

'Amy called.'

'Where are the kids?'

'The kids are fine.'

The kids are fine. Rosie's face is still unfamiliar, wrong. Amy called. Tommy's wife.

Oh God.

'What is it? Where's Tommy?'

'Tommy's home. Nothing happened to Tommy. She called about you.'

'What about me?'

Joe's heart is racing but it doesn't know where

84

to, as if he's searching the rooms of a house he's never been in, frantic, not knowing what he's looking for.

'She said Tommy's worried about you. He's worried something's wrong.'

'With me? What's he worried about?'

Rosie pauses and lifts her empty wineglass. She stops before it reaches her lips, realizing she already drained it, and lowers it back to her lap.

'He's worried you might have a drinking problem.'

'That's crazy.'

She stares at him.

'Jesus, Rosie, I don't. You know I don't. I'm not a drinker. I'm not my mother.'

He can't help but see the irony in the empty bottle of wine in front of her, but he resists the urge to make a crack, to deflect this unjust accusation by attacking her. Meanwhile, he's dying for that Corona.

'Then is it drugs?' she asks.

'What?' he asks, his voice too high and too loud, making him sound guilty when what he really feels is outrage. 'What would make him even think such a ridiculous thing?'

He waits. Whatever it is, she's thinking it, too. What the fuck is going on?

'Don't get mad.'

Instead of dissipating, the flood of sick apprehension for his kids and then Tommy is still coursing through him, hunting for something to do. Anger begins swelling in his chest, one storm colliding with another.

'I come home after a sixteen-hour day and get

accused of being a druggie. I'm fuckin' mad, Rosie.'

'He cares about you. He says you've been acting weird, not like you.'

'Like how?'

'Like you've been sloppy with procedure. He said you staggered getting out of your cruiser the other day and fell down.'

'My damn knee.'

'Your reports all come back rejected, and it's taking you hours to turn them in.'

That's true.

'He's worried about you, Joe. I am, too.'

'Because of what Amy told you?'

'Yeah,' says Rosie, but she's not finished. She searches Joe's face, testing the waters. There is more here. He opens his palms, trying to soften his demeanor, giving her space to speak her mind. He moves over to the couch and sits down next to her so he's not standing over her. Maybe she needs another glass of wine. He could sure use that Corona.

'I've been seeing things, too,' she says. 'I'm worried, too.'

So now she's his wife and a detective.

'Like what?'

'I don't know; it's like you're not you. You're always so fidgety, and you're late all the time and you never used to be. And your temper, your temper — '

'I'm fine. I'm just tired and cranky, and I've been puttin' in too many overtime hours. We need a vacation, hun. What about a trip to the Caribbean, wouldn't that be nice?'

Rosie nods and stares at the coffee table.

'I'm not drinkin', Rosie. I promise. And I'm definitely not on drugs. You have to trust that about me.'

'I know. I believe you.'

'Then what are you worried about?'

Rosie holds the gold cross on her chest between her thumb and finger and rubs it over and over, a stereotype Joe recognizes as prayer.

'I think you should go see a doctor.'

Rosie's tough. She's the wife of a cop. She knows full well that every time Joe leaves for work, he might not come home. She knows that Joe keeps a copy of his will and a handwritten good-bye letter to Rosie taped to the inside door of his police locker, just in case. She knows how to cope with a mountain of worry strapped to her back and still stand up straight. But here she is, looking small and vulnerable, like a little girl up too late and afraid to go back to sleep because of monsters under the bed. He has to show her they're not real.

'I'm fine, but okay, I'll prove it to you. I'll go to the doctor and get checked out. I'll even take a drug test if you want.'

He holds her in his arms and rocks her, protecting her from this invented, fictional threat, whatever she's imagining is wrong. *It's okay, baby. There aren't any monsters here.* She cries in his arms.

'What time did Amy call you?'

'Around eight.'

Good God. Rosie's been whipping herself up for hours. He shakes his head, pissed at Tommy for putting her through this.

'It's okay. Let it out. I'm okay, but I'll go to the doctor if that'll make you feel better. Maybe he can fix my bum knee.'

Joe cradles her face in his hands, wipes the tears and black mascara streaks on her cheeks with his thumbs, and offers her his love in a tender smile. She smiles back, but hers still isn't speaking the truth. She knows how much he hates doctors. He hasn't seen one in twenty years. She doesn't believe him.

'I will, Rosie. I don't want you to worry like this. I'll make an appointment tomorrow. I promise, I'll go to the doctor.'

She nods and exhales, but she still feels stiff in his arms. Scared and unconvinced. She doesn't believe he'll actually go to the doctor. But he will. He'd do anything to make Rosie feel safe. He'll take care of this.

'I'm okay, darlin'. I promise.'

She nods and doesn't believe him.

7

A cold, creeping dread whispers in Joe's ear as he and Rosie wait to cross Fruit Street. A taxi whizzes by too close to the curb and splashes slush onto Joe's jeans and sneakers. He looks over at Rosie. The cabbie got her, too. Joe grabs hold of Rosie's bare hand, and they dash across the street together.

They're heading over to the Wang Ambulatory Care Center at Massachusetts General Hospital. Joe's been to the General innumerable times, but always as a law enforcement officer on duty, always in front of the main building along with EMS or in the ambulance bay inside the ER. A few times, he's guarded prisoners in the psych ER. He was here on Marathon Monday, ushering the bomb victims — legs impaled with metal, shredded, bleeding, missing — into the hands of the surgeons. Nothing in his training or experience prepared him or any officer for the carnage they witnessed that day. He's never been in any other part of the hospital while on duty, and never anywhere here as a civilian.

He's wearing sneakers and jeans and his thin black coat that isn't even close to warm enough for this weather, and he looks just like all the other people making their way to the Wang entrance, people who need surgery or chemotherapy or dialysis or some other serious medical attention. He's following the sick and wounded into a hospital, and he despises his ordinary jeans and cheap coat. He might as well be naked.

He's still holding Rosie's hand, but he's lagging behind now, like a recalcitrant child being led to the principal's office or church, tethered to her steady progress toward the elevators. An unashamed germophobe, Rosie pushes the UP button with her sleeve pulled down over her hand. They wait. They get on the elevator alone. They say nothing and stare at the numbers lighting left to right. The light stops on the number seven. *Ping.* The elevator doors open. Here they are.

The Movement Disorders Unit.

Joe went to see his primary care physician in November, almost two months ago, a quick visit that amounted to nothing but this referral. If it had been up to Joe, he would've blown off this appointment. He went to the doctor, as promised. Duty served. But Rosie insisted and she meant it, and Joe's learned that when Rosie means it, acquiescence is the most efficient route to his future. So here they are, at the office of some fancy movement specialist. Seems like complete overkill for a tired man with a bad knee.

They enter the waiting room, Rosie lets the receptionist know Joe is here, and they sit down. Joe checks out the cast of characters on display, and the bashful dread that breezed by him outside on the sidewalk now penetrates him fully and with ease, like cold liquid coursing through his veins.

An elderly woman with paper-thin bluish-white skin is slumped in a wheelchair, staring at the floor with her cloudy eyes. The younger woman next to her, her daughter perhaps, is reading a magazine. A man, younger than the elderly woman but older than Joe, around sixty maybe, with a full head of gray hair, glasses, and the saggy face of a walrus, is seat-belted into a reclined wheelchair, his head dropped to one side, looking at nothing. Although someone must be, no one appears to be accompanying him. Another guy is sitting in one of the waiting room chairs, so he can presumably walk. His mouth is hanging open as if permanently unhinged, like dead Jacob Marley without the handkerchief knotted around his head. His wife or sister or nurse dutifully wipes the drool dripping from his mouth with tissues she retrieves from her purse. It's an ongoing, constant leak. A white towel draped across his chest absorbs whatever liquid she misses.

Everyone, including Joe and Rosie, is silent, and Joe's not sure whether the others are capable of speaking or choosing not to. Joe observes each person long enough to gather these basic descriptive details but then purposefully averts his eyes. He doesn't want to get caught staring. The cold dread is now an insistent tingling, a foreboding chant in his bones.

This is a room full of invalid zombies. This is purgatory, a wretched place of indefinite and possibly interminable waiting between heaven and hell. Then again, Joe can't imagine anyone here destined for anything good. There is no heaven here. This room is a holding cell for the damned, and while Joe feels bad for the misfortune of these poor souls, he wants no part of it.

This is a mistake. His winter coat suddenly feels torturously tight around his chest, and now he's hot, too hot, and he should just take the damn coat off, but he knows that won't help. The buzzing chant in his bones is now practically deafening, screaming at the top of its lungs. *You are in the WRONG PLACE at the WRONG TIME, buddy. Get the fuck out of here NOW.*

'Joseph O'Brien,' calls a young woman at the door to hell. She's wearing gray scrubs, holding a clipboard, waiting for him. There's no hint of human joy on her face or in her posture.

Rosie, who had been knitting, packs up her yarn and needles in a hurry and stands first. Joe copies her, but instead of bolting, he follows her and the angel of death into an examination room. Again, he and Rosie sit side by side. Joe avoids looking at the examining table and focuses on the closed door, reviewing in his mind the quickest route out of the building — left out this door, then the second right, through purgatory, left in the hallway, elevators on the right. The door swings open.

'Hi, I'm Dr. Cheryl Hagler.'

She's standing before Joe, completely obscuring his view of the door, his fantasy of escape. Dr. Cheryl Hagler. Cheryl. This is his doctor. A woman. Rosie didn't mention that. An intentional omission. He's sure she's a fine doctor. And smart, too. Hell, he'd be the first to

92

admit that Rosie, Meghan, and Katie are all smarter than he is. He looks down at his jeans and sneakers. He doesn't want to be here, seen like this in front of anyone, never mind a woman.

Joe stands and shakes Dr. Hagler's hand. She has a firm handshake, which Joe appreciates. In black heels, she's Joe's height and looks about Joe's age. She's wearing a white lab coat, which is too big in the shoulders and misbuttoned by one, revealing nothing of what she's wearing underneath but for a round silver loop dangling from a silver chain on her breastbone. Her black hair is loosely collected in a bun, but it's sloppy, nothing like the tight, perfectly round knobs of hair he sees on Meghan. She's attractive, but Joe gets the sense that her appearance is the last thing this woman cares about.

As she sits in the chair across from Joe and Rosie, she slides the black-rimmed glasses from the top of her head to the bridge of her duckbill nose and flips through the papers on the clipboard. She then places the clipboard on her lap, tucks her glasses back on top of her head, and clasps her hands, extending her pointer fingers into the shape of a steeple. Joe straightens in his seat, trying to take up more space.

'So tell me what's going on,' she says as if they're old friends having casual dinner conversation.

'Not much.'

She taps her pointer fingers and waits for Joe to change his story, elaborate, or pass the rolls. He says nothing.

'It says here you've been having some issues with falling, dropping things, staying on time and organized.'

'Oh yeah. Well, yeah, that.'

'What do you think is causing the falling?' she asks.

'I injured this knee a while back.'

Joe lifts his right knee off the ground to show her. He then begins wiggling that leg. Dr. Hagler refers back to the pages on the clipboard and then looks at Joe and Joe's wiggly leg.

'Do you ever have any dizziness or double vision?'

'No.'

'Any numbness in your arms and legs?'

'No.'

'Any tremors?'

Dr. Hagler holds her right hand out and shakes it, demonstrating.

'No.'

'Any headaches?'

'No.'

'Any trouble with strength?'

'No. I feel a bit more tired than usual.'

'Are you getting enough sleep?'

'Yeah.'

'What do you do for work?'

'I'm a Boston police officer.'

She nods and writes something down.

'How are things going on the job?'

'Good. I mean, I guess I'm having some issues I never used to have, like being late and getting all the details right in my reports. Guess I'm not as young as I used to be.'

Dr. Hagler nods and waits, and Joe feels pressured to fill the silence, like it's still his turn.

'And sometimes I'm a bit of a spaz. Y'know, some drops and stumbles. I think it's my knee here.'

Joe lifts his right leg again.

'Are you worried about losing your job?'

'No.'

Not until this moment.

'Any personality changes?'

Joe shrugs. He wasn't expecting this kind of question.

'I dunno,' he says, turning to Rosie. 'Whaddaya think, hun? Am I still the same ole prick I've always been?'

He's smiling, joking, but Rosie isn't. She says nothing and folds her arms over her chest, probably embarrassed that Joe said 'prick' in front of a woman doctor.

'Rose, have you noticed any changes in Joe's personality?' asks Dr. Hagler.

Rosie nods.

'Like what?' asks Dr. Hagler.

'Yeah, he's got this short fuse. You never know what's going to set him off, and he can go from like zero to sixty in nothing. I don't mean to make him sound like a jerk. He's a good man, but he's got this weird temper, and it's not like him to be like that.'

'How long has he had this weird temper?'

Rosie hesitates, thinking. Joe expects her to say maybe a few months.

'Six, seven years.'

Jesus, really?

'Any feelings of depression, Joe?' asks Dr. Hagler.

'No.'

'How's your stress level right now? On a scale of one to ten, ten being the highest.'

Joe thinks for a few seconds.

'Five.'

'Why is it five and not one?'

'It's never one.'

'Why is that?'

'I'm a cop. We're trained to never relax.'

'Even when you're not on duty?'

'Yeah, I can't turn it off.'

'So is it always at five?'

'I'd say it's typically around three.'

'So why the extra two?'

Waiting in purgatory. Being questioned by a woman doctor in civilian clothes. That would do it. And if that's not enough, he's apparently been a prick with a weird temper for at least six years.

'This isn't exactly a day at the spa here,' says Joe.

'Fair enough,' says Dr. Hagler, smiling. 'Rose, is there anything else you've noticed in Joe?'

'Well, like I'll ask him to do something, and he forgets. Like picking up milk on his way home or fixing the kitchen cabinets.'

'Honey, you just described every healthy guy on the planet.'

Dr. Hagler smiles. Joe looks at her left hand, her gold wedding band. She gets it.

'Okay, anything else you can think of, Rose?'

'He's always fidgeting, but not like normal moving around. It looks weird. He keeps knocking things over and dropping things. He broke my last wineglass a week ago.'

She's still mad about that. It's subtle, and he's not sure Dr. Hagler can detect it, but Joe can hear the sharp edge in Rosie's voice. She doesn't appreciate having to drink her wine out of a jelly jar or a plastic cup. He needs to buy her a new set of glasses.

Joe doesn't appreciate this doctor asking Rosie questions about him as if she's the star witness under interrogation in an organized crime investigation. Rosie's an intensely private woman. She doesn't mention Patrick's shenanigans to her brothers or even her priest. She doesn't tell anyone that JJ and Colleen are having trouble conceiving. She keeps her secrets and business in the house and would rather burn all of her Oprah videos than air her family's unironed laundry in front of the neighbors. So it throws Joe more than a little off balance to hear Rosie so eagerly exposing his 'weird' behavior, almost as if she's getting some mileage out of ratting him out.

'Like right now,' says Rosie.

Dr. Hagler nods and writes something down. What's going on here? Joe's not doing anything but sitting perfectly still in this damn chair, listening to his wife accuse him of being weird. And now the good doctor agrees. This interview is starting to feel conspiratorial.

Rosie taps his arm. He looks over at her. Her hands are clasped in her lap. Her face is pointed straight ahead, focused on Dr. Hagler. Then he notices his left elbow leaping out to the side, bumping up against Rosie's arm. He squirms in his seat, trying to create more space between them. These damn chairs are for midgets, and they're too close together. He looks down and observes his feet performing some sort of soft-shoe show on the floor. Okay, so he's a little fidgety. He's nervous, for cripes sake. Everyone fidgets when they're nervous.

'Do you drink, Joe?' asks Dr. Hagler.

'A couple of beers, sometimes a little nip of whiskey, but no more than that.'

He could sure use one right now.

'Any drugs?'

'No.'

'Let's talk about your family of origin. Any brothers or sisters?'

'One sister.'

'Older or younger?'

'Eighteen months older.'

'And how's her health?'

'Good, I guess. I don't really know. We don't keep in touch much.'

'How are your parents?'

'My father died of prostate cancer about nine years ago. My mother died from pneumonia when I was twelve.'

'Can you tell me more about your mother? Do you know what led to the pneumonia?'

'I'm not sure. She was living up in Tewksbury State Hospital when she died.'

'What was she there for?'

'She was an alcoholic.'

As he says the words aloud, he knows his answer doesn't make any sense. Alcoholics go to

98

AA, not Tewksbury State. Not for five years.

'Was she ever diagnosed with anything other than the pneumonia?'

'Not that I know of.'

'What did she look like when you went to visit her?'

Joe thinks, trying to conjure an image of his mother from the hospital, a peculiar exercise, since he'd spent years doing the exact opposite, trying to erase every second of what he'd witnessed there. He sees her now. She's in her bed. Her legs and arms and face are writhing into disturbing, inhuman shapes.

What appears in his mind most vividly, though, are her bones. His mother's bones protruding from beneath her cheeks and jaw, poking out the top of each shoulder, her rib cage, her knuckles, her kneecaps. He remembers his mother's skeleton. In the end, it became easier to imagine the white bones beneath her skin than the round, fleshy face and figure she used to have. It became easier to believe his mother was no longer really there, that the woman in that bed was a haunted corpse.

'She was real skinny.'

'Uh-huh. How about any aunts, uncles, cousins on your mom's side? Any health issues there?'

'My mother's family stayed in New York when she moved to Boston and married my father. She didn't speak to them. I've never met any of them.'

Why is this doctor so interested in the health of his mother and her family? What does any of

99

this have to do with his knee? Joe looks at the wall behind Dr. Hagler, at her framed diplomas and certificates of excellence. Yale School of Medicine. A residency at Johns Hopkins. A fellowship at the National Institutes of Health. Dr. Hagler might be book smart, but she'd sure make a shitty detective. These questions are a fat waste of time.

Joe reads Dr. Hagler's framed credentials again. Neurology residency. Neurology fellowship. Wait, she's a *neurologist?* He thought he was seeing a movement specialist. An orthopedic doctor. Why the fuck is he talking to some brain doctor?

'Look,' says Joe, offering to help her out. 'I twisted my knee a few years ago, and it's never been the same. I think that's what's causing my balance and falling problems.'

'Okay, let's have a look at a few things.'

Finally, but he can't see how this lady is even remotely qualified to evaluate his knee. Dr. Hagler rises to her feet, leaves her clipboard on the counter, and stands directly over Joe. She holds her hands out in front of her in closed fists, as if she's about to play a game of Guess Which Hand.

'Look at my hands, and then look at the finger that pops up.'

Dr. Hagler points her right index finger, then her left, then left again, right, left, right, right. Joe follows all this pointing with his eyes. No problem. It's a Whac-A-Mole game with eyes and fingers instead of a mallet and moles.

'Great. Now, are you a righty or lefty?'

'Righty.'

'Hold your left hand flat, palm open, like this.' Dr. Hagler demonstrates.

'Then, with your right hand, I want you to touch your left hand with a fist, then a karate chop, then a clap. Like this.'

She shows him the sequence several times through. He copies her once.

'Great, now do that over and over. Ready, go.'

Fist, chop, clap. Fist, chop, clap. Fist, clap. Wait. Fist. Wait. Chop. Wait. Clap. Fist. Fist. No. Fist. Wait. Fist, chop, fist.

Man, it's harder than it looks. Dr. Hagler performed the movements one after another without pausing between sets, without breaking the steady rhythm, without error. But she probably does this with patients all day long. She's well practiced. He'd like to see her try her hand at loading and unloading a gun. And what does any of this friggin' nonsense have to do with his knee?

'Now I'd like you to get up and walk heel-to-toe across the room and back.'

Joe's been on the other end of this request more times than he can count. He wonders whether he'll be asked to recite the alphabet forward and backward next.

'What is this, an OUI?' he asks.

Joe spreads his arms out like airplane wings and walks heel-to-toe across the room. No problem. He rushes things and gets a hair sloppy on the way back, but nothing he'd book anyone for. Again, no problem.

'Great. Now I want you to tap each finger to

your thumb, starting with your index finger down to your pinkie and back. Like this.'

Joe touches each finger to his thumb. He's slow, careful, and deliberate in choosing and landing each finger, wanting to be sure he nails it.

'Yes, that's it. Now try doing it a bit faster, and keep repeating it.'

She demonstrates. It's Joe's turn, and this time, he trips up and can't recover. His fingers go out of order or freeze up.

'I'm no Beethoven,' says Joe.

He looks at Rosie, and her face has gone ashen, her eyes withdrawn.

Dr. Hagler retrieves her clipboard. She slides her glasses back over her eyes and writes in Joe's chart. She then sits down, places the clipboard on the counter, removes her glasses, and sighs.

'Okay, you have some symptoms here. Your movements don't look completely normal. It's possible that you have Huntington's disease, but I want to do some blood tests and an MRI.'

'An MRI of my knee?' asks Joe.

'No, not your knee. Your head.'

'My head? What about my knee?'

'Dr. Levine checked out your knee and found it to be stable. Your knee looks fine, Joe.'

'But my head doesn't?'

'We'll do the MRI and the blood work and go from there.'

'Wait,' says Rosie. 'What's Hunningtin's disease?'

'Hun-ting-ton's,' says Dr. Hagler. 'It's an inherited neurological disease, but let's not get ahead of ourselves. We'll do the MRI and the blood work. We'll do a genetic test to confirm whether or not it's Huntington's, and if it is, we can treat the symptoms, but we can talk about all that next visit if that's what we're dealing with.'

Moments later, Joe and Rosie are led back into purgatory, where a new set of lost souls waits in silence, and Rosie schedules Joe's appointments with the receptionist. His next visit with Dr. Hagler isn't until March, exactly two months from today. Rosie asks for something sooner, but the receptionist says it's the soonest she has.

They proceed through the automatic doors of the Wang building, and the biting January air rushes at them. Joe takes a deep breath. Even polluted with car exhaust, the cold air feels fresh and healthy in his lungs. He pauses on the sidewalk, the air blowing against his face, moving through his lungs, and he feels real again. Whatever just happened in that building wasn't real.

Rosie leads him to their car on the fourth floor of the garage. Joe's grateful that she came with him as he admits to himself and not aloud to Rosie that he couldn't remember where they parked. They get in, and Rosie hands him the garage ticket.

'At least we know my knee works,' says Joe.

Rosie doesn't comment. She's frowning, her eyebrows knotted, tapping her iPhone screen with her finger.

'Whaddaya doin', hun?' asks Joe.

'Googling Hun-ting-ton's disease.'

'Oh.'

Joe drives the dizzying spiral out of the garage. It's a quick, unmemorable drive back to Charlestown and then the longer hunt for a parking space. As Joe zigzags up and down the hilly streets of their neighborhood, he keeps glancing at Rosie, her attention still buried in her phone. He doesn't like the shape of her face, her frown deepening, ruining her pretty mouth. He doesn't like that she's not sharing any of what she's reading. She doesn't say anything to reassure him. She's not saying anything at all. She taps, frowns, reads, and says nothing.

He finds and doesn't mess with two parking spaces 'reserved' with trash barrels before finally landing a spot only a block away. They walk home in silence. They dump their coats and shoes in the front hallway. Joe goes straight to the kitchen. He pulls the largest jelly jar from the cabinet and pours a glass of wine. He grabs a can of Bud from the fridge and looks for Rosie.

The living room shades are drawn, making it feel like early evening instead of noon. Joe doesn't flip on the light. Rosie is wrapped in her ivory afghan on the couch, reading her phone. Joe places the jar of wine in front of her on the coffee table and sits in his chair. Rosie doesn't look up.

Joe waits. Pictures of the kids from their high school graduations and JJ's wedding hang on the wall over the couch. There are pictures all over the room — baby photos on the fireplace mantel, more baby photos on the side tables, pictures of Joe and Rosie on their wedding day on the hutch. He likes the pictures. It's all the other crap he could do without.

Scattered among the standing frames are all sorts of figurines — angels, babies, Snoopy and Woodstock, Jesus and Mary, St. Patrick, Miss Piggy and Kermit, too many frogs. Rosie has a thing for frogs. And then there's the year-round Christmas carolers, which might not seem too out of place now in January but are plain ridiculous in August. Rosie loves them all.

Years ago, Joe actually considered staging a burglary, a clean heist of all the knickknacks, a mysterious crime that would go unsolved. But Rosie only would have replaced every little statue with more of the same, and so in the end, the plan would've left Joe back where he started but with less money in the bank.

All this decorative crap makes the room feel crowded and tacky if you ask him, but no one ever does, and it makes Rosie happy, so he's resigned himself to living with it. As long as he has his chair, the TV, and his side of the bed, he doesn't complain. The rest of the house belongs to Rosie.

When Joe lived here as a kid, this living room looked and felt much different. The couch and chairs were wooden frames with thin cushions, much less comfortable than what they have now. He remembers each year's awkward school photo hung on the wall on either side of Jesus on the cross: Joe on the left, Maggie on the right. There were no figurines.

His parents were chain smokers, and every wooden surface held at least one ashtray, many made and painted by Joe and Maggie in school as holiday gifts (ah, the seventies). There was the tube TV with two dials and rabbit ears, the TV trays, and always an issue of *TV Guide* and the newspaper on the coffee table, which was permanently stained and almost spongy to the touch with waterlogged rings all over. Some of the many scars left by his mother's drinking.

Joe holds the remote but doesn't turn on the TV. Today's *Patriot Bridge* is on the coffee table, unopened, but he doesn't feel like reading the paper. He drinks his beer and watches Rosie. She says nothing and frowns. He says nothing and waits. He waits.

Ice-cold dread in his veins.

Ominous chanting in his bones.

Purgatory has followed them home.

8

Joe is in the kitchen wielding a screwdriver, tasked with replacing the cabinet hinges that are bent beyond repair. He begins with tightening the ones that are merely loose. The cabinets, like everything else in their house, are old and worn out, but Rosie blames Joe for the broken hinges, says he's been too rough when opening them, yanking too hard on the handles. He doesn't agree, but he doesn't care either. It's not worth fighting about.

He's actually grateful for the job, something to keep him busy and out of Rosie's hair for a bit. Ever since Rosie shared with Joe what she learned on the Internet about Huntington's disease, Joe's been trying to scrub every word of it out of his mind. None of it rings true. He doesn't have some friggin' rare and fatal disease. No fuckin' way.

Huntington's. It's pure malarkey, and Joe won't give it any stock. Police officers deal in facts, not speculation, and the fact is, this doctor threw out this big, scary medical word without having done any real medical tests, without knowing a damn thing. It was an offhand, irresponsible remark. It's practically malpractice, to put a word like that out there, into their innocent heads, with no facts to back it up. It's complete bullshit is what it is.

While Joe refuses to think about Huntington's

beyond calling it bullshit, Rosie has done pretty much nothing but think about it. She hasn't confessed her new obsession to Joe, but it might as well be tattooed across her forehead. A Sunday church-goer her entire life, she's been at Mass every morning since Joe's doctor's appointment. Her couple of glasses of wine with supper is now at least a whole bottle beginning at four o'clock. The scarf she was knitting is now a queen-size bedspread and still growing. She's up every night way past midnight, watching old Oprah episodes while ironing anything with a seam. And normally a constant gabber, Rosie isn't talking.

The whole point of going to the goddamn doctor was to stop Rosie from worrying about him, and now look at her. A hundred times worse. Joe twists the screw he's working on with extra muscle, unleashing his infuriation on the tiny screw head, but the tip slips out and then fumbles out of Joe's hand entirely, dropping to the floor. Joe grinds his teeth. He steps down off the kitchen chair, retrieves the Phillips head, then winds up and pitches it back to the floor as hard as he can. He retrieves the screwdriver again, sighs, and resumes his business with the cabinet hinge.

He'd like to help Rosie out, to reassure her and protect her from this needless worrying, but a small part of Joe is afraid of what she's thinking, so he doesn't open up the conversation. Maybe she knows something he doesn't. He doesn't want to hear anything more until his next appointment, when the doctor admits that his tests came back fine and everything's normal. And an apology. There'd better be a fuckin' apology in there.

But while he's been doing his best to avoid falling down the dark, muddy rabbit hole of Huntington's disease, he has been thinking a lot about his mother. Joe stops turning the screwdriver and runs his index finger over the scar by the outside corner of his left eye. Six stitches when he was five. It's a thin white line now, and only visible when Joe's face is sunburned or emotionally pink.

His mother threw a potato masher across the room. Joe doesn't remember what he'd been doing before the throw, if he'd provoked it, if his mother had been mad or frustrated about anything. His memory begins with the shock and flashing pain of being struck in the face with something hard and heavy. Then the sound of Maggie's scream. Then the bright red blood on his fingers, the darker red soaked into the wet face-cloth he pressed to his head while his father drove to the hospital. He remembers sitting alone in the backseat. His mother must've stayed home with Maggie. He has no memory of the stitches. He remembers his father saying he was lucky. A centimeter to the right and Joe would've lost his eye.

Joe likes to believe that the scar by his eye is the only thing he got from his mother, a single souvenir of her madness. Aside from his sleepy-lidded blue eyes, Joe's the spitting image of his father, and he grew up assuming he'd descended straight from the O'Briens. He has his father's and grandfather's walnut-brown hair that lightens to blond in the summer, the same thin smile, broad chest and shoulders, and ugly feet, the unfortunate pasty-to-pink skin. He even has the same voice. People used to mistake Joe for his father on the phone all the time. He has the O'Brien work ethic, bullheadedness, and sense of humor that keeps everyone in the room laughing and at arm's length.

What if he inherited more from his mother than blue eyes and this scar? Alcoholism has always been a real concern, which is why he keeps his drinking under tight control. If his mother gave him a genetic predisposition for addiction, if that beast lurks within him, he simply won't feed it. While he's often wondered what it'd feel like to get rip-roaring drunk, he's never indulged in actually finding out. He'll never be a drunk like his mother. But what if beneath the scar by his eye, beneath the white, hardened skin, he carries an uglier, more insidious heirloom?

Did his mother have Huntington's? Is that why she lived at Tewksbury State?

Joe remembers going to visit his mother in the hospital after church on Sundays. At first, these were reasonably pleasant car rides. Joe and Maggie loved road trips — to Stowe in the fall for apple picking, to Good Harbor Beach in Gloucester once every summer, to some suburb every now and then to visit cousins on his father's side of the family. Granted, they weren't going to pick apples or swim in the ocean, but those rides to Tewksbury didn't seem so bad at first. Hospitals were places people went to get better. This was when Joe was seven years old, when he still hoped she'd come home, when he could still imagine the mother she'd been before — buying him ice cream from the truck at Good Harbor, the sound of her voice singing in church, her arm curled around his shoulders as she read Hardy Boys mysteries to him before bed, the cat-whisker crinkles next to her eyes when she laughed at something he said.

But she didn't get better, and in fact she was worse and somehow farther away in the same bed each time he saw her, and those fond memories of a happy, tender, sober mother began to feel vaguely imagined, a fiction he'd wished for or dreamed about, and soon he only remembered her drunken rants, and then only what she looked like lying in that bed. She was emaciated, contorted, grunting or silent. She was grotesque. The woman in that bed would never be able to read or sing or smile at him again. The woman in that bed was nobody's mother.

The atmosphere in the car changed. Normally, Joe and Maggie would play I Spy games and horse around. Their play would invariably turn too loud or too violent, and their father's hand would suddenly be in the backseat with them, swatting blindly, aiming to smack whatever body part it could reach. But now, Joe didn't feel like spying for anything. Maggie must've felt the same way, because they didn't talk or play games or even fight. Joe stared out the window and watched the trees blur by in silence. He thinks the radio must've been on, tuned to NPR or

111

Magic 106.7, but he doesn't remember that. He remembers only the blurry silence.

And the way home was always worse. On the way to Tewksbury, there was the hope, however deluded, that his mother might be better this week. Or the memory of how bony and listless she'd been the previous week would have faded some. A particularly gullible kid already, Joe could easily trick himself into thinking his mother might be cured this Sunday.

The big, fat, hideous truth of that Sunday would sit next to him on those car rides back to Charlestown, taking up way too much room in the backseat, crushing his spirit. If Joe wasn't entirely stripped of hope when he buckled his seat belt, his father would soon rob him of whatever was left. Even if Joe purposefully looked away and couldn't see his father's face in the rearview mirror, even if he didn't actually see the strongest man in the world crying, he always knew it was happening. Even with the wind and the car engine roaring in his ears, Joe would hear his father's breath catching, and he'd know. Joe remembers looking over at Maggie, checking for permission to cry, too, but she just stared, stone-faced, out the window. If Maggie didn't cry, he wasn't going to either.

His mother was a drunk in the loony bin, his father cried like a little girl in the car, and Joe and Maggie stared out the car window.

This went on for years.

Joe can't recall specifically the last time he saw his mother. He remembers watching a nurse feed her, his mother's head dropping, her mouth stretched open, the mashed potatoes and gravy dribbling down his mother's chin, spilling onto her bib and the floor. That could've been the last time. He remembers feeling disgusted and ashamed.

Joe assumed his father became ashamed, too, because they stopped going. At least, Joe and Maggie stopped. Joe can't remember what his father did. He remembers going to Aunt Mary Pat's and Uncle Dave's instead of the hospital after church. He remembers stuffing himself with Dunkin' Donuts and playing basketball at the park with his cousins. He remembers feeling relieved not to have to see the sick woman in the bed anymore.

He doesn't remember what she looked like when she died.

Joe's thoughts are interrupted by Rosie entering the kitchen. She's wearing a Town Yoga T-shirt, baggy gray sweatpants, and the fluffy pink socks she wears around the house in the winter months. She pulls a bottle of Chardonnay out of the fridge and walks over to the counter next to Joe. He assumes she's approaching him to say something. She's going to thank him for finally fixing the cabinets or ask him a question or just offer a friendly hello and maybe even a hug.

He's wrong. She opens the cabinet in front of her (without comment about the perfect, new hinges), pulls out a wineglass (no words of thanks to Joe for the new glassware), grabs the bottle opener from the counter, and leaves the kitchen. Joe sighs and looks over at the clock on the wall. Four o'clock.

He can't take another month of this. She's torturing herself over nothing. Tap your fingers. Clap your hands. Do the Hokey Pokey. That doctor doesn't know shit. He wishes he could convince Rosie. He's about to go after her, to sit her down and confront this unsubstantiated worry she's burdened with head-on, but he stops cold in front of the sink.

While he'd bet a million bucks this fancy doctor doesn't know shit, he's still not sure about Rosie. What does she know that has her so scared?

Joe stares out the kitchen window and says nothing.

9

Today is Evacuation Day, a public holiday in Boston commemorating the withdrawal of British forces from the city in 1776, George Washington's first military victory in the Revolutionary War. It sounds historically significant, a day for visiting the Freedom Trail and waving the American flag, but in truth, it's a well-played game of smoke and mirrors, a tidy and politically agreeable excuse for what's really going on here. Evacuation Day just so happens to fall on St. Patrick's Day, and Boston's Irish use the sanctioned day off to celebrate their proud heritage. This year, it also happens to be on a Monday, which means that Boston has been stinking drunk for three days.

As luck would have it, Joe has today off. In years past, if he was home on St. Patrick's Day, he'd be at Sullivan's, Charlestown's neighborhood pub, before noon, his hand hugging a glass of Glenfiddich or a pint of thick and creamy Guinness. On any other day, he limits himself to a shot and a couple of beers, but on this one day a year, he allows himself the pleasure of whatever he wants. He'd be sitting at the bar with Donny and a bunch of other Townies Joe doesn't see much of anymore now that their kids are all grown, swapping stories about the good old days. Sully would have Irish music playing on the jukebox — 'Song for Ireland,' 'Wild Colonial

115

Boy,' 'On Raglan Road.' Joe's favorites. By midafternoon, he and Donny would be arm in arm, singing along, each off-key note bleeding with sincerity.

He'd always walk home before things got too drunk and too rowdy, in time for supper — corned beef and cabbage, boiled until every molecule had loosened and separated, recombining to form some yet unnamed, tasteless compound closely related to glue. NASA should study Rosie's corned beef and cabbage.

But as luck would also have it for Joe, in addition to being St. Patrick's Day, today is the date of his second appointment with Dr. Hagler. So Joe is not sitting at the bar at Sullivan's, drinking Guinness and singing with Donny. Instead he's sitting in a small chair in the Wang Center, in the Movement Disorders Unit, where no one is celebrating the evacuation of the Brits from Boston or the snakes from Ireland. No one here is celebrating a damn thing.

Joe feels as if he's aged ten years in two months, but Dr. Hagler looks exactly the same. Same glasses on her duck nose, same loose bun and lab coat, same silver loop on a chain. It's as if he and Rosie are visiting a hospital museum, and Dr. Hagler is part of a living exhibit, here every day, open Monday through Friday nine to five, Saturday and Sunday noon to six.

Dr. Hagler recites a cursory recap of what they did during Joe's last visit and asks Joe and Rosie whether they have any questions. They don't. She's all business, stiff and no smiles, a palpable change in demeanor from two months ago. Joe's stomach tenses and hollows out. He tries smiling at Dr. Hagler, hoping to coax a smile in return, but her lips remain a tight line. This is not good. A cool prickle skates across the back of Joe's neck. He rubs it, trying to erase the sensation, but it persists. Dr. Hagler places Joe's medical report down on the desk, clasps her hands, and looks directly at Joe.

'I have the results of your blood work. Your genetic screen came back positive for Huntington's disease. Your neuro exam and some mild changes in your MRI are both consistent with this.'

A silence fills the room like a flash flood, and they're all submerged, breathless. This lasts exactly one second and forever. Then Rosie is sobbing, venting deep, ugly wails, sounds that Joe has never heard come out of her. Dr. Hagler passes Rosie a box of Kleenex. Rosie mops her face with wads of tissues, struggling to compose herself. Joe rubs Rosie's back up and down with the palm of his hand, trying to help, not sure whether he's more stunned by the anguished cries emanating from Rosie or by what Dr. Hagler just said. What did Dr. Hagler just say? His head feels numb, unresponsive. He rubs Rosie's back and can't think. His police training kicks in. Ask questions.

'So I have Huntington's disease?'

'Yes.'

'What is it again, exactly?'

'It's an inherited neurodegenerative disease that causes you to lose control over your ability to move. It also affects thinking and behavior.

This is why you've been fidgety and falling and dropping things, having trouble organizing your reports, remembering things. It's also the reason for the irritability, the temper outbursts.'

'You said 'inherited.' So what does that mean, I have this in my DNA?'

'Yes.'

Joe took biology his freshman year of high school, about a million years ago. He thinks he got a C in the class. But he remembers enough to put two and two together.

'I got this thing from my mother, then?'

'Yes.'

'So she died of Huntington's.'

'Yes.'

There it is, spoken aloud by a medical professional. *Ruth O'Brien drank herself to death.* Not a word of it was ever true. Ruth O'Brien died alone, a silent, writhing skeleton in a state hospital bed, while her children ate donuts and played at the park with cousins. She died of Huntington's disease.

And now it's his turn.

Joe's lungs feel constricted and rigid, as if he's been shot in the chest, and he's bleeding out, only the blood is cold mercury pulsing from his heart. Drained of oxygen, his head goes fuzzy. Rosie's crying sounds dull and distant. He has to fight through the fear. Keep asking questions.

'Is it always fatal?'

'Yes. But it doesn't go there overnight. The symptoms will come on slowly, and we can manage many of them.'

'How long do I have?' he hears himself ask.

'We can't say exactly, but it's typically ten to twenty years.'

In ten years, Joe will be fifty-four. Fifty-four. One year away from retirement and enjoying the good life with Rosie. For some reason, he looks at his watch. He thinks back. He remembers dropping the crystal pitcher, smashing glass all over Sunday supper. Was that a year ago? Rosie claims he's had a weird temper for at least six, seven years. Has he had Huntington's all that time? How many years has he already used up?

Inherited. Passed from mother to son. That son became a father.

'We've got four kids,' says Joe. 'Are — ' He knows his question, but he can't find sufficient air to carry the words. They hang suspended in his throat along with a new fear, massive and impatient, rudely shoving its way to the front of the line.

'Are they all going to get this from me?'

'Huntington's is caused by something called an autosomal dominant mutation. If you get one copy of the bad gene, you get the disease. That means each of your kids has a fifty-fifty chance of inheriting it.'

'So two of our four kids will have this, too?' asks Rosie.

'No, no, it's like flipping a coin. It doesn't matter what happened on the previous tosses. Each time, it's a fifty percent chance of being heads. None of your kids may have it.'

'Oh God, no,' says Rosie. 'No.'

Her crying, which had dwindled some during

119

Joe's Q&A, now loses all pretense of trying to stop or even behave. Joe knows exactly where her head went. All of their kids could get this. This is the possibility she's now envisioning as if it were prophecy. She's sitting next to Joe, buried in too many sopping-wet tissues, losing everyone she loves.

Joe reaches over, threads his fingers between Rosie's, and squeezes her hand. She squeezes back but doesn't look at him.

'How old are they?' asks Dr. Hagler.

'Oldest is twenty-five, youngest is twenty-one,' says Joe.

'Any grandchildren?'

'Not yet. The oldest is married.' JJ and Colleen. They're trying. The disease was passed from mother to son. That son became a father. And so on. And so on.

'It will be important to talk with them, let them know what they're facing, especially with respect to family planning. There are things that can be done, medical procedures, to ensure having a baby who is gene negative. And there's genetic counseling and screening if they want to know their own risk status.'

'What's risk status?'

'They can have the same blood test you had, but this time it would be presymptomatic, to find out if they're gene positive or gene negative.'

'So they can find out now if they're going to get this later.'

'Yes.'

'Does the test tell you when you'll get it?'

'No. The average age of onset is thirty-five, but

you're a bit older. If any of them are gene positive, they're probably looking at around that age, but don't quote me on that.'

'If any of them find out they have this thing, if they take the test and it's positive, can they do anything about it to prevent it from happening?'

'No. Unfortunately, as of now, no.'

A genetic crystal ball. Exoneration or the death penalty for each kid.

'So what do we do now?' asks Joe.

'I want to prescribe a neuroleptic for the temper flare-ups. It's a low dose, just a whiff. I don't want to snow you. Rosie, if you don't notice a difference, let me know; we can go a bit higher.'

Joe bristles at the thought of taking any pills. He doesn't even take a vitamin.

'I also want to get you started on physical therapy for help with strength and balance, and speech therapy for slurring and swallowing.'

'I don't have any problems with slurring or swallowing.'

Dr. Hagler meets Joe's eyes and pauses, conveying her reply without words. Yet. He doesn't have problems with slurring or swallowing yet. This is coming.

'It's good to stay ahead of it. Think of it as preparing for battle. Like training to become a police officer.'

In his police academy training, Joe learned how to carry and aim a firearm; procedure for responding to domestic calls, robberies, traffic accidents, and shootings; how to think at least six steps into any given scenario; how to imagine every possible scenario. Now he will be training to swallow.

'And then there are clinical trials. We're lucky to be here in Boston, where there's a lot of exciting research happening. There are many potential treatments being discovered in animal models, and we're trying to turn those into treatments for people. The key is participation. There's a trial ongoing now, a Phase II study that I'd like to enroll you in if you're willing.'

'Phase II, what does that mean?'

'It means we're testing for safety.'

'So it might not be safe?'

'It was found safe in mice. The next, necessary step is to determine if it's safe in people.'

'I don't like the sound of that, Joe,' says Rosie. 'They don't know what it does. What if it does something horrible to you?'

Joe doesn't know the first thing about science. He pictures the Frankenstein monster and a team of frizzy white-haired doctors poking him with needles. Then he pictures his mother. His future. He thinks of JJ, Patrick, Meghan, and Katie. Their future. He'd chop off his own head and donate it to science right now if it'd save his kids.

'I'll do it. Whatever it is. Sign me up.'

'But Joe —'

'There's no cure for this thing, right? So how are they gonna cure it if they don't have any guinea pigs?'

'That's exactly right, Joe,' says Dr. Hagler. 'There's real hope in the pipeline for HD, but we need people to participate in the research. I have

122

the trial information here for you so you can both look it over and decide, and I strongly recommend it, and there's also information on support groups. I encourage you both to talk to other people in the Huntington's community.'

'So how fast is this going to go?' asks Joe. 'I know you said ten to twenty years for the whole thing, but how soon before, you know?'

He's thinking about his mother's chronology, trying to do applied math. She was in Tewksbury for five years. Joe has eleven years until retirement. She died when she was forty, so she was thirty-five when she was first admitted to twenty-four-hour care. He's forty-four now. The numbers spin in his head.

'This disease moves slowly. It's not like flipping a light switch or like catching the flu and bam, you have it. You have time.'

'Jesus,' says Joe, raking his hands over his face. 'I really thought I just had a bad knee and was maybe a little tired and stressed-out lately.'

'I'm sorry. I know this is a shock to you both, especially since you weren't aware of your mother's Huntington's.'

Even though the doctor had told him his knee was fine, he'd still been imagining knee surgery as his worst-case prognosis. A couple of weeks off from work at the most with lots of rest, then back into the fire, good as new. Huntington's wasn't even in his vocabulary, never mind a possibility. Now it's his reality. He can't imagine the first step, never mind six, into this scenario. How many steps are there between now and Tewksbury State?

The fuzziness in Joe's head has spread throughout his body. He's numb all over. If Dr. Hagler placed a mirror in front of him right now, he knows what he'd see staring back at him — the flat, expressionless mask of a man in shock. He's witnessed trauma on the faces of too many crime and accident victims, an unflappable exterior running on autopilot, an eerie antithesis to the unbridled psychological and physiological terror raging on the inside.

'What do I do about my job?'

'I think we should be realistically optimistic there. You don't have to tell everyone yet, and I would advise that you don't. You don't want to get fired or denied disability. There are laws now to protect you, but you don't want to spend the time you have in a court battle. I'd confide in maybe one other officer, someone you trust not to tell anyone and to be your mirror. This person can help you decide when it's no longer possible for you to safely continue in your job.'

Joe nods. He's scenario playing, and he sees all the less-than-desirable and immediate possible outcomes of disclosing his diagnosis. He can tell Tommy and Donny. No one else. Tommy knows how to keep a secret and play him with a straight bat when he needs it. Joe trusts him with his life. Same for Donny. No one else on the force can know, not until he figures things out. He needs to secure at least a partial pension so Rosie will be taken care of when he's gone. Ten years. Maybe more. Maybe less.

But this is going to get worse. Falling down, dropping things, messing up his reports, showing up late, his weird temper. Slurring his words. Everyone is going to think he's a drunk. Fuck it. Let them think what they want. Until he's sure that Rosie will have what she needs, this disease is a secret.

Ruth O'Brien drank herself to death.

Like mother like son.

★ ★ ★

Joe and Rosie get home from MGH with plenty of time for Joe to join Donny and friends at Sullivan's, but he's feeling too fragile, transparent. He's worried it would take only one Guinness to crack him wide open, and he'd be spilling his diagnosis all over Donny and the rest of the bar. No, he's not going to Sullivan's this St. Patrick's Day. But he can't stay home either.

Rosie's at the kitchen sink, peeling potatoes. She's stopped crying, but her eyes are still pink and swollen. She's determined to put on a good face and look normal when the kids show up for supper. Joe and Rosie agreed that they need a little time before dropping the HD bomb on the kids. And Joe would never want to ruin their St. Patrick's Day.

'I'm going for a walk, okay?' asks Joe.

'Where you going?' She spins around, a half-naked potato in one hand and the peeler in the other.

'Just out. A walk. Don't worry.'

'How long will you be gone? Supper's at four.'

'I'll be back before then. I just need to clear my head. You okay?'

'I'm fine,' she says, and turns her back to Joe. He hears the flick, flick, flick of the potato peeler.

'Come here,' he says.

Joe places his hands on her shoulders, turns her toward him, and wraps his big bear arms around her back, pressing the slim length of her up against him. She turns her head and rests it on his chest.

'I love you, Joe.'

'I love you, too, hun. I'll be home soon, okay?'

She looks up at him with her bloated face and heartbroken eyes.

'Okay. I'll be here.'

Joe grabs his coat and walks out the front door, but before his feet hit the sidewalk, he stops and dashes back in. He dips his fingers in Rosie's holy water and looks at the painted blue eyes of the Virgin Mary while he signs the cross. He'll take all the help he can get.

On his way to the Navy Yard, he stops at the packie and picks up a bottle of Gentleman Jack. It's not Glenfiddich, but it'll do. As he hoped it would be, the Navy Yard is quiet and empty. There are no bars here since Tavern on the Water closed. The Toonies are all at the Warren Tavern, and the Townies are at Sullivan's or Ironsides. His kids are all at Ironsides, Patrick behind the bar. And Joe is a lone Irishman in the Navy Yard, sitting on a pier, feet dangling over the edge, facing the beautiful city he's loved and protected for more than half his life.

He woke up this morning just like on any other day. And now, just a few short hours later, he has Huntington's disease. Of course, he had

Huntington's disease this morning before he went to see Dr. Hagler. He's still the same guy. The only difference is in the knowing. The veil of the initial shock has lifted, and the knowing is beginning to fuck with his head.

Keeping the bottle of Gentleman Jack concealed in the brown paper bag, Joe unscrews the top and pulls back a generous swig and then another. It's a raw, gray March day, in the low fifties but much chillier when the sun hides behind the clouds and the wind comes surfing in over the water. The whiskey feels like a glowing coal in his belly.

Ten years. He'll be fifty-four. That's not so bad. It could be worse. Hell, it's more than anyone is guaranteed, especially a police officer. Every single time he's dressed in blue, he knows he might not come home. That's not just a noble sentiment. Joe's been kicked, punched, and shot at. He's chased after and confronted people who were hammered and doped up and pissed off, armed with knives and guns. He's been to the funerals of his fellow officers. All young men. He's been prepared to die in the line of duty since he was twenty. Fifty-four is old. It's a fuckin' luxury.

He gulps another nip and exhales, enjoying the burn. It's the certainty he hates, for one thing. Knowing he has only ten years left, twenty tops, that it's 100 percent fatal, makes his situation hopeless. Certainty eviscerates hope.

He could hope for a cure. Maybe those doctors will discover one within the next ten years. Dr. Hagler said there were promising things in development. She used words like *treatment* and *research*, but, and he listened for it, she never once said the word *cure*. No, Joe's not going to hold his breath for a cure for himself, but he'll climb a mountain of hope every day for his kids.

His kids. He knocks back another couple of gulps. They're all in their early twenties. Still kids. In ten years, JJ, his oldest, will be thirty-five. The average age of onset. This friggin' disease will be about done with Joe as it's starting in on them. Maybe they'll all get lucky, and by the grace of God, none of them will get this. He knocks three times on the pier.

Or all of them could have it, already hibernating inside them, waiting to crawl out of its cave. JJ's a firefighter trying to start his own family. Meghan's a dancer. A dancer with Huntington's disease. A tear rolls down Joe's face, hot on his wind-chilled cheek. He can't think of anything less fair. Katie's hoping to open her own yoga studio. Hoping. If she's gene positive, will she stop hoping? Patrick doesn't know what the hell he's doing yet. He might need the better part of the next ten years to figure his shit out. How on God's earth are he and Rosie going to tell them?

He's also hung up on the how of it, his dying. He's seen exactly what this disease does to a person, what it did to his mother. It's a relentless fuckin' demon. It's going to strip him of everything human until he's just a rack of twisting bones and a beating heart in a bed. And then it will kill him. Getting shot at and not running away takes bravery. Walking into a domestic dispute, breaking up a gang fight, chasing a suspect in a stolen car takes bravery. He's not sure he's brave enough to face year ten of Huntington's. And there's honor in dying as a police officer on duty. How will he find the honor in dying with Huntington's?

He hates the thought of putting Rosie and the kids through this unthinkable ordeal, through what he and Maggie and mostly Joe's father witnessed, powerless. Shit. Maggie. Does she know anything about this? Did his father know? Did letting everyone think his mother was a drunk carry less shame than branding her name with Huntington's? If his father knew about HD, who was he protecting?

Everyone in Town blamed her. His mother's tragic predicament was her own damn fault: She's a lush. She's a bad mother. She's a sinner. She's going to hell.

But everyone was wrong. She had Huntington's. Huntington's destroyed her ability to walk and feed herself. It mutilated her good mood, her patience and reasoning. It strangled her voice and her smile. It stole her family and her dignity, and then it killed her.

'I'm sorry, Mum. I didn't know. I didn't know.'

He silently cries and wipes his wet eyes with his coat sleeve. He exhales and tips back one more glug of whiskey before capping the bottle. Standing on the edge of the pier, he looks down past the tips of his sneakers at the black harbor water. He reaches into his front pocket and pulls out his change. He sorts out four quarters, warm and shiny in his cold, pink hand. Each kid has a fifty-fifty chance.

He flips the first quarter, catches it in his left hand, and then turns it over on the back of his right. He removes his left hand, revealing the coin.

Heads.

Joe throws it as far as he can. He follows its flight with his eyes, sees the point where it enters the water, and then it's gone. He flips the second quarter, catches, turns, reveals.

Heads again.

He chucks that one into the water, too. Third quarter.

Heads.

Fuck. He winds up and pitches the coin high into the air. He loses sight of it and doesn't see where it lands. Joe holds the last quarter in his hand, thinking of Katie. He can't flip it. He fuckin' can't. He sits back down on the edge of the pier and cries into his hands, releasing pained, vulnerable, boylike sobs. He hears the voices of people walking in the shadows of Old Ironsides. They're laughing. If he can hear them laughing, they can definitely hear him crying. He doesn't fuckin' care.

He's soon emptied out. He dries his eyes, takes a deep breath, and sighs. Rosie would call that a good cry. He'd always thought that was a ridiculous expression. What could be good about crying? But he feels better, if not good.

Joe stands, opens his right hand, and again considers the fourth quarter sitting in his palm.

He shoves it into his other pocket, down to the bottom where it'll be safe, grabs his bottle of whiskey by the neck, and checks his watch. It's time for supper.

He walks the length of the pier, whiskey playing in his head and legs, his cheeks raw from the wind and tears, with every step praying to God and the Virgin Mary and St. Patrick and whomever will listen for a dollar's worth of good luck.

PART II

The mutation associated with Huntington's disease (HD) was isolated in 1993, mapped to the short arm of chromosome 4. This historic discovery was made by an international collaboration led by a team of neuroscientists in a laboratory in the Charlestown Navy Yard. Normally, the trinucleotide cytosine-adenine-guanine (CAG) is repeated within exon 1 of the Huntingtin gene thirty-five times or fewer. The mutated gene has thirty-six or more CAG repeats. This expanded genetic stutter results in too many glutamines in the Huntingtin protein and causes the disease.

Every child of a parent with HD has a 50 percent chance of inheriting the mutated gene. The discovery of this mutation made genetic testing possible for anyone living at risk. The test definitively determines genetic status. A positive test result means the person has the mutation and will develop HD. To date, 90 percent of people at risk for HD choose not to know.

10

It's Sunday afternoon, and Katie skipped both yoga and church. Church doesn't really count. She hasn't been to Sunday Mass in years, but the thought of possibly going before deciding not to go is still a habit, maybe even a guilty pleasure. She was brought up strict Irish Catholic, which most memorably involved confessing an invented assortment of harmless sins on Saturdays to the priests, eating wafers of Christ's body on Sundays (no wonder she's vegan) and loaves of shame every day of the week, attending parochial school, where she learned from the nuns that sitting fully clothed on a boy's lap could get a girl pregnant, and saying the Angelus every evening before supper. Protestants were evil, monstrous people and somehow probably contagious, and Katie grew up fearing them, praying to God she'd never see one, never actually knowing what a real-live Protestant looked like. She could recite the Our Father and Hail Mary before she knew how to spell her name. She never understood how Jesus dying for her sins on Good Friday resulted in candy delivered by a bunny on Easter Sunday, and she'd always been too afraid to ask. This remains a mystery. And every day smelled of incense, prayers lifting in swirls of smoke, floating up to God's ear. She liked the incense.

Yoga is Katie's real religion. She found it by

accident. It was three years ago, her first year out of high school, and she'd been waitressing at Figs. She walked by Town Yoga every day on the way to work and one afternoon, curious, popped inside to grab a schedule. By the end of her first class, she was hooked. Her dad likes to say she drank the Kool-Aid, chugged a whole pitcher of it. She saved up her tip money to pay for her two-hundred-hour certified teacher training that winter and has been teaching yoga ever since.

She loves the physical practice, the postures that teach grace, resilience, and balance. Plus her abs and biceps are wicked awesome. She loves the mindful breathing, the flow of prana, which promotes a sense of grounded calm over reactive chaos. She loves meditation, which, when she can actually do it, clears the toxic trash heap in her head, silencing the negative self-talk — that cunningly persuasive voice that insists she's not smart enough, pretty enough, good enough — as well as the fictional gossip (it's always fictional), the constant doubt, the noisy worry, the judgments. She loves the sense of oneness she feels with every human being within the vibrating notes of ohm. And every day still smells of incense.

She can't remember the last time she missed Andrea's Sunday morning Vinyasa. She knows she'll regret sleeping through it later. But right now, well after noon and still lazing in bed, *her* bed, with Felix, she regrets nothing.

She's been dating Felix for a month and a half, and this is the first time he's spent the night at her place. They met the first Tuesday in April.

It was the first week of Roof Deck Yoga, classes taught outside on the fenced-in wooden patio behind the studio. Katie likes teaching outdoors, sunshine warming muscles, fresh air breezing against bare skin, even if that air sometimes smells of diesel and garlic chicken from Chow Thai.

She'd never seen him before. She didn't know him from high school or the bars or waitressing. The majority of her students are Toonies and women, so the few good men always stand out. Felix stood out more than anyone.

He practices yoga in shorts and no shirt. Bless him for that. He's tall and lean with a small waist and defined but not bulging muscles. His head and chest are shaved smooth, and she remembers, that first class, both were shining with sweat in the sun. As she stood with one foot on his mat, assisting him in Downward Dog, her left palm on his sacrum, her right hand sliding along the length of his spine to his neck, she found herself wanting to trace the black lines of the tribal tattoo on his shoulder with her fingers. She remembers blushing before stepping back and calling out Warrior I.

He came to class the following Tuesday, this time indoors due to inclement weather. He lingered a long time in the room after Savasana and took even longer gathering his things. He asked her a few questions about the schedule, about pass cards, and purchased a coconut water. When she asked whether there was anything else, hoping there was, he asked for her number.

They both dove in headfirst. Like most Toonies, Felix owns a car, which means they aren't stuck going to Ironsides or Sully's, and their relationship has remained mostly private, blossoming outside the scrutiny of the Townies. They go to dinners in Cambridge and the South End. They've been to Cape Cod and New Hampshire, and they even went to Kripalu for an R&R weekend. He goes to her Tuesday and Thursday classes every week, and they both take Andrea's class on Sunday mornings. The one place they'd never been together is her apartment. She's told him it's because his place is so much nicer. It is. And he lives alone. Her sister, Meghan, goes to bed so early. They'd disturb her, and she needs her sleep.

But the real reason Katie hasn't risked having Felix stay at her place has to do with her parents, who live on the first floor of their triple-decker. Felix Martin is not a nice Irish Catholic boy from Charlestown. Felix Martin is from the Bronx and was raised in the Baptist Church. A real-live Protestant. And, oh yeah, Felix Martin is black.

It's the religion, Katie would like to believe, and not the beautiful color of his skin that her mom, in particular, would object to. It's never been overtly stated, but Katie knows her mom expects her to marry a Murphy or a Fitzpatrick, someone similarly pale and freckled and baptized as an infant in the Catholic Church and, ideally, whose family is from Town and maybe even descended from the same village in

Ireland. Wouldn't that be lucky? Katie's never understood what would be so gloriously fortunate about this fate. So she and her husband could hang their identical family crests on the wall? So they could trace their family trees back through the branches and find themselves hugging the same trunk? So she can marry her cousin? A nice Irish boy from the neighborhood, from a good Catholic family. This is the future her mom imagines for her. Her mom has certainly not imagined Felix.

Her dad would probably be fine with both Felix's race and religion. It's his affiliation with New York that wouldn't sit well. Felix is a passionate fan of the Yankees. He might as well worship Satan.

So Katie has successfully steered her overnights away from Cook Street. Until last night. She and Felix went to a new vegan restaurant in Central Square. She had the most delicious vegan pad thai and too many basil lime martinis. It was late when they returned to Charlestown. Felix found a parking space on Cook Street, so it only felt natural that'd they go to her place. They didn't even discuss it. He simply followed her to the front stoop and up the stairs.

Meghan is already awake and gone. Katie heard the water running in the pipes and Meghan's footsteps squeaking the hallway floorboards hours ago. She opened her eyes only long enough to register that her bedroom was still dark. Meghan has a matinee performance today at noon and before that a rehearsal, then hair, makeup, costume, and the painstaking process of preparing another pair of new pointe shoes.

Meghan is the other reason Katie hasn't been in a rush for Felix to stay over, and Katie's more than a little relieved that Meghan isn't home right now. For one, there's the potential for either judgment or teasing, and as her older sister, Meghan has historically acted 100 percent entitled to either option. But the more subconscious and unflattering reason has to do with a jealous insecurity in Katie so deeply and long embedded, it might very well be congenital.

Meghan always gets everything. She got the naturally skinny body, the prettier hair, better skin, better grades, the talent for dance, and the boys. Meghan always got the boys.

Every crush Katie had in high school went unrequited because every boy she liked was crazy for Meghan. Everyone in Town is still crazy for her. Katie can't go to the post office or the hairdresser or Dunkin' Donuts without someone there telling her how wonderful it must be to have such a remarkable, accomplished sister.

The Boston Ballet! Isn't that something? Yes, it is. Now can we all please talk about something else?

Her parents and brothers never seem to tire of gushing about Meghan to anyone who will listen, and they never miss her performances. Her mom has given Meghan a pink rose after every dance recital and performance since she was three. It's their mother-daughter tradition. Meghan keeps the petals in glass bowls displayed all over their apartment. Homemade potpourri. Meanwhile, no one ever gives Katie flowers, she doesn't have a mother-daughter tradition, and not one member of her family has taken a yoga class.

Well, now Katie has the boy. Not Meghan. But if her life so far has taught her anything, Felix will take one look at Meghan and toss Katie aside for the better O'Brien sister. Lying in bed next to Felix, Katie can admit to herself that this fabricated drama sounds more than a touch paranoid and even preposterous, yet she's still relieved that Meghan isn't home.

'So this is your place,' says Felix, lying on his back, looking at everything around them.

Katie yawns, trying to see her things as if they were new to her, how Felix might be interpreting her purple bedspread and floral sheets, her childhood dresser and collection of Hello Kitty figurines, her fuzzy throw rug from Pier 1 Imports, the cracks in the plaster walls that spread like river tributaries from floor to ceiling, her cheap, once-white window shades yellowed like old teeth, and the tacky green curtains her mother made and recently ironed.

'I like all the quotes,' he says.

'Thanks.'

She's handwritten twenty-one inspirational quotes on her walls with a black Sharpie. Most come from the mouths of master yogis such as Baron Baptiste, Shiva Rea, and Ana Forrest. There are also quotes from the poems of Rumi and the teachings of Buddha, Ram Dass, and Eckhart Tolle.

When she was growing up, her mom used to try to feed her spiritual wisdom from the

141

Gospels according to Matthew, Mark, Luke, and John, but those words left her feeling hungry. Too many of the Catholic psalms passed right by Katie's ears, unabsorbed, discarded as outdated, esoteric, irrelevant. She couldn't relate. Through the spiritual teachings of yoga, Buddhism, and even poetry, Katie has found the words that nourish her soul.

Plus, yoga teachers love quotes — affirmations, intentions, words of enlightenment. Yoga is about creating balance in mind, body, and spirit so that life can be lived in peace, health, and harmony with others. The quotes are quick cheat-sheet reminders to focus on what matters. Whenever Katie's thought DJ gets stuck on a negative playlist, she borrows from a quote on her wall, consciously replacing her own default doom and gloom with prepackaged, time-proven positive words of wisdom.

She reads:

'You are either Now Here or Nowhere'
— Baron Baptiste

'I especially like your bed,' Felix says with a devilish smile, and kisses her.

Her bed once belonged to a woman named Mildred, the sister of their neighbor Mrs. Murphy. Mildred actually died *in this bed*. Katie had been completely skeeved out by the prospect of inheriting Mildred's bed, but she'd been sleeping on a futon mattress on the floor, and Mrs. Murphy was offering it to her for free. *What? You gonna turn down a perfectly good free bed?* Katie's mother had said. Katie had wanted to argue that a woman had just died in it, so it wasn't exactly perfectly good, but Katie was broke and in no position to argue. She smudged it with incense every day for weeks and still prays to Mildred each night, thanking her for the comfortable place to sleep, hoping she's happy in heaven and that she won't be visiting for any naps or slumber parties. She's surely rolling over in her grave right now if she can see the naked black Protestant in her bed. Katie kisses Felix and chooses not to tell him about Mildred.

'I feel bad that we skipped class this morning,' says Katie, carting out her guilt.

She learned guilt right along with her manners. Please. *I want something.* Guilt. Thank you. *I have something.* Guilt. *I'm kissing a beautiful naked man in Mildred's bed while my oblivious parents watch TV two floors below me.* Guilt. The ability to attach guilt firmly by the hand to any positive emotion is a skill cultivated by the Irish, a fine art admired even more than Meghan's pirouettes. Katie's been fully awake for about five minutes, and guilt is already sitting wide-eyed at the table, grinning with that shiny crown on its head.

'We had some spiritually enlightening exercise last night,' Felix says, smiling, flashing the dimple in his left cheek that she's crazy for, hinting at another go.

'I'm starving. You hungry?' she asks.

'Ravenous.'

'You want breakfast or lunch?'

'Either. Whatever you've got.'

Oh. She was thinking of getting out of her apartment, maybe going to Sorelle's. Last night in the safety of the late, dark hour and with a few martinis at the helm of her normally tightly navigated ship, the possibility of bumping into her parents seemed like a faraway continent. But now it's well into the next day, and her mom could easily pop by to say hello or to have a cup of tea or simply to remind her that it's Sunday and supper is at four o'clock, as it always is. Her dad could be out on the front stoop, walking Yaz. Shit.

Katie looks over at her alarm clock. Her mother probably won't come up. She suppresses the urge to hustle Felix out before they're caught and instead dresses in underwear and a Red Sox T-shirt. Felix throws on his boxers and follows her down the narrow hallway into the kitchen.

Her apartment has the same footprint as her parents' unit, the house she grew up in, and it's similarly lame. Worn, dirty-looking-even-after-mopping linoleum floor, a Mr. Coffee on the avocado-colored Formica counter, a secondhand kitchen table, and two mismatched chairs. No stainless steel, no soap-stone, no espresso machine here. Not like Felix's place. His bedroom, kitchen, and living room feel so mature, so independent, so real.

He's a bit older, twenty-five. JJ's age. He has an MBA from Sloan and works in business development for a start-up company that turns trash into fuel. He makes a lot more money than she does.

She stands in front of two open cabinets, not

144

finding much, wishing she'd grocery shopped yesterday.

'Granola and bananas okay?'

'Sure,' says Felix, having a seat at the table, tipping his head to examine the pictures magnetized to the fridge door.

'Herbal tea or coffee. The coffee won't be any good.'

'Tea is good. Those guys your brothers?'

'Yeah, that's JJ on the left, Patrick on the right.'

She wishes she had the money to fix this place up. Yoga instruction, she's realized, is an 'in-debt career.' She teaches five classes a week and makes six dollars a head, capping at seventy-two dollars a class. Even if she manages a handful of Toonie privates or a bachelorette party here and there, she barely makes enough to pay rent and eat. She still waitresses on the side, but it doesn't change her life. Plus there are the expenses — yoga clothes, music for class playlists, books, attending workshops and retreats. That may not sound like much, but it's enough to put her in the red when she makes only four hundred dollars a week. She could never afford health insurance. Thank God she's healthy.

'Which one's the firefighter?'

'JJ.'

The only way out of this financially strapped existence is to open her own studio. But she's friends with Andrea, the owner of Town Yoga, and Charlestown already has two studios. There aren't enough bodies in this small neighborhood to support a third. Plus Andrea would be pissed.

But Katie sees this as a sign rather than an obstacle, because it gives her the perfect reason to marry her dream of running her own studio with her other, bigger dream.

Moving out of Charlestown.

It's not that she doesn't appreciate having grown up here or love many aspects of living here now. She's proud of being Irish. She's proud of being stubborn and tough and street smart. Her cousins from the suburbs always seemed so spoiled and sheltered with their scheduled, supervised play dates and Martha Stewart summer camps. Charlestown is real life in the real world. There's no Pollyanna bullshit here, and Katie's grateful for that.

It's just so insular. Everyone knows everyone here, and no one ever does anything or goes anywhere outside of a few square blocks. Seriously.

Every weekend before Felix, she was either at the Warren Tavern, Sullivan's, or Ironsides, and really it's always Ironsides. Outside of her immediate friends, she's JJ's little sister or Officer Joe O'Brien's daughter or the dancer's sister or even Frank O'Brien's granddaughter, God rest his soul. It's the same people week after week, complaining about the same things — parking spaces, the Yankees, the weather, the revolving-door drama of who is hooking up or breaking up, and they're always talking about the same cast of characters, guys they've all known since they learned how to tie their shoes. If she doesn't do something drastic, she's going to end up like everyone else here — married to an Irish

Townie, saddled with a handful of freckled, copper-headed kids, still living upstairs from her parents.

The teachings of yoga have opened her eyes to concepts and possibilities beyond St. Francis Church and this tiny Irish neighborhood — Buddhism, Tibet, the Dalai Lama, Hinduism, India, Bhakti, Sanskrit, Shiva, Ganesh. The philosophies of a vegan diet and Ayurveda introduced a new mindfulness around health and eating, choices other than bangers and mash and blood sausage. She grew up with the Ten Commandments, a list of Thou Shalt Nots that insisted on obedience motivated by a fear of hell and God's wrath. The Eight Limbs of Yoga offer a gentler code for living soulfully. Unlike the domineering Thou Shalt Nots, the yamas and niyamas are reminders to connect with her true human nature, to live in peace, health, and loving harmony with everyone and everything. She mumbled along to the hymns in church as a girl because she knew the words and her mother insisted. Now she attends kirtans instead of mass and her heart sings.

And the people within the yoga community, hailing from all over the planet, are so exotic to Katie — Asian, Indian, African. Hell, Californian is exotic to Katie. There are mala beads instead of rosary, Krishna Das concerts instead of Mumford and Sons, tofu instead of hamburger, kombucha instead of Guinness. She's intuitively drawn to what she isn't, naive and enthralled.

She knows she's only scratched the surface. She's tasted a small sample of thought, tradition, and living foreign to the way she was raised, the way everyone here lives generation after generation without questioning, and her curious soul is hungry for more.

She remembers being young, around seven or eight, and standing on the Freedom Trail, each sneaker on a brick, following the red line with her eyes as it snaked along the ground, out of Charlestown. To freedom! She didn't know then that the trail simply went over the bridge and into the North End, another small ethnic neighborhood in the same city. In her imagination, the redbrick line was constructed by the same mason who designed the Yellow Brick Road in *The Wizard of Oz*, and so it obviously led to somewhere magical. When she was little, this magical place had houses with farmer's porches and two-car garages and grassy yards with swing sets. It was a land with trees and ponds and open fields and people who weren't Irish and who didn't know her since birth.

She still dreams of living somewhere over the rainbow in a different zip code with the space to breathe and create the kind of life she wants, a life not predetermined by where and how her parents or even great-grandparents lived. A life she chooses and freely defines, not one inherited from her parents. Someday.

She's a big 'someday' talker. *Someday, I'm going to own my own yoga studio. Someday, I'm going to live in Hawaii or India or Costa Rica. Someday, I'm going to own my own house with a yard and a driveway. Someday, I'm going to leave this neighborhood. Someday something great is going to happen.*

'Am I ever going to meet them?' asks Felix.

'Who?'

'Your brothers, your family.'

'Yeah, sure, someday.'

'How about today?'

'Today? Ah, I don't know if they're around.'

'What about this supper you always go to on Sundays? When am I going to get invited to that?'

'Sweetie, you don't want to come to Sunday supper, believe me. It's a duty, it's not fun. The food is horrible.'

'It's not about the food. I want to meet your family.'

'You will.'

'What is it? You ashamed of me or something?'

'No, definitely no. It's not you.'

She's about to pin the blame on her parents, on her mother's Catholicism and her father's singular obsession with Boston teams, or on Meghan's irresistible feminine mystique, but then the real reason presents itself, clear and unavoidable. She's the reason. She's standing in an old T-shirt and underwear, barefoot in her tiny kitchen, her feet cold on the dingy linoleum floor, and she doesn't feel worthy of being with him. She's practically twitching with discomfort over revealing this much of herself to him, as if the more of her he sees, the less of her he'll realize there is. Her kitchen exposes her lack of sophistication, her bedroom a lack of maturity, her living room a lack of elegance. The thought of adding her parents and brothers and where

149

she grew up, the real Charlestown, not the Pottery Barn Toonie version, of him seeing her lack of education and culture, the statues of Mary and Jesus and Kermit the Frog in every room and the jelly jars her parents use as glassware, makes her feel far more naked than she was ten minutes ago.

And if he sees all of her, maybe he won't love her. Boom. There it is. They haven't said that word yet, and she's sure as hell not saying it first. For all her yoga training in vulnerability and living authentically, she's still a chicken. What if he meets her family and they're incapable of embracing a Yankee-loving black Baptist, and he takes this into consideration along with the substantial list of everything else about her that isn't perfect and decides that he can't love her. She's not worthy of his love.

She's standing at the counter with her back to him, pouring granola into mismatching bowls, thinking about Felix rejecting her, and her body doesn't know the difference between the real deal and simply rehearsing this shit. It's monkey-mind madness, and she knows better than to invest energy in this completely invented story, but she can't help herself. She predicts their breakup in blow-by-blow, excruciating detail, always initiated by him, at least once a week and three times since they woke up today, every imagined split pulling more threads from her heart, knitting into a bigger, tighter knot in her chest.

Coward. She should own who she is, where she's from, and how she feels about him. She loves Felix. She should tell him and introduce him to her family. But the risk feels too big, the cliff too high, the chasm between what they have now and what they could have too wide. Like jumping could kill her.

'Another time. Really, I don't even know if my dad and JJ will be there today.'

Felix's mouth goes tight, and he lowers his head as if he's searching for meaning in the ugly pattern on the linoleum floor.

'You know what, I'm not hungry. I should get going.'

He leaves the kitchen and returns in a moment, fully dressed.

'See ya,' he says, and barely kisses her on the cheek.

'Bye.'

She should stop him, invite him to supper, apologize. Instead she says nothing, paralyzed and mute, and lets him go. Shit.

She sits at her crappy kitchen table, stunned to be suddenly alone, and doesn't touch her oatmeal and banana. She wishes she'd gone to Andrea's class, that Felix had stayed, that she wasn't such a stupid coward, that she knew how to walk her yoga talk. The kettle whistles, jolting her out of her seat. She pours the boiling water into one mug and leaves the other empty on the counter. Sipping her green tea, she replays what just happened and rehearses what she might say to him next. She hopes he'll forgive her and call her later. She hopes to God she didn't just end their relationship, that she didn't just lose him. But mostly, she hopes he didn't bump into her parents on his way out.

11

Katie is sitting between Patrick and Meghan on the couch in her parents' living room, wondering what Felix is doing. She almost invited him to Sunday supper today, had the words ready and wrapped in her mouth, but at the last second, she chickened out and swallowed them instead. He hasn't brought up meeting her family since they fought about it last week, so the issue seems dropped for now. But she's going to have to bring him one of these Sundays. She can't keep Felix a secret forever.

JJ and Colleen are sharing the love seat opposite her, their legs and bodies pressed against each other, JJ's arm draped over Colleen's shoulders. They look so happy. Katie wishes Felix were here.

Her mom glides into the room, practically tiptoeing, places a six-pack of Coors Light and a chilled bottle of Chardonnay on the coffee table without a word or looking at anyone, and returns to the kitchen. She's back a moment later with a bottle opener and three jelly jars and leaves again. Everyone looks at one another. That was weird.

They aren't allowed to start drinking until supper is ready. It's a strict rule. Patrick shrugs, leans over, grabs a beer, and cracks it open. Katie twists the bottle opener into the cork and pulls it free. JJ takes a beer, and Katie pours a glass of wine for Meghan.

'Wine?' Katie asks Colleen.

'No thanks, I'm good for now.'

'Where's the remote?' asks Patrick.

'I dunno. You live here,' says JJ.

The boys search the room without getting up off their asses.

'Pat, go put it on,' says JJ.

'Nah, you do it.'

'I'm comfortable here with Colleen. Get up, see if anyone's playing.'

'B's aren't on till tonight.'

'Go see what else is on.'

'I'm still lookin' for the remote.'

Patrick leans back into the couch, his heels together, knees spread out, and sips his beer. Katie shakes her head. Her brothers are pathetic. The room does feel strange, oppressive even, with the TV off. In fact, Katie can't remember ever being in this room without it on. It's as if they're missing their fifth sibling, the one who never shuts up and demands all the attention.

Colleen pries herself out of the love seat, marches over to the table with the angels and frogs, and returns with the remote.

'Thanks, hun,' says JJ, grinning at Patrick as he turns the TV on.

He's flipping the channels, not landing anywhere, but the light and noise coming from the screen give them all a common purpose, and the room instantly feels brighter, familiar again. Katie sighs and smells Windex. That's weird. It usually smells like whatever animal her mom is boiling this week. Her obsession with ironing

153

aside, her mom isn't exactly famous for domestic tidiness. Wiping all the dusty figurines and surfaces down with Windex typically only happens when they're having company. Katie inhales again. Only Windex.

With the exception of bacon, which somehow bypasses everything she knows and believes and still makes her mouth water, she has a hard time stomaching the smell of Sunday suppers. But the house doesn't smell like bacon or chicken or lamb. Has her mother finally figured out how to remove the taste *and* smell from food?

The front door opens, and her dad stands before them in the living room, carrying a plastic bag and three pizza boxes, smiling as if he's Santa delivering a sack of toys.

'I've got pepperoni, plain, vegan cheese and veggie for Katie, and a salad for our little rabbit.'

'Where'd you get it?' asks Katie.

Papa Gino's doesn't do vegan anything.

'The North End.'

'Wow, really?'

Her mom brings in a stack of paper plates and napkins, and they start peeling off hot slices of pizza.

'Wait, we're eating in here?' asks Meghan.

'Yeah, why not?' says her mom.

'Is there a game on?' asks Katie.

'Not 'til tonight,' says Patrick.

Pizza and beer in the living room for Sunday supper sounds like a party, but Katie tenses. This never happens, not unless there's an important game on. Something's off.

Her dad sits in his chair, her mom in the

wooden rocker. He's drinking a beer, and she's holding Yaz, but neither of them have plates of pizza in their laps. Her mother's face is pale and distracted. She's looking in the direction of the TV but not at it, rubbing Yaz with one hand and the crucifix on her necklace with the other. Her dad is fidgeting in his chair. He looks nervous.

The room suddenly feels stranger than it did with the TV off. There's an electric energy in the room, and Katie goes still and cold as it passes through her. She feels an animal intuition, an instinctive pinch in her nerves. Thunderclouds gathering. A lion waiting in the brush. Songbirds silencing before taking flight. Something is coming. Something bad.

Patrick is stuffing his face with pepperoni pizza, chewing with his mouth open. It's got to be him. It's always him. He's done something illegal, and either he has to come clean now, or their dad has to arrest him. But Patrick looks totally chill.

Maybe it's her. They saw Felix. That's it. Here comes the lecture. They're not going to let her stay here under their roof for practically free if this is how she's going to behave. Shacking up with a black man who isn't Catholic or Irish or from here. What will the neighbors think? Doesn't she care about her reputation and her family's good name, if not her soul?

She'll have to choose between her family and Felix. Maybe. Maybe this kind of ultimatum will be a blessing. They'll be doing her a favor. *Good. I'm gone. Outta here.* Just the kick in the pants she needs. She could live with Felix until she finds a place of her own. But where would she go? She's not ready. She hasn't saved up enough money to leave Charlestown, and she can't afford to live here on her own either. Shit.

Her mother gets up, takes the clicker from the love seat arm, and points it at the TV, shutting it off. JJ looks up at her in protest, but the stricken look on her face stops him from complaining. No one does. No one says a word. She sits back down in the rocker and clutches her crucifix.

'Now that we're all here together, your mom and I have something we want to tell you,' says her dad.

He's trying to talk, but the words aren't coming. His face floods pink and twitches, struggling with itself. The air in the room thins, and the bottom of Katie's stomach drops out, her insides and two bites of pizza sinking without a floor. This isn't about Felix. Her dad clears his throat.

'I had a medical test, and we found out I have something called Huntington's disease. It means I'll have trouble walking and talking and a few other issues over time. But the good news is it's slow and will take at least ten years.'

Huntington's disease. She's never heard of it. She looks to her mom to gauge how bad this is. Her mom is squeezing her crucifix in one hand and hugging herself with the other as if she's holding on for dear life. This is really bad.

'So you'll start having trouble walking in ten years?' asks Meghan.

'No, sorry. I have some of the symptoms now. I already have it.'

156

'It'll take ten years for what, then?' asks Patrick.

'For him to die,' says Colleen.

'Jesus, Coll,' says JJ.

'No, she's right. You've seen this at your job,' says her dad, checking with Colleen.

Colleen nods. Colleen's a physical therapist. Seen what? What has she seen?

'So you know the next part of this speech, huh?' says her dad.

Colleen nods again, all color drained from her face, which is clenching as if in pain, scaring the shit out of Katie.

'What next part, Dad? Ma?' asks JJ.

Her dad looks to her mom.

'I can't,' she whispers. Her mom reaches over and pulls a tissue from the box on the side table. She dabs her eyes and wipes her nose. Her dad exhales forcefully through pursed lips, as if he's blowing out candles on a birthday cake, as if he's making a wish.

'So this Huntington's thing is hereditary. I got it from my mum. And so you kids. You kids. Each of you has a fifty-fifty chance of getting it, too.'

No one moves or says anything. Katie forgets to breathe. Then her mom starts crying into her tissue.

'Wait, fifty-fifty chance of getting what? What is it again?' asks Meghan.

Her dad, their rock, their protector, always so sure of everything, looks physically fragile. His hands are shaking. His eyes are wet and pooling fast. His face grimaces as if he's just sucked on

157

a lemon, struggling to hold back his tears, and it's turning Katie inside out. She's never seen him cry. Not when his dad died or when his friend on the force was shot and killed or when he finally came home the day after the marathon.

Please don't cry, Dad.

'Here.' He pulls a stack of pamphlets from his jacket pocket and lays them on the coffee table next to the boxes of pizza. 'I'm sorry, I can't talk.'

They each pick up a copy and start reading.

'Fuck,' says Patrick.

'Language,' says her mom.

'Ma, I'm sorry, but fuck language right now,' says Patrick.

'My God, Dad,' says Meghan, clutching the pink silk scarf wrapped around her neck.

'I'm sorry. I'm praying every minute that none of you get this,' says her dad.

'Is there anything they can do to treat it?' asks Meghan.

'They have some medications to ease the symptoms, and I'll do PT and speech therapy.'

'But there's no cure for this?' asks Patrick.

'No.'

Katie reads.

Huntington's disease manifests in motor, cognitive, and psychiatric symptoms that typically begin at age 35–45 and advance relentlessly until death. There is currently no cure or treatment that can halt, slow, or reverse the disease's progression.

158

Her dad has Huntington's. Her dad is dying. Ten years. This can't be happening.

Each child of an affected parent has a 50 percent chance of developing the disease.

Symptoms typically begin at thirty-five. That's in fourteen years. And then she might be dying of Huntington's disease. This can't be happening.

'If you have the gene, is that it, you'll definitely get it?' asks JJ.

Her dad nods. A tear trickles down his pink cheek.

Katie buries herself in her pamphlet, looking for the fine print, the exception, a way out. This can't be right. Her dad is fine. He's a strong, tough Boston cop, not someone sick with a fatal disease. She reads the list of symptoms again. *Depression.* No way. *Paranoia.* Totally not him. *Slurred speech.* Clear as a bell. They must be wrong. The test was wrong. A mixup or a false positive. Dead in ten years. Fuck those assholes for being wrong and making her dad cry.

She keeps reading. *Reduced dexterity.* Sometimes, but so what? *Temper outbursts.* Okay, yes, but everyone loses it once in a while. *Chorea.*

Derived from the Greek word for dance, chorea is characterized by jerky, involuntary movements.

She looks at her dad. His feet are doing an Irish jig on the floor. His shoulders shrug. His eyebrows lift, and his face grimaces as if he just

159

sucked on a lemon. Shit.

'So we can find out if we have the gene?' asks Meghan, reading the booklet.

'Yes. You can have the same blood test I had,' says her dad.

'But if we have the gene, there's nothing we can do about it. You just live with knowing you're going to get sick,' says Meghan.

'That's right.'

'Does the test tell you when it will happen?' asks Katie.

'No.'

'Fuckin' hell,' says Patrick.

'How long have you known about this?' asks JJ.

'There've been some symptoms for a while, but we didn't know about Huntington's for sure until March,' says her dad.

'You've known since *March*?' asks JJ, his jaw clamped and his hands squeezing into fists, as if he's resisting a sudden, overwhelming urge to break every ceramic frog and angel in the room. 'Why are you just telling us this now? It's friggin' *May*!'

'We needed some time to process it ourselves,' says her dad.

'It was hard getting you all together at the same time,' says her mom, defending him.

'That's bullshit — we all *live here*,' says JJ, now yelling.

'There's Meghan's dance schedule, and either you or your dad are working on Sundays,' says her mom, her voice wobbly, Yaz covered in a heap of damp, crumpled tissues on her lap. 'We

160

had to tell all of you, all at once. We couldn't tell two of you and leave the cat half in the bag.'

'Why is Mom talking about a drunk cat?' asks Patrick.

Katie laughs, knowing it's inappropriate, but appreciating Patrick for the momentary relief from the tension. But Colleen bursts into tears, hiding her face in her hands.

'It's okay, baby, it's going to be okay,' says JJ.

Rather than consoling her, this only escalates her crying, until it can't be contained inside her hands. Her head suddenly pops up, and it's Colleen, but it's not. She looks nothing like the sweet, affable sister-in-law Katie's known since elementary school. Her eyes are desperate and crazed, and her mouth is open and distorted, as if some kind of Hollywood horror movie special-effects transformation took place within her hands. JJ tries to hug her, but she won't have it. She's up from the love seat and out of the living room. The rest of them sit in apprehensive silence, listening to her feet stomp up the stairs. The door to their apartment slams, and Colleen is wailing somewhere overhead.

'What the fuck was that?' asks Patrick.

'She's scared, you jerk,' says Meghan.

'JJ, we know you two have been trying to start a family,' says her dad. 'Even if, God forbid, you carry this thing' — he stops and knocks three times on the wooden side table — 'there are medical procedures, pretty common in-vitro stuff, and they can make sure your children never get this.'

This sounds encouraging to Katie, like a real

161

honest-to-God life raft in this roiling sea of shit, but JJ doesn't seem to want to grab it, as if he's voluntarily drowning.

'It's too late, Dad,' JJ finally says. 'She's pregnant. She's ten weeks. We just heard the heartbeat.'

Shit. Katie's been expecting her brother to say those words for three years. She's imagined so many times the delighted screams and hugs, the congratulations and toasts to the health of the first O'Brien grandchild. Her mom, especially, has been waiting on the edge of her seat for this news. The baby already owns a whole wardrobe of adorable yellow and green knitted blankets and booties and the cutest little hats.

Her mom starts sobbing. She crosses herself over and over.

'So it's too fuckin' late for a medical miracle,' says JJ.

'You won't need one,' says her mom, her voice swimming in tears, sounding more devastated than convincing. 'You and the baby are going to be fine.'

'Yeah, man. You've always been real lucky,' says Patrick. 'I'd bet anything you don't have this. Million-to-one odds.'

'Yeah, JJ. You gotta stay positive,' says Katie. 'I'm so happy for you.'

JJ smiles, but he doesn't mean it.

'I'd better go,' says JJ.

'Tell Colleen I'm sorry,' says her dad, standing.

Her dad walks over to JJ. Their hugs are usually casual, manly slaps on the back, but this one is a real embrace. Her dad and JJ hold on to each other, no space between them, squeezing hard, and Katie starts to cry.

'You're gonna be okay,' says her dad, finally releasing his oldest child.

'You, too, Dad,' says JJ, wiping his eyes. 'We'll fight it, right?'

'Yeah.'

JJ nods. He'll be lucky. They'll all be lucky. Or they'll fight it. Katie scans the open page of her booklet. But how? How can they fight something that can't be prevented or cured or even treated? There are no medical miracles for this disease. She takes a deep breath and wipes her eyes. She prays to Jesus on the wall, the ceramic angels on the tables, even Kermit the Frog. If there are no medical miracles, she'll just have to pray for the good old-fashioned regular kind.

12

Katie, Meghan, JJ, and Patrick are sitting in a row on the grass on Bunker Hill, sharing a brown-bagged bottle of Jack, watching the tourists and the Toonies and the actors sweating their asses off in Revolutionary War costumes, playing their new favorite game. Some families get together and play Parcheesi or backgammon or Go Fish. They play Guess How Strangers Will Die.

'That guy.' JJ points to a bloated, middle-aged, balding man panting and lumbering up the steps. His ankles are thicker than Meghan's thighs. 'Three Big Macs away from a heart attack. Dead before the ambulance gets him to the hospital.'

'Supersize suicide,' says Patrick. He and JJ high-five. JJ passes the bottle to Katie.

Katie spots a woman about her age toward the bottom of the hill, lying on a beach towel, boobs up in a red bikini, brown skin glistening with oil. Even in the shadow of the monument and slathered in SPF 50, Katie is paranoid about burning.

'Her,' says Katie, pointing to the woman. 'Skin cancer. Twenty-six.'

'Good one,' says Meghan.

'Aw, don't off the hotties,' says Patrick.

'Too bad she's wasting the few years she's got left with that clown,' says JJ, nodding to the dude lying on the towel next to the girl. He's wearing checkered shorts and no shirt, a black, hairy carpet covering his flabby, pale torso, navel to neck.

'Eh, he'll be dead in a week. Dumb-ass veers his Prius into an oncoming semi trailer. He was texting LOL,' says Patrick, taking the bottle from Katie.

Meghan laughs. It's a horrible, morbid game, and they should stop or at least not think it's so funny. They're all going to hell for sure.

It's weirdly comforting, though. They're all going to die. Everyone on this hill. The tourists, the Toonies, the fat guy, the girl in the bikini and her hairy boyfriend, that young mother pushing a stroller, her cute little baby. Even the O'Briens.

So they might die of Huntington's disease. So what? Did they really think they were immortal, that they'd get out of this life alive? Everyone dies. Yet Katie's been living blind-folded to this immovable fact, as if by not looking she might escape her ultimate demise. Or, yeah, sure, she's going to die, but not until she's like eighty or ninety and wicked old and has lived a full, amazing life. She's been overwhelmed and distracted for the past month, fretting about the possibility of getting Huntington's when she's thirty-five, dead before she's fifty. Dead before she's done. Patrick passes the bottle to Meghan.

'Paul Revere over there,' says Meghan, referring to one of the actors. 'Holds his musket up too high on the hill during a thunderstorm, gets struck by lightning.'

The actor's sweaty face is fixed in a hard

scowl. He's leaning on the barrel of his fake musket as he spits on the ground. Families walking past him loop away, steering clear. He's not earning his Academy Award today.

'At least he dies doing what he loves,' says Katie, laughing.

Just for fun, she recently checked the statistics. A person's lifetime odds of being struck by lightning are one in 126,000. Chance of drowning is one in a thousand. Dying in a car accident, one in a hundred. Dying of cancer, one in seven. Their odds of dying of Huntington's, one in two.

'See that guy,' says JJ, aiming his chin at an old man shuffling along the sidewalk, shoulders slumped forward, head hanging down as if his neck quit its full-time job, overgrown greasy gray hair beneath a worn Red Sox cap and a gnarly beard, smoking a cigarette. 'He's gonna die in his sleep in his own bed when he's ninety-five, surrounded by his loving family.'

'Totally,' says Meghan, cracking up, handing the bottle to JJ.

Katie shakes her head. 'So unfair.'

'Fuckin' pisses me off,' says Patrick. 'God gives our dad Huntington's and lets that asshole stick around.'

They all go silent. JJ takes an impressive swig and pushes the bottle to his brother.

'So I looked into getting the test,' says JJ. 'It's not just simply giving blood. It's a friggin'long, drawn-out saga. They make you go to two touchy-feely psychobabble appointments with a counselor spread out over two weeks before

166

they'll draw your blood, and then you have to wait another four weeks before they'll tell you your results.'

'You mean you gotta talk to a shrink?' asks Patrick.

'Yeah, basically.'

'About what?'

'The weather. Huntington's, you moron.'

'Yeah, but what about it?'

'They want to make sure you understand what it is, what the test means and why you want to know, how you'll handle knowing, so if it's positive you don't go and jump off the Tobin.'

'Doesn't sound like a bad idea to me,' says Meghan.

'Yeah, so what?' says Patrick. 'What if I say, 'Yeah, I want to jump off the fuckin' Tobin,' they gonna deny me the test? It's my life. I have a right to know. I'm not doin' any of that counseling bullshit.'

'Then they won't give you the test,' says JJ.

'Fuck 'em, then. I don't want to know anyway,' says Patrick.

Maybe knowing she's going to get Huntington's would be a positive thing. Instead of years tumbling by one after another, same old drill, procrastinating on her bucket list because she thinks she has plenty of time to do it all, forever, she'll know for sure that she doesn't. Do it now. All of it. And then the next fourteen years would be awesome, better than most people's fifty.

Or maybe it wouldn't be such a good thing. Maybe she wouldn't move out of Charlestown and open her own studio or get married and have kids because they'd deserve a wife and mother who would be alive to love them and teach them and so why bother with any of it if she's going to be dead so soon? She'd be dying every day for fourteen years instead of living.

Katie imagines a time bomb ticking away inside her head, already set to a particular year, month, day, hour. Then *boom*. Huntington's will explode inside her skull, blasting the parts of her brain in charge of moving, thinking, and feeling. Moving. Thinking. Feeling. What else is there? Her yoga training tells her being. There is being. When she meditates, the goal is to not move or think or feel. Just be. This is exactly the elusive state that every yogi aspires to experience. Get out of your head. Quiet your thoughts and silence your movements. Notice your feelings but don't attach to them. Let them pass.

But Huntington's isn't the absence of moving, thinking, and feeling. This disease is not a transcendental state of bliss. It's a complete freak show — ugly, constant, unproductive movements, uncontrollable rage, unpredictable paranoia, obsessive thinking. The *boom* doesn't obliterate moving, thinking, and feeling. It fucks them all up. She imagines the detonation releasing some kind of poisonous liquid, a steady leak of toxins that eventually seeps into every nerve cell, polluting every thought, feeling, and movement, rotting her from the inside out.

Maybe she already has it. The pamphlet says symptoms can begin fifteen years before diagnosis. So, like now. She wobbled yesterday in Ardha Chandrasana. Half Moon Pose. Her outstretched arm and leg waved around like branches blowing in a hurricane. She leaned left and then compensated right and then stumbled out of the pose in front of the whole class. Was that Huntington's?

Or maybe she doesn't have it. She's totally fine, and she just lost her balance for a moment like any normal person, and all of this obsessive worrying is for the birds.

Or maybe she does have it.

Over the past many months, Katie's felt a growing impatience, as if riding a wave rising to a white, frothy crest. Everything she's ever done has been in preparation for her real life, and she's itching to get started. It's time to begin. But just when she's ready to really start living, is she going to find out she's dying? Of course, everyone is dying. That's the point of their sick little game. She knows this. But death has always been an abstract concept, an invisible ghost with no shape or texture or smell. Huntington's is real. It's a real death that she can picture, thanks to YouTube, and it has the shape of horror and the putrid smell of dread.

JJ looks exactly like their dad. The spitting image. He doesn't even look related to their mom. He has their dad's sleepy blue eyes, his stocky build, his temperament, his pink and pasty-white freckled skin. Does that mean he also has their dad's defective Huntington's gene? Katie bears an uncanny resemblance to her grandmother, a woman she's only seen in pictures. Ruth. The one who had Huntington's. Katie has her Irish cheeks and freckles, the same thin copper hair and blunt, wide nose. She's similarly thick-boned, framed with sturdy hips and swimmer's shoulders. They both would've survived the potato famine for sure.

Meghan looks and acts more like their mom. Her nose is thinner and pointier, her face is less round, her hair is darker and thicker, her frame is petite. Meghan has their mom's private nature, her patience and tenacity, her love of Broadway music and theater and, of course, dance. Patrick looks like both parents and neither. They don't know where the hell he came from.

In the ways they can see, through external physical traits and personality, Katie and JJ come from their dad. Does this mean they also have his Huntington's? Without a degree in genetics or any real knowledge to back up her conclusion, Katie assumes that it does. She inherited her dad's ugly feet; therefore, she has Huntington's. Tick. Tick. Tick. *Boom.*

'Is anyone else going to find out?' asks JJ.

'So you definitely are?' asks Meghan.

'Yeah. I gotta know. I have an appointment on Wednesday. And because of our circumstances, the baby, they're accelerating the process. I'll find out the results in a week.'

'Jesus, man,' says Patrick.

Katie's vaguely numbing Jack Daniel's buzz abruptly coalesces into a knotty ball of sickening fear in her stomach. Her mouth tastes sour. Their fun game is over. Nobody wins. This is real. Too real.

'I don't even want to say this,' says Meghan, knocking the top of her head with the knuckles of her right hand. 'But if you have it, does that mean the baby has it?'

'If I don't have it, it ends with me. The baby's fine. If I have it, the baby has a fifty-fifty chance, just like us. Colleen will be fifteen weeks when we find out. We can have an amnio to see if the baby has it.'

'And then what?' asks Katie. 'If the baby has it, would Colleen have an abortion?'

JJ hangs his head over his knees and rubs his eyes with his hand.

'I dunno,' he says, his voice hollowed out. 'Maybe. No. I dunno.'

'Ma'd have a stroke,' says Patrick.

'I know,' says JJ.

'I'm not even kidding,' says Patrick.

'I know,' says JJ.

'What does Colleen say?' asks Katie.

'She's a basket case. She doesn't want to even think about it. She doesn't want me to get the test.'

'It's gonna be negative, man,' says Patrick. 'When do you find out?'

'A week from Wednesday.'

'Okay. You're gonna be fine, the baby's gonna be fine, Ma's not gonna have a stroke,' says Patrick.

Katie and Meghan nod. Patrick knocks back a few gulps and hands the bottle to JJ.

'Course, the poor thing still might come out lookin' like you,' says Patrick.

JJ punches Patrick's shoulder and almost smiles.

'There's another thing,' says JJ. 'The counselor

guy talked a little about juvenile HD. You can get this thing full-blown at our age. It's rare, but when it starts young, it seems to be passed down through the father.'

Meghan goes weepy.

'We're learning a new routine, and I'm having trouble with it. I keep messing up the steps,' Meghan blurts out as if confessing. 'That's never happened before. Never. And I keep falling off pointe.'

'You're just stressed,' says Katie.

'What if I have it now?'

'You don't.'

'Are you guys noticing anything?'

'No,' says Patrick.

'No, nothing,' says JJ.

'Promise?'

'Honest to God,' says Katie.

'Don't worry, Meg. If anyone's getting juvi HD, it's me, right?' says Patrick.

'You don't have juvi HD, you're just an asshole,' says JJ.

'You could get the test and find out for sure,' says Katie to Meghan.

Meghan shakes her head. 'I don't think I can. I would probably jump off the Tobin.'

'Look at Dad,' says JJ. 'He's forty-four, and he's doing okay. If you take the test, find out you don't have it, then you don't have to worry anymore. You're free. If you have it, then okay. It is what it is. You worry about it in ten, fifteen years. They might have a cure for this thing in ten years, right?'

Meghan nods. 'I don't think I can do it.'

'Katie, what about you?' asks Patrick.

She sighs. Does she want to know? She does and she doesn't. Of course, finding out she's negative would be an awesome relief. But deep down, she's pretty sure she has this thing. Yet without absolute, medical proof, she can still hope that she doesn't. Knowing for certain that she's positive would probably devastate her poor mom and dad. She'd probably have to break up with Felix. She glances over at the green girders of the Tobin.

Maybe she'll just keep living 'at risk.' Put that on your Facebook status. But who doesn't live a life at risk? Her life is full of risk every day. Risk of failure if she opens her own studio, risk of failure if she doesn't, risk of never fitting in if she moves to a place where everyone isn't Irish Catholic, risk of not being loved by Felix, risk of not being loved by anyone, risk of burning in the sun, risk of being struck by lightning, risk of having HD. Every breath is a risk.

Or maybe she'll go to the first two appointments, get those done and out of the way. Then if she decides she really wants to know, she can show up and find out the results of the test. A freakin' test.

The idea of taking the genetic test itself, regardless of the outcome, makes her skin go cool and clammy. Katie hates tests. She's never performed well on them. In high school, she'd study and care and even know the material cold, but then she'd panic when faced with all those typed and numbered questions. She's a big-time choker.

173

The last exam of her senior year, a math test, she remembers celebrating after handing her completed paper over to her teacher, giddy and bragging that this would be the last test she'd ever have to take. Like the O'Briens, God has a sick sense of humor.

That last math test was on statistics. She got a C.

'I dunno,' she says. 'Maybe.'

13

Katie counted eleven red cars on the walk from Cook Street to Town Yoga. She'd tasked herself with this specific mission before she stepped foot onto the front stoop. *How many red cars will you see from here to yoga?* It's an awareness exercise she likes. Reality depends on perspective, on what is paid attention to. Without attention to red cars, she probably wouldn't have noticed any on her walk. But with an awareness to red cars held in her consciousness, she experienced eleven.

She's been trying to remember how far back her dad's weird fidgeting and clumsiness goes. A year maybe. It's hard to say. It's like asking her how many red cars she saw on the way to yoga yesterday. None. She wasn't looking for red cars, so in her experience, there weren't any.

A month ago, she didn't notice whether her dad dropped the remote control or his fork. She didn't register any ticks or weird fidgeting. Now she sees it all, and everything she sees is called Huntington's.

It's an hour before class. The studio is empty, quiet but for the whispered dialogue of this familiar space — the whir of the ceiling fan, the hum of the heater, the whistle of her breath. She's alone in the room, the lights dimmed, sitting cross-legged with her knees anchored to the floor, her tailbone propped up on a bolster, studying herself in the mirror, hunting for Huntington's.

She focuses on her eyes. Blink. Blink. A black outer ring surrounding blue surrounding a black hole. She searches her eyes. They're steady, even. This is where she sees it most in her dad. His eyes are antsy, often darting off to some distant spot, at nothing in particular. Or he's looking at her, but he's not, the focus of his gaze slightly off, fixed in an odd stare. Huntington's disease. If she looks for it, she can find it in his eyes.

Blink. Blink.

She has stubby eyelashes. Meghan's are thick and long. She wonders if she'll ever look at herself in a mirror and not wish she looked more like Meghan. She notices that her eyebrows are crooked. God, has she really been walking around like this? She resists the impulse to pop up and fetch the tweezers from her purse. An angry pimple is ready to erupt on her chin. She denies the urge to poke at it. Freckles. Short, fat nose. No makeup. This is her naked face. No mask. No hiding. Here she is. Can she see HD in her face?

Her dad's eyebrows jump up a lot, as if he's surprised by something someone said. Only no one said anything. The corners of his mouth will sometimes pull into a grimace, but he's not actually disgusted or in any kind of pain. It's an expression that flashes randomly with no emotional cause or content. Her misshapen eyebrows lie still, two caterpillars sleeping soundly on her forehead.

Her hands are resting on her thighs, thumbs

and index fingers touching in a Guyan Mudra. She's wearing two bracelets on her right wrist. One is a jade mala she uses for chanting mantras. Her favorite is Om Namah Shivaya. *I bow to my inner, true Self. I invite positive transformation.* The second bracelet is made of jasper beads and faceted with a single wooden skull. The skull represents the impermanence of all things, a reminder to be grateful for the gift of today, because there might not be a tomorrow. When she bought that bracelet only a year ago, she couldn't have imagined how freakishly relevant and morbidly real this concept would be for her. She glances down at the skull. It used to prompt her to think about her dreams, a reminder to chase them down. She won't be here forever. Now she thinks of her dad. And forever just got a whole lot shorter.

She wears a silver claddagh ring on her right middle finger, a gift from her mother when she turned eighteen. Meghan, of course, got the good one, her mother's real gold ring, the one her dad gave to her mom when they got engaged. The silver ring isn't worth as much and isn't a family heirloom. Her mom bought it at the Galleria mall. Katie wears it with the heart pointed toward her wrist, meaning she's in a relationship.

Felix. She still hasn't told him anything about Huntington's. She knows this isn't a sustainable plan, that she's being inauthentic, lying by omission, but she can't get the words to leave her mouth. Their relationship seems to be on the verge of change, on the edge of either breaking apart or becoming more serious. The slightest thing could tip the scale either way, and Huntington's sits in her mind like a two-ton boulder. She'd like to see what's going to happen between them without the cataclysmic influence of Huntington's. What might've been. Meanwhile, this secret is breeding shame within her like a viral infection, spreading fast and making her sick.

Her bare face, feet, arms, and chest are pale and uniformly dotted with freckles. She has no tattoos, but only because she can't decide what to get. That, and she's a total chicken when it comes to pain. She wonders what's going on beneath her pale, freckled skin. Muscles and tendons, bones and blood. Her heart beating, an ovary releasing an egg, her stomach digesting granola. Huntington's plotting to kill her.

She wishes she had thicker hair and longer eyelashes like Meghan's, fewer freckles, skin that could tan when exposed to sunshine, no pimples, better eyebrows, a more petite frame, prettier feet. She wants to look away, to get up and do something. She stays. It's probably been only ten minutes, and she's finding it hard to face herself for this long. She could stay for an hour in meditation with her eyes closed, but open is another story. Here she is, all of her. She feels self-conscious, ridiculous, judgmental, worried about someone coming in and catching her.

She returns to her breathing, to the rise and fall of her chest, and her eyes. A black outer ring surrounding blue surrounding a black hole.

Blink. Blink. No subtle shiftiness. No red cars yet.

She stands, still facing the mirror, and presses her right foot into her left thigh. Vriksasana. Tree Pose. She places her hands in prayer position at her heart, then inhales, reaching her arms up as if they're branches extending to the sky. This is her favorite pose. She is grounded, balanced where she is, but she's also growing, reaching, changing.

She lifts her head up to the tin-paneled ceiling but looks beyond it, imagining a vast starry night sky above her, and sends out a prayer. With arms outstretched like a satellite dish, she closes her eyes, hoping to receive some kind of divine answer.

Suddenly, some invisible force knocks her off balance. Her arms and torso tilt right in an attempt to compensate, but she can't recover and falls out of the pose. Shit. She tries to brush it off. So she lost her balance. This happens, especially if she closes her eyes. She'd normally compose herself and then rebuild the pose, but this time, her heart jams. Was that a symptom? A sign from God? Is this how it will begin for her, falling out of Tree Pose? Her first red car sighting.

Trying not to freak out, she starts over, lifting her left foot and pressing it against her right thigh. Tree Pose, the other side. She extends her arms overhead, spreading her fingers, every muscle in both arms and her standing leg ignited, active, strong. She will not fall. She stares herself down in the mirror, refusing to blink. Her eyes are fierce, her body in control.

She inhales. She exhales. She stays and stays. Her arms tremble, her standing leg burns and begs for mercy. She gives her arms and leg no say and stays.

Finally, she throws her exhausted arms up to heaven and says, 'I'm a fuckin' oak tree. You see me?'

She waits a moment more, then slowly lowers her left foot and plants it with purpose on the mat next to her right foot. Staring at her eyes in the mirror, she presses her hands together in prayer and lands them in front of her heart.

Namaste.

14

Patrick just left. He was reluctant to go, but if he calls in sick for work again his boss might can him, so he had to leave. Meghan left a couple of hours ago for rehearsal at the Opera House. Katie thinks she was relieved to get the hell out of this claustrophobic living room, to have a nonnegotiable call time on a stage where she can become completely absorbed in something beautiful.

And then there were three. Katie and her dad are watching the evening news, waiting for news. Her mom is knitting a green-and-white blanket. She might be listening to the TV, but she never looks up at it. She's waiting, too. They all thought JJ and Colleen would be home by now. Katie holds her phone in her hand, expecting it to vibrate any second. It never does. She's too afraid to call or text them.

The evening news is probably not the best form of entertainment or distraction for any of them right now. The screen bombards them with one depressing, terrifying, catastrophic story after another. Wildfires in California that can't be controlled, hundreds of homes destroyed, over a dozen people missing or killed. A father from Dedham goes on trial for murdering his wife and two children. Car bombs in Pakistan killing thirty-two civilians. Wall Street in a nosedive. Politicians throwing tantrums.

'Dad, can we watch something else?' asks Katie.

'Sox aren't on until seven thirty.'

End of discussion. Her parents have over a hundred cable channels, but the news and the Red Sox are apparently the only two options available. She doesn't press him. But the news is too stressful for Katie, as if each story adds a log to the fire of the living room's collective anxiety. She decides to watch her dad instead.

He's in constant motion, more than usual. She notices how he tries to make it all look normal. He'll stitch the tail end of whatever part of him flings or pops or twitches into some kind of larger, meaningful-looking action. He's become quite the improvisational choreographer. It's always the strangest dance she's ever seen.

His right leg snaps out as if he's kicking away an invisible pesky dog. So he follows his foot and stands up. Standing, he must mean to go somewhere, so he walks over to the windows. He pulls the shade, sticks his nose in, and peeks out at the street. He stays there for a few seconds, muttering to himself. It makes sense that he would get up to look for signs of JJ and Colleen, but Katie's onto him. The impulse to rise out of his comfortable seat began with an involuntary leg thrust, not with a premeditated plan to look out the window.

As he returns to his chair, there's an extra bit of jostle in his step. She listens to the newly familiar jingle of change in his pocket as he walks. The sound of HD.

She continues watching him, and he's more

182

mesmerizing, and in some ways more horrifying, than anything on the news. He's like a train wreck or a car accident or a house fire, and she's the eyewitness, the rubbernecker who can't look away.

Next, his left arm flings up as if he's a nerdy student raising his hand in class. Then he bends his arm at the elbow and scratches his head as if he just happened to have a little itch. This is one of his signature moves. If you didn't know he had Huntington's, you'd think this guy must have a raging case of dandruff or head lice, or he's just plain weird. He doesn't seem to be consciously aware of his involuntary ticks or even his oh-I-totally-meant-to-do-that improvisations. He doesn't glance over at Katie to see whether she noticed. He doesn't seem embarrassed or fazed in any way. He simply continues watching the news as if nothing mentionable just happened. Nothing to see here. Certainly not any symptoms of an inherited, progressive, lethal neurodegenerative disease with no cure.

He keeps fidgeting and crazy dancing in his chair and watching the news with his wife and his daughter as if this were a normal Wednesday evening, and it's starting to bug the piss out of her. As if any evening or anything at all could ever be normal again.

Then the front door opens and Katie's heart stops. Maybe the earth stops. Time seems to have. The sound of the evening news fades to a muted murmur. Her mom stops knitting and looks up. Even her dad goes still.

JJ and Colleen appear holding hands in the

living room, two numb-eyed zombies who've just returned from a visit to hell. Their faces are puffed and splotchy. No one says anything.

Katie's afraid to make a sound, afraid that any noise might push time past this exact second. Maybe what she's seeing isn't real. Maybe what's about to happen won't. The room is eerily silent, still, an unshaken snow globe on a shelf.

And then her mom starts bawling, and JJ's on his knees in front of her, hugging her with his head in her lap on top of her knitting.

'I'm sorry, Ma. I'm sorry,' he says.

And then her dad throws the remote control across the room. It hits the wall behind the TV and shatters. The batteries go spinning on the wood floor. Her dad's face is in his hands, and Colleen is standing alone looking like a paper doll, and Patrick and Meghan don't even know what's happening. This is actually happening.

Katie sits on the couch, watching the most tragic news of the day unfolding live in front of her, the sound of a scared little girl repeating the word *no* inside her head over and over and over and over.

15

Katie's sitting cross-legged on the living room couch in her apartment, sipping hot green tea, watching Meghan sew a ribbon into the arch of a shiny satin baby-pink pointe ballet shoe.

'I can't believe you're drinking tea. It's like a million degrees out,' says Meghan, who is sitting tall on the floor with her legs in a straddle split, facing Katie.

'It's freezing in here,' says Katie.

They own only one window-box air conditioner, and it's installed in the living room. Even with it blasting on the coldest setting all day, bedroom doors kept open and an unobstructed shot down the hallway to the kitchen, the other rooms never cool down. The living room is the only bearable space in their apartment when the temperature outside hits anything over eighty.

'You coming tonight?' asks Meghan.

There's an expectation in Meghan's voice, the question not really asking, an assumption that Katie will be in the audience to see Meghan dance in *Swan Lake*, if not tonight, then before the end of the run. Meanwhile, Meghan has never been to Katie's yoga class. No one in her family has. They all bend over backward and spend a small fortune to see Meghan in every show, but no one has done so much as a single Downward Dog in the yoga studio.

'Yeah.'

'You're not wearing that, are you?'

Katie's in black cropped yoga pants and a neon-yellow racerback tank top. Curtain is at seven. It's three o'clock now. Meghan will probably leave within the next half hour for stage rehearsal, hair, makeup, and getting into costume, but Katie has at least three more hours to get ready before she needs to leave.

'Yeah, I'm wearing lululemon to the Opera House.'

'You might.'

'I wouldn't, okay?'

'Just checking.'

Done sewing the ribbons on one shoe, Meghan grabs the Bic lighter from the floor near her pointed bare foot and singes the cut ends, the smell of burnt fabric reminding Katie of Sunday suppers and the quilted potholders her mother accidentally leaves on the burners.

'You should wear that sleeveless black dress that Ma bought you,' says Meghan.

'I don't need you to tell me what to wear.'

'It looks nice on you, and you never wear it.'

'You act like I don't know how to do anything.'

'Jeez, never mind. Wear whatever you want.'

'Thanks for permission to dress myself.'

Katie hears the familiar clipped note in her own voice, her cue to storm off, and she's about to catapult off the couch when she remembers how sticky-hot the other rooms are. She shouldn't have to sit here and subject herself to her sister's fashion judgments and overall bossiness, but she refuses to be chased out of the

186

only comfortable room in their apartment. Katie sighs, resigned to being stuck in the same room with Meghan. She wants to turn on the TV or grab a book to read, do something other than watch Meghan, who is now scratching up the bottom of her pointe shoe with a pair of scissors, but she doesn't feel like moving. Katie sips her tea and watches Meghan. Even doing virtually nothing, Meghan is the star of the show.

A message vibrates on Katie's phone. She lifts it and reads. It's Felix.

What's up for 2nite?

She types.

Teaching a private at 7. Meet u @10?

K. A3 hr private?

Have to shower and get all pretty 4 u.

U r already pretty. Shower at my place.
I'll join u. ☺

She blushes.

☺ K.

She feels guilty, lying to Felix, but it's a white lie, a harmless fib. If he knew she was going to the ballet tonight, he'd justifiably want to go with her. They saw the Alvin Ailey American Dance Theater perform in Boston in April, and she and

187

Felix were both blown away — the graceful power, the raw, earthy quality of their movements, all that juicy second- and third-chakra energy, so different from the floaty, sweet meringue prettiness of Meghan's ballets. At one point during *Revelations*, Katie looked over at Felix and his eyes were wet with tears. This is one of the things she loves about him, that a dance can make him cry. He's an MIT numbers nerd who would totally dig *Swan Lake*. But her entire family is going tonight, and she's still not ready to introduce him to everyone, especially with all that's going on now with JJ and Colleen.

'So am I ever going to meet this guy you're seeing?'

Katie looks up, stunned, half believing Meghan was somehow able to divine her thoughts.

'What guy?'

'The guy you just texted.'

Katie looks down at her phone and then up at Meghan, knowing her sister couldn't possibly read the screen from across the room. 'That was Andrea.'

'Fine,' says Meghan, obviously not believing her. 'The guy you're having sex with.'

'What?'

'I'm not stupid. I know you don't sleep here at least three nights a week.'

Physically exhausted from the long, intense hours of practice, rehearsal, and performance, Meghan goes to bed early, typically by nine thirty, and she rises with the birds, dressed and out the door before Katie opens her eyes. So

188

even on the nights Katie stays home, Meghan doesn't witness Katie going to bed or getting up in the morning. All Meghan sees is a shut bedroom door. Katie assumed her absence, like most everything else about her, went unnoticed by Meghan.

'And I know Mystery Man has stayed here at least twice now.'

'Wha — '

'Toilet seat up.'

'Oh.'

'So what's the deal? Who is he? Why all the secrecy?'

Katie sips her tea, knowing the jig is up, but still buys a moment before answering. Meghan is working on the skin-toned elastics, sewing them close to the heel. Even in a plain white T-shirt and gray shorts with zero makeup on, Meghan looks elegant, beautiful. She's an easy roommate, tidy, always washes her dirty dishes and puts them away, and when she's here, unless their apartment is an oven and they're cloistered in the living room, she spends most of her time in her own bedroom. They don't see each other much, and when they do, it's typically in passing, the conversation limited to the logistics of living together, often reiterations of notes written on the kitchen chalkboard. *We need more toilet paper. Do you have any quarters? Mom's looking for you.*

'Well?'

It's this damn heat wave, trapping them together in the air-conditioned living room, prodding them via forced proximity into the kind

189

of sisterly conversation Katie would rather resist.

'I dunno.'

'Don't worry. I'm not Ma. What's his name?'

'Felix.'

'Felix what?'

Katie hesitates.

'Martin.'

'Hmm.'

'What?'

'Not O'Martin or McMartin? I take it he's not from here.'

'No.'

'A Toonie.'

Katie nods.

'What's he look like?'

'I dunno. He's cute.'

'Okay. What else?'

'I dunno.'

'What does he do?'

'He's in business development for this company that turns trash into fuel.'

'Smarty pants. How'd you meet?'

'Yoga.'

Meghan smiles at Katie while bending the shank of her shoe, forcing it toe to heel, working it over and over. The shoe crunches audibly as she does this, its stiff architecture breaking in, softening. It amazes Katie that these shoes will be worn only once. All this sewing and cutting and bending to get them supple and quiet and perfectly fitted for Meghan's feet, and after tonight, the shoes will be considered 'dead.' Meghan's feet are so strong, the integrity of the ballet shoe will be ruined after a single performance, sometimes even after a single act. They'd actually be dangerous to wear a second time.

There seems to be a goading quality in Meghan's stretched-out smile, the repetitive crunching of the shoe, the baited silence. Meghan wiggles her blistered, pretty toes.

'I don't interrogate you about who you're seeing,' says Katie.

'I'm not seeing anyone.'

Meghan says this as if not seeing anyone is the right thing to do, given their circumstances, which of course implies that Katie is doing the wrong thing, recklessly having a boyfriend when she might have HD.

'Well, I don't make fun of you for not having a boyfriend.'

'I'm not making fun of you. Jeez, you're so sensitive. I just want to know what's going on with you.'

'Well, now you know.'

'Am I ever going to meet secret, invisible Mr. Martin?'

Katie shrugs.

'You could bring him tonight.'

'No thanks.'

'What? Are we not good enough for some fancy Toonie?'

'You know what, Meg?'

'Oh, relax.'

'Whatever.'

Meghan turns her attention to the second shoe. She lays two ribbons and a short band of wide elastic on her thigh, cuts a length of thread,

191

and begins stabbing one end at the eye of a needle. It won't find the hole. She stabs and stabs, but the tip of the thread still slips past the eye. Her hands begin to shake. Meghan places the needle and thread down on the floor in front of her, clenches her hands into fists, rolls her shoulders up, down, and back, and then looks up at Katie. Meghan's forehead is beaded with sweat. The room is freezing cold.

'Listen, I need you to do me a favor,' says Meghan.

Katie raises her eyebrows and waits, silently incensed that Meghan has the nerve to ask her for anything right now.

'Will you watch me tonight, like really watch me, for, you know, anything weird? Even something really small and subtle.'

'Meg, you're fine.'

'I know, but I'm feeling really spooked,' Meghan says, nodding to the sewing needle and unattached thread on the floor.

'You just did the other shoe no problem. I watched you. And I couldn't thread that tiny thing. Just try again.'

'But you see how Dad doesn't know half the time that he's even moving at all and he's like all over the place?'

'Yeah.'

'I'm so scared of that.'

'I am, too. You don't have HD, Meg.'

'I know, but now JJ — '

'Even if we're HD positive, we wouldn't be symptomatic yet,' says Katie, trying to convince herself as much as her sister.

192

'Right. Probably not. I know. But still, I can't stop worrying about it being there, that it's starting and I don't even know it. Like having spinach in your teeth and everyone is too polite to say anything. I want you to say something.'

'Okay.'

'A tremor, any movement that looks even slightly off, I want you to tell me.'

'Okay.'

'You promise?'

'Yes.'

'I think I have to go see that genetic counselor.'

'Really?'

'Yeah. The stress of not knowing is making me crazy.'

Katie nods.

'Yeah, but what if you're HD positive?' asks Katie. 'Won't that just make you crazier?'

'At first I thought so, but now I dunno. I think knowing, either way, would give me some measure of control. Right now, the whole thing feels so completely out of control I can't stand it.'

'Yeah, you're kind of a control freak.'

'I get it from Dad.'

As soon as she says this, the blood drains from Meghan's face. Katie feels it, too, the cold terror in wondering what else they each inherited from their father.

'What about you? You think you'll get tested?' asks Meghan.

'I dunno. Maybe.'

'Have you told Felix about all this?'

'No.'

'I don't blame you. I can't imagine involving someone else in this shit. Poor JJ and Colleen.'

'I can't believe — '

'You know what? I can't even talk about this right now or I'll cry. I have to get ready.'

'Fine. You brought it up.'

But Katie would like to talk about it. She'd like to talk about JJ being HD positive, how she thinks of him differently now, as if he's someone who's already sick or damaged or even contagious, how she's kind of afraid of him, which is ridiculous, but she can't help it. She'd like to talk about Colleen and her pregnancy and how worried Katie is about the baby, that she can't believe they decided to keep it without having the amnio to find out whether it has the mutation. She'd like to talk about how scared she is of being HD positive, too, that she imagines HD like a seed buried deep inside her, already beginning to germinate, the first buds growing on a creeping vine, spreading through-out her entire body.

She'd like to talk about HD with Meghan, before Meghan's call time tosses her out of this small, chilly living room. But Meghan has returned to the needle and thread, and Katie wouldn't dare interrupt her. As it's always been, Meghan is the big sister, the driver of any conversation between them, and Katie's the little sister, still not old enough to touch the wheel.

Meghan threads the needle this time on the second try. She exhales loudly. Katie watches as she stitches a pink ribbon to the inside of the arch. Still seated in a straddle split, Meghan's toes on her right foot point and flex, point and flex, up and down, up and down, while she sews. Katie's sure she's doing this on purpose, that she's seen Meghan do this sort of seated exercise many times before, but what if she's not? If it's an exercise, why isn't she giving her left foot a turn? What if moving her right foot right now isn't volitional, and she's not aware of it? What if it's HD? It's not. It can't be.

Meghan's foot continues to point and flex, and Katie stares in stupefied silence. Just two minutes ago, Katie promised to tell her if she saw anything suspicious. She'd have no problem pointing out spinach stuck between her sister's teeth, but she can't bring herself to mention the possibility of HD in Meghan's foot. Is this how it's going to go for all of them? She imagines Sunday suppers, everyone grimacing and fidgeting, bumping into each other and knocking things over, five giant pink elephants squeezed into that tiny kitchen and no one saying one word about it.

Meghan lights the end of the ribbon, and her foot stops. Katie holds her breath, waiting for Meghan's foot to start up again, but it remains still. She watches Meghan go through the rest of the process without any questionable movements, disruption, or comment.

'What time is it?' Meghan asks, inspecting her shoes, satisfied with her efforts.

Katie checks her phone. 'Three twenty.'

'Okay, I gotta go. I'll see you tonight.'

'Good lu — '

'Don't.'

'Sorry. *Merde*.'

'Thanks.'

Meghan gathers the needle, thread, scissors, and lighter, and off she goes. *Merde*. And they all think yoga is weird. Yogis would say *Namaste*, which means *I bow to the divine in you*. Actors would say *Break a leg*, which Katie agrees would be a particularly inappropriate wish for dancers. And Katie gets that saying *Good luck* is tempting fate. This is why she knocks on wood all the time. But *merde* makes no sense. *Merde* is French for *shit*.

Katie sits alone in the cold living room, aimlessly scrolling through her Facebook news-feed on her phone. Andrea posted a video of Krishna Das chanting in India. Katie taps PLAY, and although her eyes stay focused on the screen, what she's really seeing is her sister's foot pointing, flexing, pointing, flexing, pointing, flexing. The green tea in her stomach turns, becoming a pool of hot sewage.

Merde.

★ ★ ★

Felix opens the door to his apartment wearing a Yankees T-shirt, white linen shorts, and a pleased smile of surprise.

'Hey, you're early. It's only seven thirty. What happened to your private?'

'She canceled last minute,' says Katie.

'I hope you charged her anyway.'

'Nah, it's okay.'

'Come on in.'

Katie kicks off her flip-flops, drops her bag at the door, and follows Felix into the kitchen. His apartment is central air-conditioned, and her bare feet feel refreshingly cool on the smooth tile floor. She sits on one of the bar stools while Felix pulls a bottle of white wine from the fridge.

'How's this?' he asks.

Katie nods. Ziggy Marley is playing on his iPod. She swivels in her seat to the music and fondles one of the red apples in the white ceramic bowl on the soapstone bar counter while watching Felix work the bottle opener into the cork, admiring his strong hands. He pours two glasses of wine and gives her one.

'Cheers,' he says, and they clink glasses. The wine is cold, crisp, tangy. Katie considers the wine and the elegant heft of the glass in her hand and would bet that what she's holding is worth more than what she would've earned tonight had she actually had a private scheduled.

'So it's early now. Should we go out for dinner?' he asks.

'It's so hot out there. Can we just stay in?'

'Yeah. Good,' he says, sitting down next to her. 'It's been a long week, and I don't really feel like venturing back out. I can make us a salad or we can order something.'

'Okay.'

'You look all ready to hit the town, though.'

She's wearing the sleeveless black dress that Meghan told her to wear.

'I'm all sweaty from the walk over.'

'Looks like you could still use that shower,' he

says, smiling with those eyes so liquid brown she could bathe in them, and he leans over and kisses her.

She holds the back of his smooth, bald head with her hand and pulls his kiss deeper into her. His hands reach up under her dress, up her thighs, and his kiss reaches deeper, and she pulls his Yankees shirt up over his head and drops it to the floor. He does the same to her dress.

They're standing now, and she kisses his neck, tasting his bergamot soap and salty sweat, running her hands along his shoulders, down his arms, across his smooth, muscular back. She's kissed and touched and tasted every inch of him, and yet every dimple and crease, each scar and tattoo still feels intoxicatingly new. She unzips his shorts, and they fall off his thin hips to his ankles. He's not wearing any underwear. She wiggles out of her black thong, and he unhooks her bra.

They kiss and grab and hold each other, and Katie loses herself in him — the taste of white wine in his mouth, his hot hands, the bass of the music from his iPod thumping through her. He leads her by the hand to the bathroom. As Felix lets go of her grasp to turn the shower on, Meghan pops into Katie's consciousness, and for the slightest moment, a stone-cold guilty pang interrupts her libido, sickening her.

She couldn't go. She's holding too many secrets as it is — HD from Felix, her family from Felix, Felix from her family. She couldn't bear the possibility, the responsibility, seeing Meghan stutter onstage, a misstep, that right foot pointing and flexing when it shouldn't, because she knows she wouldn't have the guts to tell Meghan about it. And then she'd have yet another secret to carry, and her hands are already too damn full.

The glass door steams up. Katie steps into the shower, and Felix follows her. Hot water rains down on her head. Felix's dark brown hands rub slippery, liquid soap on her ghostly white breasts. She inhales the sweet smell of citrus as Felix presses up against her from behind, and the fact that she's not at the Opera House with the rest of her family fades to an inconsequential footnote.

16

Katie and the genetic counselor are killing time, waiting for the neurologist. She pulls out her cell phone, hoping to absorb herself in some kind of mindless distraction. The battery's dead. Well, then. She tucks her phone back inside her bag and casually browses the room, attempting to avoid eye contact and the potential for any more pointless small talk, but there's not much to look at in here. The counselor's office is small and impersonal, not at all what she expected. For some reason, she'd imagined something similar to her high school guidance counselor's office, which was overly cheery, trying-way-too-hard-to-be-cool uncool. She remembers the fish-bowl full of M&Ms, the antibullying and school spirit posters. EVERY KID MATTERS, GO TOWNIES! His collection of Bruins bobbleheads. The entire office was a forced smiley-face emoticon with exclamation points on every flat surface.

This place is definitely more subdued on the positivity front. The genetic counselor has his framed diploma on the wall. Eric Clarkson, MSW. Boston College. Next to the diploma is a Huntington's Disease Society of America HOPE poster. There's a tall, pink orchid in a pot on the windowsill and a framed photograph of a yellow Lab on his desk. She checks out his left hand. No ring. No wife or kids or even a girlfriend established or loved enough to own a spot in a frame in his office. Just a man and his dog and his pretty flower. No M&Ms. No *rah rah rah!*

He's kind of cute. She tucks her hair behind her ear and wonders how she looks. In her rush to get here on time, which clearly wasn't necessary, she didn't put on any makeup. Now she wishes she had. Good God. How can she be sitting here, worried about how she looks? First of all, she has a boyfriend. Second, she's here to find out whether she has the gene for a fatal disease. He's a genetic counselor at the hospital, not some cute guy at Ironsides.

The door opens. A woman enters the room and says hello to Eric. She's wearing a white lab coat, glasses, and high heels. Her black hair is pulled into a loose bun. She reads whatever it says on her clipboard and then looks up at Katie.

'Kathryn O'Brien?' she says, extending her hand and shaking Katie's. 'I'm Dr. Hagler. We're going to do a quick neurological exam before you begin talking with Eric, okay?'

Katie nods, but she's faking it. Wait, what? There's a test *before* the test? Her heart tightens.

'All right. Can you stick out your tongue for me?'

Katie sticks out her tongue. She watches Dr. Hagler's eyes studying her tongue. What is her tongue doing? Is her tongue doing something wrong?

'Okay, now follow my finger with your eyes.'

She does. Or at least she thinks she does. Shit. This is happening. She's being tested to see whether she's showing symptoms *now*. She feels blindsided, tricked. She remembers now that

201

Eric mentioned something on the phone about a quick neuro exam, but the words went in one ear and out the other without registering. She conveniently ignored whatever that meant. She thought today would only be a preliminary visit, a conversation about whether she wants to find out if she's gene positive, whether she's destined to get Huntington's disease fourteen years or so down the road. This was an appointment with a *genetic counselor*, not a neurologist. Even as she and Eric sat waiting for the neurologist, it honestly never occurred to her that a doctor would be checking her to see whether she's got this thing *now*.

'Hold your left hand flat, palm open, like this. Then, with your right hand, I want you to touch your left hand with a fist, then a karate chop, then a clap. Like this.'

Dr. Hagler shows Katie the sequence three times through. Katie copies her three times, doing exactly as the doctor did, maybe a touch slower. Does that matter? Is that bad?

'Now walk heel to toe over here in a straight line.'

Katie stands up, and the blood drains from her face. Her head feels airy, cool, dizzy. Her heart is beating too fast, panicking. She needs to breathe. She's not breathing. Breathe.

You can walk heel to toe, for God's sake. You can walk on your HANDS if she asks you to.

Katie walks across the room heel to toe with arms outstretched in a T, as if she's walking across a tightrope or being busted for an OUI. Dr. Hagler writes something down. Did she not nail it? Should she have had her arms down? Dr. Hagler continues with the exam, and each task makes Katie feel as if she's in big trouble, one wrong move away from a death sentence.

'Now name as many words as you can that begin with the letter *B*. You have one minute. Go,' says Dr. Hagler, looking down at her watch.

B is for, *B* is for . . . Nothing. No words. Her mind is completely blank.

'Blank. Ball. Boston. Blood.'

Think. She can't think of any more words starting with *B*. What does that mean? Why didn't JJ warn her about this? She could've prepared, practiced. Man, she hates tests. This is bullshit.

'Bullshit.'

'Okay, time,' says Dr. Hagler.

That totally sucked. Katie's face is flushed hot, and her heart is beating as if she's in a full sprint. Beating. B. Damn it.

You don't have HD, but we did diagnose you with STUPID. Sorry, there's nothing we can do for that.

'All right, Kathryn. It was nice to meet you. I'm going to leave you now with Eric. Do you have any questions for me before I go?'

'Wait, uh, yeah. What just happened?'

'You had a neurological exam.'

'To see if I'm showing symptoms of Huntington's?'

'Yes.'

Katie examines Dr. Hagler's face, trying to discern the answer to the terrifying question blinking in her head like a neon sign without having to verbalize it. Dr. Hagler and her infuriatingly impassive face are standing by the door. Katie can't let her leave without knowing. Did she pass or fail? She closes her eyes.

'Am I?' asks Katie.

'No. Everything looks normal.'

Katie opens her eyes to Dr. Hagler's smiling face. It's the most reassuring, honest-to-God smile Katie's ever seen.

'Okay, then. Take care.' And Dr. Hagler is gone. Namaste.

Eric raises his eyebrows and claps his hands together.

'Shall we?' he asks.

She's not sure. To be honest, she'd really like to lie down. She's not showing any signs of HD. All that time studying herself in the mirror, tormenting herself over every nervous fidget, or that major full-body twitch she sometimes gets just before falling asleep, hunting for Huntington's. She can stop. She doesn't have it. For now. This is really good news. But that neuro exam was like surviving fifteen rounds in a boxing ring. She's been declared the winner, but she still got knocked around. She's not sure she's ready for anything more than a nap.

She nods.

'So your father has HD and your oldest brother is gene positive. I have your family's medical history from JJ, so we don't need to go through that again. Let's talk about why you're here. Why do you want to know?'

'I'm not sure I do.'

'Okay.'

'I mean, sometimes I think living with the constant uncertainty is worse than knowing that I'm going to get it.'

He nods. 'So how've you been dealing with the uncertainty?'

'Not that great.'

The questioning, the stress, the anxiety are always there, like an annoying radio station playing too loudly in the background that she can never turn off or completely tune out. She becomes gripped with panic many times a day — if she loses balance in a standing pose in class, if she drops her keys, if she forgets her phone, if she catches herself jiggling her foot. Or for no reason at all. It can simply be that there's enough time and space for her mind to wander — waiting for class to start, waiting for her tea to steep, watching some inane commercial on TV, trying to meditate, listening to her mother talk. Her thoughts beeline to HD. She's like a teenager with a mad crush on a bad boy, or a junkie fantasizing about her next hit of meth. She can't resist her new favorite yet destructive topic and obsesses about it every chance she gets. HD. HD. HD.

What if she has it now? What if she gets it later? What if all of them get it?

'Are you feeling depressed?'

'That's kind of a ridiculous question.'

'How so?'

She sighs, annoyed that she has to spell it out for this guy.

'My dad and brother have a fatal disease, and I might have it, too. This isn't exactly the happiest time in my life.'

'Your brother has the gene. He doesn't have the disease yet.'

'Whatever.'

'It's an important distinction. He's the same guy he was the day before he found out his gene status. He's a perfectly healthy twenty-five-year-old.'

Katie nods. It's so hard for her to look at JJ now and not see him differently. Doomed. Sick. Dying young. HD. HD. HD.

'And you're right, it's totally normal to feel a bit depressed with all that's happening. Have you ever been depressed before?'

'No.'

'Ever been to see a psychiatrist or psychologist for any reason?'

'No.'

'Are you on any medication?'

'No.'

One of the symptoms of HD is depression. Some people with HD begin with the physical symptoms, the movement changes she was just tested for by the neurologist, but some people begin with the psychological symptoms years before any of the chorea sets in. Obsession, paranoia, depression. She can't stop thinking about HD, she's convinced that God has cursed her whole family with this disease, and she's sad about it. Is her less-than-bubbly mood of late the first sign of HD creeping through the cracks, or is it what any normal person under these totally abnormal circumstances would feel? Which comes first, the chicken or the egg?

It's a circular mind fuck.

'I'm pretty sure I have the gene,' says Katie.

'Why's that?'

'JJ looks exactly like my dad, and he has it. I look like my dad's mother, and she had HD.'

'That's a pretty typical assumption, but there's absolutely no truth to it. You can look exactly like your dad or your grandmother and not have inherited the HD gene.'

She nods, not buying one word of it.

'This might be a good time to go over some basic genetics.'

Eric walks over to a white board on the wall and picks up a black marker.

'Uh, do I have to write this down?' She didn't bring a pen or paper. JJ didn't warn her about any of this. She wishes Meghan had gone first. Meghan would've told her everything.

'No, there's no quiz or anything. I just want to help you understand how the inheritance of HD works.'

He writes a list of words on the board.

Chromosomes. Genes. DNA. ATCG. CAG.

'The genes we inherit from our parents are packaged inside structures called chromosomes. We all have twenty-three pairs of chromosomes. Each chromosome pair consists of one that came from Mom and the other from Dad. Our genes are arranged along the chromosomes like beads on a string.'

He draws these strings and beads on the board. They look like necklaces.

'You can think of genes as recipes. They're the body's instructions for making proteins and everything about you from eye color to disease susceptibility. The letters and words that make up the gene recipes are called DNA. Instead of the A-B-C alphabet, the DNA alphabet letters are A,T,C,G.'

He circles these letters on the board.

'The change underlying Huntington's involves these DNA letters. The Huntington's gene is located on chromosome four.'

He points to a dot on one of the necklaces.

'There is a sequence, C-A-G, that repeats over and over in the HD gene. On average, people have seventeen CAG repeats in the HD gene. With Huntington's, there are thirty-six or more CAG repeats. This expansion of the gene is like changing the recipe, and the altered recipe causes the disease. You with me so far?'

She nods. She thinks so.

'So let's look at your family tree. Remember, we inherit two copies of every gene, one from our mother and one from our father. Your dad inherited a normal copy of the HD gene from his father, but he inherited an expanded copy from his mother, who had HD. Huntington's is what's called a dominant disease. You only need one copy of the altered gene to inherit the disease.'

He draws a square next to a circle on the board and draws a line between them. He writes *grandfather* over the square and *grandmother* over the circle and draws a line between them. He then shades in the circle black with the marker. He draws a line like a stem down from her grandparents to a shaded square labeled *father* and connects her dad's square to an unshaded circle labeled *mother*.

'Now there's your generation.' He draws squares for JJ and Patrick, circles for Meghan and Katie. He blackens JJ's square, and the sight of it blackens Katie's stomach. She shifts her focus to her circle, empty for now. She closes her eyes for a moment, a white circle emblazoned in her mind's eye, holding on to it. A symbol of hope.

'Each of you inherited a normal copy of the gene from your mom. Remember, your dad has one normal copy of the HD gene from his father and one expanded copy from his mother. So each of you inherited either his normal copy or the expanded copy. If you inherited the normal copy from your dad, you will not get HD. If you inherited the expanded copy, you will develop HD if you live long enough.'

'So that's how each of us has a fifty percent chance of getting this.'

'Exactly,' he says, smiling, seemingly pleased that she followed his biology lecture.

So it really does comes down to random chance. Shit luck. Nothing she has done or will ever do can affect it. She can eat a vegan diet, practice yoga every day, have protected sex, stay away from drugs, take her vitamins, and sleep eight hours a night. She can pray, hope, write positive affirmations on her bedroom walls, and light candles. She can meditate on an empty, white circle. None of it matters. There it is on the board. She either already has the gene or she doesn't.

'Fuck,' she says. Her eyes widen and she

presses her lips together, her mother's voice in her head scolding her with a harsh *Language!* 'Sorry.'

'That's okay. You can say 'fuck' in here. You can say anything in here.'

Her lips part and she exhales. She feels that she has to be so careful now, especially around her family, worrying about what not to say, what not to notice. Sunday suppers in that cramped kitchen are particularly excruciating, where every spoken and withheld word seems to stomp on a minefield of eggs, crushing them into sharp shards that slice her lungs, making it painful to breathe.

There's a noticeable pause in conversation. The air in the room fills with something. An invitation. A promise. A dare.

'When I was a kid and we played truth or dare, I always picked dare,' says Katie.

'So you were a risk taker.'

'No, not at all. It was just the better choice, better than having to admit some embarrassing truth about myself.'

'What was so embarrassing about you?'

'I dunno normal stuff.'

The baby of the family, she was forever trying to keep up with her older siblings. JJ, Patrick, and Meghan knew about sex, drinking, pot, everything before she did, and her ignorance made her feel stupid. And it was particularly difficult following Meghan. Katie spent most of her childhood faking what she knew, hiding what she didn't.

'This feels a little like truth or dare,' she says.

Truth: Find out whether she is going to get Huntington's disease or not.

Dare: Live without knowing, wondering every other second whether she already has it.

She never liked that game. She still doesn't want to play it. Eric nods, seemingly impressed and contemplative, as if this comparison had never occurred to him before.

'Tell me,' he says. 'What would it mean to find out you're gene negative?'

'Uh, that would be amazing. Biggest relief ever.'

Duh.

'How do you think it would affect your relationship with JJ?'

Oh. The lightness from her imagined, obvious relief drops into an unliftable weight in her lap.

'And what if his baby has it?'

'He's not finding out.'

'In eighteen years, his kid can get tested. What if your niece or nephew is positive? How will that be for you?'

'Not good,' she says, lowering her head.

'What if Meghan and Patrick are positive, and you're negative?'

'Jesus,' she says, leaning forward to knock three times on Eric's desk. 'Why are you painting the worst possible picture?'

'You said being negative would be the biggest relief ever. See how it's not that simple?'

'Yeah, I see it.'

Thanks a fuckin' lot.

'What would testing positive feel like?'

'Rainbows and kittens.'

211

'How would you handle it?'

'I wouldn't jump off the Tobin, if that's what you're getting at.'

This is getting too intense. She squirms in her seat. Eric notices. Fuck this. This isn't mandatory. She can get up and leave anytime she wants. She doesn't have to be polite to Eric. She doesn't have to care what he thinks. She doesn't have to see Eric ever again.

'So, what would you do? Would anything in your life change?' he asks.

'I dunno. Maybe.'

'You in a relationship?'

She shifts to the edge of her seat and eyes the door.

'Yeah.'

'What's his name?'

'Felix.'

'Does Felix know about this?'

'No. I don't want to lay it on him until I know what's what.'

'Okay.'

'Don't judge me.'

'No judgment here. Let's make it more abstract. You want to get married someday?'

'Yeah.'

'Have kids?'

She shrugs. 'Yeah, probably.'

'What if you're HD positive?'

She thinks about JJ and Colleen. She doesn't know whether she could've made the decision they made, whether she would've kept the baby. But Katie can find out before becoming pregnant. She could do that in vitro thing where they test the embryos for the mutated HD gene and only implant the embryos that don't have it. She could have Huntington's and have babies. It's not exactly chocolate and peanut butter, but she could make the combination work.

Or not. Felix doesn't deserve to sign up for a wife who is destined to get this hideous disease. He doesn't deserve a wife whom he'll have to take care of — feed her, push her in a wheelchair, change her diapers, bury her — by the time she's fifty. She thinks of her mom and dad, and she starts picturing their immediate future. She squeezes her eyes shut for a second and clenches her teeth, chasing the images away.

Why should Felix be stuck with that kind of future, knowing it from the get-go? At least her parents have had twenty-five years together without knowing. No guy should have to be saddled with that kind of burden before even getting started.

A realization hits her hard, and an overwhelming urge to cry swells fast within her, filling to the top of her throat. She swallows several times, grinding her molars, holding it down. Maybe being HD positive would be the perfect excuse, irrefutable proof that she's unlovable.

'I dunno. These questions are all way ahead of where I'm at anyway. You're not married,' she says, as if accusing him of something. 'You planning to?'

'I'd like to someday, yeah,' says Eric.

'How old are you?'

'Thirty-two.'

'Okay, so you could get hit by a bus when

you're thirty-five. Dead. Done. You still wanna make plans? You still wanna get married someday?'

Eric nods. 'I understand your example, and you're right. We're all going to die. And who knows, I might get hit by a bus when I'm thirty-five. The difference is, I'm not sitting in someone's office, asking a counselor or a doctor or a psychic to tell me approximately when and exactly how I'm going to die.'

Katie thinks of the last ghost in *A Christmas Carol*, the grim reaper pointing to Scrooge's future gravestone. She never did read the book for English class like she was supposed to, but she's watched various versions of the movie on TV every year at Christmastime. Scrooge in his nightgown and nightcap, shaking in his slippers, begging for a different outcome. That scene always scared the living shit out of her, gave her vivid nightmares when she was little. Now the nightmare is real, and the creepy ghost's name is Eric Clarkson. He's even wearing a black shirt. All he needs is a hood and sickle.

'I don't get why I have to answer all these questions. It's my business what I do with the information and how I'll live my life. If I say the wrong answer, you gonna tell me I can't find out?'

'There are no wrong answers. We're not going to deny you the test. But we want you to understand what you're getting into and have the tools to deal with it. We feel some responsibility for how you're going to react.'

She waits. Eric says nothing.

'So what happens now?' she asks.

'If you still want to go ahead and find out, you can come back in two weeks or anytime after that. We'll talk again, see how all this is sitting with you, and if you still want to know, I'll walk you to the lab and they'll draw your blood.'

She swallows.

'And then I'll know?'

'Then you'll come back four weeks after that, and I'll tell you the result of the test.'

She does the math. Six weeks. If she goes through with this, she'll know whether she's HD positive or negative by the end of the summer.

'Can't you just tell me over the phone?'

'No, it has to be here. In fact, we want someone to come with you for support, and not one of your siblings, because your news either way might be too hard on them given that they're also at risk. I also wouldn't recommend JJ or your father. Bring your mother or a friend.'

She wouldn't bring her mother. If the news is bad, her mother would be more of a mess than Katie. She'd end up supporting her mother, not the other way around. The other possibilities are equally unappealing. Felix. Andrea. Another teacher from the studio.

'But no one outside our family knows about this. Can't I just come alone?'

'I don't recommend it.'

'But it's not a rule.'

'No.'

She can't imagine whom she'd bring, but it's two appointments from now. Maybe by then she'll have told Felix. Maybe she doesn't want to

215

know. Maybe she won't even go through with this. A lot can happen in six weeks. If she gets to that last appointment, to the day of reckoning, she'll either figure out whom to bring or come alone. She'll cross that bridge when she gets to it.

Truth or dare, little girl. What's it going to be?

17

Outside Katie's bedroom window, the day is flat, colorless, grim, a perfect reflection of her mood. She checks the calendar on her phone. Today is September 30. Katie could've gone to her second genetic counselor appointment two months ago, but she blew it off. Eric Clarkson just called. His voice mail was gently casual, as if coaxing a shy child hiding behind her mother's leg, reminding her that he's still there and available to talk if she's still wrestling with the idea of genetic testing. He didn't need to call. She thinks about Eric Clarkson probably more than she thinks about Felix, which isn't good for many reasons. She knows he's there and how to get in touch with him. She deletes the message.

She's avoiding pretty much everyone right now — Eric Clarkson and her second appointment, her dad, JJ and Colleen, Meghan, the other yoga instructors, even Felix. She's been going to three yoga classes a day, but she's all business about it, getting in and out with as little eye contact and chitchat with the other yogis as possible. Her body is wicked kickass strong from all the exercise, but her mind has been completely disconnected from her practice. Her mind is junk.

She has no self-discipline, no control over her thoughts. They're like big, hyper, untrained dogs chasing foxes into a dark forest, and she's holding on to their leashes, tethered to their reckless decisions, being dragged everywhere they go. Meditation should take care of this. It should rein in the wild dogs. Heel. Sit. Be the fuck still. Good dogs. But she can't seem to stay focused.

Alone in her bedroom, she sits on her meditation pillow and reads the strange, beautiful graffiti on her walls. She's scrawled many more inspirational quotes in black Sharpie on the walls from floor to ceiling over the summer, hoping her exterior world would seep into her consciousness and perk things up in there. Her mom isn't too pleased that she's been marking up the walls, but Katie can't see the harm in it. She's never been crafty and doesn't want to waste money she doesn't have on buying posters or painted boards. A two-dollar Sharpie and her walls are all she needs. They can easily paint over everything if she ever moves. When she moves. When. Someday.

She reads the three quotes directly in front of her.

'The pain that you create now is always some form of nonacceptance, some form of unconscious resistance to what is.'
— Eckhart Tolle

'Life is a near-death experience. Stumble around in giddy gratitude while you still can.'
— Jen Sincero

'What we think, we become.'
— Buddha

She thinks about HD. All the time. Constantly. The creepy, dark forest is teeming with it. HD. HD. HD. She's a skipping vinyl record, and she wishes someone would smack her.

'What we think, we become.'
— *Buddha*

She's becoming HD. This self-sabotaging, obsessive habit has to stop.

She settles into a comfortable cross-legged seat on her pillow and closes her eyes. She begins Ujjayi breathing, creating an ocean wave rhythm through her nose, in and out, in and out. On the next inhalation, she mentally says the word *so*. On the exhalation, she mentally hears the word *hum*. In, *so*. Out, *hum*. *So hum* is actually short for the Sanskrit *So aham*, meaning *That I am*. She's breathing in and out, so-humming. That I am. That I am. So hum. So hum.

The mind loves words. Feeding it a restricted script of *So hum* keeps it focused, absorbed in essentially nothing, holding it still. When thoughts and sensations arise, when the dogs start barking, she's supposed to notice them, let them float by her like wispy clouds on a passing breeze, and then return to inhaling *so*, exhaling *hum*.

At first, it's working. *So hum. So hum.* Her mind is a clear glass of water, empty and clean. But then the dogs get a whiff of something scrumptious and take off for the woods.

HD. HD. HD.

She should call Eric Clarkson back. It's rude

to ignore him. But she's not sure whether she wants to know. What if she's gene positive? What if she has HD like her dad and JJ?

And so the storytelling begins, a hallucination of a fictional future starring Katie and the O'Brien family, her mind an Academy Award-winning screenwriter, director, and actress. There are no romantic comedies or Hollywood endings in here. These epic tales are always extremely dark, invariably playing out the worst imaginable possibilities. And her sick, addicted mind loves every gruesome, dramatic second of it.

Her thoughts time travel, trying on a future wardrobe of Katie and Katie's life, where nothing is pretty. Her dad and JJ are dead. Her mom sells the house because she can't afford it alone and moves in with one of Katie's uncles just before having a nervous breakdown. Patrick is a heroin addict. Meghan kills herself. Katie has HD.

She breaks up with Felix to spare him. He marries a perfect woman and has two beautiful, perfect children, and they live in the penthouse of one of those fancy condos in the Navy Yard. Katie imagines sitting on a bench alone, watching them walk and laugh and play in the park.

She never opens her own yoga studio because she waited too long and then became symptomatic. Her balance was the first to go, so she lost her job right away. She ends up homeless.

People are disgusted by the sight of her. She's mistaken for being drunk in public and gets picked up by the police. It's Tommy Vitale, her dad's best friend, but instead of helping her, he locks her up. He says if her father were alive, he'd hunt her down and kick her ass for not fighting to live, for giving up and letting HD ruin her like this. He says she should be ashamed of herself. And she is. She's ruined and ashamed.

She's a thirty-five-year-old homeless, unloved woman with HD.

She's a forty-five-year-old homeless, unloved woman with HD.

She dies alone, ruined and ashamed with HD.

Wait, she's not breathing. *So hum* is gone. She's forgotten to breathe, and she's sweating, and her heart is bathing in a pool of adrenaline. Shit. This is what happens. This is why she's a mess.

She needs to get a grip, get present. Let go of the leash. No more getting dragged through the creepy, dark forest, lured into a future that may never happen. The future, good or bad, is a fantasy. There is only this moment, right now.

Right now, she's a twenty-one-year-old yoga teacher sitting in her bedroom, and she doesn't have HD. She has an amazing boyfriend and a decent apartment, and her dad and JJ are still alive, and Patrick isn't a junkie, and Meghan is fine, and none of the drama she just experienced in her head is real.

None of it was real. She takes in a deep breath and lets it go, softening her panic-squeezed ribs, calming her anxious heart. She straightens her spine, places her palms on her thighs, and tries again. No more dogs. No more madness. This time, she begins by setting an intention.

'I am here now. I am healthy and whole.'

Instead of *So hum*, she repeats her intention in her mind over and over. Inhale, *I am here now*. Exhale, *I am healthy and whole*. Inhale. Exhale.

The dogs are gone. The forest dissolves into a sunlit meadow. Inhale, *I am here now*. Exhale, *I am healthy and whole*. The meadow brightens until there is only white light. There is white light and breathing in and out. And then there is nothing, and in that still space of nothing, there is peace.

Peace. Peace. Peace.

And then she thinks, *I'm doing it!* And with that thought, she's instantly ejected from that blissful, empty place. But that's okay. She smiles. She was there. It exists.

A space inside her where there is no HD.

She opens her eyes. Felix is sitting cross-legged in front of her, grinning at her face.

'Are you real?' she asks.

He laughs. 'As real as they get, baby.'

'How long have you been here?'

'About ten minutes. Your sister let me in.'

And so Secret Invisible Mr. Martin is finally revealed. She wonders what Meghan is thinking right now, whether her mind is as blown as Katie suspects it is. She's sure to hear an earful as soon as Meghan gets her alone. She feels nervous, beetles scattering in her stomach.

'So how was meeting Meghan?'

'Fine. She seems nice. It was just for a second. Good to know she actually exists.'

'So, ten minutes. Really?'

'Yeah.'

She had no awareness of his presence, his bare knees only a couple of inches from hers. And she had no sense of time passing. If she had guessed, she would've said she'd been sitting in meditation for only a few moments.

'Hey, I have news,' he says. 'The Biofuel project rolled out so well in Boston, we've been contracted to implement the same model in Portland, Oregon. The CEO wants me to go and oversee it.'

Katie feels her face drop.

'No, don't be upset. I want you to come with me.' She looks into his eyes, trying to catch up with him, searching for more.

'I love you, Katie. You're always talking about leaving this place, opening your own studio. Let's go for it. Portland's a great city. What do you think?'

His words sit between them like an unwrapped gift, his face bursting with confident anticipation.

'Wait,' she says. 'You love me?'

'Yeah,' he says, squeezing both of her hands, his eyes tearing. 'I do.'

'I love you, too. And I'm not just saying it back to say it. I have for a while. I've just been too scared to go first.'

'Chicken.'

'I know. I'm working on it.'

'So what do you think? You up for this adventure with me?'

Portland, Oregon. She doesn't know the first

thing about it. Maybe Portland is the place she's been dreaming of, a city where there's space for her to grow without limitations; where she can live without being judged for dating a black man; where people don't look at her sideways for eating vegan; where she wouldn't feel mostly invisible in the capacious shadow of her older sister; where she wouldn't live under the oppressive and not-so-subtle expectation that she'll marry a nice Irish boy from Charlestown and raise her many children Catholic; where people have ambitions beyond working in civil service, staying out of jail, raising a family, and getting hammered every weekend at the local bars; where she wouldn't feel inadequate because she's not a ballerina, weird because she doesn't particularly care about Tom Brady or the Bruins, or uppity because her highest aspiration in life isn't to be Mrs. Flannagan or Mrs. O Apostrophe Whatever; where she wouldn't feel ashamed of who she is.

Portland, Oregon. The other side of the country. Another world. Her own studio. A man who loves her. This could be her dream, laid out right in front of her for the taking.

Take it.

But what if she has HD and becomes symptomatic, and Felix can't handle it, and he leaves her, and she'll be left all alone out there? What if Portland is like Charlestown, and there isn't enough room for another yoga studio? What if she opens her own studio and it fails? The timing doesn't feel right. Her dad's HD is going to get worse. JJ's, too. They're going to need her.

It would be selfish to leave now. What if Meghan and Patrick are HD positive? What if she is?

Let go of the leash, girl. Don't ruin your life with thoughts that aren't real.

Okay, here's what's real. She's a yoga teacher, daughter, and sister. She is sitting across from a brilliant, beautiful man she loves who loves her back. He's just asked her to move across the country with him. She wants to say yes. She is here now. She is healthy and whole.

And she has a second appointment to keep with Eric Clarkson.

She stares into Felix's brown, hopeful eyes, so exquisitely gorgeous and naive, and she's terrified of the change she's about to see in them. She takes a deep breath and lets it go. She inhales again, and on her next exhale, she holds on to his hands, looks into his eyes, her vulnerable heart facing his, and tells him what's real.

18

Katie hands Eric a present wrapped in blue paper and a white ribbon. As he's tugging on the ribbon, she suddenly wishes she could take it back. Giving her genetic counselor a gift seemed like a good idea back at home, but watching him open it here in his office, she feels weird, inappropriate, lame.

He tears off the paper, revealing a three-by-five white index card in a black frame. In Katie's neatest writing, the card reads:

'Hope is the thing with feathers
That perches in the soul
And sings the tune without the words
And never stops at all.'
— Emily Dickinson

Eric smiles as he reads it. 'Wow, thank you. This is great.'

'I thought it would be good for your office.'

'It's perfect,' he says, standing the frame on his desk, facing Katie. 'And my birthday was just last week.'

'Cool.'

'So,' he says, studying Katie for too many discomforting seconds, dipping his toe into conversation as if they're on an awkward second date, the possibility of a third looking highly unlikely. 'I'm glad you came back.'

Katie laughs.

'What's so funny?' asks Eric.

'You kinda need people like me to come back or you'd be out of a job.'

'I'm not worried about my job, Katie. I've been worried about you.'

At first she feels flattered, special as the subject of his concern and care, but she backs away. Concern is a thin hair on the head of pity.

'How was your summer?' asks Eric.

'Good.'

'How's your dad doing?'

'He's okay. You can definitely see his symptoms. Those spastic, jerky movements — what are those called again?'

'Chorea.'

'Yeah, his chorea is getting more obvious. He's disorganized and forgetting stuff, and then he gets frustrated with himself and blows up at someone, usually my mom.'

'How's your mom doing with it?'

Katie shrugs. 'Okay.'

'Is your dad still working?'

'Yeah.'

'Does anyone at the police department know about his HD?'

'Just his best friend there. He has another friend, an EMT, who knows, but no one else does. It's a secret.'

Tommy Vitale and Donny Kelly are keeping an eye on her dad. For now, they agree that he's okay to work, and no one else has to know. Honestly, she can't imagine that he can go on as a police officer much longer. And at the same time, she can't imagine her dad not being a police officer. Her dad is getting hard to imagine, even when he's sitting in his chair, right in front her.

They decided as a family back in May that they wouldn't tell anyone in Town. This kind of news would spread like the plague. If it leaked, every Townie and Toonie would know within the week, maybe even the same day. Her dad doesn't give a shit what people in Town think about him, but it matters for JJ. If the guys at the firehouse know about her dad's HD, it wouldn't take a genius after a little Googling for them to figure out that JJ might have it, too. Then they'd start watching him, treating him differently, maybe passing him over for promotions. It wouldn't be fair to JJ. So they all swore themselves to secrecy.

And then she told Felix.

'So how about you? How are you doing?' he asks.

'I'm okay.'

She hesitates, holding back, protecting herself from being exposed. She bobs her cross-legged foot up and down and reads the Emily Dickinson quote.

'When I didn't hear back from you after two weeks and then a month and then two months, I figured I'd never see you again.'

'Yeah, well, for a while there, that was the plan,' she says. 'Nothing personal.'

It's not like she was playing hard to get. Eric holds up his hands as if he's being held at gunpoint.

'Hey, I get it. This is tough stuff.'

'Do you see that a lot? People come in one time and then disappear?'

He nods. 'Yeah, over half. Not unlike my stats following a first date.'

Katie laughs.

'Plus it was summer,' says Eric. 'No one wants to find out if they're HD positive in the summer.'

'And now it's October,' says Katie.

'Yes, it is.'

'And here I am.'

'Here you are.'

'On our second date.'

Eric smiles and taps his fingers on his desk. A flirtatious energy passes between them. Katie blushes.

'So what brought you back?'

Katie switches her crossed leg, buying time.

'I told Felix.'

'This is the guy you were seeing back in July?'

'Yeah.'

'How did he take it?'

'Better than I thought he would. He didn't break up with me on the spot, so that was good.'

'Sounds like a good guy.'

'He is. He told me he loves me.'

She blushes again and looks down at her claddagh ring, feeling silly.

'But I don't think he really gets it,' says Katie. 'He's read the little HD pamphlet I gave him, but he refuses to read anything else or Google it or anything. He says he doesn't need to know more now. I think he's in denial.'

'Or maybe you are.'

'How am I in denial? I'm *here*.'

And, she'd like to point out, it took some undeniably huge balls to come back here, but she decides not to say *balls* to Eric.

'About Felix and how he feels about you.'

Katie rolls her eyes.

'Yeah, he loves me and I love him, and that's all great, and I'm really happy. But *if* I have this, I'm going to change. A lot. I'm not going to be the same girl he loves right now, and I wouldn't blame him for not loving me with HD.'

'Does your mom still love your dad?'

'Yeah, but she's like a serious Catholic. She has to love him.'

'Devotion and a commitment to marriage vows are different than love. Has your mom stopped loving your dad?'

When they walk Yaz together, they hold hands. She notices them kissing more than they used to. Her mom dotes on him. She doesn't yell back when he blows up, and she doesn't seem to hold it over him after. She calls him 'sweetie' and 'my love.' Her calls her 'hun' and 'darlin'.'

'No. But he's not that bad yet.'

'True. Look, I've seen a lot of families with HD, and based on what I've seen, your mom is going to hate HD, not your dad.'

'Felix's boss wants him to move to the company's new office in Portland, Oregon. He wants me to go with him.'

'Do you want to go?'

'I dunno. That's what I'm trying to figure out.'

'And do you think your gene status will influence this decision?'

'I dunno, yeah, probably. But even if I don't

230

have HD and actually especially if I don't, I shouldn't leave Charlestown. I feel so selfish even thinking about leaving now and abandoning my dad and JJ when they need me.'

'JJ is perfectly healthy. He might not be symptomatic for ten years or more. Your dad's still working. He's not in a wheelchair or needing outside assistance. Sounds like your mom and his friends have things well in hand. How long would you live in Portland?'

The Biofuel project in Boston lasted three years. Felix thinks the rollout in Portland would take roughly the same amount of time.

'I dunno, at least a couple of years.'

'So what's holding you back?'

Her eyebrows lift as she shoots him an exasperated look, a gesture stolen from her mom's playbook. *Don't play dumb with me, young man.*

'Your unknown gene status,' he says.

She nods.

'Okay, so what happens if you're gene negative? Would you go?'

She thinks. It wouldn't have to be forever. If her mom and dad need her help, she can adjust her life when that happens. If she doesn't have HD, she has no reason not to go. She loves Felix. She can't bear the thought of losing him.

'Yeah, I think I would.'

A nervous thrill rushes through her after hearing herself voice her truth aloud, and a stupid smile spreads across her face.

'Okay, and now the other possibility. What if you find out you're gene positive?'

231

And just like that, her smile retreats. The nervous thrill is shuttled into memory.

'I dunno. I feel like not going and breaking up with him would be the right thing to do.'

Eric nods.

'So you think that's what I should do?'

'No, no, I'm just listening, understanding your thoughts.'

'What would you do?' asks Katie.

'I can't answer that for you. I'm not in your shoes.'

Katie looks down at her feet. She's wearing black Toms.

'Plus, I don't think Felix would want to live with me,' says Eric.

'Very funny.'

'You don't have to be a martyr, Katie. If you're gene positive, you could have fifteen to twenty years with no symptoms. That's a long time. A lot of things can change in that amount of time. There's plenty of real hope in the research being done. We could have a really effective treatment or cure by then.'

Fifteen to twenty years. Enough time to hope for JJ and for her, Meghan, and Patrick if they're gene positive. Too late for her dad.

'It'd be a shame to end an important relationship, to cut a man you love out of your life because of a disease that, if you're going to get it, won't even interfere with your life for maybe another decade or more. Maybe there's a cure in ten years, and HD will never interfere with anything. And then you gave up Felix and Portland for nothing.'

'Sounds like you're trying to convince me to get the test.'

'No, I didn't mean for you to hear that. I'm not here to influence your decision either way. I'm here to help you process the potential impact of every possible outcome. I'm just trying to paint a picture for you, to show you that your life doesn't have to stop or go off the rails if you take the test and find out it's positive.'

'Yeah, but it still doesn't seem fair to Felix,' says her Irish Catholic guilt.

'Not to be a downer here, Katie, but you're really young. You're only twenty-one. I know you guys are in love, but chances are, you two don't end up happily ever after, together forever. Chances are, you'll love a few more guys before it all works out. And none of that has anything to do with HD. It's just life.'

She's not realistically thinking about marrying Felix, but, to be honest, in the back of her mind, just for fun, she's trying on gowns. And Felix would look so totally hot in a black tux. It could happen. Her mom was married with three kids when she was Katie's age. She wonders what her chances are of ending up with Felix. Probably not as likely as her chances of getting Huntington's.

'Have you been in love before?' asks Katie.

'Yeah,' says Eric, hesitating, as if he has more to say but is unsure of whether it's appropriate to share it. 'I've loved three women. Really loved them, but none of them lasted. Relationships are hard. At least they are for me.'

'This is so weird. I mean, I don't really know

you, and we're talking about stuff I don't talk about with anyone.'

'That's my job.'

'Oh,' says Katie, visibly deflated.

'I didn't mean that it's not personal. We're sharing really intimate stuff here. I get what you mean. You can't really make this kind of decision without rolling up your sleeves, stripping off the armor, and going in deep.'

'Which decision? Moving to Portland with Felix or taking the test?'

'Both.'

Katie nods. Eric waits. The air between them swells with a sticky silence.

'One thing we didn't talk about last time when we went over the genetics that you should know. Remember we talked about the expanded HD gene. Thirty-five or fewer CAG repeats is a negative result and means you won't get HD. Forty or more CAG repeats means you will definitely get HD. Well, the test isn't completely black-and-white. There's a gray area.'

Eric pauses. Katie's stomach tightens, and she braces herself. She has no idea what he's about to say, but her intuition is sounding every alarm.

'If you have thirty-six to thirty-nine repeats, it's a result I can't interpret. This is called a reduced penetrance allele. This is the gray area. With thirty-eight or thirty-nine, you probably have a ninety percent chance of getting HD in your lifetime if you live long enough. It's probably around seventy-five percent if you have thirty-seven CAG repeats and fifty percent for thirty-six repeats, but none of this is exact. We can't really say for sure when the number is between thirty-six and thirty-nine.'

He waits, exploring Katie's face for how this new information is landing in her. It landed like a fuckin' drone attack. She never saw it coming. It was a big fat lie of omission. A bait and switch. She's so pissed, she can't even find the words. She takes a deep breath. There they are.

'So let me get this straight. I could take the test and get an answer that's not an answer.'

'Unfortunately, yes.'

She can't believe it. This can't be right.

'So I could go through all this bullshit, decide I want to know, and then if the result is gray, I'll essentially still be at fifty-fifty.'

'Yes.'

'Well, that fuckin' sucks.'

'It does. But it's the best we have.'

'You should've told me on our first date.'

She hears what she just said. She's too pissed to blush.

'I mean appointment.'

'I know. I'm sorry. Sometimes, I find it's too much information to lay out on the first visit. Has any of this helped?' asks Eric.

It did right up until everything went gray.

'I dunno.'

'You don't have to decide anything today. But if you want, we can walk down to the lab, have your blood drawn, and sent for the test.'

'And then I'll find out if my CAG count is black, white, or gray.'

'Yes. And in four weeks, if you still want to know, you can come back, and I'll tell you your

235

results. Here's how that visit will go down if you decide to go through with it. You and *the person you bring to support you* will be called in from the waiting room. I won't know your results before you come in, so whatever my face is doing when you first see me means nothing. If I smile or look distracted or whatever, it doesn't mean anything. I'll ask you whether you still want to know. If you say yes, then I'll open your envelope, read your results, and then tell you the news.'

She tries to picture them in this same office in four weeks. Eric has a white envelope in his hand. He opens it. And the winner is . . .

'So what do you want to do? Do you want me to escort you to the lab for a blood draw?'

Truth or dare, little girl. What'll it be?

'Hope is the thing with feathers
That perches in the soul
And sings the tune without the words
And never stops at all.'

'Fuck it. Yeah, let's do it.'

19

Katie is heaving deep, wild sobs as she scribbles over another word with a black Sharpie. She's frantic yet determined to be thorough, to destroy every letter. She pushes hard against the wall, stabbing at the words as if she were holding a knife instead of a pen, wanting to kill them all, and she's frustrated with the impotence of the soft, fine tip.

She presses harder, as hard as she can muscle, ignoring the burning ache in her right shoulder, annihilating every lying word. She draws over each letter until it's unrecognizable, eliminating the evidence of what she once believed in. She believes in nothing now. Her bedroom is chilly, but she's a furnace fueled by anguish, hot from feverish exertion and the enormity of the job, the front of her shirt damp with sweat and tears.

Finally, she's inked over every last letter. No more quotes. No more false hope. She steps back. Her bedroom walls are covered in black, jagged, outraged explosions, like an artist's abstract interpretation of war. Her walls are at war. A better reflection of her reality, she thinks.

She catches her reflection in the mirror over her dresser. Her cheeks are stained with mascara, twin black streaks running the length of her face. An impulse seizes her, impossible to resist, and she takes the Sharpie to her skin, tracing the mascara trails, running the indelible black marker from eye to jawbone, up and down, up and down. She studies herself in the mirror without expression.

With the marker still in her hand, she scans the rest of her room to see whether she's done. She finds one more thing. She stands on her bed at the headboard and attacks a peaceful meadow of white space, a stretch of wall yet unaffected by the black war. She writes the letters *CAG* over and over in a horizontal line until there are forty-seven. Forty-seven CAGs.

The number of CAG repeats dancing inside the mind of her only sister.

⋆   ⋆   ⋆

She couldn't sleep in her room after that. She's been staying with Felix for the past three days. She couldn't face what she'd done or even Meghan just yet. To say that Felix is worried is an understatement. He actually took two sick days off from work to stay with her. She sank into his bed and didn't move for much of anything. He brought her food, which she ate, but only because he insisted. He wiped a facecloth soaked in rubbing alcohol on her cheeks until her skin was raw and finally clean. She slept and cried and stared at his walls.

Innocent, neutral, gray-green walls. He has a giclée print of Rockport Harbor, a cheerful image in bright Crayola eight-pack colors. Red, yellow, and orange buoys. A green boat. A blue sky. There's the photograph Felix took of the USS *Constitution* at sunrise, the historic warship in the foreground, the modern city in the background, black and silver lines against a blushing sky. Finally, there's a black-and-white woodblock print of the New York City skyline, Felix's hometown, a place Katie has never been. His walls comforted her, providing refuge from the walls of her bedroom, of blotted-out lies and a deadly DNA recipe, from the invisible walls surrounding and closing in on her and her family, threatening to crush them all.

She's living in a horror movie, and this hideous monster is on a rampage, tearing through the O'Brien family tree, chopping off branches and tossing them into the chipper. And the beast won't be satisfied until there's nothing left but a stump, the only evidence of their existence to be traced by her mother's grief-stricken finger along the concentric rings.

First her grandmother and her dad. Then JJ. Now Meghan. Meghan's going to get HD. She imagines Meghan with chorea like her dad has, unable to dance, and it shreds Katie's insides. She closes her eyes, but she can still picture Meghan with chorea, and Katie wishes her imagination would go blind. Meghan's going to die with HD. Katie can't imagine her life without Meghan. She can't. She won't.

For three days, she found refuge in Felix's bed, snuggled under a heavy blanket of guilt and shame. She's been treating time like an easy, abundant commodity, something she could cavalierly afford to waste. Underneath Katie's petty jealousy of her older sister, there's an honest admiration and respect she's been aching but unable to express. Behind the constant comparison and competition, there's the memory of friendship and sisterhood she misses. Outwardly, Katie's shown Meghan mostly hostility and resentment for several years. But inside, beneath the armor that has so effectively kept them apart, there's love.

In truth, Katie has longed to be close with Meghan for years, but taking responsibility for her role in their rift and raising her hand to go first felt too daunting. She's such a coward. Instead, she's procrastinated, content to stay in the familiar habit of envying Meghan, believing her mind's invented story of the sister who got everything and the sister who got nothing, playing the role of Meghan's opposite and adversary, the victim. She assumed she had forever to fix things between them. And now, like her dad and JJ, Meghan is HD positive.

It's time to let this shit go.

Today, Katie rejoined the world. She taught her nine thirty Vinyasa class and then took Andrea's Hour of Power at noon. It felt good to move, to go through the motions of a regular day. Hearing the familiar cues and moving through the asanas began stitching her back together.

She's almost home now, climbing the stairwell to her apartment. It smells of fresh paint. The door to her bedroom is partly open. She sees a paint-splattered drop cloth on the floor through the crack.

She pushes the door open and stops on the

threshold, stunned. Meghan is standing there, holding an uncapped Sharpie. She turns to face Katie. She's smiling.

The black explosions and the forty-seven CAGs are gone. Her room has been repainted a robin's-egg blue, Katie's favorite color. To her amazement, every quote is back on the wall in roughly the same location where it had been, now in Meghan's handwriting.

'Don't be mad,' says Meghan.

'How?' asks Katie. 'You have them all. You put everything back.'

'I sometimes sit on your bed when you're not home and read your walls. I have for a long time, even before all this. The quotes help me, and I really need them now.' She pauses. 'I think you do, too. Please don't give up on me.'

Meghan walks over to her sister and folds Katie into her arms. Katie hugs her back, overwhelmed with relief, gratitude, and love. Their estranged bodies fit together easily, their embrace a favorite memory. Katie steps back and wipes her eyes.

'I won't. I promise,' says Katie. 'I miss you, Meg.'

'I miss you, too.'

'I didn't know you valued or even noticed any of this. Actually, I thought you thought my yoga quotes were stupid.'

'Where did you ever get that?'

'I dunno. You guys always tease me about the juice cleanses and the chanting and the Sanskrit words.'

'It's mostly JJ and Patrick who tease you. We

don't mean anything by it.'

'Yeah, but you've never even been to one of my classes.'

'I didn't think you wanted me to. You've never asked me to come, and I assumed that meant you didn't want me there.'

Katie's been waiting for Meghan to attend one of her classes, and when this never happened, she assumed Meg thought yoga was beneath her, that Katie was beneath her. And all this time, Meg's been waiting for an invitation.

'I definitely want you there,' says Katie.

'Then I want to go.'

'It's not that big a deal. My classes aren't exactly *Swan Lake*.'

'It's a huge deal. You're a yoga teacher. That's so cool. I'd love to take one of your classes. But the only pose I know is Dancer's. I'll probably make a fool of myself.'

Katie shakes her head, smiling. Meghan's never made a fool of herself in her life. Katie thinks about HD, about her dad stumbling, falling, grimacing, dropping things, looking like a fool to anyone who doesn't know what he has. Meghan's future.

'I'm so sorry, Meg.'

'It's okay. It's not like I'm dying tomorrow.'

'No. I know. I meant, I'm sorry for being such a jerk to you for so long.'

'Oh. Me, too.'

'I wish I didn't waste so much time.'

With the Sharpie still in her hand, Meghan walks back over to the wall and finishes the quote she was replacing when Katie walked in.

'Being deeply loved by someone gives you strength,
while loving someone deeply gives you courage.'
— Lao Tzu

'Let's start from today. Okay?'
Katie nods. 'Wait, what's this?' she asks, pointing.

'Stay in the fight.'
— Boston Police Department

'That's from Dad,' says Meghan. 'There are a couple more additions.'
Katie's eyes travel the perimeter of her room until they land on the wall just over her mirror. She laughs, and Meghan laughs readily in response, knowing what Katie is reading.

'These demons don't know who they're fucking with.'
— Patrick O'Brien

And then there is her mom. The lengthiest quote in the room, written in cursive above her headboard where the deadly chain of CAGs had been three days ago. The prayer of St. Francis.

Lord, make me an instrument of Thy peace;
Where there is hatred, let me sow love;
Where there is injury, pardon;
Where there is error, truth;
Where there is doubt, faith;
Where there is despair, hope;
Where there is darkness, light;
And where there is sadness, joy.

O Divine Master, Grant that I may not so
 much seek
To be consoled as to console;
To be understood as to understand;
To be loved as to love.
For it is in giving that we receive;
It is in pardoning that we are pardoned;
And it is in dying that we are born to eter-
 nal life.

'Thank you, Mom,' Katie whispers when she finishes reading. She's moved by the divine wisdom of this entire prayer, but five particular words sing like a choir in the center of her heart.
Where there is despair, hope.

PART III

The progression of Huntington's disease typically runs ten to twenty years and can be divided into three stages. Early-stage symptoms typically include loss of coordination, chorea, difficulty thinking, depression, and an irritable mood. In middle-stage, planning and reasoning difficulties worsen, chorea becomes more pronounced, and speech and swallowing are compromised. In late-stage HD, the affected person is no longer able to walk, talk intelligibly, or move effectively and is completely dependent on others for care and the activities of daily living. The person with HD retains comprehension, memory, and awareness throughout all stages. Death is most often caused by complications of the disease, such as choking, pneumonia, starvation, and even suicide.

Despite the fact that the genetic mutation, the singular cause of HD, has been known since 1993, there are still no effective therapies that prevent or slow the progression of the disease.

Huntington's disease is commonly called a family disease. Due to HD's autosomal dominant inheritance and protracted course, parents, siblings, children, and even grand-children within a single family might all experience different stages of the disease at the same time. Often as one generation is nearing end-stage, the next generation begins.

20

The smell of Sunday supper permeates their bedroom. Joe can't identify what boiled animal or vegetable he's detecting, and it's not actually an appealing odor, but it triggers his hunger anyway. He stands in profile in front of the mirror and pats his relaxed stomach, now flattened to the shape it used to temporarily take when he sucked it in as far as he could. His love handles and gut are gone. His physical therapist told him he needs four to five thousand calories a day to maintain his weight. Even with medical permission to eat all the donuts and pizza he wants, he's rapidly shedding pounds. Constant fidgeting burns calories.

Joe's just arrived home after a day shift. Changing into civilian clothes, he's removed his gun belt and pants, but he's stuck in his shirt. His fingers are flicking, playing Mozart on an invisible flute over the buttons of his uniform shirt, ignoring Joe's commands, refusing to cooperate. He's concentrating on his fingers as if he were aiming to thread the world's smallest needle, trying to will his thumbs and index fingers to work the simple buttons, but no amount of focus will stop them from goofing around. Heat is building inside him, and he's holding his breath, losing patience, about to rip the goddamn shirt in half.

'Joe! Supper!'

Fuck it. He'll change later. He throws on a pair of gray sweatpants and walks into the kitchen.

The table is set, and everyone is gathered around it but Katie. Colleen's chair is pushed back a considerable distance from the table to make room for her enormous pregnant belly. Her swollen, socked feet are propped up on JJ's lap. The poor girl looks as if she could pop any minute, but her due date isn't until December. She needs to hold the little bugger in for one more month.

Joe prays every day that their baby is healthy. Ten fingers and ten toes and no HD. But once the baby is born, the decision to know his or her gene status will belong to the baby, not the parents, and the youngest age eligible for testing is eighteen. So they won't know if JJ's baby carries the HD gene until he or she is an adult, and then only if he or she wants to know.

Eighteen years. Joe probably won't be here. And if he is, he probably won't be *here*, living in their triple-decker on Cook Street. He'll be either dead or in an assisted-living facility, and either way, he'll likely never know the fate of his grandchild. Will this cursed disease extend its wicked tentacles into the next, innocent generation, or will this lineage of HD end with JJ? He prays every day that it ends with JJ.

And Meghan. God, he's having a hard time accepting that she's got this monster hiding in her DNA, too. Meghan's going to get HD. It's a bleeding wound in Joe's gut that no surgery can fix, and the pain at times is almost unbearable. He prays, sometimes through tears, that she'll dance into her forties without so much as a whisper of HD. He prays and hopes for all of his kids, and on good days, he believes. But the future weighs on him, on all of them. And the guilt. It's a miracle Joe can stand upright with all the guilt he's carrying.

Rosie places a basket of soda bread and a stick of butter on the table.

'Are we starting without Katie?' asks Meghan as she adjusts the wrap of the black wool scarf around her neck.

'She has one minute,' says Rosie, threatening the second hand of the clock.

Joe takes a sip of what he expected to be water through his straw and is surprised by the tingly, crisp taste of beer in his mouth. He swallows and looks to Patrick, who is wearing a sly grin. Joe winks at him and sucks up another sip. Everyone else at the table has been given a glass jelly jar filled with water. No beer until supper. Joe's 'glass' is an opaque, plastic Dunkin' Donuts to-go cup with a lid and straw. He's accidentally dropped, sloshed, and even flung too many glasses and mugs. Rosie grew tired of picking up the shattered mess, and he certainly can't be unpredictably smashing glassware or tossing hot coffee into the air once there's a baby around, so he now drinks everything out of one of these plastic, lidded cups. At times, it's felt downright humiliating, a grown man restricted to drinking from a sippy cup, but now he's seeing the upside. Beer before supper.

Katie appears on the threshold of the kitchen, looking stiff and terrified. She's not alone.

'Everyone,' says Katie, clearing her throat. 'This is Felix.' She pauses. 'My boyfriend. Felix, you've met Meghan. This is JJ and Colleen. That's Patrick. And my mom and dad.'

Felix smiles and says hello to everyone. He shakes hands with JJ and Patrick.

'Hi, Mrs. O'Brien. Mr. O'Brien.'

Rosie smiles. 'Welcome, Felix.'

Joe stands. He and Felix shake hands. Joe pats him on the shoulder.

'Hey, Felix. Good to see you again. Glad you finally made it to supper,' says Joe.

'I'll go get him a chair,' says Meghan.

'Wait, *again?*' asks Katie, her head swiveling from Felix to Joe and back.

'Hun, I'm your father and a cop. You think I don't know for a second if someone's been coming in and out of this house for the past six months?'

Katie blushes, and her eyes don't know which way to go.

'Why didn't you tell me you already met my dad?' Katie asks Felix.

He shrugs and smiles. 'I was kind of looking forward to this moment.'

'I suppose you did a background check on him,' says Katie.

'Yup. He's clean,' says Joe. 'We'll have to beat that Yankee thing out of him, though.'

'She must really like you if she's bringing you to supper,' says JJ.

'Or she's trying to scare you off,' says Patrick.

251

'Ignore them,' Katie says to Felix. 'Felix works for Biofuel.'

'We know,' says Joe. 'Felix and I are pretty well caught up these days.'

'What? How?' asks Katie, her voice shrill.

'We chat when we walk Yaz,' says Joe.

'Are you kidding me?' asks Katie.

'Sometimes, I just so happen to be on the stoop when he's leaving. Quite early in the morning, most of the time,' says Joe, enjoying every second of this.

Rosie tells Felix to please have a seat and hands him a plate. Rosie's playing it cool now, but the lid completely blew off her kettle when she first found out about Felix from Joe. She took it personally. She's consciously and specifically taught both girls what to look for in a man. He should be a man of faith from a good family, have a steady job, and ideally live in Charlestown. Joe pointed out that Felix is, in fact, all of these things, but Rosie just scoffed at him and simmered.

He knows the fine-print subtext of her 'suitable husband' lessons. Being a man of faith can only mean being Catholic, preferably a parishioner of St. Francis Church. Being from a good family means being Irish. Having a steady job means working for the post office, the fire department, the police, BEMS, the MBTA, or Logan Airport, not for some highfalutin corporate company she's never heard of. And living in Charlestown means born and bred. Townie, not Toonie.

Rosie sits and says grace. Meghan passes a

252

beer to everyone but Colleen. Today's supper is ham, baked potatoes, boiled turnip and spinach, and salad. Joe grabs the salt shaker.

'Felix, do you eat meat?' asks Rosie, holding the platter of ham.

'I eat everything,' says Felix.

'So you thought before today,' says Patrick.

'Don't be fresh,' says Rosie, passing the platter to Felix.

'Ma, I won't be here for supper next week,' says Meghan. '*Nutcracker* rehearsals.'

Rosie nods. 'Okay. Felix, how is everything?'

'Delicious, thank you.'

The ham is rubber, the potatoes are rocks, the turnips are unrecognizable, and the spinach looks more like what Joe hawks up when he's got the flu than an edible vegetable. This young man has some damn fine manners. And he must really like Katie.

'We're gonna have a high chair in here soon,' says JJ, his broad shoulders slouched and elbows tucked awkwardly close in front of him. 'How are we all gonna fit in this kitchen?'

'We'll fit,' says Rosie.

'How?' asks JJ.

'We'll fit,' Rosie says again.

Joe agrees with JJ. He looks at Colleen and Felix. It's time for a change here.

'I'm thinking of taking that wall down,' says Joe, happy with the idea of making room for his expanding family, a high chair at the table, a playpen in the corner, an extra seat for his daughter's boyfriend.

'What?' asks Rosie. 'You'll do no such thing.'

253

'Why not? I could turn that wall into a bar with a nice stone countertop and some stools, open it up to the girls' old bedroom, make that a dining room. I bet you could sit ten comfortably in there.'

'No.'

'You could — that room's much bigger than this room. If we move all the crap out of there and — '

'You're not doing that.'

'Why not?'

'Taking down the wall? Building a stone counter? Are you crazy? You don't know how to do any of that. You'll make a huge mess.'

'Ye of little faith.'

'More like ye of vast experience.'

It's true, his past attempts at home improvement haven't exactly been episodes of *This Old House*.

'I'll get Donny over to help. We could replace these crappy old floors and the countertop, too.'

'I'm handy,' offers Felix. 'I could help.'

'Yeah, I'll work on it with you, Dad,' says JJ.

'I want to demolish the wall,' says Patrick.

Joe offers up his sippy cup, and the four men toast to their new construction job.

'No one's demolishing anything,' says Rosie.

'Why not, Ma?' asks Meghan. 'I think it would look awesome. And you don't use our old room for any real purpose.'

Meghan's right. The girls' old bedroom is where Rosie stores the Christmas decorations that don't stay out all year, boxes of old clothes, and all kinds of junk. They could clear it out, relocate everything to the basement or a closet or give it all to Goodwill. Joe could knock down the wall and give them a proper dining room. The idea excites him. Their kitchen is tired and outdated. It needs to be renovated. This is just the kind of project he needs, something big and manly and meaningful. Something to keep him from going batshit crazy when he can no longer work. He hates to face it, but that day is coming. It's either knocking the wall down or watching Rosie's *Oprah* tapes all day, every day. Rosie's going to have to come around on this. He's going to need a sledgehammer.

'We can talk about it later,' says Rosie.

'Dad, you working another shift tonight?' asks Patrick.

'No.'

'Why you still in uniform?' asks Patrick.

Joe slams his sippy cup down on the table. 'Why don't you mind your fuckin' business?'

Everyone goes silent. The clinking of silverware stops. Patrick holds his beer midair and doesn't move. Katie's eyes are wide, unblinking, her drawn face the color of the baked potatoes. Joe doesn't look at anyone else.

Heat rushes through him. For a fragile moment, he recognizes that his reaction was too big, his anger inappropriate, that he was wrong to snap at Patrick and should apologize, but in a flash, all reasonable thoughts are gone, eviscerated by a screaming, boiling-hot rage.

He pushes back from the table to stand, but the push is dramatic and too forceful, and the chair crashes to the crappy linoleum floor. Joe then stumbles over the upturned legs as he backs up, and now both the chair and Joe are on the ground.

A mocking laugh leaks out of Patrick before he strangles it.

Now riding the back of humiliation, Joe's rage accelerates. He stands, lifts the chair by two legs, and smashes it against the floor. The legs crack off and several of the back spindles break apart. He tosses the chairless legs to the ground and marches off to his bedroom.

He paces and paces, wanting to scream or break something else or rip his hair out or scratch his skin off or throw that statue of the Virgin Mary through the fuckin' window. He paces and paces, and he's praying that no one comes in, that no one he loves steps in front of this burning rage that's tearing through him, that doesn't belong to him. He feels possessed, a puppet strung to the sadistic hand of the devil.

He paces, and the white-hot rage consumes him, the pressure building and blistering and pressing against his every molecule, and he's sure he'll physically explode if the rage doesn't leave him in some other way. He paces, searching for a safe place to send it.

He catches his reflection in the mirror. His uniform shirt. He grabs the shirt at the midline and rips it wide open as if he were Clark Kent called upon to save the world. Buttons pop off and scatter along the wood floor. He stares at himself in the mirror. His face is red. His eyes look crazy. He's breathing fast and hard through his mouth, fogging up the mirror. There is no

Superman *S* on his chest. Just a Kevlar vest over a Hanes white T-shirt over an ordinary man.

He removes his uniform shirt, throws it to the floor, and sits on the bed. He's cooling down. His rapid breathing is slowing, and he can feel the red draining from his face.

Rosie steps into the bedroom and approaches him as if she were dipping a toe in the water's edge at Revere Beach in May. He meets her eyes and then lowers his to the floor, landing on a button.

'Sweetie,' says Rosie. 'I just called Dr. Hagler. I think we need to up the dose of your Seroquel.'

Joe sighs and stares at his fallen button. As a police officer, self-control is vital to everyone's safety. Every cop he knows is a control freak. He doesn't know whether the job made them this way, or whether they were all drawn to law enforcement because they already possessed this trait. Either way, cops need to be in control.

Joe is out of control. More and more, HD is at the wheel, and Joe is sitting handcuffed in the backseat. He hates pills. *Hates* them. The Seroquel dampens his HD temper, but it also dampens everything else. He feels sapped on these pills, as if his body's been dipped in molasses, and even his thoughts are submerged too deep for him to bother with the effort of dredging them out. But he hates sitting helpless in the backseat more, and he can't muscle HD out of the driver's seat on his own.

'Good idea,' says Joe. 'I'm sorry, darlin'.'

Rosie sits next to him on the bed. 'It's okay. I know.'

257

He leans against her, and she hugs him. He kisses the top of her head and hugs her back. As he holds Rosie in his arms, his breathing returns to normal, and any residual anger drifts away. He's back. He kisses her head again and exhales in her embrace, grateful for Rosie's love and patience.

But Joe worries. His HD is going to get worse. How much love and patience can one person have? Even a saint like Rosie might not possess a reserve deep enough to stand up against HD, to put up with this escalating madness for years. At some point, the Seroquel dose can't go any higher. He can live without effective meds, but he can't imagine a life on this earth without Rosie's love and patience. He kisses her again and prays she's got enough in her.

21

The sky is clouded over, and the morning light is dull. Joe and Katie are walking Yaz. This is more of an expression than actual description these days. Yaz is old. He's recently lost the mojo in his scamper and doesn't have the stamina to walk up the steep hills of Charlestown. So Katie carries him, tucked in the crook of her elbow like a furry football, and Joe and Katie walk.

It's Wednesday, and Joe has the day off. Katie doesn't teach until noon. The chilly, damp November air is harsh and unwelcome against the exposed skin of Joe's face and hands. They haven't seen any joggers or mothers pushing strollers or even any other dog walkers. Town feels oppressively quiet today, and the dreary, subdued mood of the neighborhood seems to permeate father and daughter. They haven't shared a word since they left the stoop.

They reach Doherty Park, and Katie releases Yaz to the ground. Yaz sniffs the grass, investigates the empty benches, and takes a whiz against the trunk of a tree. Murphy's sitting in his spot on the far bench, holding court for at least a dozen pigeons clustered at his feet.

'Hey, Mayor,' calls Joe. 'What's new?'

'New York, New Jersey, New Mexico.'

Joe chuckles. He's been chatting with Murphy at this park for years and doesn't know a damn real thing about him. Still, Joe looks forward to these amusing if inconsequential exchanges and finds comfort in Murphy's consistent presence, a soldier at his post. One of these days, Joe will stroll through this park and Murphy won't be here. Joe imagines the pigeons gathered beneath the bench, waiting, expectant, hungry, and then simply gone, relocated to another park, devoted to some other kind soul with time and bread. Joe sighs, watching Yaz amble through a pile of gold and brown leaves. Here every day and then one day gone, for Murphy, for Yaz, for Joe. For Katie. And the pigeons don't give a shit about any of them.

'Hey,' Joe says to Katie. 'I'm sorry about losing my temper in front of Felix.'

'That's okay.'

'That wasn't really me.'

'I know, Dad.'

'Hope I didn't scare him off.'

'No, it's good. He should see what this thing looks like. He should know what he's getting into.'

Joe flashes to a memory of his mother's bony, contorted body, seat-belted into a wheelchair in her room at Tewksbury State Hospital, and wonders whether even Katie knows what she's getting into.

'He seems like a good man.'

'He is.'

'I like him.'

'Thanks, Dad. Me, too.'

A young woman walks briskly toward them on the path with her leashed dog, a black Lab. The woman seems to be fixated on Joe, her intent

260

and trajectory aimed directly at him, but when she's close enough to make actual eye contact, she looks away. Her dog veers off the path to check out Joe and Katie on the grass, wagging its tail as it sniffs their shoes.

'Guinness, come!' the woman says, yanking the leash.

She walks right past Joe and Katie, her eyes glued to the horizon. She doesn't smile or nod or say hello. Katie's posture stiffens, visibly defensive or embarrassed or both. Joe doesn't ask.

He's generally not aware of his chorea on his own. It's somewhat like pen tapping or foot jiggling or knuckle cracking or any other number of annoying physical habits normal people have that they might not be conscious of until someone asks them to stop. But it's actually more than simple obliviousness. Dr. Hagler says he's got something called anosognosia, which as far as Joe can tell is just a fancy medical word for clueless. It seems in addition to the slew of symptoms he's already got, HD is crawling into his right hemisphere, causing anosognosia, stealing his self-awareness. So he doesn't know he's moving when he's moving. He sees his lurching limbs and facial contortions through the mirror of the guarded, unforgiving stares of strangers. Then he knows.

At first they stare, curious, trying to figure him out. Is he drunk? Mentally impaired? Is he harmless or violent? Is he contagious? Deranged? Before they get too close, they decide their best course of action is to look away, to pretend not to see the revolting display of human disability before them, and they move along as quickly as possible. To the uneducated or unloving eye, Joe is horrifying, unacceptable, and then invisible.

Joe thinks about JJ and Meghan, about strangers and even friends and neighbors looking at his kids with this kind of contempt and disgust, and it makes him want to sit down next to Murphy on the bench and cry. This is what happened to his mother. Everyone assumed she was a drunk. She did drink, but Joe believes a more plausible chain of events now. She probably drank to cope with what was happening to her without her permission or control, to hide from the hideous changes in her mind and body that she had no explanation or name for, to anesthetize herself against the cruel judgment in her neighbors' eyes and the fear in their footsteps as they walked away.

He sighs. A white puff of vapor dissolves into the gray morning. Katie's staring at the ground with her arms crossed.

'So, where are you at with the genetic testing?' asks Joe.

'I did the first two appointments, so I can go anytime now to find out, but I'm not sure I want to know.'

Joe nods. He's not sure he wants to know either. He slides his right hand into his front pocket and finds the quarter, the same one he's been carrying since St. Patrick's Day. He's been careful not to lose or spend it. He likes reading the words beneath George Washington's chin, as if they were a personal message meant for him. *In God We Trust*. The year on the quarter is 1982, the year his mother died. He holds that quarter in his hand every day, rubs it between his thumb and finger, and prays for no more Huntington's. Patrick, Katie, his unborn grandchild. No more. The quarter is his superstitious symbol of hope, but his need to touch it and wish for fewer than thirty-six CAGs has become almost a compulsion. He fingers the quarter now, concealed inside his pocket, smooth and worn.

Please, God, no more Huntington's.

'Felix is moving to Portland,' says Katie.

'Maine?'

'Oregon.'

'Oh. When?'

'Not sure yet. Probably sometime in the next six months.'

Six months. Joe looks over at Murphy. One day here, the next day gone.

'Are you thinking of going with him?'

'I dunno. Maybe.'

Joe nods, working through what that would mean.

'Would you live with him there?'

Katie hesitates. 'Yeah.'

Well, that can't happen. Rosie's already a wreck. If Katie moves to Portland with Felix, Rosie might have a legitimate nervous breakdown. She's already convinced that she's going to lose everyone. Her husband has Huntington's, and two of her kids are definitely HD positive. Patrick's hardly ever home. Never mind that

Felix isn't Irish Catholic and what the neighbors would think; if Katie leaves, Joe's not sure Rosie could handle the void. She'd protest Katie moving to Somerville, never mind the other side of the country. Portland might as well be a city on the moon. It would feel like losing her daughter, like a death. With all that Rosie faces losing, Katie leaving home and living with a man out of wedlock would create an unnecessary pain, an avoidable suffering that need not be inflicted.

Joe has to convince Katie to stay, but he's unsure of how to approach her. It's an odd transition as a parent, being a father to his baby girl who is now a young woman. Katie was just a cute little kid, Meghan's happy-go-lucky side-kick, a blink ago. Back then, it was his right and responsibility to tell her what to do. Brush your teeth. Go to bed. Do your homework. Don't talk to your mother that way.

Don't move to Portland with your boyfriend.

He's not sure he still holds the authority to make this kind of forbidding demand without meeting overt rebellion. It's going to require a softer touch.

'Hey, you know I like Felix, and I'm all for trying on the shoes before you buy them, but you know living in sin would make your poor mother crazy.'

'Yeah, I know.'

'And living all the way across the country with all that's going on, to not have you around. You really haven't known him that long. Maybe you could go a little slower, try things long distance at first, do Skype or Facebook time or whatever you kids do.'

'Yeah, I could, but he doesn't want to do long distance.'

'Well, don't let him pressure you into doing something you don't want to do.'

'I'm not. I don't know what I want to do.'

She sounds overwhelmed, like she's unsure of so much more than her future residence.

'Would your genetic test results influence your decision?'

'I dunno. I think that's one of the reasons I'm afraid to find out.'

'Honey, I'm sorry to have to say this, but for the sake of your poor mother and the family, I don't think you should go with Felix to Portland. It's too serious, too fast anyway. It's just not the right time, okay?'

Katie hangs her head and fiddles with the bracelets on her wrist as she studies the ground. Just as Joe assumes she either didn't hear him or forgot his question, she looks up.

'Okay.'

'Thanks, hun. I think it's for the best, for everyone. If you and Felix are meant to be, the two of you will work it out.'

She nods, her face expressionless. Joe exhales, feeling like he just dodged a bullet. That was fairly easy. Katie's in agreement and not upset, and he protected Rosie from more tears. And he's protecting Katie, too. Living with her boyfriend in an unfamiliar city where Katie has no family sounds like a bad plan any way he slices it, even without considering HD. She's only twenty-one. She's too young. Granted, he and Rosie were eighteen when they married, but times are different. They don't know each other well enough. Joe and Rosie don't even know his parents. It's too risky. Katie's got enough risk to deal with.

'And listen, if you decide to find out, I know the genetic counselor probably told you not to bring me, but if you think it's too much for Felix and you don't want to go alone, I'd be happy to go with you if you want me there.'

'Thanks, Dad. I don't think I'm ready to know.'

'Okay. If and when you ever are, I'm here for you,' says Joe, rubbing his quarter. 'And I'm praying for you, every day.'

'Thanks, Dad.'

Joe's got that genie-in-his-gut feeling that sees the truth light-years before his head does. He doesn't want to jinx anything, so he doesn't share his prediction aloud, but he'd bet his lucky quarter and everything he's got that his baby girl is okay.

Please, God, no more.

22

Sleep is a blissfully peaceful respite from Huntington's. When Joe sleeps, there are no involuntary thrashes, wiggles, or twitches. His body lies still in a normal state of slumber all night. Apparently, chorea will only tie on its tap shoes when there's an audience. Even the devil inside him needs a good night's sleep.

The alarm wakes him, and he opens his eyes to a new day. He feels rested, reset, a tabula rasa. Before he pushes back the covers, he's still thirty years old, a young man, ready to attack the day and capable of anything that happens. Bring it on.

Then he stands, and every muscle in his body feels stiff and wound tight, shortened several inches. He's bent over at the waist, groaning, rubbing his lower back, and his right knee refuses to straighten, and he remembers that he's forty-four. He hobbles to the bathroom. He looks in the mirror, and he's definitely forty-four, and he wonders how that happened. Then his shoulders shrug without instruction to do so, and he remembers that he has HD. Shit.

He studies his puffy-eyed morning face in the mirror as if he's meeting this man for the first time. Short, unremarkable brown hair. No sign of balding. Wrinkles at the corners of his eyes and creases like parentheses cupping each side of his mouth. Joe rubs the black, brown, and white stubble on his chin. He has a strong chin, like his father's. The droopy skin of his eyelids makes him look sleepy even when he's wide awake. He leans in closer to the glass and looks deep into his own eyes. Blue, the color of morning sky. His mother's eyes.

He's forty-four, and he has Huntington's. Every morning it's the same drill, the same shocking, soul-sinking revelation. He sighs and shakes his head at the poor bastard in the mirror. The poor bastard in the mirror can't believe it either.

Joe's on for shift 3, evening duty, and has only one necessary task on his agenda to accomplish before then. He showers, dresses in sweatpants, a hooded Patriots sweatshirt over a BPD T-shirt, a Red Sox cap, and sneakers. Patrick is still sleeping, and Rosie has already gone to work.

She left his sippy cup and a plate of scrambled eggs and bacon on the kitchen table for him. He takes the cup and sucks on the straw. His hot coffee is ice cold. He downs the whole thing, ignores the eggs and bacon, blesses himself with holy water at the front door, and leaves the house.

He walks to Bunker Hill Street and crosses in front of St. Francis Church to the top of the Forty Flights stairway. He reads the sign, dedicated to Catherine and Martin O'Brien, no relation.

TO MASS AT ST. FRANCIS DE SALES
DAYS AND NIGHTS
THEIR STAIRWAY TO HEAVEN

Joe stands at the edge with his hands on his hips, staring down the steep, concrete steps to the bottom. It's an intimidating descent, but not as imposing as its misnomer implies. The stairway is actually seven flights of ten steps each. Joe has no idea how anyone got forty flights out of seven or ten or even seventy. Townies aren't known for their proficiency in mathematics.

Joe rubs the palms of his hands together, ready to go. Needing something constructive to do with his anger and fear, Joe's been running these steps every day since finding out that Meghan is HD positive. He's running for JJ and Meghan, to prove that he can, to wear out the demon inside him, to stay in the fight.

He runs down, then up, down, then up. He runs up the seven flights for the third time, and he's got a stabbing stitch in his side. His lungs feel like bags filled with gravel. He skitters down the stairs, and his quads are on fire. He keeps going, running up and down, punishing his muscles, flushing the anger out of his blood.

This is his daily private PT session. Focus, balance, coordination, strength, control. He's even heeding the imagined admonition of Colleen and Vivian, his physical therapist, gliding his hand along the black iron railing as he ascends and descends, just in case. Of course, at Spaulding, he's on a soft, cushy blue mat, and every move he makes is supervised. Joe knows Colleen and Vivian wouldn't actually approve of this activity, railing or not. Rosie wouldn't like it either. Good thing none of them know a damn thing about it.

He'll readily admit that a slip here could be a mistake he'd regret. A fall could result in a broken leg or back, and either would lay him up for a long time. Or he could fall and crack his head. Lights out. Game over. That wouldn't be a bad way to go, considering the options. *Officer Joseph O'Brien died on These Forty Flights, his Stairway to Heaven.* It has an enticingly poetic ring to it.

But he won't fall. He can handle this. Despite the involuntary ticks popping all over him while he runs, he's in control. He focuses on the precision of each step even as he tires, pressing and lifting, each foot landing with a tap on the concrete, creating a steady drumbeat that echoes through his center, inspiring him, cheering him on despite the burn beneath his ribs and the weariness in his legs. Keep going. Stay in the fight.

He's fatigued, sucking wind. He harnesses Patrick's rebellious attitude. *These demons don't know who they're fucking with.* He thinks of Katie and lengthens his breathing, gathering stamina. He pushes up another flight and another, maintaining his pace for JJ and Meghan.

He pictures his mother, strapped to her wheelchair, wearing a bib, a nurse feeding her lunch. His mind runs wild with this memory and others like it, faster and harder than his legs up the stairs. His mother grunting like an animal, unable to speak intelligible words. His mother wearing a helmet while a nurse struggles to get her onto the toilet. His mother weighing ninety pounds. Then his mind's a master magician, and abracadabra, every image of his mother is now Joe. Joe in a wheelchair, Joe wearing a bib and a helmet, Joe being fed and showered and hoisted onto a toilet, Joe unable to tell Rosie or his kids that he loves them.

That last imagined thought chokes the air from his lungs. He runs up the next flight unable to breathe, his heartbeat pounding his skull like a drum. This is his future. This is where he's going, and there's no running from it.

But not yet, he reminds himself. Not today. His lungs insist on air, and oxygen rushes in, feeding his starved muscles. Joe asks his legs to pump harder. They respond. He's not in a wheelchair today. Today, he is alive and well.

A pack of teenage boys gathers at the bottom of the stairway, wearing their tough gangsta pusses and pants hanging below their tighties. Joe will never comprehend what's so tough about underwear. These kids don't have a clue. They glare at him, likely annoyed that he's invading their hangout and repulsed by Joe's chorea, wishing this sweaty, weird old man would get the fuck off their stairs. Joe feels the pinch of embarrassed self-consciousness, but he pushes past it. He's doing this, whatever it looks like, in front of a bunch of punk teens or not. He considers asking them why they aren't in school today but decides to leave them alone.

It's a cold December morning, in the low

forties, but Joe's now steamy hot. He wipes his forehead, slick with sweat. He decides to make a quick pit stop after ascending the next flight to remove his Patriots hoodie. He's panting and pushing up each step, almost there. Then the ball of his right foot misses the edge of the next step and skids out from under him. His heart and lungs jump and stay suspended, weightless in his chest. He's falling. Before he has a chance to think, his hand reaches for the railing. It slides at first and then catches, wrenching his shoulder but saving his body from slamming prone onto the concrete, tumbling down the Forty Flights.

He hangs there for a few seconds, dangling from the railing by one arm, lying on his stomach, feet splayed out several steps below him, waiting for his heart to calm the fuck down. He releases the railing and rolls over, taking a seat on the step. Looking down the length of the staircase, he rubs his shoulder and counts. Thirty-five. That would've hurt. The teenage boys stare at him with flat, uncaring eyes and say nothing.

If Colleen or his physical therapist or Rosie had seen that little stunt, they would not be pleased. But they didn't see it, and he caught himself. He may be a decrepit old man with Huntington's, but he's got the reflexes of a gazelle. Still in the fight, baby.

Woop, woop.

Joe turns. A cruiser is parked at the peak of the stairwell. Then he sees Tommy standing at the top, looking down at him with his arms crossed over his chest.

'Training for the Olympics?'

'Yeah.'

Tommy trots down the steps and takes a seat next to Joe. Joe stares straight ahead past the bottom of the staircase, down Mead Street. The punk boys are gone. They must've heard the siren and taken off. Tommy sighs.

'This isn't the smartest thing you could be doing.'

'It's for my application to Harvard.'

'I'm not going to be able to talk you out of doing this.'

'No.'

'You wanna ride home?'

'Yeah, man. Thanks.'

Tommy offers Joe a hand, and Joe takes it. There's an extra moment in their clasp before they release, an unspoken exchange of respect and brotherhood. When they reach the top of the stairs, Joe taps the Forty Flights sign with his fingers, a promise to return tomorrow.

Keep going.

Stay in the fight.

23

It's early in the morning, not yet six o'clock, and Joe is dressed and ready, sitting in his chair in the living room, waiting for Rosie and the girls. The shades are still drawn, the room dark, lit only by the TV, which is tuned to QVC. Rosie must've been up in the middle of the night again. He'd like to watch the news, but the remote is on the ironing board, and Joe can't motivate out of his seat to fetch it. Two women with high, nasal voices are yammering on and on about the miracle of furniture coasters. Joe hasn't moved a piece of furniture in this house since getting rid of the cribs a million years ago, but the ladies win him over. This innovation is pure genius. And it's only $19.95. He's searching his pockets for his phone when Katie walks in.

She mumbles a sleepy hello and plops herself onto the couch. She's wearing her typical uniform of black yoga pants, UGGs, and a hoodie, but something about her is different. Her face is clean. Joe can't remember the last time he saw his little girl without makeup on, especially around her eyes. She wouldn't agree, but Joe thinks she looks better without it. Less is more. She's a naturally beautiful girl.

He'd like to chat with Katie, to find out what's new with her and how she's doing, but he can't seem to start a conversation these days. He waits for her to throw the first pitch, but she's got her eyes closed. Her breathing is long and steady, in and out, her face placid. Her eyes remain shut. Joe studies her and wonders whether she's fallen asleep. Maybe she just doesn't want to watch QVC. Maybe she just doesn't want to watch her old man.

Damn it. The coasters are gone. While Joe was watching Katie, QVC moved on to the next item, a device that folds clothes. He has no interest in this one. Meghan is still upstairs, and Rosie is in the bathroom doing her hair, a multi-step process that Joe has learned cannot be rushed or skipped over. They don't know where the hell Patrick is, and they're not waiting on him. Meghan appears, looking urgent, bundled in a puffy black coat, a black hat, and a fuzzy white scarf, a pocketbook slung over her shoulder.

'We ready? Where's Ma?' she asks.

'Two minutes,' calls Rosie from the bathroom.

Meghan hovers on the threshold. Katie's still asleep or meditating or ignoring all of them. Rosie finally walks into the living room, the chemical scent of aerosol hairspray blowing in with her like a tornado.

'What's that smell?' asks Rosie, her nose scrunched up, detecting something other than hairspray.

Joe hadn't noticed anything before, but now he does. He zeroes in on Yaz lying at the foot of Rosie's rocking chair, sitting in a puddle of diarrhea.

'Shit,' says Joe.

'Language,' says Rosie.

'Just describing what I'm seeing,' says Joe, pointing to Yaz.

'Gross,' says Meghan.

'Aw, not again,' says Rosie, retreating in a hurry to the kitchen.

Yaz hadn't had an accident in the house since he was a puppy until last week or so, and now it's an everyday occurrence. Yaz lifts his head and meets Joe's eyes, and Joe could swear Yaz is apologizing. Yaz returns his head to the rug, helpless and ashamed of what he's done, breaking Joe's heart.

Katie gets up and squats down next to Yaz. 'Poor baby.' She carefully scoops him into her hands and carries him into the kitchen.

Rosie returns with a bottle of Windex, paper towels, and a can of Lysol.

'At least it wasn't the couch again,' says Rosie, wiping the floor.

Katie returns with Yaz wrapped in a towel. 'What should I do with him?'

'Put him on his bed and let's go,' says Rosie, spraying Lysol and waving her hand through the air.

'Where's Pat?' asks Meghan.

'We're not waiting for him,' says Rosie.

Rosie herds them toward the front door. Pausing in the foyer behind the girls, Joe dips his fingers in the holy water above the statue of Mary and signs the cross. Rosie does the same, then looks up at Joe and smiles.

'Here we go,' says Joe.

And they're off to the hospital.

* * *

They exit the elevators on the fourteenth floor of the Blake Building, and a palpable relief lightens Joe's step as he walks down the hallway behind Rosie. They make their way past the waiting room inhabited with people slumped in their chairs, looking as if they've been there all night. Despite the languorous appearance of its residents, it's a room expecting celebration. The sleepy people here are accessorized with Mylar balloons and stuffed animals and vases of cheery flowers. Nothing like the gateway to hell on floor 7 of the Wang Center.

Rosie stops, and Joe follows her into a room where they find JJ and Colleen sitting upright together in a hospital bed. And there he is. Joseph Francis O'Brien III, swaddled in a white blanket, wearing one of the two thousand mint-green infant caps Rosie knitted for him, cradled in Colleen's arms.

Wasting no time, Rosie makes a beeline for the baby. She hugs and kisses JJ and Colleen, but it's the baby she's after.

'Can I hold him?' asks Rosie. 'I just sanitized my hands.'

'Sure,' says Colleen.

Rosie scoops her grandson into her arms, and her face becomes a memory, a picture from their photo album twenty-five years ago, an expression of uncomplicated joy and love Joe hasn't seen in a long while. Rosie removes the cap and glides her fingers over the baby's bald, somewhat coneshaped head.

'He's perfect,' she says, tears in her eyes.

'Congratulations,' says Katie. 'He's so cute.'

'I wanna hold him next,' says Meghan. 'How are you feeling, Colleen?'

'Okay.'

Colleen's face is without makeup, swollen and splotchy. Her hair is damp at the hairline, happiness and exhaustion fighting for the spotlight in her eyes. She actually still looks pregnant, a significant bump at her midsection protruding beneath the bedsheets, but Joe's not dumb enough to mention it.

'She's a champ,' says JJ. 'Sixteen hours of labor, forty minutes of pushing, no drugs. She tore a little — '

'TMI, JJ,' says Meghan, holding up her hand.

'Thank you,' says Colleen's father, who is sitting in a visitor's chair near the window. 'I know I didn't want to hear that next part again.'

'Sorry, Bill,' says Joe, walking over to shake Colleen's father's hand. 'I didn't see you over there.'

'No problem. I've got three daughters. I'm used to going unnoticed in a room.'

Joe laughs. 'How about the little champ's stats?'

'He's seven pounds, eight ounces, twenty-one inches,' says Colleen.

Joe stands beside Rosie and studies his grandson's sleeping, puffy eyelids, his round button of a nose, his delicate, pursed lips, his dimpled chin, his pink face, his bald cone head. In truth, he's an ugly little thing, and yet he's the most beautiful sight Joe's ever laid eyes on.

Joseph Francis O'Brien. A name now passed down three generations. Joe's at once bursting with pride and wishing they'd picked Colin or Brendan or any of the other fine Irish names on their list, names having no association with Huntington's. Joe hopes his name and an ugly Irish mug are the only two things this baby inherited from him.

When Joe's kids were born, he remembers thinking they each began with limitless possibility. Each pink-headed baby was a blank slate. But now he's looking at his grandson, only a couple of hours old, and he's wondering whether everything is already mapped out, the parameters preset, his future predetermined, written in the stars before his cord was cut. For Joe's mother, for Joe, for JJ and Meghan, Huntington's disease was inevitable, fated before they took their first breaths. How many times will this story repeat itself? A repeated DNA sequence causing a tragically repeated life story, generation after generation after generation.

Birth. Huntington's. Death.

Beginning. Middle. End.

Rosie unwraps the folds of the blanket to reveal the baby's tiny feet, and while she's kissing his toes, Joe is skipping over the baby's entire life, imagining him as a man with Huntington's. Rosie rewraps the sleeping, ugly, beautiful baby and passes him to Meghan's ready arms, and Joe is imagining the baby as a shriveled, not-yet-old man, dying alone in a hospital bed with no one to hold him.

While Rosie fits the green knit cap back onto

baby Joseph's misshapen head, Joe tries to divine the number of CAGs strung together inside there, fearing the worst. *Please, God, don't let him have what I gave to JJ.*

Joe takes a deep breath and shakes his head, trying to rid himself of this overpowering feeling of doom, but it's got the gravitational pull of a large planet. He should feel happy. He looks around the room. Everyone is smiling. Everyone but Joe and the baby.

'Whatsamatta, Joe?' asks Rosie, elbowing him.

'Me? Nothin',' says Joe.

He's got to snap out of it. They're not cursed. Inheritance is random. Shit luck. *Be lucky, baby boy.* Rosie eyes him with suspicion and annoyance.

'Would you like to hold him, Joe?' asks Colleen.

'No thanks,' says Joe.

It's one thing to drop and break a crystal pitcher, his cell phone (he's on his third), many wineglasses and jelly jars, but he'd never forgive himself if he dropped his newborn grandson. He'll keep his clumsy, disease-ridden paws off this innocent baby and enjoy him from a safe distance. Both Rosie and Colleen's father seem relieved by Joe's answer. Joe notices Bill keeping a ready, watchful eye on him. Joe doesn't blame him one bit. A grandfather's protective instinct. Good man.

Patrick shows up carrying a white teddy bear, smiling through a busted-up face.

'Jesus, Pat,' says Meghan.

'Bar fight. You should see the other four guys.'

His right eye is swollen shut. He's got a shiner ripening purple and green under the other, and his lip is torn open at the corner.

'Your lip is bleeding,' says Katie.

'I'm fine. Congratulations,' says Patrick to Colleen, handing her the bear. 'Good job, brother.'

'Look at you,' says Rosie. 'You need stitches.'

'I'm fine,' says Patrick, touching the baby's blanket, having a look.

'You can't be in here near the baby like that,' says Rosie, swatting at Patrick's hand.

'I'm not gonna get blood on the baby.'

'You're already in the hospital. Go down to the ER,' says Rosie.

'Ma, I'm not spending the next twenty hours in the ER.'

'That's not going to close on its own. Don't argue with me. Meg, go with him.'

'Aw, why do I have to go with him?' asks Meghan. She kisses baby Joseph on the head and snuggles him into her soft scarf.

'Because I said so,' says Rosie.

'Fine,' says Meghan, passing the baby to Katie. 'You suck, Pat.'

'See what you have to look forward to?' Rosie says to Colleen and JJ.

Joe watches Patrick shuffling out of the room, escorted by his younger sister, and Joe knows it's time to have a sit-down with his son. Patrick rarely comes home after his shift at the bar, and they have no idea where he goes. They're not aware of a girlfriend. As much as Joe and Rosie aren't fans of his all-nighters and sleeping around, that behavior isn't so extreme for Patrick. It's the fighting. He's been in a number of brawls in the past month, and that's new. Joe thinks Meghan's gene status is hitting Patrick particularly hard. Joe sighs.

Colleen's mother and sisters return from the cafeteria, carrying trays of coffee. There are hugs and congratulations and gushing, and cups of coffee are passed to Bill and JJ, and the room is now a party, loud and crowded.

'I'm sorry, you guys, but I'm really tired,' says Colleen. 'You mind if Joey and I take a little nap?'

Of course, everyone understands. Katie passes baby Joseph back to his mother. Colleen's sisters make a plan to check on her in an hour. Joe kisses Colleen on the head.

'You done good, hun.'

'Thanks, Joe.'

Katie and Rosie decide to go to the cafeteria for breakfast. Joe and JJ begin heading to the main building to check on Patrick in the ER, but JJ asks Joe to join him outside for a few minutes instead. Joe follows JJ away from the General a couple of blocks to a bench where they take a seat, and JJ pulls two cigars from his coat pocket. JJ raises his eyebrows, offering one to Joe.

'Absolutely,' says Joe.

Joe's not a smoker, and he actually hates the nasty taste of a cigar, even a supposedly good one, but he's never passed up an invitation to smoke a stogie. For Joe, the cigar is never the point. Smoking a cigar is all about male bonding, the guy equivalent of shopping or mani-pedis. JJ lights the cigars, and they both take a couple of puffs.

'I have a son,' says JJ, marveling at the sound and truth of the words.

'Yes, you do. You're a father now.'

'It's amazing, isn't it, Dad?'

'It is.'

'Do you remember this moment with me, when I was born?'

'I do. Best day of my life.'

JJ crosses his right ankle over his left knee, swings his arm over his dad's shoulder, and puffs his cigar between his teeth.

'You know I love you and Mom. And Pat and Meg and Katie. And I love Colleen. But I don't even know this baby, and the love — ' JJ clears his throat and wipes his suddenly wet eyes with the back of his hand. 'It's bigger. I'd lie down in traffic for him right now. I didn't know it could get bigger.'

Joe nods. 'This is only the beginning.'

Wait until he grabs your finger, smiles at you, says he loves you, cries in your arms. Shares a cigar with you after the birth of his first child.

And a bigger love swells inside Joe, pushing aside the overwhelming fears of every horrible thing that will and might be, making room for every magnificent thing that is and might be. This is only the beginning, and there's more to the middle than Huntington's. HD will be Joe's death, but his life and JJ's and Meghan's lives and the life of this beautiful baby boy, whatever his fate, is about a million other things that have nothing to do with HD.

Joe puffs on his stogie, hating the bitter taste but loving the sweet experience, soaking in this magnificent moment in JJ's life. The birth of his first child. A son. Joe's grandson.

And then it hits him. This is a pretty fuckin' magnificent moment in Joe's life, too. Right here on this bench with his son on a cold December morning in Boston. Proof that even a life cursed with Huntington's can be magnificent.

'This is only the beginning, JJ.'

24

It's only ten degrees outside. Ten. That's a shoe size, for cripes sake, not a temperature. And the wind feels like an angry woman who won't shut up — relentless, caustic, making an already uncomfortable situation kiss the feet of unbearable. It's got to be *minus* ten with the windchill.

And the snow has just started. Boston is supposed to get two to three inches, not enough to cancel school or release the kids early, but enough to cause plenty of auto accidents, as if the people of this city have never dealt with this shit. Bostonians are no strangers to winter nor'easters and blizzards. It's the second week in January, and they've already endured three major winter storms, each dumping more than six inches of snow on the city. Drive slower, or better yet, stay off the friggin' roads. No one learns. Vehicles will be skidding into one another, careening down the steep, narrow roads of Town, ricocheting off parked cars like pinballs. Joe's favorites are the tinker toy cars, the Fiats and Smart cars, and the old rear-wheel-drive tankers, both kinds spinning in place, stranded in the street, blocking traffic.

Joe's standing in the middle of the road, at the busy intersection of Bunker Hill and Tufts Street, assigned to crossing-guard duty for the elementary school, filling in for the civilian crossing guard who called in sick this morning.

This person could actually have the flu. A nasty stomach bug has been sweeping through the station, knocking anyone who flirts with it down for a week. But Joe suspects this crossing guard, feeling perfectly chipper, checked the weather forecast for this morning and said, *Fuck it. I don't get paid nearly enough to stand outside in that.* Joe's not sure he does either.

He's wearing his heaviest police jacket under a fluorescent lime-green vest, a hat, white mittens, and long johns underneath everything, but it's all useless against this kind of cold. The air is a thousand sharp blades slicing his exposed face. His eyes won't stop watering, and his nose is running its own marathon. Tears have frozen solid between his eyelashes, icicles are accumulating on his cheeks, and snot is crusted on his upper lip. Jesus, even breathing hurts. Every inhale flash freezes the lining of his lungs, refrigerating him from the inside out. His fingers and toes have gone numb. He's a frozen slab of meat directing traffic.

Global warming, my ass. Those polar bears should relocate to Boston Harbor.

The kids waiting on the sidewalk are dressed in a colorful assortment of hats, mittens, coats, and boots, strapped to backpacks printed with superheroes, princesses, or Boston sports teams, holding the gloved hands of parents. Joe stops morning-commute traffic, waving the shivering kids and parents across the street as quickly as possible. He'd normally offer a friendly 'Good mornin'' here and there, a smile for the kids, and many 'Have a nice day's. The parents often go first, saying, 'Thank you.' But it's just too damn cold for conversation today, and no one says anything.

After escorting their children to the front door of the school, a cluster of mothers have accumulated at the sidewalk. Joe waves them across, but four of them remain at the curb. Joe urges them forward with one hand, holding off an impatient school bus driver with the other. *Come ON, ladies.* This isn't the kind of day to be chitchatting or dillydallying outside. They stare at him. He sees them seeing him, but they don't budge. A couple of them are on their phones. Friggin' people can't walk and talk at the same time. Joe gives up and waves the bus on.

A cruiser pulls up, lights flashing, and parks opposite the school. Tommy and Artie DeSario get out and approach Joe. Artie's wearing white mittens and a fluorescent lime-green vest.

'Hey, Joe,' says Tommy. 'Artie's gonna take over your duty here. Give him your cruiser keys and come with me.'

Artie avoids Joe's eyes. Artie's jaw is set and his feet spread wide. He's all business. Parents and kids still on their way to school pause in their mad dash to get inside. Joe feels the eyes of the moms at the curb on him, wondering what's going on. Joe wonders, too. He does as requested, but he doesn't like the sound of this one bit.

Joe gets in the cruiser with Tommy. Tommy starts the engine but doesn't go anywhere. Joe assumes they're headed to the station, only two blocks away, but he has no idea why. He waits for Tommy to say something while his skin thaws in the blessedly warm car. Tommy stares through the windshield, watching the kids and parents crossing the street, now under Artie's supervision. Or maybe his vision is focused on the snowflakes hitting the windshield, the wipers clearing them aside every few seconds.

'So we got several 911s for an officer drunk-directing traffic.'

Tommy looks over at Joe now, sorry to be the messenger.

'Shit,' says Joe. His chorea and anosognosia. Involuntarily moving and unaware of it.

'Yeah.'

'It couldn't have been that bad. It's friggin' cold out there, man. I'm just moving around to get the blood circulating so I don't freeze to death.'

Tommy pinches his lips together and again stares at the windshield.

'It's not just these 911 calls. A lot of rumors are flyin' around the station.'

'Like what?'

'Drugs. Drinking. Some kind of nervous breakdown.'

Joe shakes his head, grinding his teeth, seething. He had no idea people were talking, but he shouldn't be surprised. Police officers gossip more than a bunch of friggin' old ladies. Still, he can't believe that no one had the guts or decency to say something to his face.

'You know I love you like a brother, man.' Tommy pauses and taps the steering wheel. 'I think you've gone as far as you can go here.'

No. No way. Over a little chorea, bullshit rumors, and some bogus 911 calls? It's Mount Friggin' Everest cold out there. Give Artie ten minutes, and he'll be dancing around, doing whatever he can to keep warm. See if Artie doesn't look hammered in ten minutes.

A rage sparks deep inside Joe, in the marrow of his bones, catching fire easily, blazing throughout his body, consuming him in betrayal. Fuck Tommy. Yeah, they agreed that Tommy would be his mirror and let him know when it was time to tell everyone at the station about his HD, but Joe didn't think Tommy would give him up so quickly. Over a friggin' school crossing. Not in a million years would Joe do that to him. Tommy's been like a brother to him, and now he's fuckin' Cain, and Joe's Abel. Fuck it. He doesn't need Tommy's support. Screw his fellow officers, too. He doesn't care what they think. He doesn't need any of them. Joe clenches his teeth and his fists.

He's still got Donny. He and Donny go back to when they were kids, since the beginning. They're Townies. Donny'll have Joe's back to the end.

'This is fuckin' bullshit,' says Joe, staring at Artie through the windshield, trying to Jedi-mind him off balance, hoping to witness a full-body shiver, something.

Tommy nods. 'I'm sorry, man. Sergeant McDonough's over from A1. He's waiting for you.'

Tommy slips the cruiser into drive, and Artie

waves them on, his feet solidly planted on the road, his steady white mitten holding the kids and parents on the sidewalk, utterly unaffected by the cold. And he doesn't look at Joe as the cruiser passes.

★ ★ ★

A15 is a substation with a small, skeleton staff and normally no supervisors. When Joe walks in, he's face-to-face with Sergeant Rick McDonough, who looks unmistakably pissed to be there. Rick has been Joe's supervisor for more than ten years. They have a decent working relationship, but it doesn't extend beyond that. Joe knows he's married with two kids, but Joe's never met them. No one knows much about Rick's personal life. He keeps to himself, never joins the guys for beers after a shift. Rick can be an anal son of a bitch when it comes to procedure, and he's overly concerned with what the media has to say about them.

Joe says nothing, follows Rick's lead into an office, where Joe shuts the door, and they both take a seat.

'You want to tell me why we just had to pull you off a school crossing?' asks Rick.

Rick watches Joe with his thin, gray eyes, both patience and authority held firmly in his posture. His style has always been no-nonsense but fair. Joe looks into the face of his boss and the anger that was coursing through Joe in the cruiser drains, leaving him wrung out, utterly exposed, pinned, and too exhausted to fight his way out of

290

this corner. He thinks, wishing he could have a conversation with Donny first, racing through his options before he opens his mouth.

If he doesn't confess his HD, if he shrugs and gives Rick nothing, as Joe's supervisor, he'll be left with no choice. Rick won't sweep this under the rug. He'll go by the book. He'll send Joe to Boston Medical Center for a urinalysis, and the incident will go on Joe's record. Of course, the urinalysis will come back negative for drugs and alcohol, so if Joe keeps his mouth shut, he won't lose his job. But everyone's going to know he was pulled off a school crossing. If rumors were flying before this, they'll be on a rocket to the moon now.

Joe fidgets in his chair. He glances around the small, windowless room, aware of the closed door inches behind him, Rick's eyes studying him. *I think you've gone as far as you can go here.* Fuck Tommy for being right. Rick still waits, going nowhere, his hands clasped on the desk. Maybe it'll be better if everyone knows. Maybe they'll make accommodations for him. This situation is still workable. Maybe he won't lose his job. His life. Joe blows an exhale through his mouth, summoning courage and any luck God's willing to throw his way.

'I have Huntington's disease.'

A moment passes between them. Rick's thin eyes go blank. Joe stiffens.

'What does that mean?'

They're both about to find out.

25

It's just after noon the next day, and Joe's indulging in a fourth Guinness at Sullivan's. Two men and Kerry Perry are drinking bottles of Bud at the bar by the front window, arguing about the Bruins. The guys are Townies for sure, regulars, Joe surmises by the familiar ease they have with Jack, the owner, but Joe doesn't know them. They're younger, probably started high school well after Joe graduated. Kerry is Joe's age. She was one of the 'hot' girls, a cheerleader whom every guy had a thing for at some point. Joe had an unrequited crush on her just before he started seeing Rosie. She's twice divorced, had kids with both dads. She still looks all right, but there's a coarse edge to her once sweet, soft, girly features and a belligerence in her stance, as if she's been cheated out of something life once promised her. Kerry catches Joe's gaze, and her severely made-up eyes flirt with him, inviting him over. Joe tosses her a brief smile and, uninterested in Kerry or the Bruins, quickly makes his way to the empty back of the pub.

He tucks himself inside a dimly lit booth against the brick wall below the 2004 World Champions Red Sox poster. He'd hoped Varitek and Foulke would improve his foul mood, and they might've lifted his spirit for that hair-thin moment when he first sat down three beers ago, but the boost didn't stick. He can't relate to feeling like a champion or to the unparalleled joy in that beloved memory today. He sucks the dense, foamy head off the top of his Guinness, a sublime moment he typically savors, but, as with the three beers before, it gives him no pleasure.

The dispute about the Bruins is getting boisterous, more passionate than violent. Kerry chimes in, her voice a screeching, whiny alto. Joe sips his Guinness and wishes they'd all shut the fuck up.

Only Donny knows he's here. Rosie thinks he went to work. He hasn't told her what's going on. Tommy knows and Donny knows. Hell, all of A1 and A15 probably know. Bunch of friggin' drama queens. But Rosie doesn't know a thing. He can't bring himself to tell her.

Rick gave him time off until the department physician reviews Joe's medical records, released yesterday from Dr. Hagler. Joe's got an unshakable, bad feeling about what is to come. Joe tips back several gulps of Guinness, aiming for numbness.

First off, there's the Seroquel and Tetrabenezine. According to department policies and procedures, Joe's supposed to report in writing any and all prescription medications he's taking. So he's in violation there, but punishment, if any, would be a slap on the wrist at most. It's the thought of this doc reading the dirty laundry list of HD symptoms, symptoms he'll easily match up with Joe's behavior, that feels like raw meat rotting in Joe's stomach.

Loss of balance, reduced dexterity, chorea. What if Joe needs to use his gun and his hand involuntarily contracts, squeezing the trigger, killing a civilian or fellow officer? What if he loses control of his cruiser by suddenly giving it gas or turning without intention and runs down a pedestrian? Impulsivity, dysexecutive syndrome, which means he gets stymied by complex problem solving and reasoning, and extreme mood swings, what Rosie still refers to as his 'weird temper.' Can they trust Joe to stay in complete control, to remain levelheaded, to follow precise procedure, to protect the people of this city and have the backs of his fellow officers?

No, no they can't. Joe's queasy stomach tightens. He takes another swig of Guinness. It doesn't help.

So what will this mean? Best-case scenario, the doc will probably recommend to the commissioner that they take away Joe's department-issued gun. He'll be relegated to desk duty. He won't be allowed to deal with prisoners or the public. He'll be banned from overtime and detail work. He'll be answering phones and shuffling paperwork. He'll be a friggin' secretary. Desk jobs are typically reserved for officers coming back from an injury. It's a temporary post, a transition back to real duty. For Joe, it'll be a transition out of duty.

And desk duty is his best-case scenario, what will happen if he's lucky. Worst case, they'll ask him to turn in his badge immediately. That possibility churns the contents of Joe's stomach, and he swallows several times, fighting the sudden, embarrassing urge to vomit. Losing his service weapon and badge now. That'll kill him faster than HD will.

Joe downs the rest of his Guinness, despite roiling protests from his stomach. He walks back to the bar, ignores the stares of Kerry Perry and her goony friends, and orders a Glenfiddich, no ice. Back in his seat, Joe brings the glass to his nose, then his lips. The buttery smell. The clean, peaty taste. Still, no joy.

Donny shows up and slides into the booth facing Joe. An EMT, his brother in brown, Donny's dressed for duty.

'You comin' or goin'?' asks Joe.

Donny checks his watch.

'I'm on for shift three, but I gotta check on my mum before. I got some time. You see Kerry Perry out front?'

'Yeah.'

'She still looks good.'

'Eh.'

'So what's happenin' here?'

'Just havin'a coupla drinks.'

'You're a friggin' lightweight. You've had more than a couple.'

'So what?'

Joe's tired of trying to control everything, of staying in the fight. Fuck it. He tips his head back, drains the Glenfiddich, and slams the empty glass down on the table as if he's John Wayne. It takes about a second for him to register the singeing pain tearing down the length of his throat. He grinds his teeth, biting the burn, determined not to sputter or gasp.

'Okay, tough guy. You don't think Rosie has it hard enough dealing with your anger and your breakin' shit and worryin' about her future and your kids without you comin' home shit-faced in the middle of the day on top of it all?'

Joe hears him, but he doesn't want to. Donny's words float in and out of Joe's head, which is now hovering above him, a balloon on a string.

'I get it, OB,' says Donny. 'I'd do the same thing. And you'd be here talkin' sense into me. Arm-curl therapy can't be your plan. Whatever decision comes down at the station, you're not drinkin' your face off in Sully's every day.'

'This is just one day, for cripes sake.'

'Good. Go nuts today. But that's it. I'm just callin' it now. This isn't your plan. I'm not carryin' your sorry drunk ass outta here every day.'

Joe laughs, but then he can't remember what was so funny, and he feels like crying. He rubs his face with his hands and exhales, trying to regroup. Donny waits.

Joe looks across the booth, intent on being pissed at Donny for bossing him, but he can't do it. The bald guy across from him with the busted-up nose and the BEMS uniform is also the kid from kindergarten with the wiffle haircut and the Incredible Hulk T-shirt. He's the loyal pal who played shortstop in Little League, point guard in basketball, and left wing in hockey, who hopped the church fence with Joe and skipped out on confession on Saturdays, who also liked Rosie in high school but stepped aside so Joe could have a shot. Joe looks at Donny, a serious, respectable grown man sitting across from him in Sully's, and he remembers spaghetti and meatballs at Donny's house on Wednesday nights for years, too many blind-drunk Bunker Hill Day parades, standing beside him on his wedding day and through his divorce, watching their kids grow up together.

'What do you think I'm lookin' at?' asks Joe.

'Aside from my handsome face? Desk job for now, probably. I don't think they'll terminate you right off.'

Joe nods, appreciating his friend for not pulling any punches, still wishing for some other possibility.

'How much sick time you got?' asks Donny.

'About ten months.'

'How many years of service you at now?' Donny counts on his fingers. 'Twenty-four?'

'Almost twenty-five.'

'How much pension would you be entitled to?'

'I dunno.'

'If they put you on desk, can you go out on disability?'

'I dunno.'

'Okay, man. You need to look into this shit. Now. It's time for a plan. You gotta make one before they make it for you.'

Joe nods.

'And this definitely ain't the plan,' says Donny, pointing to Joe's empty glass.

'All right, all right. The friggin' horse is dead.'

'You wanna talk to my boy, Chris?'

'The lawyer?'

'Yeah.'

Joe nods. 'Yeah. Text me his number.'

Donny checks his watch. 'I gotta go.' He sighs.

'This time of year is brutal. Yesterday we had three suicides. You wanna ride home?'

'Nah, I'm gonna hang out for a few, then I'll go.'

'Lemme take you home.'

'Go. I'm fine.'

'If I come back and you're still here, I'm gonna kick your skinny ass.'

Joe laughs. 'I can still take you.'

Donny stands and slaps Joe's shoulder. 'Go home to Rosie. I'll come by in the mornin'.'

'I will. See ya, man.'

Donny leaves and Joe is alone again. Although Donny's company was comforting, he also confirmed Joe's worst fears. They're going to take away Joe's gun. Eventually, if not straightaway, they're going to take away his badge. Joe touches the glock on his hip with the heel of his right hand and then places the same hand over his chest against his civilian shirt, where his badge would be if he were in uniform. The thought of losing either is like facing the surgical removal of a vital organ. Taking his gun is cutting off his balls. Losing his badge is excising his heart.

He thinks about what he's missing on patrol duty today, what he'll be missing tomorrow, next week, next year. Standing on his feet for eight hours outside in freezing or sweltering temperatures, getting shot at, missing the final championship games of his beloved sports teams, missing holidays with his family, dealing with lying druggies and murderers and all kinds of crazy shit, being despised by the very people he's risking his own well-being to protect. Who wouldn't want to be done with that? Joe. Joe wouldn't. If he wanted a safe, temperature-regulated desk job, he would've been an accountant.

He's a police officer. Never give up. Stay in the fight. The Boston Police Academy beat those tenets into every fiber of his being. Turning in his gun and badge is giving up, turning his back on who he is. Joe closes his eyes, and every thought in his head finds a seat next to the word *failure*. He's failing his fellow officers, his city, his wife, his kids, himself. Without his gun and badge, he'll just be taking up space, a sack of stumbling skin and bones causing everyone a whole lot of heartache until he's rotting in a box.

This was never his plan. His plan was to work for thirty-five years and retire at the young age of fifty-five, to live the good life he earned with Rosie, to enjoy their grandkids, to earn a full pension that would take care of both of them and then Rosie through old age after he's gone. He can't make it to fifty-five. Not even close. He'll get a partial pension, maybe some disability. Maybe not. He'll use up his sick time and whatever time his fellow officers might generously donate to him. And then what? Rosie will still be a young woman with no one providing for her. And Joe's future medical expenses could cost them everything.

He doesn't want to go home and tell Rosie what's going on. He doesn't want to deliver one more piece of bad news to her world. He can't stand being the source of her pain. And their kids are going through a perverse and unimaginable hell over this. He's spent his life protecting the city of Boston, and his very existence has put his own children in harm's way. Unless medical science comes up with something fast, JJ and Meghan are going to die young because of him. The light in Joe's soul dims every time this reality enters his consciousness, killing him a little every day.

This time of year is brutal. Joe knows exactly what Donny's referring to. It's January, just after the holiday season, a time for family and gift giving and celebration for most, a time of unbearable depression for others. The days are cold and dark by four thirty. Joe and Donny have responded to a lot of suicides over the years, and winter is sadly the most popular season. Joe won't miss that part of his job. Discovering the bodies. Sometimes the body parts. A teenager overdoses on heroin. A mother swallows a bottle of prescription pills. A father leaps off the Tobin. A cop eats his gun.

That last one is how he'd do it, if suicide were his plan.

26

Joe and Rosie are sitting in the law office of Christopher Cannistraro, waiting for him to get off the phone. Chris is Revere's 'famous' ambulance chaser, but he also dabbles in real estate, family law, disability. He's got one of those cheesy commercials airing ad nauseam on daytime television, a close-up of Chris with his gel-slicked black hair and shiny face staring directly into the camera, pledging to fight if you or anyone you know has been injured in an accident. Joe imagines he was aiming to sound sincere and determined, a noble champion of the wronged, but in Joe's opinion, he comes off as a sleazeball.

But Joe would never go to some lawyer he didn't know from Adam. With the exception of district attorneys, lawyers as a category make him uneasy. DAs are on the same side as the police, so they're okay in Joe's book. The rest of them strike Joe as greedy, fast-talking scammers at best. The worst are the public defenders. Joe knows they're a necessary cog in the wheel of justice, but that doesn't keep Joe's blood from boiling every time they get some scumbag off on a ridiculous technicality when anyone with a brain cell knows the guy did it. All that police work wasted because some lawyer with a twisted moral compass in a cheap suit thinks he's the star of friggin' *Law & Order*. Joe honestly doesn't know how they sleep at night.

But Chris isn't a public defender. He and Donny met at Wonderland, used to bet on the dogs and celebrate any winnings together over pizza at Santarpio's. Chris helped Donny through his divorce, got him joint custody, and kept him from getting financially raped by Donny's ex. If Donny trusts him, that's good enough for Joe. He won't need a second opinion.

Chris's desk is cluttered with so many stacks of manila folders, Joe can only see him from the shoulders up. He's wearing a gray suit, white shirt, and blue tie, a pencil balanced on his right ear, reading something on the screen of his outdated, large desktop computer while he listens and loudly 'yah's and 'uh-huh's to whoever is talking on the phone. The bookcase next to Joe is packed with impressive-looking textbooks. Joe wonders whether Chris has read any of them, or whether they're just for show. He suspects the latter.

Joe checks his watch and Chris notices. Chris holds up his index finger and lets the person on the other end know he's got to go.

'Sorry about that,' says Chris, standing and offering his hand to Rosie and then to Joe.

'No problem,' says Joe. 'Thanks for seeing us.'

Chris pulls a folder from the top of one of the piles and shuffles through the papers inside it. He then shuts the folder, returns it to the top of the pile, and taps his fingers on his desk as if playing chords on a piano, a silent musical prelude.

'Okay,' he says finally. 'This isn't my area of

expertise, but I promise I've done my homework and looked into all your options. Here's what you're looking at. You've put in twenty-five years. You're on desk duty now. I don't know how much longer you can stay on, but you need to leave *before* they terminate you. I can't stress that enough. You get fired, you get nothing. And yeah, we have GINA now and could sue them, but you don't wanna spend the time you got left hangin' out with me.'

GINA, the Genetic Information Nondiscrimination Act, makes it illegal for employers to terminate an employee based on genetic information. Of course, it's still perfectly legal for any employer to fire someone if he can't do his job safely and effectively. Someone like Joe.

'No, I don't. No offense,' says Joe.

'Hey, most days, I don't wanna hang out with me either. So you quit before they fire you.'

Joe nods.

'You'll use all of your sick time first. How much you got?'

'Ten months. I can probably get some more from my fellow officers.'

'Then you go out on Ordinary Disability Retirement. You'll get thirty percent pension.'

'*Thirty?* That's it?'

''Fraid so.'

Joe looks over at Rosie, her mouth hanging open and wordless, her face drained of color. He suspects he's got the same dumb expression painted on his. Full retirement is eighty percent. They can barely make ends meet on what he's pulling home now. He hasn't seen a raise in years. Thirty percent. How is Rosie going to live on that? He assumed he wouldn't get full pension, but he was hoping for more than this. Twenty-five years of sacrifice and service, and it only adds up to a miserable 30 percent. Joe doesn't know whether to cry or throw the heaviest law book on the shelf at Chris's slick head.

'Fuck,' says Joe.

'I hear ya. Unfortunately, that's not the worst of it. Here's the kicker. Looking at what's ahead for you healthwise and assuming you'll need assisted living, your entire retirement pension, what little it is, will end up going to a nursing home or the state if you go to a state hospital.' Chris pauses. '*If* you stay married.'

Chris again taps his fingers on the desk, invisible piano keys plinking a suspense-building musical interlude, and waits. Joe scratches his stubbled face and rubs his eyes. He replays what Chris just said in his head, trying to figure out which part was more incomprehensible.

'What are you sayin'?' asks Joe.

'I'm saying the only way to protect your thirty percent pension from being handed over to nursing care or the state will be to get divorced. You need to sign over one hundred percent of your pension to Rosie, deed the house and any other assets to her, too. Basically, we have to leave you with nothing and Rosie with everything. Otherwise, it'll be gone. They'll take it all.'

Joe and Rosie sit in horrified silence. He thought they came to this appointment with his eyes open, braced for any possibility, prepared to

304

make some hard legal decisions about their future. Disability. Power of attorney. Advance directives. Feeding tube. DNR — Do Not Resuscitate. But he didn't anticipate this. Not for a second. He feels completely unprepared, as if he'd been looking out for a train scheduled to approach on the eastbound track and they've just been annihilated by the west-bound freighter he never saw coming.

'No,' says Rosie, her arms crossed. 'We're not doing that. We can't get divorced. There has to be another way.'

Joe takes a moment to process this new information, a scenario he never considered but should have. He nods to himself. There's no friggin' justice in it, but it's the right thing to do. He's not taking Rosie down with him. If getting divorced is how he can protect and provide for her, however unfair and fucked up that is, he's doing it. He refuses to leave her widowed and bankrupt on top of it.

'It's just on paper, hun.'

'Are you crazy? No. This is completely ridiculous. And it's a sin. My parents would turn over in their graves.'

'It won't be real in our hearts or in the eyes of God. I think we need to listen to Chris, here.'

'No way. I'm not divorcing you, Joe. That's just nuts. I think we should talk to someone else. This guy doesn't know what he's doing.'

Joe glances at Chris, ready to apologize for Rosie's offensive comment, but Chris's expression is unperturbed. He's probably heard a lot worse.

'Chris, can we have a minute alone?' asks Joe.

'Sure.'

Chris checks something on his computer screen, then spins his chair around, gets up, and leaves his office, shutting the door behind him.

'Rosie, it's not real. It's just a piece of paper. It doesn't mean anything.' Joe hears himself, and suddenly he's a defense attorney, arguing technicalities.

'Our marriage certificate is a piece of paper. It means something,' says Rosie, her voice pursued by fear and anger.

'Rosie, waking up next to you every day for twenty-six years means something. Raising our four beautiful kids means something. Telling you I love you every day while I can still speak means something. This piece of paper just protects you. It keeps the money I earned for us in your pocket instead of the state's. It means nothing about you and me.'

He can't protect JJ and Meghan. He can't change whatever will happen with Patrick and Katie. But he can do this for Rosie, his beautiful bride, who deserves so much more than 30 percent and a divorce from a husband with Huntington's. No one deserves a husband with Huntington's.

Joe looks down at his hands, at his thirty-five-dollar wedding band, the most valuable thing he owns. They can take his marriage on paper, but they can't have his ring. They'd have to saw it off his cold, dead finger first. He holds up his left hand and taps his simple wedding band with his thumb. He reaches for

Rosie's left hand and holds it in his.

'These stay on. God will understand, Rosie. This isn't a sin. The bigger sin would be to lose the pension and the house and everything to this disease and leave you alone with nothing to take care of you.'

Tears spill down Rosie's pale face. She looks into Joe's eyes, searching for a way out of this dark corner she's being forced into. Joe squeezes her hand, a gesture meant to assure her that he's in that corner with her. She squeezes back, holding on tight.

'Okay,' she whispers.

'Okay,' he whispers back, pressing his forehead against hers. A perverse version of *I do*.

After several minutes of silence, there's a gentle knock on the door and then it opens a crack. 'You need more time?' asks Chris.

'No,' says Joe. 'No, we're all set.'

Chris returns to his seat, taps his fingers on his desk, and waits.

'Okay,' says Joe. 'We'll get divorced.'

'Really sorry I didn't have better news for you guys, but I think that's the smart decision. I'll draw up those papers right away.'

'Then what happens?' asks Joe.

'You'll both sign. We'll get a court date. It's lopsided but uncontested. If the judge has any questions, I'll explain that you have a terminal illness. It'll go through. You'll be legally divorced in' — Chris flips through the pages of his day planner — 'three months.'

Twenty-six years. Undone by a couple of signatures and three months. Joe rubs his chin, digging the pads of his fingers into the rough skin of his face, reminding himself that he's real, that this decision was about him and Rosie and not some other poor slob, some other lovely wife. It's the right thing to do. And it doesn't mean anything.

As Joe goes to stand to fetch the box of tissues by the bookcase for Rosie, his legs wobble, unable to support the vertical weight of him, as if he no longer has bones, and he grabs on to the edge of Chris's desk, catching himself from falling. Even though Huntington's is the reason they're here in this office, he still feels embarrassed to be so exposed, so physically vulnerable in front of Chris, to be the kind of man who won't be able to keep his job or his wife, who literally can't even stand on his own two feet.

And then it hits him. Agreeing to sign their divorce papers does mean something. Agreeing to divorce Rosie means he's agreeing to Huntington's. All of it. They're preparing for the tail end of this beast. End stage. Joe's death. The certain reality of his grim future is a two-by-four to his chest and a steel-toed boot to the crotch. Denial has now left the building.

His service weapon. His job. His wife. His family. His life. He's going to lose everything.

Breathless, his pitiful heart feeling heavy and useless, he wants to surrender, to slip alone into a black tar pit of defeat. But then Rosie's standing beside him, her face still wet with tears, holding on to his arm. She's steadying him, assuring him that he's not alone, and the bones restack in Joe's legs; his heart remembers itself.

Their divorce means something, but it doesn't mean everything. HD is going to take his gun, his job, his dignity, his ability to walk, his words, his life. It's eventually going to take JJ and Meghan. But he'll be damned if it takes Rosie from him. Whatever the Commonwealth of Massachusetts says, whatever a judge or even God decrees, whatever HD takes from him, nothing can take away his family or his love for Rosie. He'll love Rosie until the day he dies.

27

Felix is leaving for Portland on Monday. Not for good. He's only going for the week to help with setting up the new office, interviewing some potential new employees from the West Coast, meeting with the mayor and various people in Energy, Waste Management, and City Planning, preparing for the Big Move.

The Big Move is happening June first, four months from now, and Felix has already begun packing up his apartment. Katie is curled up on his couch, drinking Chardonnay, watching him remove books from his bookcase, stacking them into cardboard boxes.

'You wanna watch a movie?' she asks.

'Yeah, lemme just finish up this shelf.'

'I don't get why you're doing that now.'

'One less thing I have to do later.'

She shakes her head, not comprehending him. If she were in charge of packing, those books might get thrown into boxes four *days* before the move, but not a minute before then. It's not simply that she's a procrastinator. What kind of person wants to live in a living room full of brown cardboard boxes for four months? What if he wants to read one of those books before June? She shakes her head again. She imagines all of her books packed into moving boxes, and her stomach sours. If she were moving to Portland in four months . . . The sentence hurts too much to finish it.

'What do you think about next week?' asks Felix, holding a copy of *Bunker Hill* by Nathaniel Philbrick.

'Whaddaya mean?' asks Katie, playing dumb.

'Are you coming with me?'

'I dunno. I'd have to find subs for all my classes, and it's kind of last minute.'

'Jesus, Katie. You've known about this trip for weeks. You're totally dragging your feet. I think you don't want to come, and you're afraid to tell me.'

She's afraid of a million things right now.

'That's not it.'

'Then come with me. We'll explore Portland together, see what's there. You'll love the microbreweries. We can go hiking, maybe find a cool space for your yoga studio. And we need to look for an apartment. The move is coming up fast, and we still don't have a place to live.'

She winces without meaning to with every 'we' and hopes he didn't see her. He 'we's' her all the time. He's being positive and hopeful, even charmingly persuasive if she's in the right mood, but today each 'we' rubs her the wrong way, a bra strap on a sunburn, a callous assumption on the edge of bullying.

She hasn't told him she's not going.

'I'm okay with you picking out an apartment without me.'

'I think we should do that together. Let's go find a place, and then we can really start imagining our future there.'

The only place she can imagine her future

with any clarity is in a nursing home. And there's no 'we' there.

'I'm not sure I'm coming,' she says, tiptoeing toward the real answer.

Felix stops packing and rubs his bottom lip with his thumb. He has beautiful lips.

'Do you mean Monday or June?'

Katie hesitates. She doesn't want to talk about June. She wants to drink wine, snuggle on the couch, and watch a movie.

'Both.'

Felix pinches his lips. He stares at her hard, as if he's trying to see through her eyes, into her mind or maybe her soul. Or maybe he's trying to see whether he sees Huntington's in her eyes.

'This is about HD,' he says.

'Yes.'

He leaves the books and boxes and sits down next to Katie on the couch.

'What about HD is keeping you from coming with me to Portland on Monday?'

'I dunno.'

'You know you don't have HD now, even if you're gene positive.'

'I know.'

'And you might be gene negative, so all this planning around you having HD someday might be a colossal waste of time.'

'I know.'

'Then come with me!' he says, smiling, trying to persuade her with his dimple. That usually works.

'It's not that simple.'

'You know you could line up the subs if you wanted to.'

She shrugs out of instinct, feeling like a kid in trouble with her parents. When cornered, it's better to say nothing.

'If you get the test results, and it's positive, are you breaking up with me?'

'I don't know.'

Maybe. Probably.

'Jesus. You don't know if you're coming with me on Monday. You don't know if you're moving with me in June. You don't know if you're going to find out your test results. You don't know if you're breaking up with me if you have the HD gene. What the fuck do you know, Katie?'

She doesn't blame him for getting frustrated and mad at her, but she can't stand it. She hangs her head and stares at her claddagh ring, imagining her lonely finger without it. She wants to shrug or say *I don't know* again and avoid him. She'd like to avoid everything — her test results, thinking about June, watching her dad fidget and fall, thinking about HD, being a depressing source of anger and frustration for Felix. Maybe she should break up with him now. His life would be so much easier without her.

Sometimes it feels as if Huntington's is the only thing she knows. Her head is filled with thoughts of nothing else. HD. HD. HD. She looks up at Felix, his brown eyes focused on her, waiting, wanting her, and she wants him, too. And then she's struck in the heart with what she knows other than HD, the unavoidable truth and the courage to speak it.

'I love you.'

Felix softens. He hugs her and kisses her gently on the lips.

'I love you, too. I know what you're going through is terrifying and unfair and really hard. But you have to go through it. Right now, you're just standing still. You're sinking in it. Let me hold your hand and go through it with you.'

Katie nods. 'You're right. I want to do that.'

Felix smiles. 'Good. I love you if you do or don't have the gene, but I'm not doing a long-distance relationship. I'm not interested in seeing you on FaceTime or Facebook. I want to be in this with you, in person. All or nothing.'

'But — '

'I'm sorry, but at least I'm being clear on what I want. Can you get clear for me? For us?'

'It's like you're giving me an ultimatum.'

'I'm *leaving* in *four* months,' he says, his outstretched hand pointing out the cardboard boxes. 'You don't seem to grasp this. I feel like you're deciding not to decide, and then the day will come, and I'll go and you'll stay because you never decided what to do.'

He's right and he's wrong. He knows her so well. She's totally stuck. She can't make any decisions. Does she get her results, or live not knowing her genetic fate? If she gets her results and she's gene positive, does she break up with Felix or stay with him? Does she move to Portland with Felix against her dad's wishes, abandoning her family in their time of need, or does she stay in Charlestown?

If she had to give an answer today, she'd honor

her father and stay. Interestingly, if HD weren't in the picture, her dad practically forbidding her to move with Felix might've pissed her off just enough to send her packing. But HD is smack dab in the center of the picture, and her dad's influence gives her one more valid reason to pause, legitimizing her stagnation.

To be or not to be, that is the question. And so far, the answer has been radio silence. But she grasps that whatever she decides or doesn't decide, Felix is moving in four short months. She grasps this every hour of the day.

'I'm sorry. I don't know what to do,' she says.

'About the test results?'

'For one thing.'

'I think you should find out.'

'You do? You didn't even want me to do the testing.'

'Not knowing isn't exactly sitting well with you. You're living like you've been handed a death sentence.'

'I am?'

She didn't think he noticed.

'Yeah. I think you need to be okay, really authentically okay with not knowing, or you need to find out.'

So true. But which one should she choose? That's the million-dollar question. She spends hours every day internally arguing the pros and cons of either decision. Ignorance is bliss. Knowledge is power. Living in the moment is enlightened. Planning for the future is responsible. Prepare for the worst. Hope for the best. By the end of each day, the tally is either even on both sides or too dizzying to count, and she collapses into bed, exhausted from the effort.

'If it's negative, would you move to Portland with me?'

Katie considers his question as if she's working through a profound and sacred riddle. It's a strange shift in perspective, imagining a gene-negative outcome, free of Huntington's, when so many synapses in her brain have been devoted to practicing the opposite. Then there's her father's voice, the one she's always trusted and tried her best to obey, telling her to stay. Staying in Charlestown. The idea feels like a noose pulled tight around her neck. Staying. She's shackled to a future as predetermined as her risk of HD.

She looks into Felix's eyes and sees an invitation to freedom. Freedom from Huntington's, freedom from the smothering limitations of this neighborhood, freedom to love and grow into who she really is. If she's gene negative, this is her chance. Sorry, Dad.

'Yeah,' she says. 'I would.'

A wide, immensely excited smile spreads across Felix's face. She feels excited, too, realizing what she just admitted aloud, but the thrill is quickly seasoned with fear and guilt. She told her dad she wouldn't go. Leaving would break her mother's heart. JJ and Meghan are gene positive. Who does she think she is, imagining her life gene negative? Why should she be granted such a freedom? Felix hugs her, unaware of the obstinate torment within her, and holds on to her shoulders.

316

'That's progress! Excellent. Okay, so now we know what's holding you back. What about if it's positive?'

Felix's hands suddenly feel unbearably heavy on her shoulders, pinning her down.

'I dunno,' she says, knowing.

'Okay; we can cross that bridge if we find ourselves on it. How about just coming with me to Portland this week? Think of it as a vacation.'

Katie presses her temples with her fingers. She's got a screaming headache. She could use a vacation, an escape. But she could go all the way to Fiji, stay in a five-star hotel situated on a private beach, and she'd still be thinking about HD. There is no escape.

'I really can't.'

'Fine.'

Felix rises abruptly and returns to the bookcase.

'You still want to watch a movie?'

'I don't care.'

Katie watches him packing another box, not looking at her. From what he's told her about his job, she imagines Felix as a powerful and effective manager at the office. Her refusal to see things his way must be making him crazy. But he doesn't look like a man throwing a tantrum, taking his ball and leaving the playground because he didn't get what he wanted. His shoulders are turned and slumped, his eyes downcast. Her heart tenses, her blood pulsing hard against her temples as she understands his face. He looks scared. In all her self-centered fear, it never occurred to her that he could be scared, too.

'I'm sorry, Felix. Will you be going out there again before June? Maybe I could come next time.'

Felix shrugs. A taste of her own medicine.

'I'm just not ready to go next week. I didn't find any subs.'

He says nothing.

'Go pick an apartment without me. I trust you. I'll love anything you love.'

June first is a Monday. Katie imagines waking up that morning, her books still displayed in her bookcase, her clothes still hanging in the closet, her suitcases not packed, kissing Felix good-bye as he leaves for Logan Airport, staying behind and standing still out of fear of being HD positive. She loves him, and he deserves a life that isn't cursed with Huntington's. But what if she doesn't move, she doesn't open her own yoga studio, she breaks up with Felix, and it turns out she's HD negative?

She will have given up everything for nothing.

28

Yaz stopped walking three days ago. Joe didn't have to convince Rosie of anything. She agreed. It's time. Rosie already said her good-bye. She knows this is the right thing to do, but she can't bear to see it happen. Joe thanks God she has baby Joseph to keep her distracted, or she'd be an inconsolable mess.

'Who's driving?' asks Katie.

'You do it,' says Meghan. 'I don't wanna go. It's too sad.'

'Gimme the keys,' says Patrick. 'I'll drive. You and Katie stay here. Me and Dad'll do the dirty work.'

Katie hands the keys to Patrick, and Joe leads the way to the front door, trying to pretend this conversation about driving had nothing to do with him. But he knows he's the reason for every word, and despite his feigned ignorance, he feels shamed and helpless.

Two weeks ago, Joe was asked to turn in his service-issued weapon. Three days later, upon recommendation of the department physician, Rick informed him that they had to notify the Registry of Motor Vehicles that Joe was no longer medically fit to be behind the wheel. Rick then elaborated. If Joe were ever to get into a car accident and hurt someone, a scenario the physician and Rick apparently deemed imminent and likely, and the injured party were to find out that

Joe has Huntington's *and* the Boston Police Department knew about his illness, they'd be liable. Allowing Joe to drive, even off duty, would be inviting tragedy, a huge lawsuit, and a media shit storm. So, Rick notified the RMV before notifying Joe, and the state revoked his license to drive.

With no service weapon and no driver's license, Joe didn't need an interpreter to read the writing on the wall. He officially and unceremoniously quit his job four days ago. And then, as if in an act of solidarity, Yaz quit walking. It's been a fuckin' awful week.

Joe still has a license to carry and legally owns his personal handgun. But he suspects that this license, too, will go. Somewhere, someone has already yelled out *Timber!* and the tree is on its way down.

So Patrick is driving, and Joe and Yaz are in the passenger seat. It's a short distance to the vet's office in Somerville, but they're in traffic and facing at least a half dozen lights, plenty of time for Joe to have a conversation with his son. Joe notices Patrick's knuckles resting atop the steering wheel, cut up and pink, like raw steak. The intention to speak is there, but Joe still sits in heavy silence, patting Yaz's head. It often takes tremendous internal work for Joe to initiate talking, yet another act in the three-ring circus that is HD. He imagines pushing a granite boulder up Bunker Hill, a grueling, painstaking, sweaty task, and he can only squeeze the first syllable of what he wants to say out his mouth after he's reached the peak and gravity takes over the job. The damn rock is finally rolling downhill.

'What's goin' on with you, Pat?'

'Nothin'.'

'What's with all the fightin'?'

Patrick shrugs. 'Bar's been rowdy.'

'Don't you guys have bouncers?'

'Yeah. They've been outnumbered. I'm just givin' 'em a hand.'

'Is that all there is to it?'

'Yeah.'

'We haven't seen you in the mornin' in a while.'

Patrick looks straight ahead and doesn't acknowledge that anything has been said. Katy Perry is singing 'Roar' on Kiss 108. The windows are steaming up. Having Huntington's burns a ton of calories, and in doing so emits a lot of heat. Joe now fogs up every car he rides in. Patrick flicks on the wipers and turns the defroster setting to HIGH. The sounds of rushing air and Katy Perry fill the car. Joe feels himself sinking back into the cozy bed of silence, the conversation fading to black. He has to resist and keep talking, or else he'll find himself back at the bottom of the hill, tasked with yet another boulder.

'Where you been stayin'?' Joe asks, rephrasing in the form of a direct question.

'Here and there.'

'You got a girlfriend?'

'Not really.'

'Then where you been sleepin'?'

'Mostly at this girl's place.'

'This girl's not your girlfriend.'

Patrick shrugs. 'Not really.'

Joe shakes his head. 'You using?'

'What?'

'Are you takin' drugs?'

'Jesus, Dad. No.'

'Don't bullshit me, Pat.'

'I'm not. I'm just drinkin' with friends after work. No big deal.'

'Stay away from that shit, Pat. I mean it.'

'I don't need this lecture, Dad. I'm not doin' drugs.'

'Your poor mother has enough to worry about.'

'Don't worry about me. It's all good.'

The wipers and defroster aren't making enough of a difference. Patrick leans forward and wipes the windshield with his hand, creating a complex web of wet finger streaks on the glass amid the fog. Joe watches Patrick drive, trying to figure out whether he believes his son. He can't get a bead on him. Even sitting right next to him, at arm's distance, it feels as if Patrick is miles away. And still running.

Joe can't really blame him. Patrick's a young man with plenty to run from — the impossible truth of what's going to happen to his father, his brother, and Meghan; the 50 percent chance that it could happen to him, Katie, and baby Joseph; feeling anything real with this girl he's sleeping with; pulling her innocent life into this horrific nightmare; feeling anything real with anyone.

'There it is,' says Joe, pointing. 'Right there.'

Patrick pulls into the parking lot and gets out. They're here. Patrick is standing in front of the car, hands stuffed inside his coat pockets, appearing blurry through the watery, fogged windshield, waiting. Joe cradles Yaz in his arms and kisses his soft, matted head, wishing there were more to do before going through with this. Joe wraps a green fleece blanket neatly around Yaz's frail body. He takes his index finger to the steamed passenger door window and writes.

Yaz was here.

Then he kisses Yaz again and opens the door.

★   ★   ★

Back home, Joe is sitting in his living room chair, drinking his fifth Budweiser, strapping on a comfortable buzz. Yaz's dog bed is empty but for the small discoloration where he used to sleep, and it's surreal that he's no longer here. Gone. Just like that. Joe presses his shirtsleeve against his eyes, mopping up his tears.

He's watching the evening news. They're in the middle of the sports, recounting the Bruins' pitiful loss last night to the Canucks, when Stacey O'Hara cuts in with breaking news.

An unidentified white male walked into the lobby of Spaulding Rehabilitation Hospital in Charlestown just after five o'clock, carrying a black backpack; it was seized and found to contain a fully loaded semiautomatic weapon. The unidentified male then shot off several rounds with another gun he had hidden in his coat, wounding one Boston police officer before being restrained and taken into custody. The gunman's motives are unclear. The officer was taken to Massachusetts General Hospital. His condition is not yet known. We'll bring you more details as this story unfolds.

An electric jolt shoots through Joe's numb brain. He texts Tommy, then Donny. He stares at his phone, his heart pounding in his tight throat, waiting forever. He runs down the list of everyone else. Rosie and Colleen are upstairs with the baby. But what if Colleen dropped by work today for a visit with her coworkers to show off baby Joseph? He texts Colleen.

Where r u?

He texts Rosie.

Where r u?

The news continues, moving on to the weather. Mother-fuckers. It's cold outside. End of story. Go back to Spaulding. *Which officer? What's his status?*
Joe's attention goes back and forth between the blue map of Massachusetts on the TV screen and the screen of his phone, neither communicating a fuckin' useful thing. *Officer in trouble.* Joe can hear the heart-stopping sound of those three radioed words inside his head, but it's an auditory memory from another day. *Officer in trouble.* Joe should've been there. He should be out there instead of sitting in his living-room chair, still wearing yesterday's T-shirt and

sweatpants, a passive witness to the aftermath on TV. A waste of friggin' oxygen.

Joe's phone dings. A text from Colleen.

We're upstairs. Rosie and Joey are napping.

Joe texts her back.

K. Thx.

Joe's phone dings again. It's Tommy.

I'm OK. Sean shot in stomach. In surgery at the General.

Fuck. Joe throws his phone across the room, knocking a porcelain angel off the end table. It lies on the floor, beheaded. Joe's eyes then wander to the left of the body, landing on Yaz's empty dog bed. And then it's all too much for him. Rosie's broken angel, their dead dog, his fellow officer shot and fighting for his life, Joe sitting in the living room, unable to do a damn thing about any of it.

He gets up and marches into the kitchen, and he's stopped cold in front of Yaz's dog dishes on the floor, still full of food and water. They need to be emptied and washed, and then what? Thrown away? Joe can't do it.

He turns and faces what remains of the wall that separates the kitchen from the girls' old bedroom. He began the renovation project three days ago, the same day Yaz stopped walking. At first it felt good to replace one job with another, but almost immediately he found he had no enthusiasm for it, and instead he parked himself in his chair in front of the TV, consenting without resistance to the very life he'd dreaded. So the wall is partially demolished, pissing Rosie off every time she walks in or out of the kitchen, mocking Joe during breakfast and supper.

He stares at the damaged wall, avoiding the TV and the sudden, palpable absence of Yaz, and he feels that familiar, primal rage stretching its long, hairy arms, awakening inside him. The rage clenches its fists, threatening that idiot white male for aiming to kill innocent people, good people who've devoted their lives to the healing of others, people like his daughter-in-law, mother of his grandson. They could've been there.

The rage stands and curses at that idiot white male for shooting Sean. The rage seethes, disgusted with the news reporters who Joe can hear are now talking about Lindsay Lohan instead of giving him an update on the condition of his friend. Sean has to survive. He has a wife, a family.

The rage beats its chest and howls at Joe for quitting his job. It should've been him at Spaulding instead of Sean. He didn't stay in the fight. He gave up. He quit so he could stay home in sweatpants, drink beers, and watch TV. He's not Boston Strong. He's a friggin' coward.

The rage roars deep within him, and an ungodly sound vibrates into every corner of his being, heard by every cell. Joe retrieves the sledgehammer from the broom closet and goes to work on the wall. He winds up. *Slam.* He winds up again. *Slam*. He winds up and falls backward onto the floor. He gets up, swings, and *slam*. The sound of the hammer making contact and the physical experience of each impact are immensely satisfying, better than hitting a baseball with the sweet spot of a bat.

He's breathing in drywall dust, heaving and hacking, swinging and falling, swinging and pounding and falling. *Slam*. Bits of wall crumble onto his dirty white socks. *Slam*. He hears his voice yelling nonsense, his voice grunting, the wall breaking apart. *Bam. Bam. Bam.*

Finally he's exhausted, and Joe drops the sledgehammer to the floor. He rubs his eyes and sits on the bed. The bed? He's not in the kitchen. The room is dark. He's in his bedroom. The walls. There are bashed-in holes all over the bedroom, pieces of bedroom wall all over the bedroom floor.

He counts. Nine holes. Shit. How did that happen?

He staggers out to the hallway. The entire length from living room to kitchen is littered with hammered holes. He approaches the living room as if investigating a crime scene. The room is intact but for the beheaded angel. He returns to the kitchen. The wall is gutted, destroyed.

Joe rakes his fingers over his sweaty face. What the fuck just happened to him? He was literally out of his mind. What if Rosie or Patrick had been here? Would they have been able to talk sense into him and stop him, or would he have taken a swing at them? Would he have hurt them? Is he capable of that?

Joe walks back into his darkened bedroom and absorbs the senseless destruction before him. He was completely out of control. The thought scares the bejesus out of him. He looks down at his hands. They're shaking.

What if Colleen or JJ had walked in with the baby while Joe was in the middle of his rampage? He can't stand the thought of it. He sits on the edge of the bed, surveys the mess, and cries. Rosie's going to kill him.

Somebody should.

His phone dings.

Sean's out of surgery. Condition stable. He'll be OK.

Joe types:

Tiding bed she it there.

Damn autocorrect. Midget keyboard. Friggin' spastic fingers. He's text slurring. He tries again.

Thx. B safe out there.

Joe exhales and thanks God, grateful that Sean is going to survive. Then he sees the vandalized walls, the godawful mess he made, and gratitude is swiftly supplanted by unbearable shame for what he's done, for what he has, for who he is.

He's an officer who's no longer an officer. He's not protecting the city of Boston. He's not protecting anyone. JJ and Meghan will get HD, and it's his fault. Patrick and Katie and baby Joseph, God bless him, are all at risk, and it's his fault. He's never even held his own grandson, too afraid of some unintended, unpredictable movement hurting him. He can't provide for his wife but for a pitiful 30 percent pension, not enough to live on. He's about to divorce her.

He can't protect Boston or his fellow officers or his family. He looks at the holes in the walls. He just smashed the shit out of his own home. He's a home wrecker.

So what's left for him? Wither in a disgusting stew of shame for years in the living room and then the state hospital, some poor nurse wiping shit off his skinny ass every day until he starves or develops pneumonia and finally dies? What's the point? Why put them all through the miserable shame of it all?

Joe thinks of Yaz. He lived a good, full life. And then, when his quality of life drained away, they didn't make him suffer. Yaz's end was peaceful and dignified, fast and painless. Five seconds after the vet's injection, he was gone.

It was the humane thing to do. Joe takes note of the word *human* in *humane*, and yet that kind of 'human' compassion is reserved only for animals, not for people. There is no five-second injection option for Joe. Doctors aren't allowed to be humane with humans. Joe and everyone like him will be expected to suffer and suck it up, to endure zero quality of life while being a burden to everyone held dear until the bitter, gruesome end.

Fuck that.

Joe walks over to his dresser. Police sirens wail outside, stretching, floating, drifting into the distance. Joe pauses to listen. Silence.

He opens the top drawer and removes his handgun, his Smith & Wesson Bodyguard. He removes the trigger lock and holds the gun in his hand. He curls his fingers around the handle, appreciating the power packed into its light weight, the natural fit of it in his palm. He ejects the magazine and eyeballs it. Six rounds, plus the one that's already in the chamber. It's fully loaded. He snaps the magazine back into place.

'Joe?'

He looks up, startled.

'What are you doing?' asks Rosie, standing on the threshold of their bedroom, illuminated by the hallway light.

'Nothing. Go back to JJ's.'

'Joe, you're scaring me.'

Joe looks at the black holes and dark shadows all over the walls, at the gun in his hand. He doesn't look at Rosie.

'Don't be scared, hun. I'm just makin' sure it works.'

'It works. Put the gun away, okay?'

'This doesn't concern you, Rosie. Go back to JJ's.'

Joe waits. Rosie doesn't budge. The primal rage stirs inside him. He swallows and grinds his teeth.

'Joe — '

'Go, I said! Get outta here!'

'No. I'm not going anywhere. Whatever you're doing, you're going to have to do it in front of me.'

29

The gun is still his plan. Joe didn't promise Rosie anything. She talked him off the ledge the other night, but he's still enamored with his decision, the control it offers him. The idea of cheating HD out of its fiendish end fills Joe with a sense of justice, even sweet victory. He's going to go out on his own terms. He's not going to give HD the diabolical satisfaction of finishing him off. The good guy will win in the end, and HD will lose. Of course, the good guy wins by dying, but at least this way, he deprives HD of taking the credit. It's a classic tale of good versus evil. Disney could make a friggin' movie out of this shit.

He opens his top dresser drawer and goes through the familiar steps. He cradles the gun in his hand, removes the trigger lock, ejects the magazine, counts the rounds, pops the magazine back into place, snaps the trigger lock, returns the gun to the dresser, and shuts the drawer. Before letting go of the knobs, he slides the drawer open once more, allowing himself one more visual of the gun, confirming its presence, and then he shuts the drawer.

He exhales, absorbing the delicious satisfaction in knowing that his gun and the bullets are still there. The relief rushes through him, so fast and thorough, better than the endorphin high he feels after running the Forty Flights. He wishes the feeling would last. It never does.

He checks the gun many times a day. Often many times an hour. He can't stop. In a few minutes, the relief will have completely evaporated, and he'll be nagged by that addictive uncertainty. What if the gun is gone? What if the bullets are gone? It's irrational. He knows they're in the dresser. He just checked it. But the doubt gets more insistent, a doorbell ringing faster and louder in the center of his head over and over, and it won't stop until he answers the friggin' door.

Check the gun. *Check the gun. Check the gun!*

So the only way to rid himself of the compulsive thought is to check the friggin' gun. So he does. There. It's done. The gun is there. The bullets are there. But the maddening uncertainty finds its way back to him within minutes, like an eager dog that has just fetched a stick, never tiring of the game no matter how many times Joe throws it.

He grabs another Bud from the fridge, acknowledges the three empties from earlier this morning on the counter, and returns to his chair in the living room. He realizes that drinking beers and checking his gun isn't a responsible combination, but he shrugs it off. He can do what he wants. He can handle it.

He hears the front door open and footsteps approaching from down the hall. Rosie's at work. It's probably Donny or Tommy, coming to lecture him about the gun and drinking and scaring Rosie. He's been expecting this. He sits up straighter in his chair, defiantly holding his can of Bud, sloshing some onto his sweatpants, ready to defend his plan and actions to Donny or Tommy. They'll understand. He looks up, and it's Katie. He's not ready to defend anything to Katie.

Katie eyeballs him up and down with her hands on her hips and says nothing. She turns, walks over to the windows, and slingshots the three shades up to the ceiling. Natural light floods into the room. Joe squints and turns his head, offended by the sunny day. He hadn't realized how dark it had been in the living room. Dust particles float and sparkle in the air over the coffee table, which is littered with a stack of unread *Patriot Ledgers*, two empty bags of chips, this morning's forgotten sippy cup of coffee.

Katie turns and walks straight to Joe. She takes the clicker from the arm of Joe's chair, shuts off the TV, walks the clicker over to the TV cabinet, and leaves it there.

'Hey,' says Joe.

Katie says nothing. She pulls the rocking chair over and sets it directly in front of Joe. She sits, and then, remembering, backs up a careful foot. She knows now from experience not to plant herself too close to her dad. She might get HD-slapped in the face, punched in the ribs, kicked in the shins, knocked over. He elbowed Rosie square in the nose last week, gave her a shiner. He can still see the bruised discoloration beneath her eye, even under the makeup she applies to hide it. The poor woman looks abused.

In so many ways, she is.

'Mom told me what happened,' she says, staring into her father's eyes, unwavering.

Joe says nothing. He'd like to stop her right there, to tell her that her mother shouldn't have shared that with her, that she shouldn't worry or that it's none of her business, but the words are locked up inside the prison cell of HD. Instead, he looks into his daughter's blue eyes, determination and fear fighting for dominance in her gaze, both keeping her glued to her seat. Katie waits, probably anticipating resistance, but then his silence waves her on.

'I'm not going to tell you any clichés or quote some famous dead guy and go all yoga on you. What I'm going to say comes from me.'

She pauses, taking note of the can of Bud in his hand. At first he's indignant. He can do what he wants. But then her fierce blue eyes turn so disappointed in him, he can't stand it. He places the can on the side table.

'Here's the thing, Dad. You've taught us kids so many things that've made us who we are. You taught us right from wrong, respect for others, our work ethic. You taught us about honesty and integrity, and how to love each other. Yeah, we all did okay in school, but our real education came from you guys. You and Mom have always been our first and best example of what to do.'

Joe nods, touched.

'JJ and Meghan are going to get this. Pat and I might get it, too,' she says, a surge of fear crashing through her voice, aerating each word, and Joe wants to do anything to protect his

334

daughter from that distraught sound. But he's the powerless cause of that sound, and it kills him. Katie presses the inside corners of her eyes with her index fingers. Joe's arm flings out, knocking his hand against the side table, accidentally bumping the can of Bud over onto the floor.

Katie jumps up and dashes off to the kitchen. She returns with a roll of paper towels and mops up the puddle of beer on the floor.

'Thanks, hun,' says Joe.

Katie returns to her seat in the rocking chair, locks eyes with her dad, and takes a deep breath before continuing.

'We don't know anyone else with HD. You're the only example we have. We're going to learn how to live and die with HD from you, Dad.'

Joe averts his eyes and thinks about his plan. His perfect plan. It's the humane decision. He'll be teaching them the humane thing to do, the victorious way out. The gun. He should check the gun.

'I'm not telling you what to do, Dad. I don't have the answers here. None of us do. We don't know what's right and wrong when it comes to HD. But whatever you do, that's the advice you're giving us.'

The gun is the plan. That's the right thing to do. That's what he'll be teaching his kids. He'll be teaching them to kill themselves before HD does. The gun is the plan. The gun. He should check the gun. He wants to get up and go to the dresser, but Katie's still locked in on him. Check the gun. It's an itch he can't scratch, intensifying every second he sits in his chair. Resisting the pull is agonizing.

'And okay, so I am going to go a little yoga on you,' says Katie, her voice still shaking. She scootches the rocking chair toward Joe so that they're touching knee to knee. She leans forward and places her hands on Joe's thighs. 'If you end it now, you're avoiding a future that hasn't happened yet. You still have reasons to be here. I still want you to be here. We all do. We need you, Dad. Please. We need to learn how to live with this.'

Her penetrating blue eyes land on him, determined and loving, and he sees the unguarded little girl in her, the three-year-old Katie, a part of her own history she doesn't even remember that Joe has the distinct and rare privilege of knowing. Suddenly, all thoughts of the gun disappear, and there is only Katie, his brave, beautiful daughter, this grown woman who loves him enough to face him like this, his baby girl. And a relief sweeps through Joe's core that is bigger and deeper than every gun check combined. He bursts into tears and doesn't try to hold them back. Katie's crying, too, and they're face-to-face, two blubbering messes, and there's no shame in it. There's no shame anywhere.

Something inside Joe awakens. He remembers teaching JJ how to zip his coat and throw a baseball, showing Patrick how to look both ways before crossing the street and to ice-skate. He taught Meghan to snap and whistle. He taught Katie how to play chess. He remembers the first time she legitimately beat him. He taught them about money, how to drive a car and change a flat tire, the importance of being on time, of always giving 100 percent. The responsibility of being their father has been his honor, and it continues, even when his kids are no longer children. They will always be his kids. He could end HD for himself today, but this part of his legacy will carry on in them.

He's been nothing but a sorry sight, sitting in a dark living room, wearing dirty sweatpants, drinking beers before noon, checking his gun all day and night, scaring the shit out of everyone. This is not the example he wants to set. And right there, a new plan coalesces, whole and obvious, powerful and unequivocal. This is what he is here to do. He will teach his kids how to live and die with HD. This is the right thing to do, the real humane decision.

Joe wipes his face with his shirtsleeve and sighs. 'You wanna get outta here?'

Katie's wet eyes light up. 'Yeah. Where to?'

'How about the yoga studio?'

Katie's entire face pops with surprised delight, as if he's just offered her a winning lottery ticket. 'Really?'

'Yeah, it's on my bucket list.'

'You're going to love it, Dad.'

'Do I need one of those fruit roll-up mats?'

'I have one for you.'

'I got no idea how to do it, so go easy on me.'

'That's the beautiful thing about yoga. You just need to know how to breathe.'

Joe notices the automatic rise and fall of his

337

chest. Breathing. Today, he can still do that.

'Hey, Katie.'

She waits.

'Thank you, hun.'

'You bet, Dad.'

'How'd you get to be so smart?'

Katie shrugs and smiles. 'Mom.'

Joe laughs, leans forward, and hugs his baby girl with all the love and pride he's got.

30

Rosie's in the kitchen hunting for candles while Joe and the rest of the family wait for her. They're about to break bread at the first O'Brien Sunday supper in the new dining room. Joe's sitting at the head of an oak picnic-style table from Jordan's Furniture that seats eight, plenty of room for everyone. The table and the ample elbow room it affords is an improvement, but Rosie's still not happy. The wall separating the kitchen from the girls' old bedroom is gutted and gone, destroyed in Joe's rampage, but he hasn't gotten around yet to replacing the wall with the promised bar counter. And they're crowded in a different way from how they were in the kitchen, now by the cardboard boxes of old clothes and holiday crap yet to be stored elsewhere or donated, stacked up against the walls, hovering too close to the backs of everyone's chairs. And there's no overhead light in here. The girls had desk lamps when this was their bedroom. At four o'clock on a February afternoon, the room is only partially lit by the bright kitchen and dim hallway.

'Got 'em,' says Rosie, returning to the table, victorious, with a devotional candle in each hand.

The picture on the glass container of the first candle Rosie places on the table is of the Virgin Mary, Undoer of Knots. The second is St.

Michael killing the devil with his spear. Rosie lights both candles with a single match, and the room isn't noticeably brighter.

'How's that?' she asks.

'Very romantic,' says Meghan.

'Maybe I should get a lamp from the living room,' says Rosie.

'Sit down, Ma. It's fine,' says Katie.

Rosie acquiesces, delivers a perfunctory grace followed by a mumbled, collective 'Amen,' and then supper begins. Joe watches Rosie passing a platter of lamb a bowl of boiled turnips, her movements all business, her hair still damp from a late-afternoon shower, her emerald eyes dull in the shadows cast by the Virgin Mary candle; her presence at the other end of the table feels removed. She probably wouldn't speak to Joe for a week if she knew he was thinking this, but she looks much older than forty-four.

His HD is already wearing her down — the impending divorce, the episode and obsession with the gun, the holes in the walls, his constant calling and texting to check on her. She's heartsick about JJ and Meghan and worried to distraction over Patrick, Katie, and baby Joseph. Plus she hasn't been getting her beauty sleep. She's been doing night duty three nights a week up at JJ's, sleeping in their guest bedroom, ready with a bottle or a lullaby for baby Joseph whenever he wakes, giving JJ and Colleen a reprieve from the round-the-clock responsibility of caring for a newborn. On top of everything, she's working thirty hours a week now, up from twenty, which she says is no big deal, but Joe can see that it's all starting to take a toll on her.

JJ and Colleen keep disappearing from and reappearing at the table, bending down at the waist and popping back up, fussing over baby Joseph, who is sitting in a reclined, vibrating, oscillating seat on the floor. Neither JJ nor Colleen have eaten a bite of supper.

'He's fine, you two,' says Rosie.

'I'm just adjusting his head,' says JJ.

Colleen wipes the smallest speck of white spittle from the corner of baby Joseph's mouth with a blue cloth and then sticks a pacifier in it. He sucks the thing like a pro for a few seconds, but then he stops and the pacifier tumbles to the floor. JJ bends down and snatches the pacifier from under the table and is about to plug baby Joseph's mouth again, but Colleen stops him with her hand.

'Don't — it touched the floor. Hold on, I have another in his diaper bag,' says Colleen, taking the contaminated pacifier from JJ and sliding sideways out of her chair.

Meanwhile, baby Joseph seems perfectly content to Joe. The child might actually doze off if JJ and Colleen would leave him the fuck alone. New parents. Each generation has to learn for themselves.

'Where's Felix?' asks Joe.

'Portland,' says Katie without elaborating.

'I thought he wasn't going until June,' says Patrick.

Katie says nothing.

'He's not,' offers Meghan. 'He's just there for the week.'

Katie keeps her eyes downcast, focused on eating her salad. Felix hasn't missed a Sunday supper since the first time Katie brought him back in November. Joe likes the guy. He's smart and ambitious, but he doesn't seem to be a workaholic and doesn't talk incessantly about his job. He's still a fan of the Yankees, which is a problem likely to persist, but he's watched the Bruins in the living room a few times now with Joe, and Joe caught him actually cheering for the Bs at least once, so there's hope for him. Other than the Yankees, he doesn't appear to have any objectionable vices. Felix was brought up Protestant, but Joe's not holding that against him. He's salt of the earth, not at all the pretentious Toonie Joe expected. He's got good manners, and he treats Katie well. Joe can tell by the way Katie lights up whenever he's in the room. Katie doesn't resemble Rosie much, but something about her looks just like Rosie, especially when Rosie was young, whenever Felix is around.

Joe studies Katie eating her salad, her face drawn and heavy, the opposite of lit up, and a regret seeps through Joe like a poison. He's basically ordered Katie to break up with this fine young man, a man she obviously loves, to protect Rosie. He looks at Rosie and the sledgehammered holes framing her exhausted face in the hallway wall behind her. He's not exactly protecting Rosie from a damn thing. Why should Katie have to bear that burden? Life is too short, one of the many lessons HD is ramming down his throat, whether he likes the taste or not.

A moldy hunk of rock-hard potato suddenly lands in the middle of JJ's plate with a crash that startles everyone.

'Jesus, Pat. Ma asked you to clean off the ceiling last week,' says JJ.

It's getting increasingly improbable for Joe to transport food from a fork or spoon to his mouth without some HD spaz attack sending it elsewhere. His hand will twitch or his fingers will release the utensil or his arm will fling wildly, causing his food to go sailing onto someone's face or shirt or the wall or the ceiling. Most of the food that hits the ceiling falls right back down, but Rosie's mashed potatoes, which Joe has always said resembled glue, stick and stay there. Joe looks up. Globs of hardened mashed potatoes from previous suppers hang like stalactite chandeliers all over the ceiling.

'I forgot,' says Patrick.

'You didn't fix the holes in the hallway walls either,' says JJ, who patched, sanded, and painted over the holes in the bedroom.

'I've been busy. I'm workin' on it.'

'You're not that busy, for Chrissake,' says JJ.

'I don't see you doin' anything around here to help.'

'I don't live here for free, moochin' off Ma and Dad. Least you could do is lift one of your lazy-ass fingers and help them out.'

'You don't exactly pay real rent, and you have your own place.'

'You know what?' yells JJ, his face now an incensed shade of pink. 'I have a wife and a baby, but I'll do it. I'll clean the ceiling and fix the rest

343

of the holes, since you're a totally worthless piece of shit.'

'JJ,' scolds Rosie.

'No, Ma. I'm sick of him not being held accountable for anything. You tell 'em your big news yet, Pat?'

Patrick says nothing, but his eyes are trying to murder JJ from across the table.

'You gonna tell 'em, Patty boy?'

'Shut the fuck up, JJ.'

'Language. JJ, stop it. Pat, what is it?' asks Rosie.

'Nothing, Ma. There's no news. I'll clean the ceiling after supper.'

'Oh, there's news. Pat knocked up this girl he's been shackin' up with.'

The room goes heart-stopping silent. Joe stares at St. Michael killing the devil on the candle, and then, gripping his fork like a spear, he lifts his gaze to Pat. His son's pale, freckled face. Pat's sullen blue eyes. His slumped shoulders and messy hair the color of lightly steeped tea.

'Tell me that's not true,' says Joe.

Patrick hesitates, then nods. 'Least that's what she says.'

'Who says, Pat? Who is this girl?' asks Rosie.

'Ashley.'

'Ashley who?' asks Rosie, her words overly controlled, her eyes closed. Joe guesses she's praying to God for patience and the strength not to kill her son.

'Donahue.'

'Kathleen's daughter?' asks Rosie.

'Niece,' says JJ.

'And why haven't we met her?' asks Rosie.

Patrick shrugs. 'We were just messin' around. It wasn't anything serious.'

'Well it's fuckin' serious now,' yells Joe, hot rage licking each word. 'How can you be this totally fuckin' irresponsible? Your mother gives you the goddamn rubbers, for Chrissake, and you still get this girl pregnant.'

'You got Ma pregnant, and you guys were only eighteen.'

'And I did the right thing and married her. What if you have HD? Did you ever think of that? You might've just passed it on to some innocent baby.'

'No one yelled at JJ for maybe passing it on to his baby.'

'You shut your stupid fuckin' mouth right now,' warns JJ. 'I'm *married*, and I didn't know about HD before *my wife* got pregnant.'

'Have you told her you're at risk for HD?' asks Rosie.

'No.'

'You're taking that test and finding out,' says Joe, pointing his fork at Pat's head.

'No, I'm not.'

'That girl deserves to know,' says Joe.

'I don't want to know. I'm not takin' it.'

'You're taking it, and you're marrying her,' threatens Joe.

'I'm not. I'm not takin' the stupid test, and I'm not marryin' Ashley.'

'You have a responsibility to that young woman and your unborn child.'

345

'I can be the kid's father without getting married. I don't love her.'

Rosie stands. 'I can't take this anymore. I can't do this,' she says, looking at Joe, avoiding Patrick, her voice vibrating high and hollow. She throws her napkin on the table and leaves. The bedroom door slams, and another piece of petrified potato falls from the ceiling, landing with a clunky thud on the table next to the Mary candle. Baby Joseph whimpers. Colleen picks him up and tries to soothe him with the pacifier, but he won't keep it in his mouth. Meghan hugs her thick, gray scarf to her ears as if she's trying to hide inside it.

'Goddamn it, Pat. How could you do this?' asks Joe above baby Joseph's wailing. 'How?'

Patrick says nothing. The hot rage swimming through Joe cools and coalesces into a dense helplessness that settles in his center. This disease is a fuckin' plague, spreading, wreaking evil havoc however it pleases, and there's not a damn thing Joe can do about it but witness the devastation. Pat is sitting there, arrogant and ignorant, making a bad situation worse, and Joe can't stomach the sight of him.

Joe dumps his fork onto his plate and fumbles clumsily out of his seat, hurrying out of the dining room before his four grown children can see him cry.

31

Joe's been practicing yoga with Katie for a few weeks now. He dutifully takes what Rosie calls his 'God-knows-what's-in-'em pills' twice a day as part of a randomized, double-blind clinical trial. He signed up to participate in the HD Human Biology Project. He's been praying in church for all of them, especially now for Patrick and his unborn child, asking for guidance, grace, and good health. Joe's making real progress on the kitchen bar counter with the help of JJ, Patrick, and Felix. He's even staying away from predinner beers and his gun. He's doing his best with each day he has, mindfully showing his kids how to live honorably with HD.

But thinking ahead is where he gets muddled. The dying part. Any possible ending to HD sucks. Pneumonia. Starvation. Lingering as a barely living corpse until God finally, mercifully opens the pearly gates to heaven. What kind of honorable example can he provide his kids for how to die with HD? He can't figure it out, and it scares the shit out of him, to be passively heading into a future where he'll be completely out of control, vulnerable, and without a plan.

But he has time. As Katie would say, 'You are either Now Here or Nowhere.' So today he is still here, living with HD, trying not to think about the dying part.

Joe and Katie are standing on their mats in the

yoga studio. Katie's leading him through a class she customizes just for him. A 'private,' she calls it. She does this sort of thing on a regular basis for a couple of women, both Toonies. One is a world-famous doctor at Mass Eye and Ear who works long hours. Katie teaches her twice a week at 9:00 p.m. The other apparently can't get to the scheduled group classes due to various conflicting weekly hair, nail, and therapy appointments, plus she doesn't like to sweat in front of anyone, and paying for privates with Katie is really just so much simpler.

And then there is Katie's client with Huntington's disease. Her dear old dad. Joe and Katie are side by side, facing the mirror, which he's learned isn't the typical configuration for a normal class. Katie teaches everyone else from the front of the room, oriented toward the wall with the Buddha painted on it. But she's placed Joe in front of the mirrored wall so he can see what his body is doing with his eyes. It definitely helps.

Most of the time, his mind's eye, his sense of proprioception, is either asleep on the job or blindfolded. Add a dash of anosognosia, and he's unaware of what he's unaware of. He typically has no idea what his legs and arms and hands are doing or where they are in space until he falls down or crashes into a wall or hits someone or breaks something. Yesterday he went from sitting comfortably in his chair, happily watching the Bruins, to finding himself sprawled out facedown on the floor. He's his own stuntman, the star of a slapstick comedy. Only the show ain't so funny.

Huntington's has a sick sense of humor.

And it's not just the chorea, anosognosia, and lack of proprioception that get him into trouble. The extraordinary and most often inappropriate force he's able to generate without conscious awareness astounds everyone. Twice now, he went to lift the toilet seat to take a piss and tore the lid clear off. If only he could harness his superhero powers for good.

Katie stands at the top of her mat, her pale feet planted hip-distance apart, legs parallel. Looking in the mirror, Joe watches his similarly pale feet fidgeting, stepping on and off the mat as if he's stomping on an invasion of ants. After Joe's episode with the gun, Rosie tattled on him, and Dr. Hagler lowered Joe's dosage of Tetrabenazine. There's a black-box warning for depression and suicidal tendencies right on the label, affecting about 20 percent of those who take it. Fuckin' brilliant. Depression is already a symptom of HD, yet another chocolate in a delightful boxed assortment. So let's give people facing a brutal terminal illness who probably already exhibit depression a drug that can exacerbate that depression and cause suicidal ideation. That's a great fuckin'idea. But if Joe wants to treat his chorea, and he does, Tetrabenazine is the best and only thing they've got.

Joe likes to imagine Tetrabenazine as a pharmaceutical army of patrol officers chasing down the HD bad guys who commit chorea, catching, cuffing, and locking them up. So with less Tetrabenazine on duty now, Joe's got more bad guys on the loose inside him committing heinous acts of chorea. He's moving around a lot.

But Rosie's happy with the trade-off. No more suicidal obsession with the gun. Joe would argue that it was Katie and not a drug adjustment that pulled him out of that dark hole, but Rosie's too traumatized to hear anything about upping the dose again. They're all just going to have to live with more chorea. More chorea, less gun.

The compulsion to check something remains, but Joe's obsession with his gun has transferred to his phone. He texts Rosie probably a hundred times a day. The need to check on her and be sure she's okay feels as urgent as the need for oxygen, and he suffocates while waiting for her to reply. So if she doesn't return his text within a few seconds, he texts her again. And again. He knows he's driving her nuts, but he can't stop.

'Arms up.'

Joe copies Katie, and they are now moving 'together' through something called Sun Salutations.

'Forward Fold.'

Katie swan-dives her arms, and her hands press flat on the mat, her nose to her knees. Joe's arms flail down, and his fingers dangle in front of his shins, about a mile from the floor. Katie's body is a jackknife. Joe is Quasimodo.

'Halfway lift.'

Already there, darlin'. Then Plank pose. The Push-up. Up Dog. Down Dog. As usual, they hang out here for a bit.

'Relax into the pose. Where can you try less?'

Joe laughs. 'There's nothing but trying hard here, honey.'

Katie looks as if she could stay in this position forever, but Joe's grunting and panting, blood flooding into his sweaty pink head, praying for Down Dog to be over.

Katie laughs. 'You can be in Downward Dog, hating every second of it. Or you can be in this pose, peaceful and nonreactive, breathing calmly. Either way, you're in this pose. You decide the quality of your experience. Be the thermostat, not the temperature.'

Wise words, but Joe's wishing his lovely daughter would shut the fuck up and move them out of Down Dog. His arms are trembling. His feet are still busy annihilating invisible ants. He pushes hard into the mat with his hands, but his right hand does something the left hand doesn't, and Joe collapses onto his stomach. He gets up onto his knees, wipes his nose with his shirtsleeve, and pushes back up into Down Dog.

'You okay, Dad?'

'Yeah. So what comes after Down Dog?'

Katie laughs again. 'Step to the top of the mat.'

Joe lowers to his knees and crawls forward. Katie is waiting for him there. He stands.

'Arms up. Hands to heart.'

Amen.

They do it again. And again. Joe is huffing and wobbling, flailing and falling. Katie is graceful, fluid, strong. She makes it look effortless. Even without HD, Joe wouldn't have looked anything like her. Every second for Joe is packed with sloppy exertion, his muscles straining, his brain scrambling to copy the shape of Katie, judging his every pitiful inadequacy. This shit ain't for sissies.

But he sticks with it, and the repetition is his friend. His muscles begin to predict what will happen next. He knows the choreography to this dance. Katie seems to sense this, and her cues start to focus more on the breathing.

'*Inhale*, arms up. *Exhale*, Forward Fold. *Inhale*, Halfway Lift. Exhale. Inhale.'

And then, something magical happens. Moving moves to the background. Joe becomes a breathing body that happens to be moving. He's breathing slow, steady, long inhales and exhaling through his nose, just like Katie taught him, and he finds a stillness within the moving. He's in the zone. No more ants. No more falling. The bad guys who commit chorea have fled the city.

He's had five privates with Katie now, and this is the first time he's experienced this kind of moving stillness, this momentary waking pause from chorea. He used to have to run the Forty Flights to the point of exhaustion, falling on the steps over and over, skinning his knees and elbows and hands, becoming a bloody mess before chorea waved its white flag. This is better. And a whole lot safer.

After the Sun Salutations, they move to the floor. Three Cobras. Two Locusts. And then Bridge. He dreads Bridge. He lies on his back, feet planted, knees bent, and, on Katie's cue, presses his hips to the sky. Or least up a bit.

'Hold the pose, not your breath. Stay here for ten.'

Joe's legs tremble. His throat feels constricted, thin. He squeezes his face and grunts, sputtering his breath. He tightens every muscle he can find, fighting to keep his ass off the ground, to stay in the pose, to stay in the fight.

'The pose begins when you want to get out of it. Quiet your reactions. Quiet your thoughts. Quiet the struggle. Witness and breathe.'

Joe finds his face first and unclenches his jaw. He breathes and mindfully relaxes everything but his feet, which he pushes into the ground. He watches his stomach rise and fall. Rise and fall. And here he is, almost comfortable in Bridge.

Stay in the Fight worked for Joe as a patrol officer. It's even worked for Joe at times as a husband and father. But it doesn't quite work as a man with HD. Stay in the Fight is a struggle. It's war. Despite the Seroquel and his inadequate dose of Tetrabenazine, he still exhibits chorea, loss of coordination and proprioception, OCD, paranoia, impulsivity, anosognosia, wild swings in mood with an unconscious predilection for anger, and dysexecutive syndrome. And slurring. The slurring has started. He has no real weapon to fight HD. He'd never admit this to Donny or Tommy or any of the guys, but maybe, instead of Stay in the Fight, his approach to HD should be to Stay in the Pose.

Katie mercifully cues Joe to release his Bridge. They move on to Seated Forward Fold. Happy Baby. Spinal Twist.

And finally, his favorite, Savasana. Dead Man's Pose. The irony of this position's name is not lost on him. Joe lies on his mat, his arms at his sides, his legs wide, feet splayed, eyes closed. Breathing. Letting go of all effort. Surrendering everything, allowing every pound of him to be held by the mat and hardwood floor beneath him, which feels in this moment somehow more comfortable than his bed mattress.

Sometimes Katie reads an inspirational passage from one of her yoga books while he's in this pose, but today she says nothing. Without looking, he can feel her presence on her mat next to him. Joe breathes, not forcing or expecting anything, and he sinks in, releasing his body and thoughts, emptying out.

And in that empty space emerges an image of his mother. A memory. She's in her shared room in the state hospital, sitting in a padded, reclined wheelchair, a white seat belt over her chest, a black seat belt tight around her waist. She's wearing a short-sleeved blue shirt, swimming on her emaciated frame, a fluorescent-yellow paper bracelet sporting the words FALL RISK around her translucent wrist. Her wrists are pronated, her bony fingers curled and rigid.

She's sputtering, grunting, pushing out low, wild-animal growls. Her face squeezes fast and tight as if she's been unexpectedly punched. She grunts again and throws her chin up to the ceiling. Her mouth hangs open. Drool drips from her bottom lip onto her blue shirt.

Joe is eleven. He's disgusted, ashamed,

repulsed. He turns his head and looks away. He wants to leave.

The pose begins when you want to get out of it. Quiet your reactions. Quiet your thoughts. Quiet the struggle. Witness and breathe.

Stay in the Pose.

Joe lies in Dead Man's Pose and begins to relive the same vivid memory of his mother, but it shifts, as if God has reached into his brain and rotated it a few degrees.

Not like that. Like this.

His mother's wheelchair, the seat belts, her blue short-sleeved shirt, the yellow bracelet, the growls, the drool. Instead of looking away, Joe meets her eyes with his, and he sees his mother's eyes smiling at him. Her face winces, and she grunts, but now Joe's eyes are connected to hers, unafraid, and the guttural animal sounds become human, intelligible.

'Eh ew.'

Thank you.

His mother is thanking the nurse for feeding her lunch. She's thanking his father for brushing her hair. She's thanking Joe and Maggie for the pictures they drew for her.

And before they leave for another week, his mother gathers all the strength she has to produce a sharp groan.

'Eh uh ew.'

I love you.

The last words Joe heard his mother say, words he didn't comprehend until now, were *Thank you* and *I love you*. Gratitude and love.

Joe replays the memory, and he sees his

355

mother again and anew. Unable to walk or feed herself, unable to defend her reputation from the rumors that she was a drunk and a sinner and a bad mother, unable to live at home or hug her kids or tuck them into bed at night, she's smiling with her eyes at Joe. In the end, his mother wasn't just a living corpse waiting to die in a hospital. She was a wife and mother who loved her family, grateful to see them and still love them for as long as she could.

Tears stream down Joe's temples, wetting his hair as he remembers his mother, no longer the grotesque monster he despised and blamed and was ashamed of. She was Ruth O'Brien, his mother, a woman who had HD through no fault of her own, who gave her family love and gratitude when she had nothing else to give.

After all these years, he sees his mother. Re-membered.

I love you, Mum. Please forgive me. And Joe's heart swells, knowing it's already done. He is loved and forgiven.

And, like a lightning strike, there is his example. His mother before him. The lesson that she passed down for him to pass on to his children — the courage to face every breath with love and gratitude.

'Okay, Dad. Let's wiggle our fingers and toes. Stretch your arms up overhead, and when you're ready, come to a seated position.'

Joe and Katie are now sitting cross-legged, eyes open, seeing each other in the mirror. Katie's face is wet with tears, top.

'Let's bring our palms together at our hearts.'

356

Joe copies Katie. They sit for a moment in silence, in prayer.

'The light within me bows to and honors the light within you. Namaste.'

'Namaste,' says Joe, smiling at his daughter in the mirror. 'I love you, Katie.'

'I love you, too, Dad.'

'Thank you, sweetie.'

Love and gratitude.

32

Joe's standing in the front foyer, trying to understand what he's seeing, or rather, what he's not seeing. The marble blessing font is gone. He's staring at two screw holes and a patch of white paint in the shape of the font twenty years brighter than the white wall surrounding it, unable to imagine who would do this. A few months ago, he might not have even noticed its absence. The holy-water sacramental has always been Rosie's thing. But as Joe's HD symptoms have worsened, he figures water blessed by God is probably as effective as anything modern medicine's got for him and a hell of a lot cheaper. So for the past few months, he's bought into this devotional act, anointing himself in the name of the Father, the Son, and the Holy Spirit when leaving or returning home. One morning, when no one was looking, he actually removed the straw from his sippy cup, dunked it into the font, and drank a little. It couldn't hurt.

He tosses his keys onto the hallway table and goes to high-five the Virgin Mary, another ritual he's become almost obsessively attached to, but he's left hanging. She's gone, too. There's nothing on the table but his keys and the ivory doily where Mary used to stand. Have they been burgled by some crazy Catholic?

He finds a similar scene in the living room. The crucifix is missing from the wall above the fireplace. Jesus, St. Patrick, St. Christopher, the angels, the prayer candles, even the Christmas carolers and the manger scene have all disappeared. Only the frogs, the babies, the Snoopys, and their family photos remain. To Joe, the room looks better without all that religious crap, but his skin goes cool. The statues and candles don't mean anything to Joe, but they mean the world to Rosie.

He continues to inspect the living room as if it's a crime scene. Rosie's ironing board is set up, but the iron's cord is unplugged, and the laundry is still a wrinkled heap in the basket on the floor. Vanished religious crap, unfinished ironing. Nothing else seems to be amiss, but then his eyes land on the TV cabinet, the final clue. The *Oprah* videotapes are gone.

Rosie's come undone.

'Rosie?'

He walks into the bedroom, and there she is, still in her pink pajamas, lying in the fetal position on the bed, her face red and puffy, her eyes sunken, her auburn hair looking like it's in an eighties rock band. He kneels down on the floor next to her and leans into the mattress like a boy saying his prayers at bedtime. His face is even with hers, only inches apart. He can feel her soft breath on his nose. She smells like wine.

'What happened, hun?'

'Nothin'.'

The Madonna holding baby Jesus is gone from the night table next to her. In its place are two bottles of Chardonnay and a jelly jar, all three empty.

359

'You're drunk.'

'So.'

'So? It's ten o'clock in the morning.'

'I don't fuckin' care.'

''Fuckin',' huh?'

'That's right,' she says, challenging him to correct her. He wouldn't dream of it.

'Whaddya do with all the religious stuff?'

'I packed it up.'

'Why?'

''Cuz I don't believe in God anymore.'

'I see.'

'I don't. I'm all done. How, Joe?' she asks, sitting up now, suddenly coming to life. She's got a rant in her that's been simmering in wine all morning, just waiting for an audience. He can see it in her outraged green eyes. 'How can I? How am I supposed to have faith in a God that would do this to our family? We're good people, Joe.'

'I know. Bad things happen to good people every day.'

'Oh, don't feed me any cliché bullshit. I was okay with you dying.'

'Thanks, darlin'. That's real sweet.'

'No, you know what I mean. I've been to too many police funerals with you. I've seen the grief on those wives' faces. I've been prepared to be one of those women since I was in my twenties.'

He gets it. The funerals always bring it home. This ain't no game of cops and robbers. This shit is real. Sometimes, the good guys get taken down. And when they lose a brother or sister in blue, every cop standing at attention, honoring

360

the lost officer in the casket, is thinking the exact same thing.

That could just as easily be me.

'I was okay when I was praying for just you,' says Rosie. 'I could handle it. Dr. Hagler said the disease is slow, so okay, that's a blessing, right? We still have time. I prayed to God to give me the strength and grace to endure this, to take care of you, to be grateful for every day we have. You know I've always believed in trusting in God's plan.'

Joe nods.

'Plus we're Irish. We know how to endure backbreaking, soul-crushing hardship. Perseverance is in our blood, for fuck's sake.'

Joes agrees. They're a strong and tenacious breed of people, stubborn as a constipated mule and proud of it.

'But then JJ and then Meghan. They have this fuckin' hideous, mutated thing in their blood and their brains, and they're going to die before me, Joe, and I can't take it. I can't.'

It's a mother's worst nightmare, and Rosie's voice cracks under the cruel weight of it. She's weeping, and Joe can't think of what to say to comfort her. He wants to run his fingers through her hair, to wipe away her tears, to rub her back and hold her, but he doesn't trust his arms and hands to do what he intends. He might punch her in the face, squeeze her too hard, poke her in the eye, or dig his fingernails into her skin, drawing blood. He knows he might, because these things have already happened. It's as if the command center for voluntary movement in his brain has been hijacked by a gang of naughty kids, and they're in there maniacally laughing as they randomly, repetitively flip the switches. Or conversely, the kids are in there with their arms crossed, some stubborn, others indolent, flat-out refusing Joe's simple and polite request to turn the proper motor sequence for hugging on. So he resists the urge to touch her, and Rosie cries next to him alone.

'I think about their funeral services, their beautiful faces and their bodies in caskets, buried in the ground, and I don't want to spend one minute on this earth knowing two of my children are buried beneath it.'

'Shhh, honey, don't go there.'

'I can't help it. I keep picturing them dead in the ground, and it's winter, and their bodies would be so cold, and I can't stand it.'

'You gotta stop imagining that. They're not dying anytime soon. You gotta keep faith.'

'I can't. The faith I had is broken. It's gone. I tried. I tried praying for them, and it started all humble and hopeful, but then it turned to begging, and then it became this full-on rage against God and the angels and the church. What if Katie and Patrick and baby Joseph get this, too? I could lose everyone, Joe.'

Joe notices Rosie didn't include Patrick's unborn, illegitimate bastard child in her list of 'everyone.'

'They won't. You won't.'

'I'll tell you right now, I'm crawling into the casket with the last one. They're gonna have to bury me alive because I won't go on alone.'

'Rosie, honey, this isn't good for you to think like this. You gotta focus on the kids living.'

'What if the girls never get married and have families because of this? What if JJ and Colleen decide they shouldn't have any more children?'

'They can all do that genetic in-vitro thing. Or they could adopt.'

'What if JJ becomes symptomatic and he loses his job? How will he support his family? Who's going to teach Joey how to play catch and hit a baseball and all those father-son things?'

Her voice is spiraling higher with each question, and Joe fears she's going to what-if herself into a full-blown drunken panic attack.

'He's not symptomatic, and we have to hope that he won't be for at least another twenty years. And Colleen can teach Joey that stuff, too. Have you seen her throw? She's got one helluvan arm.'

'I think I see it happening in Patrick.'

'It's not. You're just scared and imagining the worst. Look, there's so much hope to have for our kids. Those scientists are gonna find effective treatments and a cure for this thing.'

'How do you know? What if they don't?'

'They will. I have faith in them. There are all these really smart people right down the street in the Navy Yard labs who are dedicating their entire lives to figuring this out. They already know the mutation, and that's the only thing that causes HD. It's gonna happen. They're gonna cure this someday, hopefully in time to save our kids. And hopefully no one else in our family has the gene. That's what I pray for.'

'You pray?'

'Jeez, you don't have to look *that* shocked. Yeah, I've been going to church.'

'Since when?'

''Bout a month now. I figure if there's ever a time for praying and finding some greater purpose and grace, it's now.'

'Do you go to Mass?'

'Nah. I don't need the priest and all the sitting and standing. I'd probably fall on my face and cause a fuss. I go most mornings, after the seven thirty is cleared out.'

'So what do you do?'

'Just sit and pray.'

Joe actually started going to church because of his sister, Maggie. He finally talked to her on the phone last month, told her everything. She was stunned and upset and even cried while asking about Joe's kids, which surprised him, given that she's never even met them. While Joe's grateful that Maggie hasn't noticed any symptoms in herself, he also couldn't help feeling outraged. He and Maggie each had a fifty-fifty chance of inheriting HD from their mother. Why couldn't it have been Maggie who got it instead of him? Maggie has no children. It could end with her. Why would God curse Joe's kids with this wretched disease? And to his shame, he hated Maggie for probably being HD negative. He hated God for singling him out, for giving HD to his family. Most of all, he hated himself.

Without a consciously calculated decision to do so, he walked his sorry ass into St. Francis the next morning, collapsed into a pew, and, alone in the church, prayed aloud to God. He prayed for many things that day, but mostly, he asked God for forgiveness. To his surprise, he felt almost immediately absolved, lighter, cleaner, the toxic hatred washed from his body. He's gone to church almost every morning since.

Four rows from the back on the right side, where they always sat as a family when the kids were little. He's only there each time for five minutes, tops. He could easily pray from his chair in the living room, but he likes praying in that spot, in their old pew, in St. Francis Church. He likes the columns leading to grand arches on the balcony level, fashioned after the cathedral in Limerick, Ireland; the pipe organ; the American, Irish, and Charlestown flags; the gold crucifix hanging from the ceiling; the stained glass windows and stations of the cross; the worn, red-painted wooden floors. His prayers whispered there feel official, blessed, heard.

God, please help the scientists find a cure for HD so my children don't lose their lives to this.

God, please let Patrick and Katie and baby Joseph be gene negative.

God, please let JJ and Meghan be cured, and let me live long enough to know they'll be okay. Or, if there can't be a cure yet, let them not become symptomatic until they're much older.

God, please pray for Rosie. Don't let me be too big a burden on her. Let her always feel loved by me. Please take care of her after I'm gone.

And lastly, God, if I'm not being too greedy, please let the Red Sox win the World Series, the

Bruins win the Stanley Cup, and the Pats win the Super Bowl.

Amen.

Then he signs the cross, kisses his lucky quarter, and goes home.

'How 'bout this?' asks Joe. 'I'll pray for you and the kids. You pray for me. Just me. That way you don't get overwhelmed, and everyone's covered. I know I could use the help.'

Rosie shakes her head, unconvinced. 'But why, Joe? Why would God do this to us?'

'I don't know, hun. I don't know.'

He pauses, wishing he had something wiser to offer. Where's Katie with one of her damn inspirational yoga quotes when he needs her?

'Wanna put all the Jesus stuff back?' he asks.

'No,' she sniffles. 'I can't. It still feels like a lie.'

'Okay, that's fine. We don't need it. Snoopy's still out there. We can pray to Snoopy. In the name of Snoopy, Charlie Brown, and the Holy Woodstock,' says Joe, crossing himself.

'Stop it, that's terrible.'

'Or we could use Kermit. Holy Kermit, mother of Miss Piggy.'

'Stop. That's ridiculous and blasphemy.'

'See, you still believe. Don't lose faith, sweetie.'

Joe holds on to the edge of the bed and stands, groaning as his knees crack. He flings his arms wide open, inviting Rosie out of bed.

'Come with me. Let's get you a cuppa tea.'

Rosie acquiesces. They walk together, listing and pitching, bumping off the hallway walls and each other's hips. A drunk wife and a husband with HD. They make a fine pair. As they lurch down the hallway and finally make it to the kitchen, it occurs to Joe that this is the best anyone can hope for in life.

Someone you love to stagger through the hard times with.

33

Joe's physical therapist is a young woman named Vivian. Joe calls her Viv. She has bouncy blond hair, a big, easy smile on a pretty face, and a fit but feminine body that Joe finds pleasantly distracting. Joe knows by now not to be fooled by her girly-sweet appearance. Viv is tough as nails. She shows Joe no mercy, and that's his favorite part about her.

Each week for an hour they work on balance and core strength and what Viv calls 'gait training.' That's fancy PT-speak for walking. Joe finds it more than a little demoralizing that he requires a paid professional to train him to walk. But alas, so it is.

He's on the floor mat on all fours, in what Katie would call Table Pose.

'Okay now, hold your position while I push against you,' says Viv. 'Ready? Resist me.'

Viv's hands are on Joe's shoulders, pushing him back while Joe's leaning into her hands, exerting with his legs, core, arms, all of him, really. At first he's steady, holding his Table, but he's been through this drill too many times with Viv now to celebrate. While Joe's giving it 100 percent, he knows Viv is probably only working at about 25.

'Okay, good job. Sit back on your heels and rest.'

She's giving him a break in what Katie calls Child's Pose.

'Arms stay outstretched.'

Viv massages Joe's hips and then kneads the knots out of his neck. Her small, manicured hands are surprisingly strong. She goes to work on his trapezius next. Bless her. It feels so good to be touched, and he means that in the most respectful, non-sexually harassing way.

Rosie's been avoiding him. He understands that close physical proximity to him can be dangerous. He might involuntarily throw a punch or his food or a cutting word, and any are likely to hit her where it hurts. He gets why she keeps a safe distance from him during the day. But she's also sleeping upstairs at JJ's every night now, taking care of baby Joseph so JJ and Colleen can sleep. She loves everything about being a grandmother, says she feels blessed to be able to help, that she wants to soak up every minute, even at three in the morning, because he won't be a baby for long, but Joe thinks her sleepovers are also an excuse to be where Joe isn't, that maybe she's practicing, trying on a piece of her future. Whatever her reasons, missing Rosie is hard. Harder than PT.

'Okay, break's over. Back onto your hands and knees. Let's go again.'

Viv pushes harder into his shoulders this time, and Joe is quivering with effort. She seems to know his edge and backs off before Joe quits or loses. She returns him to Child's Pose, and Joe reclaims his composure.

'Okay, last time. Back up you go.'

369

This is when she beats him. Just one of these weeks, he'd like to remain immovable against her best shot. Unfortunately, this isn't in the cards for Joe. Despite all this physical training, he'll continue to get less agile, less coordinated, weaker over time instead of stronger. He's fighting a rising tide.

'Resist, Joe. Come on. Give it all you've got. Hold me here, Joe.'

He's squeezing and leaning and pushing with all his might, sputtering and grunting, and then, as predicted, Viv forces him back onto his heels. Defeated again. Score: Viv 52, Joe 0.

Next, he's standing and joined by another therapist, George. George is also young and physically fit, which must be a job requirement. He's bald with a goatee, which makes him look angry whenever he's not smiling, and he has the most muscular forearms and biceps Joe's ever seen. The dude is Popeye.

Viv stands in front of Joe, and George positions himself behind. More games of Knock Joe Over. PTs are sadistic. Viv will catch Joe when he falls forward, George will catch him when he falls backward, and it's whoever calls it when Joe falls to the right or left.

'Lift your right foot off the ground and hold it,' says Viv, stretching her arms out like airplane wings.

Joe mirrors Viv's arms and lifts his leg probably only an inch off the ground, but in Joe's mind, he's the Karate Kid. Viv counts.

'One, two. Try again. One, two. Again. One, two, three. Okay, other side.'

Joe lifts his other leg for a similar and loathsomely inadequate number of seconds before losing his balance. He hasn't made it past 'three' in weeks.

'Now resist my hands,' says Viv, standing in a lunge with her arms extended and her strong hands pressing against Joe's hips. 'Don't let me move you from where you're standing.'

He's no match for her on this one from the first try. He steps back. They go again. He steps back. They go again. He looks down at her young, ripe cleavage as she pushes. He steps back. One more time. He's off balance but doesn't step back. He's falling over and scared for about a half second before George, his human safety net, catches him.

'Thanks, man,' says Joe.

'Anytime,' says George.

Joe studies his reflection in the mirror. It was one year ago this week that Joe was officially diagnosed with Huntington's. He's disheartened, noticing how much his body has changed in a year. Before HD, Joe's shirts were always tight on him. He had a broad, muscular chest, thick traps, biceps that stretched the sleeves of his shirts, and probably an extra ten to twenty pounds around his middle. He's only five foot nine, but he was big for a little man.

He's lost the fat around his middle, but his gut now protrudes out like a toddler's belly with no abdominal strength to hold it in. He's also lost muscle mass in his pecs, biceps, traps, everywhere. He's a skinny, short, weak, middle-aged guy with a slouched posture who was just easily beaten by a girl.

He could be the 'after' photo in a diet commercial, but not quite. No one's saying, 'Hey, Joe, you look great!' HD isn't a weight-loss plan like Jenny Craig. He looks shrunken, a bit wrung out, flaccid, the beginning of bony, sickly.

'Okay, Joe. Have a seat,' says Viv. Viv, George, and Joe all sit on the blue floor mat, facing one another like kids. 'Before we wrap it up for today, is anything else going on?'

'Nope.'

'Rosie tells me you're slurring some of your words.'

'Oh, yeah, I guess.'

Viv nods. 'Okay, let's do a few things real quick. Stick out your tongue for me and keep it out. Yup, but keep it out. Nope, it went back in. Out. Stick it back out. Your tongue's a shy little guy. There, hold it there. Now move it to the right, now the left. Back to the right. Hmm.'

Well, that felt ridiculous, and from the sound of Viv's 'Hmm,' he failed the tongue test. Physical therapy doesn't exactly beef up Joe's self-esteem.

'Hold on,' says Viv.

She trots over to her big bag of tricks, where she keeps her stash of squeeze balls, elastic bands, and probably her whips and chains. She returns to the mat with a red lollipop.

'Okay, Joe, suck on this.'

She opens her mouth, a request for Joe to follow suit. He does, and she inserts the lollipop into his mouth.

'Don't let me pull it out, okay?'

Viv pulls on the stick, and it slides without stopping right out of Joe's mouth.

'Let's try again. Don't let me take this out. Good. Good.'

And then Viv is sitting there with a red lollipop in her hand.

'Let's do it again.'

Viv slides the lollipop into Joe's mouth. This time, Joe cracks the candy with his teeth and chews. Viv pulls out a popless stick. Joe smiles. Viv shakes her head.

'What am I gonna do with you?' she asks.

'You're the mean lady taking candy from a baby,' says Joe.

'Get some lollipops and do this with Rosie at home. It'll help to strengthen your mouth and jaw muscles, and should help with the slurred speech. Sound good?'

'Will do.'

'Okay. Before you go, I think it's time we talk about getting you a walker.'

'Nah, nah. I told you not to use any *w* words with me. It's not becoming language for a young lady like yourself.'

Joe knew the *w* word conversation was coming. This is how Viv has ended his previous two sessions. At this point, *w* is for walker. Later, *w* will stand for wheelchair. Joe hates the letter *w*.

'Unless you want to talk about Vince Wilfork,' says Joe.

'We have to think about your safety. The falls are — '

'No big deal. You fall, you get back up. 'Tis

part of life, my dear.'

Viv shakes her head, patient but frustrated with him. She's pushing this walker thing on him pretty hard, but for now, he's still able to resist.

'Okay,' she relents. 'But you're not going to be able to avoid the *w* word much longer.'

A win for Joe. *W*-word conversation: Viv 0, Joe 3. Joe smiles, savoring his one and only victory of the day. Even the small ones count.

★ ★ ★

Katie walks into the lobby of the Spaulding Rehabilitation Hospital, and her dad is already sitting in the waiting area, done with his physical therapy session. She would've been on time, but she had to circle the Navy Yard a few times looking for a space, and then it took about ten embarrassing minutes to parallel park the damn car. He's watching the TV mounted on the wall and doesn't see her yet, and she pauses before approaching him.

He keeps adjusting in his seat as if trying to get comfortable, but he never does. He's in perpetual motion. His head glides around on the axis of his neck, tilting, nodding, swaying, as if someone loosened the screws connecting his skull to his spine. His limb movements begin as random but usually develop into a pattern, something close to a steady rhythm if she watches long enough. Heels up, heels down, toe tap, heels up, heels down, toe tap, toe tap, shoulder shrug, arm fling, eyebrows raise, heels up, heels down. He's boogying to music no one else on the planet can hear.

His facial contortions are the hardest for Katie to witness. They make him seem disturbed, and she's ashamed to admit that at times she has to remind herself that he's not. Even though she knows the reason behind the grimaces and facial twitching, they're off-putting. Strangers must assume he's dangerous or deranged or drunk.

That's why he wears the T-shirts. The guy who makes the TOWNIE T-shirts printed up a dozen for her dad for free. Her dad won't wear anything else now. Since JJ told the guys at the firehouse about his gene status, they have no reason to keep HD locked up in the closet. And so with JJ's blessing, her dad is on a mission to educate the world, or at least the good people of Charlestown. Gray with navy blue lettering across the center of his chest, each shirt reads:

THIS IS HUNTINGTON'S

Learn more at HDSA.org
or ask me

He came up with many more HD slogans and wanted to have a whole line of T-shirts made, but her mom put a stop to it. Most of them were definitely not PC, and her mom said being seen in public with him is hard enough without him wearing an offensive shirt. Katie thought some of them were pretty hilarious.

I have Huntington's disease. What's your excuse?

This is my brain on Huntington's

Life is Good but Huntington's Sucks Ass

You are staring at a man with Huntington's disease

Fuck you. This is Huntington's.

She walks over to him now. 'Hey, Dad, you ready?'

He slaps his thighs. 'Yup. Let's go!'

Katie holds the door open for him as they leave the building. It's an exceptionally warm afternoon, in the midsixties, a freakishly rare thing for March in Boston. Katie points her face up to the sky and closes her eyes, feeling the sun touch her nose and cheeks. The heat makes her smile. She's had enough of this winter. But she knows today is more of a cruel tease than an actual preview. No one in Boston is putting away hats and gloves and winter coats yet. It could snow a foot tomorrow. The pink and white blossoms Katie loves won't burst open for at least another month. She keeps her head tipped for another few seconds before beginning to worry about sunburn. She's not wearing any SPF.

Her dad inhales and smiles. 'What a day! You in a hurry to get anywhere?'

'Nope.'

'Wanna go for a walk?'

'Sure.'

Walking with her dad is stressful. The whole reason she drives the car to pick him up from physical therapy is to avoid walking with him. But who can resist this day?

She wants to be close enough to catch him if he starts to fall, but not close enough to catch a flying fist in the face. She gives him a fairly wide berth. She won't take her eyes off him while he walks, but he's frightening to watch. Every joint — his ankles, knees, hips, elbows, wrists, fingers, shoulders — is overly involved in the task. Each step is exaggerated, jerky, wild, almost violent. She finds herself holding her breath the way she imagines a mother does when watching her baby taking those first uncertain, wobbly steps. It's a miracle he doesn't fall. And then he does.

It happened too fast for her to react in time. She thinks he dragged the toe of his sneaker, and then he was flailing, his legs running to catch up with himself, like a cartoon character. And now he is sprawled out, facedown, spread-eagled on the sidewalk, and she's just standing over him, stunned even though she was expecting this to happen, stupidly doing nothing.

'Dad! Are you okay?'

She rushes to him now and crouches down. He pushes himself up to sitting and wipes sand and gravel from his hands and arms.

'Yeah, I'm all right.'

Katie checks him over. No blood. Wait.

'Dad, you're bleeding,' she says, pointing to the middle of her own forehead.

He dabs his forehead with his fingers, sees the blood, then wipes his head with the bottom half of his T-shirt.

'Just a little cut,' he says.

It's more than a little cut.

'Hold on,' says Katie.

She rummages through her pocketbook.

'I have a Band-Aid, but it's Hello Kitty,' she says, holding it up, assuming he'll refuse it.

'Okay,' he says, absorbing more blood with the bottom of his shirt. 'I don't think I can look any more ridiculous.'

Katie peels open the Band-Aid and gently places it over the gash, sticking it to her dad's forehead. She looks him over. Scraped palms and elbows, bloodstains all over his T-shirt under THIS IS HUNTINGTON'S, a Hello Kitty Band-Aid taped to the middle of his forehead.

'Yeah, you look a little more ridiculous,' she says, smiling.

Her dad laughs. 'Frankly, my dear, I don't give a damn. Let's walk to that park over there.'

They walk to the Massachusetts Korean War Memorial, and her dad chooses a bench. The benches are arranged in a circle, a hexagon actually, she realizes as she counts the six pillars defining this space. The names of the Massachusetts soldiers who died in the Korean War are inscribed on each pillar. Other names are inscribed in bricks along the pathway, still others in the marble benches. In the center of the hexagon stands a larger-than-life bronze statue of a soldier outfitted in rain gear.

Katie didn't even realize this was here. Most Townies ignore the historical stuff in Town. They don't climb the Bunker Hill Monument or take the tour of the USS *Constitution*. Her mom says she went on Old Ironsides for a school field trip in second grade, but she doesn't remember it. The monument is tall. The boat is old. Good enough.

She and her dad sit side by side a safe distance apart and say nothing. The sunlit marble bench feels pleasantly hot against her palms. A sparrow hops past their feet on the bricks and skitters off into the grass. She hears children's voices sailing through the warm air, presumably from a playground she can't see.

As she does whenever she has free time to think, she imagines the results of her genetic testing, printed and waiting for her on a piece of paper sealed in a white envelope in Eric's office. What's written on that piece of paper? She always begins with imagining that she's gene positive.

I'm sorry, Katie, but you will get Huntington's disease, just like your grandmother, father, JJ, and Meghan.

And then she begins believing that scenario, her mind readily running with it. A twenty-two-year-old girl tests gene positive for HD. A tragic tale. Her mind loves those.

She imagines the possibility of being HD positive many times a day. *Yes*, her mind says. *Yes, you are.* And even though she knows the story is only a possibility, a thought created by her mind that isn't real, the fear that the thought elicits is taking on a physical form inside her. The fear she carries is heavy, so heavy, and she's powerless to let it go.

She carries her heavy fear to yoga class and to

bed with Felix. She stuffs the fear deep inside, but lately, it feels like there's no more room. She's a suitcase filled to capacity, yet every day she thinks about testing positive, and so there's more fear to carry, so she must stuff more inside. She must.

The tears are always right there, ready, but she holds them in. She holds everything in. She's pretty sure that she soon won't be able to zip herself shut. The fear is crowding her out. Every time her lungs expand, each time her heart beats, they bump up against the fear inside her. The fear is in her pulse, in every shallow breath. The fear is a black mass in her chest, expanding, crushing her heart and lungs, and soon she won't be able to breathe.

For a split second every morning, she forgets. And then the black heaviness is there, and she wonders what it is, and then she remembers. She probably has HD.

So she's faking it through her days. Every cheery hello, every class she teaches, preaching about grace and gratitude and peace, every time she has sex with Felix, she's an imposter going through the motions of civilized society, pretending everything is A-okay.

Hi, Katie! How are you? Good. I'm good.

She's not good. She's a big, fat fuckin' lie is what she is. She's planning her Huntington's, rehearsing her final genetic counselor appointment, hearing the words pronouncing her doomed fate. *You are HD positive.* And she's practicing her response, strong, icy cold, even cocky. *Yeah, I knew it.* Then she moves on to imagining the first symptoms, never getting married or having kids, living in a nursing home, dying alone.

Indulging in all this negative storytelling isn't doing her any good, and she knows it. She has the tools to put a stop to it. If her thoughts can create the fear, her thoughts can eliminate it. But for some sick reason, she chooses to keep it. She's wallowing in her fear, and it feels good in that bad kind of way, like eating a pan of brownies when she's on a juice cleanse or sneaking a slice of bacon when she's vegan.

'So how are you doin'?' asks her dad.

She's about to throw him her pat reply, her tidy lie. The *Good* is in her mouth, but suddenly, she can't stand the taste of it.

'I'm scared, Dad.'

She looks down at her shoes, the balls of her feet resting on the ground, still. She looks over at her dad's. Heels up, heels down, toe tap.

'I know, honey. I'm scared, too.'

In the past, he would've tried to cover over her fear with some quick fix, like slapping a Hello Kitty Band-Aid on a bloody cut. Like most fathers wanting to protect their little girls, he would've tried to annihilate it or hide it or negate it, whatever it took for him to feel as if he removed the problem. *Don't be scared. There's nothing to be afraid of. Don't worry. It'll all work out.* He would've left her feeling still scared and alone in it. But today, to her complete surprise, he goes there with her.

She scooches over to him, hip to hip, and hugs her arm around him. He wraps his arm around her, too. Being scared together is so much less scary.

'I was thinking about you and Felix,' says her dad. 'If you decide you want to move to Portland, you have my blessing. Your mother's, too.'

'I do?'

'Live your life, sweetheart. No matter what happens, it's too short. Go do what you want with no regrets, no guilt.'

Her dad has been doing an admirable job of living well with HD, providing a positive example for his children, but this change of heart comes wholly unexpected. She appreciates his blessing, but it's the heavy black mass inside her, and not her parents' disapproval, that's been keeping her from packing her things, refusing her permission to go.

'You keep surprising me, Dad.'

'What, you think you yogis are the only enlightened ones?'

Katie laughs. Her smile lands in his eyes, and there he is, her father. If she looks for it, she can see his love for her in his eyes.

'Are you saying cops are enlightened?' she asks, teasing him.

'Oh yeah. They don't let us wear blue unless we pass Zen training.'

She laughs again.

'Let's go over there,' says her dad, nodding toward the footpath.

The path is brick and uneven and windy, and Katie's spotting her dad with every precarious step, unsure whether she has another Band-Aid should he fall, but they make it to the path's end without incident. They're standing before a small fountain, a shallow pool of water in a circle of concrete, a spigot spurting a modest splash of water in the center. Beyond the fountain is the familiar panorama of skyscrapers, Boston's Government Center and financial district.

'She's a beautiful city,' says her dad, gazing out at the horizon.

'Yeah,' says Katie, thinking it's all right, wondering what Portland might look like.

'I have something for you,' says her dad, digging into the front pocket of his pants. He produces a quarter, displaying it in the palm of his hand. 'I want you to have this, for good luck.'

He gives the quarter to Katie and then holds her hand inside his for a moment.

'Thanks, Dad.'

She folds her fingers over the quarter and closes her eyes. She imagines the black mass of fear inside her chest, takes the deepest breath she can, filling her lungs to capacity, and then exhales, breathing the black mass through her mouth, releasing it. Then she opens her eyes, winds up, and tosses the quarter into the fountain.

She looks over at her dad. His face is shocked, pale.

'I can't believe you just did that,' he says.

'What? I made a wish.'

He laughs and shakes his head.

'What did you want me to do with it?'

'I dunno. I didn't expect you to get rid of it.'

'I made a wish.'

'Good, honey. I hope it comes true.'

'Me, too.'

They stand there a bit longer before finding the car, neath the warm, sunny sky, scared and hoping together.

34

It's early afternoon, and Katie and Meghan are sitting on the front stoop. Meghan is smoking a cigarette, something she does only if there's no risk of their mom seeing or smelling it. Their grandfather died of lung cancer, and their mom goes ballistic whenever she catches Meghan smoking. Patrick is sleeping, Colleen is out walking baby Joey, their mom and JJ are working, and their dad is at PT. Cook Street is sunlit and quiet, no cars zipping down the road, no joggers or dog walkers. No one's around.

Katie hasn't chilled out with Meghan like this in ages. They live together, so everyone assumes they see each other all the time. Only rarely do they, and when they do it's mostly in sleepy-eyed good mornings as they fill travel mugs with coffee or tea, quick hellos as Katie rushes off to teach a class or Meghan dashes to catch a bus downtown, whirling by each other as Meghan packs her makeup case for a performance or Katie changes out of lululemon and into jeans and a sweater for a date with Felix, a quick hug and good night before going to separate bedrooms, closing doors before going to sleep. On the few occasions Katie is actually there. She sleeps over at Felix's apartment most nights. Even with the self-constructed barrier between them removed, she and Meghan are still in the habit of occupying separate sides of their old

385

wall. Without a reason for them to remain distant, they still haven't found their way back to being close.

'So what's happening with you and Felix?' asks Meghan, tapping loose ash from the tip of her cigarette.

'I dunno. We've been fighting a lot lately.'

She nods. 'About what?' she asks, her perfectly sculpted right eyebrow lifting at the arch. She already knows.

'He's pressuring me to decide about Portland, and it's totally stressing me out. It feels like too many things to figure out right now.'

Katie's genetic test results hang over her head like a guillotine, the pointed blade hovering inches above the tender, bare skin of her neck. But maybe she's gene negative, and so there is no guillotine. Maybe her HD gene is normal, and she'll never get HD. Maybe she's free.

She tries to imagine that sense of freedom, but she's sitting next to Meghan, her big sister, an accomplished, beautiful dancer who will get HD, and being HD-free doesn't feel like freedom. It feels unfair, tainted, rotten. She feels utterly unworthy of that freedom.

'It's like the worst possible timing,' says Katie.

'Or it's absolutely perfect,' says Meghan.

Katie studies her sister, her smooth brown hair, her green almond eyes, the five freckles on her face. Five. It would take all day and a calculator to count the freckles on Katie's face. Meghan's petite frame, her small, delicate feet. Katie places her ugly Fred Flintstone bare foot on the step next to Meghan's. Their feet don't look one bit related.

They have the same sense of humor and tastes in clothes, music, and men. Meghan gets Katie better than anyone on the planet. But, in addition to being naturally prettier and smarter and able to dance like an angel, Meghan has always been so much braver than Katie. In middle school, Katie was desperate to play one of the orphans in the production of *Annie*. In her wildest dreams, the drama teacher cast her as Annie. But she was too afraid, too loathsomely self-conscious to even mention her interest aloud, never mind try out. Meghan auditioned. She played one of the orphans. Katie hated her for it and, consumed with jealousy, didn't speak to her sister for months. She never told Meghan why.

Meghan was never afraid to flirt openly with the boy she liked, and is equally unafraid of dumping a guy's ass if she's not that into him. She knew she wanted to be a ballerina since she was a little girl and went after it, full throttle. No waffling. No wondering whether she'd be good enough or assuming she wasn't. No vague plans of maybe someday. She just claimed it. *This is mine.*

It was the same with Meghan's genetic testing. She just did it. She didn't agonize over each appointment or ignore Eric's phone calls. She didn't delay her judgment day. She arrived at Eric's office the very day her results were ready, sat opposite him along with a friend from the Boston Ballet, and received her fate.

Meanwhile, Katie is paralyzed, drowning in a

thick, creamy vegan soup of fear.

'How do you do it?' asks Katie. 'You're fearless.'

'No, I'm not. I'm scared shitless.'

Meghan inhales a long drag off her cigarette, turns her head, and blows the exhale away from Katie's face.

'But whatever; I gotta keep going. I'm a dancer. I'll keep dancing until I can't.'

'What would you do if you were me?' asks Katie, looking for advice or maybe for her brave sister to make Katie's decisions for her.

'About Felix?'

'And the test results.'

'Find out the results and move with Felix.'

'What if I'm gene positive?'

'Move with Felix and be gene positive.'

Katie blinks, stunned. Meghan didn't even pause to think about it. 'Yeah, but, wouldn't that be totally unfair of me, to get further involved with him *knowing* I'm going to get HD?'

'Jesus, don't be such a martyr.'

'I'm not,' says Katie, her voice a whiny violin. 'I just don't know if I could knowingly saddle him with that kind of future.'

'Why do you get to pick his future?'

Because. Because. Katie thinks, but she can't complete that sentence without sounding like a spoiled brat or a total moron. They sit in silence for a few moments.

'How do you think JJ's doing?' asks Katie.

'Okay, I think.'

'You see anything with him yet?'

'No, you?'

'No.'

'What about me?' asks Meghan.

'Nothing. You're fine.'

'You swear to God?'

'Yeah.'

'Thanks. I'm kinda worried about Pat. I dunno — he's got this thing going on in his eyes. Like they're kinda shifty.'

'That's just how he is.'

But Katie's been thinking the same thing. Each time she thinks that she's possibly seeing something, she sweeps it away. It can't be. But there it is. Meghan sees it, too. Patrick might already be symptomatic. Fuckin' hell.

'Has he told Ashley about HD being in our family?' asks Katie.

'I dunno.'

'Do you think he'll end up marrying her?'

'No way,' says Meghan, picking at the dead skin on her big toe. 'That's probably for the best.'

'Yeah,' says Katie, agreeing on both counts. She loves her brother, but even subtracting the possibility of HD, Patrick isn't exactly stellar-husband material. 'How about me? You see anything?'

'No,' says Meghan, then checking out Katie's feet, hands, eyes. 'You're good.'

'Every time I fall out of a standing pose in class, I think, *Is this it? Does this mean I have it?*'

'Yeah, HD totally fucks with your head. Before this, if I fell off pointe or messed up an eight count or something, I'd think, *Fuck*, and be mad

389

at myself for like a few seconds. But then I'd think, *Whatever, shit happens.* Now, if I make a mistake, I have this huge, heart-stopping, wordless moment of panic. It actually feels like I'm having a heart attack.'

'I have whole *weeks* of heart-stopping panic,' says Katie.

'You gotta let it go, or it'll make you crazy. I figure however long I have, I'm not going to let HD steal the symptomatic-free time I have. I don't know when this thing's going to hit, but I'm not going to live like I've got it before I actually do.'

Katie nods. *You are either Now Here or Nowhere.*

'I also figure most professional ballerinas are done with touring and performing in companies by the time they're thirty-five. So no reason I can't have a full-out dance career before HD sets in.'

Katie nods. 'That's true.'

'That's why I'm going to live in London in the fall.'

'*What?*'

'I auditioned for Matthew Bourne's company when they came to Boston, and I got accepted.'

'So you're going to London?' asks Katie, in total disbelief.

'I'm going to London!'

Here, Katie's been agonizing over whether to move with Felix to Oregon, guilty and scared and worried over the prospect of leaving Charlestown and her family, her comfort zone, and there is Meghan, without any drama, who just, *boom*, decides to move alone to another country.

'I can't believe you're going to live in *London*.'

'I know. I'm totally psyched. The company is called New Adventures, and they're amazing. Matthew's choreography is more contemporary and edgy, and I love his storytelling, how he combines acting and dance. You have to see *Edward Scissorhands*. It's mind-blowing. They tour all over the UK. Last year, they also performed in Paris and Moscow.'

'Holy shit, Meg. That sounds awesome. How long would you be there?'

'I dunno. At least three years.'

Katie studies her sister, and there's not one ounce of guilt or hesitation in her. Of course Meghan should go. So why does Katie feel obligated to stay?

'Do you think Mom and Dad will be upset about you leaving?'

'Nope. They already know. Dad's cool with it, and Mom's trying to be. You know how she worries. And so, I kinda need to tell you something,' says Meghan, teeing up something big and bad with her tone.

'What?' asks Katie, bracing herself.

'I'm gonna move in with JJ and Colleen for the summer, rent-free, to save up money for London in exchange for some babysitting.'

'Okay,' says Katie, relieved. That's not a big deal.

'And I hate to be the one to break it to you, but whether you go to Portland or not, you're moving out, too.'

'What?'

'Mom and Dad need to rent out our unit for real. The going rate for a three-bedroom is like four times what we pay, and they need the money.'

Shit. That's a big deal.

'When was someone going to tell me all this?'

'It just got decided like two days ago, after I told them about London. Mom's afraid to tell you. She's feels bad that Dad turned our old bedroom into a dining room, and they'd be kicking you out without giving you somewhere to go. I told her you'd probably go live with Felix, but she acted like she didn't hear me.'

'Yeah, she's practically forcing me to live in sin now.'

'Right.'

'It's kinda like the universe is telling me to move to Portland.'

'Yup.'

Katie has the sudden, overwhelming urge to move off the stoop. She can't sit still anymore.

'You wanna go for a run?' asks Katie.

'Me? Not unless someone's chasing us.'

'A walk? I need to move.'

'Nah, you go. I need a nap before tonight.'

Meghan is dancing tonight in *Lady of the Camellias*. She finishes her cigarette and stubs it out on the step.

'Don't tell Ma. See you tonight?'

'Yup.'

'You bringing Felix?'

'Yeah.'

'Good. And yoga in the morning, right?'

'Right.'

'Okay, see you later. Love you.'

'Love you, too.'

A memory flashes through Katie as she hugs her sister. It's Sunday-morning Mass, the priest's homily, and Katie's about ten years old. Father Michael is telling a story about a sick girl in a hospital. She needs a blood transfusion, and without one, she'll die. Her younger brother, the only family member with the same blood type, volunteers to donate his blood to save her. When the nurse is done drawing his blood, the brother asks, 'Now when will I die?' Of course, the boy misunderstood and he would live, but he believed that by giving his blood, he would be the one to die instead of his sister.

It's a beautiful, inspiring story, but Katie hated it, and it haunted her for years. *I'd NEVER do that for my brothers or Meghan.* She felt physically sick every time she thought about that boy, overwhelmed with guilt and shame. Her heart must be the size of a raisin. If she were a good person, she'd be more like that little boy. She must be evil. She was too ashamed to confess her thoughts to the priests. She didn't deserve absolution from this sin. She would have to go to hell.

She hadn't thought about that homily in years. And now, embracing her sister on the stoop, heart to heart, the remembered story of the boy and his sick sister takes Katie to an entirely different place. She thinks about Eric and her blood draw from six months ago now and the test result awaiting her, and an amazing thought

393

sits straight-spined and fearless at the bottom of her heart, radiating selfless love. If she could take away Meghan's gene-positive result by being gene positive herself, she would. She really would.

Tears well in Katie's eyes as she hugs Meghan a little tighter. Maybe she's braver than she thinks.

★　★　★

Katie begins by walking to the top of Cook Street, left onto Bunker Hill, then down Concord. She passes the triple-deckers, the flower boxes and oil lamps, the Irish and Boston Strong flags hanging in windows. She wonders what Portland looks like. It rains a lot there. Felix says the Columbia River is huge and beautiful, surrounded by mountains and waterfalls and hiking trails. He says it's nothing like the Mystic River. What if everything about Portland is nothing like here?

She walks down Winthrop Street, stops at the curb, and looks down. Two red bricks side by side, inlaid in the center of the sidewalk, extending in a line across the street. The Freedom Trail.

She stops, considering the bricks beneath her shoes for a moment, and then follows her impulse. She's always wanted to do this. She walks along the red line, sometimes brick, sometimes red paint, and follows it through City Square to the edge of Charlestown opposite Paul Revere Park. She pauses, looks back, and then keeps going.

Of course, she leaves Charlestown all the time. She and Felix go to dinner in Cambridge and the South End on a regular basis. She's going to the Opera House tonight. But she's never followed the actual Freedom Trail, her childhood Yellow Brick Road, with her own two feet, out of her neighborhood.

She steps onto the Charlestown Bridge and immediately hates it. The pedestrian walkway, lined in red paint, is a metal grid. Looking down, she can see the mouth of the Charles River below her feet, and her stomach feels as if it drops through her. She keeps walking, and she's terrifyingly high above the black, reflectionless water. Cars and trucks whiz by her right shoulder only inches from where she stands, vibrating the metal floor under her shoes, assaulting her ears. She pauses, tempted to turn around. She feels danger beside and below her, and the comfort of everything she knows behind her, calling her back.

No. She's doing this. She holds her eyes straight ahead and keeps going forward, one step at a time.

Soon and finally, she is over that horrible bridge. She crosses the street and, still on the Freedom Trail, stands on the corner of the North End, Boston's Italian neighborhood. She did it! She's not in Kansas anymore.

She looks back at Charlestown. She can still see the monument, the Navy Yard, the Tobin Bridge. She can practically see her house. She laughs. How pathetic.

She thinks about Meghan, living HD positive,

not using it as an excuse to limit herself in any way. Meghan is moving to London. JJ had a baby. Her dad is practicing yoga.

Felix is moving to Portland.

Katie smiles to herself, continuing along the trail into the North End and away from home, wondering where the red line goes next, having no idea.

You've had the power all along, girl. Go live your dreams.

35

It's a clear, cold April evening at Fenway, the second week of the season, and Joe isn't standing on duty outside the ballpark on Yawkey Way. He's finally, blessedly on the inside. He's sitting with Donny, Tommy, JJ, and Patrick along the third-base line, fourteen seats behind the visiting-team dugout. The tickets were a gift from Christopher Cannistraro. If Joe had known that seeing a lawyer came with awesome seats to a Sox game, he would've divorced Rosie a long time ago. He's only partly kidding.

The game hasn't started yet. Donny and Tommy leave to fetch beers and food. JJ and Patrick are flipping through the program, talking players and pitchers, batting averages and ERAs. Joe's content to just sit and take it all in, his senses enraptured with the tradition and beauty of this beloved ballpark.

The infield grass is golf-course green, the dirt like rich Georgia clay. The foul-ball lines and base bags are Tide-commercial white. The air is chilly against his face and smells clean and occasionally of hot dogs and pizza. The cheery organ music makes him think of roller rinks and carnival carousels, good old-fashioned American fun. He feels comforted by the red, white, and blue neon CITGO sign, unchanged since Joe was a boy, and his heart softens with pride as he reads the retired Hall of Fame numbers on the

397

Green Monster: 9, 4, 1, 8, 27, 6, 14, 42.

The players are on the field, warming up in long-sleeved red shirts, blue caps, and white pants worn long to the ankles. Joe misses his police uniform, the visible unity, being part of a team, one of the guys, the brotherhood. He misses all of that. A giddy, childlike wonder washes over him as the players field grounders right there in front of him. They seem larger than life, and Joe feels privileged, as if he's witnessing a notable moment in American history. Granted, it's not the presidential inauguration or even a postseason game, but still, this is something special, being here.

Donny and Tommy are back with pizza and Miller Lites. Donny reaches over Joe's chest, passing beers to JJ and Patrick, and then hands the one with a lid and straw to Joe. The ballpark is filling in, and the crowd is buzzing with anticipation.

The godlike, echoing voice of the announcer asks all law enforcement officers, firefighters, and EMS workers to stand in appreciation for all they have done and continue to do to protect and serve the city of Boston. It's the week before the second anniversary of the Boston Marathon bombings, and Boston is reliving the memories, both the horror and the heroism. The images from that Monday in April, resurrected in somewhat obscene numbers by the media, still sicken Joe's heart. Thankfully, there are new images to counter the old, inspiring portraits of the bombing victims using prosthetics to walk and run and dance again, of runners and spectators who turned out in record numbers last year, determined to show up and take the day back.

And they did. Boston law enforcement was there in full force, fiercely alert and equally determined to see the day through from start to finish in peace. It was a true, glorious win for the good guys. Boston Strong. And Staying in the Pose.

At first, their whole row is reluctant to rise, but Patrick starts fussing and calling attention to them. Donny, Tommy, and JJ stand, and, with Tommy's insistence, Joe joins them. It's a well-meant, respectful public nod, but the moment is mixed with a heavy melancholy for Joe, knowing he won't be on duty with his fellow officers on Patriots' Day this year. Joe is the first in his row to return to his seat.

They're standing again in a few minutes for the national anthem, sung by a young woman from the Cape, not particularly well, but the high notes always give Joe the goose bumps. And then it's the first pitch, and the Sox are playing ball.

The first inning is one, two, three for both teams. Top of the second, Joe glances over at Patrick just in time to see his cup of Miller Lite slide through his hand, dropping to the ground between his feet. Patrick looks down at his spilled beer and then up at Joe. They lock eyes. Patrick's face is drained of color, replaced with a pale shade of dread.

'Don't go there, Pat. It don't mean nothin',' says Joe.

'Look,' says JJ, holding his beer up on display.

'These cups are all wet and slippery, and my fingers are frozen.'

'Don't worry about it,' says Joe. But Pat is worried, and Joe knows nothing he says is going to shake it loose. 'Don't worry.'

Joe looks around Fenway, betting himself that at least a hundred people drop their drinks tonight. It doesn't mean anything. So Patrick wasn't knocked or bumped or juggling too many things in his hands or even drunk yet. So what? It doesn't mean anything. Tommy flags down one of the boys running concessions and orders another beer for Patrick.

Patrick is still refusing to take the genetic test. He says he couldn't stomach it if he knew for sure he was going to get HD, that he'd probably go on a bender and never come back. And while he professes without any kind of detailed plan that he'll be a responsible father to his child, no amount of threatening or pleading from Joe and Rosie has budged him one inch on marrying Ashley. He ain't doing it. Joe's next grandchild is going to be a bastard. Joe can only pray the little bastard will be healthy.

Not far from their seats, Joe watches the third-base coach. He's rolling back and forth from the balls of his feet to his heels. He's bouncing his knees. He's touching his hat, his face, his stomach, signaling to the runner on second.

Next, Joe checks out the pitcher. He steps off the rubber. He steps back on. He removes his cap, wipes his forehead, and fixes the cap back on his head. He spits over his shoulder. He squints his eyes and shakes his head. He nods and throws a pitch. The batter doesn't swing. *Strike*.

Joe now stays with the batter. It's Pedroia. He tugs on his left glove, then his right glove. He steps into the batter's box. He taps the tip of the bat to the plate, then loops the bat once, twice. Then every muscle goes still. Here comes the pitch. Pedroia holds his swing. It's a ball.

Pedroia steps out of the box. He tugs on his left glove, then his right glove. He steps back into the batter's box, taps the bat to the plate, and so it goes again. It occurs to Joe that playing baseball looks a lot like having Huntington's.

Pedroia and the pitcher are ready. The pitcher releases the ball. All loose energy then pulls tight into Pedey's center before the split-second intuitive decision to swing or hold. Pedroia reaches back, then swings and smacks a looping single into shallow left field. Fenway erupts in celebration.

Top of the sixth, the Sox are up 3 – 2. Joe checks his watch. It's almost nine, but the ballpark is brightly lit, tricking the senses into believing it's daytime. The city and sky beyond the park are black but for the CITGO sign and the yellow window dots of the Pru. Otherwise, there is nothing beyond the Green Monster. Only Fenway exists.

Without cause or warning, Joe jackrabbit-jumps to a stand and, with little legroom to accommodate such a forceful move, begins falling over into the row in front of them. He's going, with no way to save himself, when Tommy grabs him by the scruff of his coat collar and pulls him back into his seat.

'Thanks, man.'

'No problem.'

His chorea is worsening. The jackrabbit jump is one of Joe's new signature moves. He pops up to his feet, usually shocking the hell out of everyone in the room, including Joe, and then drops back into his chair, sometimes falling over backward. If he's got anything in his lap, it's either broken or spilled. Sometimes he jackrabbits over and over in a series of quick thrusts, like some crazy calisthenics drill. He has no control over it. He hates to think this, but he could use a seat belt.

Several people are now staring, a few even completely turned around in their seats. Donny zeroes in on the rubbernecker closest to them.

'You wanna take a friggin' picture? He's got Huntington's. Turn around and watch the game.'

The guy does as he's told. Joe suspects he's sitting there thinking to himself, *What's Huntington's? What's wrong with that guy?* And he's probably hoping whatever it is, it's not contagious.

Joe looks out at the scattered colors in the bleachers. He knows that the colors are people, but he can't see their faces. In fact, aside from the people nearest him, he can't see the faces of anyone here tonight. He can only make out the faces of the players if he looks up at the giant TV screen above the Green Monster. A ballpark full of faceless people.

Fenway seats just over thirty-seven thousand,

about the same number of people as have Huntington's in the United States. Thirty-seven thousand. It's a faceless number, and when it comes to diseases, it's also a small one. More than five million people in the United States have Alzheimer's. Almost three million women in the United States have breast cancer. Only thirty-seven thousand have HD. Drug companies aren't exactly falling over themselves to find the cure for thirty-seven thousand people when they could tackle Alzheimer's or breast cancer. The risk and cost of drug development is high. There's no big lotto jackpot to be made with HD.

Joe's thoughts turn to all the faceless people here battling illness. There are women here with breast cancer, children with leukemia, men with prostate cancer, people with dementia, people who will die before the end of the year. Joe might be the only one here with HD.

The jaded, cynical cop in Joe looks around at the faceless thirty-seven thousand and acknowledges that, statistically, there's a murderer here. There are husbands who beat their wives, people who didn't pay their taxes, people who have committed a variety of unseemly crimes. Then Joe looks to his right, beyond Patrick, and focuses on some of the faces he can see. He notices a father with his boy, about ten years old. He's got his Sox hat on backward and freckled cheeks, and he's holding his glove up, ready for a foul ball. In front of them, Joe spots a couple of old-timers, guys who've probably known each other for sixty years and have been coming here just as long. He's surrounded by husbands and wives, boyfriends and girlfriends, sons and daughters, grandkids and best friends, people with honest jobs and real lives. Real faces.

It's now two outs, bottom of the eighth. Big Papi is up. The count is three and two.

'Let's go *Red Sox*!' *Clap. Clap. Clap, clap, clap.*

Big Papi hits a fly ball hard toward the centerfield wall. There's a collective inhale and hold. It takes an unpredictable bounce off the wall, and Big Papi is standing safe at second. Fenway is on its feet, loving him.

Joe looks over at Patrick, who is hooting and celebrating, holding on to his fourth beer without a problem. See. It didn't mean anything. He's fine. His unborn child is fine.

A wave begins in the bleachers. Joe follows the concert of movement and roar around the ballpark, and the wave looks like a living organism, a jellyfish pulsing. He sees and hears it coming closer, closer, and then he lifts his arms, becoming part of it, and all of Fenway passes through him like a massive electrical current, continuing around again. *This* many Americans have Huntington's. 'Only' thirty-seven thousand. Here in Fenway, there's nothing 'only' about that number. The visceral realization gives him goose bumps.

And without a cure, everyone with HD will die. Joe pictures an empty, silent Fenway, the game still playing without any fans to witness it, and Joe's heart breaks for every single seat here. The thought is overwhelming, haunting.

It's top of the ninth, and the pitcher goes one, two, three. The Sox win it, 5 – 2. JJ is whistling. Patrick is howling and clapping.

Tommy leans over, his program folded into a tube in his hands. 'Good game.'

'Great game,' says Joe.

'Yeah, I don't remember getting Sox tickets when I got divorced,' says Donny. 'Cannistraro owes me. We're doin' this again.'

Joe laughs, agreeing, and then hoping he'll be well enough long enough to keep coming back to Fenway.

'You ready?' asks Tommy.

'One sec,' says Joe.

He takes a moment, wanting to remember this, the joy of the win, the beers and pizza, the electric energy of the crowd, a night at Fenway with his best friends and his two sons. His seat ain't empty yet. And tonight, he enjoyed every wicked-awesome second of it.

'Ready.'

They make their way to the aisle. Donny and Tommy arrange themselves on either side of Joe, JJ spotting him from behind. Joe turns his head to the field one last time.

Good night, sweetheart. It's time to go.

36

They're in the waiting room at the genetic counseling clinic. All of them. Katie, JJ, Colleen and baby Joey, Patrick, Meghan, her mom and dad, and Felix. She brought everyone. How's that for bringing support?

They've been sitting here for about fifteen minutes, one minute past forever. No one is talking or reading the magazines or even making eye contact. They're all looking vaguely at their feet or the walls. Her mom is rubbing the beads of her rosary, whispering with her eyes closed. Katie is holding Felix's hand so tight she's lost circulation in her fingers. She doesn't let go. Katie swallows, and it feels as if her stomach is in the process of turning itself inside out. She thinks she might throw up.

It doesn't help that they're all hungover and have barely slept. Patrick had the night off, and he decided that the eve of Katie's Day of Reckoning called for alcohol. Katie didn't argue. JJ, Pat, Meg, Katie, and Felix went to Sully's early and closed the place. JJ kicked things off with a round of tequila shots. Many, many beers later, Katie vaguely remembers doing shots of Jäger. They all got totally shitfaced.

'This is wicked fun,' says Patrick. 'I can see why you guys all signed up to do this.'

No one says anything.

'When we're done here, we should all go for

colonoscopies down the hall.'

'You'd like a big hose up the ass, wouldn't you, Pat?' goads JJ.

'Gross,' says Meghan.

'Boys,' her mom scolds without opening her eyes.

'Actually, I do have to take a shit,' says Patrick.

'This is why I didn't bring you to my appointment,' says Meghan.

'There a bathroom around here?'

'Out the door, go left,' says JJ.

Katie watches her mom praying. *Thank you, Mom.* Her dad jumps up, startling everyone. He does a quick dance, a little soft-shoe shuffle, and then throws himself back into his chair. A few minutes later, the waiting room door opens, and Patrick is back.

Then the other door suddenly opens, slicing the air like a guillotine blade rising, and standing before them is Eric Clarkson. His face is serious. Then, seeing so many O'Briens, he smiles. He's still smiling. He wouldn't be smiling if he were about to deliver bad news. That would be sadistic.

Katie's spirit and hangover lift, floating weightless above her for a moment before her memory sinks them back into her body. He doesn't know her test results yet either. The smile has nothing to do with HD. He's just happy to see them.

'Hello, everyone,' says Eric. 'Hey, Joe, I like your shirt.'

Her dad nods and smiles. He's very proud of his T-shirts.

'Shall we?' asks Eric, holding the door open.

Katie stands first. Still holding Felix's hand, she follows Eric down the hall, leading the O'Brien family in single file, as if they were a funeral procession or an army marching to the front line. They pile into Eric's office, and the space is too small for this many people. Katie sits in one of the chairs, and her mother takes the only other seat next to her. Everyone else stands, squished and leaning against the wall behind her.

'And I was worried you wouldn't bring anyone,' says Eric.

His office looks pretty much the same as she remembers it. His diploma, the HOPE poster, the orchid. She looks over at the whiteboard.

Chromosomes. Genes. DNA. ATCG. CAG.

A genetics 101 lesson not yet erased from an earlier appointment, another innocent soul formally introduced to the simply cruel biology of HD. Everything looks the same, with one notable exception — a framed photo of Eric with his dog and a pretty girl. She's cute. She looks a little bit like Katie. Next to their picture is the gift Katie gave to him last year.

'Hope is the thing with feathers
That perches in the soul
and sings the tune without the words
and never stops at all.'
— Emily Dickinson

She pulls down the top of her T-shirt a smidge

408

to just above her heart and drags her fingers over her new tattoo, the skin still red and itchy. A white feather. Hope. She looks down at the outside of her right ankle. A pink lotus flower. Her other tattoo. Lotus flowers blossom while rooted in mud, a reminder that beauty and grace can rise above something ugly. Something like HD. She was planning on getting only the feather, but the pain of the needle wasn't nearly as bad as she'd expected, so she got the lotus, too. Her anticipation was far worse than the actual experience. Possibly like right now.

She used to think that being gene positive would change everything. If she's positive, it will certainly affect her future. But the future is a fantasy. The present moment is all there is. Today, in this moment, if she finds out she's gene positive, it changes nothing about now. She'll still love the people in this room, and they'll still love her. She's still moving with Felix to Portland next week. Her bags are packed.

So why does she need to know?

Everyone dies. As her dad would say, *That's the price of playing poker.* Maybe it's an accident or something lethal lurking inside them — cancer, heart disease, Alzheimer's. Katie looks at Eric and his girlfriend, happy in the framed picture, and hopes he doesn't get hit by a bus when he's thirty-five. But who knows? Who knows what genetic fate might be lurking inside Eric, her mom, Felix?

So HD might be the reason she dies someday. She's done with living with the excuse of someday. She's determined to stay focused on the reason she lives now. She loves her family. She loves Felix. She loves inspiring wellness and peace through teaching yoga. She loves herself. Love is her reason for living, and that has nothing to do with HD.

So why does she need to know whether she'll get HD in the future?

She eyes the white envelope centered on Eric's desk. She has a 50 percent chance of being HD positive. A flip-of-the-coin risk. But everything in life is a risk. Moving to Portland, opening a yoga studio, loving Felix. Every breath is a risk. She envisions the quote she wrote on her bedroom wall yesterday before they all went to Sully's and got hammered, knowing the words will be painted over within the week, before the new tenants move in.

'Every breath is a risk. Love is why we breathe.'
— *Katie O'Brien*

She looks up at Eric looking at her. Here they are. Their third and last date. She could bolt like a bride with cold feet on her wedding day. She could politely say *No, thank you.* She could walk out of this building none the wiser and move to Portland with Felix. She could be a twenty-two-year-old girl and not know what letters are written in her DNA.

Or she could find out.

If that piece of paper reveals that she's gene negative, she's free of HD. No more worrying every time she drops her spoon. No more panicked dread every time she fidgets in her seat.

Her children will never get HD.

The thought of hearing Eric say she's gene positive used to terrify her. The thought became a fear that physically consumed her. But the thought is only terrifying if she chooses to be terrified. The quality of her experience depends entirely on the thoughts she chooses. Reality depends on what is paid attention to. Whether she's gene positive or negative, she's determined to pay attention to living, not dying.

Still clutching Felix's hand, Katie turns and locks eyes with her dad. His eyes go wide and round, his eyebrows hop up and hang there. An HD grimace. Possibly her future face. She reads his T-shirt. THIS IS HUNTINGTON'S. And then his eyebrows relax, and there's a reassuring twinkle in his eyes, and without words, she knows what he's telling her. *I'm with you, honey.* This is her dad.

'So, Katie. I have your genetic screening results here. You ready?' asks Eric, holding the envelope, her fate, in his hands.

She squeezes Felix's hand and looks Eric straight in the eye. She takes a deep breath in. So. She exhales it out. Hum. Every breath is a risk. Love is why we breathe.

'I am.'

Lisa's call to action

Dear Reader,

Thank you for reading *Inside the O'Briens*. Through the story of the O'Brien family, I hope you've gained a compassionate awareness for what it feels like to live with Huntington's. I also hope you'll join me in putting that compassionate awareness into action. By making a small donation to Huntington's research, YOU can be part of the progress that will lead to a cure.

Please take a moment and go to www.LisaGenova.com and click on the **Readers in Action — Huntington's** button to make a donation to Huntington's research. You'll be taken to an animated Fenway Park and a fun, interactive way to see the impact of your donation. You'll also be able to check the tally, both the number of readers who've contributed and the total dollar amount.

Thank you for taking the time to get involved, for turning your compassionate awareness into action.

Let's see how amazingly generous and powerful this readership can be!

Namaste,
Lisa Genova

Acknowledgments

First and foremost, I am profoundly grateful to the families affected by Huntington's who so openly shared themselves, who entrusted me with their most personal experiences. I spoke with people who have early-, middle-, and late-stage HD, people who are gene positive and asymptomatic, gene negative, and at risk. I spoke with the spouses, parents, siblings, children, and friends of those affected. Many have become my close and cherished friends. I owe my understanding of the complexity of living with this disease to each of them.

Thank you, Cheryl Sullivan Staveley, Kevin Staveley, Meghan Sullivan, Jeri Garcia, Kari Hagler Wilson, Lance Mallow, Kathy Mallow, Robin Renschen, Mary Shreiber, Elise Shreiber, Alan Arena, Lizbeth Clinton Granfield, Rosemary Adamson, Mark Wiesel, Catherine Hayes, Genevieve McCrea, Gail Lambert, Dr. Jeff Carroll, Matthew Ellison (founder of HDYO.org), and Michelle Muller. You showed me the humanity that cannot be found in clinical textbooks.

Thank you, Karen Baker, LICSW, MSW, who immediately knew that I needed to meet Cheryl Sullivan. A special thank-you goes to Cheryl. Cheryl, I'm so thankful for all that you taught me about HD, for all the time you spent with me, for inviting me into your home and your family. And beyond the pages of this book, I'm truly grateful for your generous and loving spirit and our friendship. And I'm deeply grateful I had the chance to know your beautiful daughter, Meghan.

Meghan died of juvenile HD in the early morning of Monday, May 12, 2014, at the age of twenty-six. Meghan was a tenacious advocate for HD, inspiringly courageous in her positive attitude, and known for her contagious smiles and huge hugs. She showed me that even in a situation that appears hopeless, love and gratitude are possible. Meghan, thank you for touching my life and countless others' with the way you lived. I think of you every day.

An enormous thank-you to the many health-care professionals who so generously took the time to help me gain an accurate picture of the neurological, genetic, scientific, and therapeutic aspects of living with HD. Thank you, Dr. Anne Young (neurologist), Dr. Steven Hersch (neurologist), Rudy Tanzi (neuroscientist), Alicia Semaka, PhD, CCGC (Canadian Certified Genetic Counsellor), Judy Sinsheimer (clinical social worker), Suzanne Imbriglio (physical therapist), David Banks (behavior specialist), and Allan Tobin (former senior scientific advisor for the CHDI Foundation).

A huge, admiration-filled thank-you to the police officers who helped me understand the day-to-day life of their jobs. When I began writing this book, I knew I wanted to raise the reader's awareness of Huntington's. After all I've learned, I hope this book also generates an appreciation and gratitude for law enforcement officers. Thank you to Officers Daniel Wallace, Richie Vitale, John Quarranto, retired officer Frank DeSario, and Detective Melissa Marshall.

A special thank-you to the Boston police officer who wanted nothing to do with me. Because of him, I met Officer Danny Wallace, who became my daily police consultant, my 'pusher,' my muse, and my dear friend. Danny, you gave so much more than I asked for, and this book is infinitely better for all that you contributed. Thank you for meeting me in Charlestown and on Cape Cod, for the ride-alongs, the trips to the stations, for explaining and reexplaining, every rambling, every photo, every e-mail and text, for reading the drafts, and so much more. I adore and admire you and am so grateful that our paths have crossed. I thank my lucky stars all the time that the first officer I met in Charlestown wouldn't talk to me. There are no coincidences, right? Danny, I'm so blessed to know you and call you my friend.

Thank you to the Townies: Jamie Kelly, Jack Sullivan, and Frank and Carol Donlan. After a long and courageous battle with cancer, Carol passed away while I was editing this manuscript. Carol, thank you for sharing your childhood stories with me, for telling me about the neighborhood and the man you loved.

Thank you to Allison Sloan, the wonderful Toonie and senior library associate with the Reading Public Library who spent a day with me, giving me the grand tour — walking through Town, introducing me to neighbors, sharing fun

415

facts both historical and current.

To better understand Katie's life as a yoga instructor, I enrolled in Jill Abraham's Power Yoga of Cape Cod two-hundred-hour yoga teacher training while writing this book. I completed the two hundred hours and was certified in May, one week before completing the first draft. For what they contributed to Katie's character and the countless ways my own life has been enriched, I am forever and deeply grateful to my fellow yogis and teachers: Jill Abraham, Leigh Alberti, Jed Armour, Katie Briody, Keveney Carroll, Rhia Cataldo, Eric Clark, Victoria Diamond, Andrea Howard, Heather Hunter, Ed Jacobs, Victor Johnson, Kristin Kaloper, Michelle Kelly, Haley King, Kadri Kurgun, Amy Latham, Alicia Mathewson, Terri McCallister, Lauren Miller-Jones, Jessica Riley Norton, Andrea Odrzywolski, Kelley Field Pearce, Heather Pearston, and John Perrone.

Thank you to Susanna Vennerbeck, formerly a dancer for the Boston Ballet, Jennifer Markham, a teacher for the Boston Ballet, Sylvia Deaton, currently in the corps de ballet at the Boston Ballet, and my beautiful cousin Lizzie Green, who attended the Boston Ballet School.

Thank you to my dear friend Greg O'Brien, who shared his love of and many books about his Irish heritage. Thank you to Rose Summers, who shared many great stories about Ireland and growing up Irish Catholic. Thank you to Beth Schaufus Gavin, my beloved Irish friend of thirty years now, who answered all sorts of questions about Irish songs, Protestants, and beer. A wink and a nod to your dad, who inspired the character of Michael Murphy.

Thank you to my amazing assistant, Kate Racette, who accompanied me to Charlestown and made those trips productive, smooth, and fun, who researched all manner of facts and figures for me, and who wears a hundred hats every day to make my writing time possible and my overall quality of life wicked awesome.

Thank you to my brother, Tom Genova, who fielded any and all questions related to Boston sports teams. Thanks again to my brother and to my lovely friend Danyel Matteson for sharing personal stories about their beloved dogs.

Thank you to Larry Lucchino for answering many questions related to the Boston Red Sox and Fenway, for explaining the important difference between a ballpark and a stadium. Thank you to Stacey Lucchino for so generously inviting me to Fenway, for seeing the possibilities in raising urgently needed money for HD research and then unflinchingly rolling up her sleeves. Thanks also to Dave and Lynn Waller for generously jumping in, for contributing your amazing talents to this worthy cause.

Thank you to Ragdale for the magnificent writer's residency and to everyone who made my time there so productive and magical — Jeffrey Meeuwsen, Regin Igloria, Jack Danch, Cynthia Quick, and Linda Williams. My gratitude and love to the generous Forever Om Yoga and Lake Forest community — Sandra Deromedi, Brian Floriani, Areta Kohout, and Jeanna Park.

A loving thank-you to my brilliant and

inspiring friend Michael Verde, who generously gave me time and space to write during the Memory Bridge retreat (memorybridge.org) at the Tibetan Mongolian Buddhist Cultural Center in Bloomington, Indiana.

Enormous gratitude to Vicky Bijur and Karen Kosztolnyik for their careful and insightful feedback on many drafts. Thanks also to Carolyn Reidy, Louise Burke, Jen Bergstrom, Jean Anne Rose, Jennifer Robinson, Marcy Engelman, Liz Psaltis, Liz Perl, Michael Selleck, Wendy Sheanin, Lisa Litwack, and Becky Prager for supporting this book in such a huge way.

A huge-hearted thank-you to my beloved early readers: Anne Carey, Mary MacGregor, Laurel Daly, Kim Howland, Kate Racette, and Dan Wallace. And then Cheryl Sullivan and Jeri Garcia. Thank you for reading, for cheering me on, for your feedback, love, and support. Cheryl and Jeri, thank you for having the courage to read this story, for trusting me, and for giving me feedback. I love you both.

We do hope that you have enjoyed reading
this large print book.

Did you know that all of our titles
are available for purchase?

We publish a wide range of high quality
large print books including:
**Romances, Mysteries, Classics
General Fiction
Non Fiction and Westerns**

Special interest titles available in
large print are:
**The Little Oxford Dictionary
Music Book
Song Book
Hymn Book
Service Book**

Also available from us courtesy of
Oxford University Press:
**Young Readers' Dictionary
(large print edition)
Young Readers' Thesaurus
(large print edition)**

For further information or a free
brochure, please contact us at:
**Ulverscroft Large Print Books Ltd.,
The Green, Bradgate Road, Anstey,
Leicester, LE7 7FU, England.
Tel:** (00 44) 0116 236 4325
Fax: (00 44) 0116 234 0205

Other titles published by Ulverscroft:

LOVE ANTHONY

Lisa Genova

Olivia Donatelli's dream of a normal life was shattered when her son, Anthony, was diagnosed with autism at age three. He didn't speak. He hated to be touched. He almost never made eye contact. And just as Olivia was starting to realise that happiness and autism could coexist, Anthony was gone. Now she's alone on Nantucket, desperate to find meaning in her son's short life, when a chance encounter with another woman brings Anthony alive again in a most unexpected way. In a piercing story about motherhood, autism and love, Lisa Genova offers us two unforgettable women who discover the small but exuberant voice that helps them both find the answers they need.

LIBERTY SILK

Kate Beaufoy

France, 1919: Jessie is celebrating the last heady days of her honeymoon. But when her husband suddenly disappears, she finds herself bereft — until a chance encounter thrusts her into the centre of the intoxicating world of Parisian high life . . . Hollywood, 1942: Lisa has come a long way from her quiet, unassuming life in London and is taking Hollywood by storm. But all that glitters is not gold, and as the smoke and mirrors of the lifestyle she so longs for shatter around her, there are some secrets she can never escape . . . Ireland, 1969: Cat, headstrong and independent, drawn to danger and passionately opposed to injustice, has no idea of the legacy that precedes her. Once past secrets are revealed, she has the chance to find out what liberty really means . . .

A DICTIONARY OF MUTUAL UNDERSTANDING

Jackie Copleton

When a badly scarred man knocks on the door of Amaterasu Takahashi's retirement home and says he is her grandson, she doesn't believe him. Amaterasu knows that her grandson and daughter died the day the Americans dropped the atomic bomb on Nagasaki; she searched for them amongst the ruins of her devastated city. So this man is either a miracle or a cruel trick. The stranger forces Amaterasu to revisit her past: the hurt and humiliation of her early life, the intoxication of a first romance, the fierceness of a mother's love. For years she has held on to the idea that she did what she had to do to protect her family . . . but now nothing seems so certain. We can't rewrite history — but can we create a new future?